THE TRUTH
ABOUT SHARKS AND PIGEONS

THE TRUTH
ABOUT SHARKS AND PIGEONS

Matt Phillips

9,95

gorilla books

First published in New Zealand in 2011
This edition published in 2015
Gorilla Books Limited, Wellington, New Zealand

Copyright 2011 © Matt Phillips

ISBN 978-0-473-18354-7

www.primatepublishing.com

Special Anniversary Ultimate Limited Edition Director's Cut

Alternate Endings!

Competitions!

Bloopers and Outtakes!

Book Soundtrack!

Cut-out-and-keep Pigeon Mask!

Deleted Scenes!

To Cathy

"Would you stop bothering me with these stories and write them down instead?"

Well, you asked for it.

Introduction to the Special Anniversary Ultimate Limited Edition Director's Cut

When I asked myself to write the introduction for this Special Anniversary Ultimate Limited Edition I was honoured. I was also a little perturbed. Is it normal to ask yourself to do things, I asked myself?

This edition celebrates the eight month and four day anniversary of the initial publication of "The Truth about Sharks and Pigeons" and is strictly limited to one billion copies. Given current sales volumes this will happen sometime between the sun collapsing into a red dwarf and all life on Earth being destroyed (or later). So lucky you – you've managed to get your hands on a copy just in time!

I have done my very best to address the inadequacies of the first edition, and have added some bonus features that will entertain and engage (possibly). These special DVD-only (note: this is a book, not a DVD) bonus features include the following:

"The Truth about Sharks and Pigeons", fully revised and updated. Thanks to all of you who recommended I hire a professional Editor (and a special thank you to those that did so without resorting to profanity). Most of all a big thank you to Allison for being that editor!

Not one, not two, not even three, but four **Alternate Endings!** That's right, you read that correctly. Amuse yourself (maybe) with what might have been.

fabric cushion on the seat, and the other had a tendency to collapse if you used it the wrong way. "Using it the wrong way" included things like sitting on it. It had never been an issue, as in all his time at the flat Bill had never had more than a single guest. That was, of course, unless he counted the time he had been burgled; the police claimed the fingerprints indicated a gang of at least three. It was the busiest his flat had ever been, and if this caused him any quirk of sadness, it was quickly swamped by the knowledge that the burglars had found nothing worth stealing, and had even seen fit to rearrange the magnetic letters on his fridge to read "wat (sic) a dump u loser."

The third seat, the one he was sitting in, had nothing wrong with it at all, other than being a green plastic garden chair. That this was his best chair was also a little depressing. It was the only chair he used when sat at the table. The eclectic chair—as he had named the one prone to burst into pieces—was just too dangerous to contemplate, and he couldn't bring himself to sit in the one with the torn cushion. That had been Ella's chair, and he still thought of it has hers, even though she had not sat in it for over a year, and likely never would again.

Likely? Even including that word was optimistic. He and Ella had dated for just over two years, and the end had been abrupt and painful. For him anyway. He couldn't say too much for her. He'd returned home from work to find her things gone and a short note, not much longer than the *Dear John* left for him by the burglars, pinned to the fridge by a magnet from the Isle of Skye. "An Enchanting Place" said the magnet; "You're dumped" said the note, or words to that effect.

In the far corner of the room was his bed, a saggy springed affair that seemed to think it had died and been reborn as a hammock. Bill actually found it rather comfortable, and if he slept in exactly the right way—a sort of twisted star formation—he avoided nearly all of the sharp edges from the broken springs. The covers were a tangled mess and would remain that way until that evening, when he would tug them into some semblance of order. While this was habit, he had read somewhere that airing your covers (ergo not making your bed), was very bad for bed bugs, and therefore very good for humans. He suspected that most self-respecting bed bugs would find a more salubrious abode, less filled with sharp metal springs, but he was sure his "bed airing" helped. The only other furniture in the room was a red fabric settee and a black pine veneer coffee table, both pointed at a fourteen-inch portable TV.

The bird's expression seemed to echo the magnetic words on his fridge: "What a dump, you loser." Bill hadn't had the heart to rearrange the letters: it was possibly the longest sentence the burglar had ever composed, and might even be needed one day as coursework. By comparison, he was certain that the pigeon was an educated bird, and as such would no doubt use exemplary spelling and grammar. And probably poop on the kitchen floor.

"It's not cheap renting in London and saving up a deposit, okay? This is the best I can do," said Bill. The bird bobbed his head in appreciation of the point.

Get a grip, thought Bill, closing his eyes and rubbing his temples. *Do not start talking to a pigeon, it can't talk back.* Abandoning breakfast he grabbed his coat and made for the door.

As usual, the bird was waiting outside, loitering in the gutter by his front door. This morning it was intently studying a fractured polystyrene box, projecting feral innocence in a way that seemed a little contrived. Ignoring the pigeon, he set off down the road at a quick jog. He didn't even turn around to see if it was following him. It probably was; it had every other day this week. It wouldn't follow him onto the Underground though.

5

At least it hadn't yet.

He arrived at the Underground station a little out of breath. An announcement informed passengers that services were subject to unspecified delays. As if summoned by this revelation the train rattled into view, wheezing and scraping like an arthritic millipede. Climbing on board Bill successfully navigated into the personal space of six complete strangers. The woman to his left had her face buried in *The Metro* newspaper. "Naked Pigeon Phenomenon," said the headline on the front of the newspaper. *Not more pigeons*, thought Bill. The article went on to explain that large numbers of naked pigeons—their bodies plucked clean of feathers but otherwise unharmed—had been turning up all over London. Bill turned his head away from the newspaper. A bit of luck today: the businessman in front was wearing an expensive-looking soft wool coat. In full-body contact with the man's back, and various body parts of five other passengers, Bill surreptitiously snuggled down into the wool coat for a nap. The last person to get on the train, a short girl with long, brown hair, was repeatedly battered by the doors before they squeezed closed behind her. *She's pretty*, thought Bill, before lapsing into a contented doze on his woolly bed.

Bill considered the ability to sleep while standing up to be a life skill that people in London should look to cultivate. The Western world was sleep deprived, everyone knew that, and those few extra minutes a day could make all the difference. He felt his woolly mattress slowly moving away from him, as its owner fought his way to the door. Opening a sleepy eye, Bill saw it was also his stop. Following the path forged by the businessman he made his way up the escalators and back to daylight.

The Underground exit brought him out onto a street choked with traffic. Looming over the scene of urban chaos was his destination: the forty-two storey Bally Brooks Bank tower. Bill was an analyst programmer at Bally Brooks Bank, and while he didn't leap out of bed eager to get to work each morning, it paid his bills. He'd joined the bank on his twenty-first birthday almost eight years ago.

He dodged around a group of pigeons, the standard filthy variety. They were engrossed in half a stale bun, heedless of the crushing potential of the suited and booted humans all around them. They weren't his favourite creatures, but he had no desire to see them squashed.

His security pass, safely tethered to his hip by a piece of elastic, granted him passage through the gate in the tower's marble-clad foyer. There was a short wait for a lift, and when one arrived people squashed themselves into it like lemmings, possibly keen to re-live their morning's journey on the Underground.

Unseen by Bill, the brown-haired girl from the train squeezed into the lift, pushing herself between the suited occupants and worming her way to the back wall. With a competent swish, the lift doors closed, the glass and metal box beginning its rapid ascent to floor thirty-six. Bill stared vacantly at his reflection in the shiny metal wall of the lift, trying to ignore the vague tendrils of hunger that were seeking to remind him of his half-finished breakfast. His nondescript brown hair was a little untidy; ideally he would have showered, had he not wasted five minutes dithering about whether or not to open the curtains. Trying not to jostle his fellow lift passengers, he raised a hand and smoothed his hair back into place. He was of average height and average build, and had been told (on more than one occasion) that his face was neither ugly, handsome, nor overly plain. He was wearing a dark grey suit and very ordinary black shoes. He was the sort of person you never noticed, the man who didn't just blend into the background, but virtually *became* the background. He was decidedly average, ordinary, and unremarkable, but it didn't bother him one bit.

The doors slid open and Bill stepped out onto the thirty-sixth floor. Peering out from the sea of suits, the girl with brown hair and pretty brown eyes watched him leave.

"Bill, don't get comfortable," called Mr Shank, a large, red-haired man, who was strolling duck-footedly down the corridor. "Those idiots in section 3C want another briefing, and you are the only one in the effing section who can speak their language." The pinprick eyes beneath the bush of red curls scowled at Bill. Bill worked in section 8G, but it was a running joke amongst his colleagues that they should be in section F based on the amount Mr Shank went on about the effing section. It was an inside joke that made them laugh. And die a little inside.

"No problem, boss," Bill called back, throwing his coat over the back of his chair and picking up his notebook and pen. This happened quite often, especially on Wednesdays. Bill was useful at briefings, mostly because his abnormal normalness lent him an uncanny ability to communicate with normal, non-techy folk.

"Oh, and there's a delivery for you in the cargo bay that you're supposed to sign for," Shank bellowed over his shoulder as he shuffled away. "Thirty minutes," he hollered, before adding "Judas!" and drifted out of section 8G.

Bill took the service lift—a battered and scratched metal box that smelled of pizza and old sweat—down to basement level one. In the basement, a heavyset man with a salt-and-pepper moustache sat in a small blue-and-grey booth opposite the lift.

"Morning, Harry," Bill greeted the man as he approached the booth. "How are the wife and kids?"

Harry looked up. The smile on his face looked tired and false, as always.

"Morning, Bill. Good thanks. Parcel for you out on the street. Delivery guy wouldn't even come in, said you had to sign in person. Strange one," said Harry, half apologetically.

"Cool. Cheers Harry," Bill called over his shoulder, already making his way to the roller shutter. He was curious about the mysterious delivery, but he was also steeling himself for the inevitable disappointment when it turned out to be something entirely boring and mundane.

The door to the street stood open, but Bill couldn't see the delivery man. Stepping outside he found himself in the narrow alley that ran down the side of the building, strewn with all manner of wind-blown refuse. He looked around but could see no one. *Maybe Harry had gotten it wrong*, he thought. As he turned to head back, he froze.

There, on a low ledge of the building, directly at eye level, sat the pigeon.

Chapter Two

Bill stared at the bird.

"Do not be alarmed," said the pigeon, alarming Bill quite dramatically. It then added, *coo coo*.

The hairs on Bill's arm stood on end. A light breeze wafted down the alley, bringing the smell of rain and last night's kebabs. Bill's mind had frozen. With a snap, it kicked back into life. Grappling desperately for his skittering thoughts, he latched onto what the pigeon had said.

"Coo coo?" he asked.

"Yes, sorry," said the pigeon, contriving to look embarrassed. Its small pink tongue licked the edges of its black beak, and it ruffled its petrol-sheen feathers self-consciously. "You seemed startled, and I thought a bit of normality might help."

"Normality?" he choked.

"Yes, you know, pigeons going *coo coo* not 'do not be alarmed.'"

"Right, okay," said Bill, though he suspected things might never be right again. Or okay. "So you can talk then?" he asked. Even as he spoke some part of his brain, some higher or lower function unperturbed by a talking pigeon, told him that this was a stupid question. He was having a conversation with a pigeon, ergo it could talk.

"Err, yes," said the pigeon, "bit of a shock, I know, but you will adjust very soon, I am sure."

"Right, okay," he repeated. He was sure he'd adjust very soon. And very soon the men with sharp needles and white coats would be here for him, or he would wake up, or the hidden camera crew would appear and point out the cleverly concealed pigeon speaker. His paranoia had finally gotten the better of him. He should have taken the time to finish his breakfast; clearly this was a low blood-sugar induced hallucination. He screwed his eyes closed. If he couldn't see the pigeon it would just go away.

"Ahem," coughed the pigeon, causing Bill's eyes to pop open. It was still there, and looking at him expectantly.

"What, sorry?" said Bill.

"I said," began the pigeon, speaking slowly as if to a very small child or someone especially stupid or hard of hearing. "My name is Clyde. It's good to meet you Mr Posters."

"Call me Bill," said Bill, slipping into the relatively comfortable waters of polite protocol.

"Okay, Bill. Now, this isn't very normal."

I'll say, thought Bill.

"It's very rare that we talk to people, but the situation really is quite urgent, and I need you to come with me."

"I can't," said Bill, somewhat dreamily. "I'm due in Judas in twenty-three minutes."

"Err . . . Judas?" asked Clyde.

"It's a meeting room. There are twelve of them on the thirty-sixth floor. They're named after . . . look, is this really important right now?"

"Oh, no, no, that's all taken care of, I assure you. Nothing to worry about."

Oh no, thought Bill. *I'm talking to a pigeon named Clyde, so I suspect my worrying days are well and truly behind me.*

"But how come you can talk?" he asked, his brain finally getting through to the important stuff.

"It really is a long story. I'll be happy to fill you in on the journey if you will just step this way," said Clyde, beckoning with an out-stretched wing. *A very clean and shiny wing,* thought Bill. *Must be a pigeon with a desk job,* he chuckled nervously inside his head. Utter shock gave way to fear, quickly swamped by the all-purpose human emotional knee jerk: overriding mistrust of anything too complicated to understand.

"Uh huh, no way, I'm not going anywhere with you, Clive, or whatever your name is. What right have you got, just flapping up to someone and talking to them, that's what I want to know? I've seen you, outside my flat. You're one of those stalker pigeons, aren't you?" *What the hell was a stalker pigeon!?* "No, I'm staying right here. You can bugger off, that's what you can do!" His voice was a half scream, half whimper, and bordered on a hazardous falsetto on the dying syllables. It was difficult to breathe.

"Go on, bugger off!" he shrieked with the last of his breath, then lurched towards the pigeon, his hands waving in a shooing motion. The pigeon staggered back, its steps wooden and ungainly, right to the far edge of the ledge where it teetered as if about to fall.

For some reason Bill couldn't inhale. It was as if his throat had closed up. He stumbled forward and caught himself on the small ledge as the world started to fade.

The pigeon looked pissed off, both wings raised in an awkward attempt to regain its balance. It seemed a very uncoordinated action for a pigeon. Bill's eyes were level with the ledge, looking up at the bird. Under its left wing, nestled among the feathers, Bill could see three flashing LEDs and a small computer port. Or at least he thought he could . . . the world was getting pretty dark.

Then a flash behind his eyes, an odd woozy feeling, and everything went black.

Chapter Three

C*alm down, act professional,* Fern told herself, trying desperately to contain her excitement. This was the moment she had been waiting for her whole life; a moment that she had begun to think would never come. Slowly she pushed her hand under the baggy sleeve of the woolly jumper, reached past the six-inch dagger strapped to her wrist, and gave her skin a pinch. No, this definitely wasn't a dream. She'd lost count of the number of times she'd pinched herself that morning, and was developing a fairly tender bruise on that part of her arm. None of that mattered though, not now.

She looked down at the man passed out on the floor. His face looked peaceful, almost as if he was in a pleasant dream. He mumbled something unintelligible—she just caught the word *pigeon*—and started to drool onto the carpet. It was remarkable how unremarkable he looked. She wasn't sure what she had expected, but all her training had left her to expect something else. Something better? No, that wasn't right. As she had followed him to his workplace that morning she had tried to put her finger on what was wrong. As she had watched Bill Posters in the lift she had realised: there was certainly nothing wrong with how he looked, it was just that he looked so . . . so ordinary!

Clyde had hopped up onto the control panel and was flicking switches and pecking buttons. She'd never been in the field with such a senior officer before, yet another reason to remember her training and to stay focused. Everything was being done in a rush. She'd been briefed just before dawn, ten minutes after they'd woken her, but the man slumbering on the carpet still had no idea what was going on. She almost felt sorry for him, but for now her excitement was blotting out all other emotions.

"See if you can wake him," said Clyde, as the door closed and the capsule slid almost imperceptibly into motion.

"Yes, sir," she said smartly, pulling a scent bottle from her pocket and crouching down next to the man, making sure to avoid the spreading patch of drool on the carpet. A couple of wafts under the nostrils and the man—Bill Posters was his name, it had a nice ring to it—began to stir, his eyelids flickering and his hands twitching. Fern reached out and patted his hand and tried to make reassuring noises. This was all going to be something of a shock for Mr Bill Posters.

Bill could feel a warm pressure on his hand, soothing words working their way into the darkness with him.

"Calm yourself. Be easy now, easy," said the voice. A face drifted into view. Deep brown eyes, freckles, vaguely familiar. The smell of vanilla.

"Where am I?" Bill croaked.

"The Underground," replied the girl, the short pretty one with long, brown hair.

Thank goodness! Just the Underground, I've been asleep the whole time! No stalker pigeon named Clyde. Wait, what's a stalker pigeon? His mind relaxed for a moment, lazing in relief. He could see squishy, cream carpet, which was damp for some reason. *Wait, this isn't the Underground. Fine, outside is dark, that makes sense, but this carriage is tiny and lined with teak, with leather armchairs and . . . gah! It's being driven by a pigeon!*

"Ah, you are awake," said Clyde, flicking a switch with his scrawny pigeon foot and turning to face him. "Fern, help Mr Posters—I'm sorry, Bill—into a chair, would you?"

Gentle hands took his arm and helped him up from the floor. The instant he got to his feet a small metal cube scuttled out from the shadows and hurried over to where he had been laying.

"What the hell is that?" Bill croaked.

The cube settled over the damp patch on the carpet and with a quiet whirring noise began sucking up the moisture.

"That is a guanodrone, Mr Posters."

The carpet was now dry, and the cube raced away back to the shadows.

"A guano-what-now?" he mumbled, the pretty girl gently guiding him into one of the leather armchairs. "Thanks," he muttered to the girl, his eyes fixed on Clyde. He wasn't sure what to do, but he felt he could at least remain polite.

"That's better," said the pigeon.

"What did you do to me?" Bill grumbled, rubbing his aching forehead.

"Do to you? Nothing! I was about to offer you a cigarette when you passed out. Do you smoke?" Clyde lifted his right wing, revealing a tiny pack of cigarettes incongruously tucked between the feathers.

"No," replied Bill, thinking he might make a point of starting very soon.

"Well then, we might as well fill you in. Run the video please, Fern."

Bill watched as the girl, Fern, opened a small hatch in the wall and flicked a series of switches. She didn't seem at all bothered by Clyde the Talking Pigeon. *What kind of a person* isn't *bothered by a talking bird? What the hell is going on?* He gave his wrist a vicious pinch, almost yelping at the sharp pain. *Bugger, that was going to bruise!* So, definitely not a dream.

The lights dimmed and a small, white screen rolled down on the wall opposite Bill. An old projector flickered to life behind his head, and the numbers 5-4-3-2-1 counted down on the screen. The number 1 was replaced by a logo that looked like a squashed rat next to a chunk of text.

"This informative video is brought to you by Squamex. Look out for our other work at the National Archives, Alderney Puffin Colony and the Museum of Intestinal Distress." A smaller line at the bottom of the screen read "Squamex, number one in informative media and industrial chemicals." The logo and text slowly faded to a picture of a man neatly dressed in a tweed jacket replete with leather arm patches.

"Congratulations!" the man began, "you are one of the privileged few who are about to learn The Truth. Over the next ten minutes you will go on a journey, a great journey!" he enthused.

He was laying it on a bit thick for Bill's liking.

"You will see what almost no one else has ever seen and learn The Truth. You will learn The Truth about the world!" concluded the gentleman, pausing as if expecting applause from his audience. Bill thought that after learning that pigeons could talk he was reasonably well equipped to learn "The Truth about the world!"

He was, of course, wrong.

"Now, I know what you are thinking," the man continued, fixing the camera with a cheesy smile. "But don't worry too much. The vast majority of what you hold dear won't be affected by what you learn today. Counselling is available, and the first-year suicide rate among new initiates is at an all-time low."

At this point Clyde had seen fit to interject. "This video was made in 1972. Since then the suicide rate has sky rocketed!" he said, fixing Bill with what was possibly the pigeon equivalent of a winning smile. It involved holding his beak half open as his feathers around the edges puffed up, his black, glossy eyes shining. To Bill's horror the pigeon then gave him a friendly wink.

The video started at what it called "The Beginning" fifteen million years ago. *A lot of back story for ten minutes*, thought Bill. The scene was set with a galaxy teeming with intelligent life. Mighty races of aliens vied for supremacy, with the video focussing on two species in particular: the Pygeans and the Sharkosians. The bias of the video maker was quite clear. The Sharkosians were baddies and the Pygeans were goodies.

The aliens discovered Earth, a beautiful planet ruled by the Dino Republic. The dinosaurs promptly formed an alliance with the Sharkosians. To regain the upper hand, the Pygeans needed a new galactic ally. This task fell to the Pygean's chief geneticist, an alien who had some very interesting ideas about apes.

The video jumped around a bit, cutting from a scene of an alien science lab to a group of humans striding out of the savannah. The early humans, with the help of some nifty Pygean technology, overthrew the tyrannical Dino Republic. The fact that not a single dinosaur survived pointed to some fairly drastic Palaeolithic genocide, something the video glossed over very quickly.

With the Dinos out of the picture, peace and harmony reigned on Earth for, okay, about two-and-a-half weeks, before the early humans turned on each other. Fearing the ensuing carnage, the Pygeans took away all their advanced technology, throwing Stone Age man back into the, well, you know. *Aha*, thought the Sharkosians, *time for some revenge*. The Pygeans, feeling responsible for the plight of their genetic experiment stepped in, and they and the Sharkosians fought themselves to a standstill over the next two hundred thousand years. It would seem that some sort of truce was eventually reached, but the details and the terms of any agreement weren't featured in the video. To protect the human race, the Pygeans left a battalion on Earth. Their mission was to guide humanity through its continued evolution and defend the primates from the Sharkosians. In turn, the Sharkosians left their own troops on Earth, waiting for an opportunity to gain the upper hand, shatter the truce, wipe humanity from the face of the planet, and return Earth to the age of the dinosaurs.

Both species would conceal their presence on Earth, working in secret from the shadows. Neither humanity's secret guardians nor their ancient nemesis would reveal themselves, except in the most extreme circumstances. Over the centuries on Earth, the battalions of the interstellar warlords underwent some changes themselves. Always watchful, keeping close to humans but not developing an affinity, the Pygeans slowly evolved to match their environment. The Sharkosians, haters of humans, always keeping a distance and preferring locations untouched by human hand, wary of any opportunity to settle an old score, also evolved to serve this purpose.

The narrator was replaced with pictures of two figures, both clearly alien: one haughty looking and proud, the other vicious and cruel. Both had grey-blue skin, large, bulbous heads, and gangly limbs. Bill knew he was looking at a Pygean and a Sharkosian, and for all their aeons of conflict there was little to tell them apart. The main difference was around the mouth. The cruel-looking figure—a Sharkosian, given the video's obvious bias—sported a double row of vicious teeth in a gaping slash of a mouth. The other figure—presumably the Pygean—had a pinched and tight mouth that protruded sharply from its face.

Bill watched the two figures began to change, shifting painfully through some 1970s version of digital morphing. After a few eye-wrenching contortions, Bill was shocked that he could instantly recognise the two figures. One from personal experience; the other from his nightmares and a trip to the aquarium when he was twelve. He glanced at Clyde, who gave him a knowing smile. Bill turned his attention back to the video; it was nearing the end. "For millennia an uneasy cease-fire has been observed," concluded the video, "right under humanity's nose. And now you too know The Truth, you have been inducted!"

Bill sat there, slack jawed. The presentation had been short, but had used all of the available special effects of the day. The entire tale had been portrayed with mighty sweeping vistas, vast fight scenes of man versus dinosaur, alien craft buzzing around Earth like bees around a hive, and of course the odd morphing sequence. The video on its own was something to behold (indeed, it featured in our galaxy's top ten public information broadcasts), but it was the content that had blown Bill away. He hadn't blinked throughout the entire presentation. His eyes, dry from ten minutes of non-stop exposure to the barren air of the teak-lined carriage, scraped painfully closed. Shaking his head he rubbed his sore eyeballs, trying to clear his mind and make sense of it all.

Taken on its own, on any given day, Bill would have sat there, chuckled, and said, "Pull the other one, it has bells on." Watching a video while he could see a talking pigeon out of the corner of his eye was another matter. And there was also the feeling, deep down, that this all made a lot of sense. Okay, so a lot of it made no sense at all, and Bill was sure it wasn't as black and white as the man in the video would have him believe, but something about it felt right. He cautiously opened his left eye. The bird was staring at him with a vacant pigeon expression, only now the look seemed to carry a hidden menace, a disguised intellect lurking beneath each shiny eyeball. How much could he trust this alien-come-skyrat? How much of this was true? Bill turned to Fern. She was human, didn't *she* find this rather odd? The pretty brown eyes were intent on him, her smile reassuring. Wait, she *was* human, right?

"Err, you're okay with all this then?" he asked her nervously.

She nodded encouragingly.

"And, err. . . you're a space-alien too?"

For a second it looked like the girl was about to burst out laughing, but she controlled herself and just shook her head.

"Nope, I'm an ordinary human, just like you. Well, not just like you, obviously, clearly we're quite different in a number of ways. Some very important ways, when you think about it, but—"

Clyde cleared his throat, half cough, half squawk, and Bill turned back to him.

"But you *are* the descendant of a mighty space-alien?" he asked the pigeon.

"More or less," replied the pigeon.

"Who helped humans defeat the dinosaurs?"

"Uh huh."

"And who watch over us and protect us while those, err . . . other ones are plotting our downfall?"

"Pretty much."

"Not in fact a scabby skyrat?"

"Not as such, no."

Bill glanced at Fern; she was still beaming encouragement at him. With a sigh he rubbed his temples, something he did when he had a headache. He didn't *actually* have a headache, but it felt like he should. This was all far too strange, but if he ignored that for a moment there was only really one question he needed answering.

"Okay, so what does all this have to do with me?"

Clyde puffed up his feathers and fixed Bill with a meaningful stare, which was no mean feat for a pigeon, especially given he had to keep bobbing his head from side to side to keep both eyes on Bill.

"Because you, Bill Posters, are of vital importance to humanity's survival."

Chapter Four

D ramatic pauses had never really had much effect on him. The pigeon sat there, chest puffed out and eyes intent, but by this point Bill had firmly suspended disbelief and had been prepared for almost anything. This fitted with the ludicrous content of the video as well.

"Right, okay, so I am the Chosen One, destined to save humanity?"

A slight pause.

"Err, not quite." The pigeon shuffled his three-toed feet. "Actually, you are the chosen 12(b)."

"The chosen 12(b)!" Bill was quite affronted. "What the hell does that mean?"

Clyde looked distinctly uncomfortable. "Oh dear, oh dear," he muttered. "This is all very embarrassing, but I can explain. You see, long ago we initiated a programme to progressively scan the genes of every new-born human, identifying those with the necessary qualities." Bill opened his mouth to interrupt. "No, please, let me finish first. Thank you," continued Clyde. Bill closed his mouth again and remained silent.

"As I said," Clyde continued, "we identify all those with the necessary qualities for great deeds. Every generation has a chosen one, but we worked out long ago that you need backups, so we also identify a chosen two, three, four, five, six, and so on, ranked in the order of their likelihood to be able to save mankind. Once the process to identify individuals was established it turned out to be very easy to extend this as far as we liked really . . ." Clyde trailed off, shuffling his clawed feet uncomfortably.

"Oh, I see," said Bill. He still felt aggrieved, but was somewhat mollified at being number twelve.

"So I am the twelfth most likely person to save mankind? That's not bad," he said, feeling his injured pride picking itself off the floor.

Clyde flapped a wingtip around his neck, as if trying to loosen a collar that wasn't there. "Err, again, not quite correct. You see, the numbers were getting quite high, so we designed a tranche system with letters, and each tranche represents a subset below the tranche above."

Bill thought he could see the logic in this, but he had a sinking feeling in his stomach, his injured pride preparing itself for another fall. "Okay, so I am in b, how many in a?" he asked.

"Each tranche has 99,999 members, but I am afraid that the lettering system is not alphabetical. You see, first we have tranche (e), who represent an exceptional chance of success, then we have tranche (v) with very high, then tranche (w) with well-above average, then tranche (a) with above average, and then—"

"Okay, okay, I get the picture," Bill interrupted. "So what is (b)?"

Clyde hesitated. He didn't look comfortable at all. "Errrrmm, below average."

"Below average! I'm the twelfth person with a below-average chance of saving humanity?"

"Correct."

After the "grave importance to the world" bit, this felt distinctly like a kick in the teeth.

"Tell it to me straight, Clyde, out of all the tranches that makes me—"

"Number 768,271," said Clyde with no hint of apology in his voice.

"Brilliant, so I'm humanity's 768,271st best chance of survival? The chosen 768,271?"

Clyde nodded.

Bill grumbled something he wouldn't want repeated, then a thought occurred. "If this is true, then why am I here and not Mr or Ms 1(e)?"

Again, Clyde looked embarrassed, coupled with some birdy emotion Bill couldn't identify. If pushed he might have gone for smug, but that couldn't be it.

"Because they are dead, Bill."

"Oh dear, I'm sorry," said Bill automatically, with some part of his brain that could calmly assimilate the news that humanity's best hope for survival was dead adding *maybe we all will be.*

"Err, 2(e)?"

"Dead, Bill."

"3(e)?"

"Dead."

The sinking feeling in Bill's stomach was back and dropping like a stone. "4(e)?"

"Dead."

"5(e)?"

"Dead."

"6(e)?"

"Dead."

"7(e)?"

"Listen Bill, this could go on for some time."

For a reason he couldn't articulate Bill felt a rising panic. "What about . . . 1(n)?" he blurted at random.

"Oh, very much alive," said Clyde, "but tranche (n) represents 'not a hope in hell, not on your nelly, no way, nu huh, not happening.'"

"Oh," the brief wave of relief fled. "What about 1(a)?" he asked, remembering this was a good one.

"Listen, Bill, suffice it to say that everyone, *everyone* higher than you is dead."

"Dear God!" gasped Bill. A minute ago he had not known of the existence of this elite group of people, but now he felt their passing like the death of a fourth favourite cousin.

"That's right, Bill, you are humanity's 768,271st best hope for survival, and you are the best we have left."

For a second Bill didn't know how to react. Hunting though a lexicon of emotions, he opted for indignation. "How could you let this happen!" he cried. "How did they die?"

"Well, some would have been of natural causes. Some, possibly even double figures. But the majority have been systematically hunted down and assassinated by the Sharkosians."

"Dear God!" said Bill again. "But how?"

If Clyde had looked embarrassed before, he was positively crimson now. Except he wasn't, as he remained grey and bluish. "Well, we keep records, and it would appear that a disc containing the names, addresses, and bank details of a large group of tranches went missing during an inter-departmental transfer." Clyde must have noticed the horrified look on Bill's face, because he added, "Oh, don't worry, yours weren't included."

Bill raised an eyebrow.

"Well, you see it was the group designated Alpha: reasonable chance of survival. Your tranche heads up group Omega—"

"No need to go on," interrupted Bill, whose passing knowledge of the Greek alphabet was enough to leave him feeling queasy. "How do you assign numbers to people anyway, what on earth are you looking for?" he huffed.

"Honestly no idea," replied Clyde.

"What do you mean, no idea?"

"Well, a computer program does it all, but to be honest no one really understands how it all works any more, it just kind of does."

"It just kind of does?" repeated Bill, heavy on the sarcasm with a side of disdain.

"No need to get offended," Clyde retorted. "I'd rather not be having this conversation either."

Bill sniffed and decided to take it on the chin for now. "So, if you don't know how it works, how do you even know that it works at all?" he asked, but Clyde had clearly been expecting this.

"Empirical evidence of course. You think this is the first grave threat the world has faced? History is littered with the work of many a great 1(e), and more than a few passable 2(e)s. Winston Churchill, Augustus Caesar, Genghis Khan, Barry Manilow—"

Bill interrupted, "Wait, you say 1(e) and 2(e)s. This whole down-to-Mr-768,271 business. This has never happened before, has it?"

A long, barren pause. Despite being in an entirely enclosed space, a whistle of wind passed through and, if it had been even remotely possible, a tumbleweed would have rolled past.

"In the early days, before we had perfected the tracking and monitoring of subjects, there was an instance where a 4(e) was called on to save mankind. Managed it too, though it all got very sticky. Lost Atlantis to the bloody Sharkosians as a result. And a 3(e) was called on not all that long ago. You are familiar with the Dark Ages?" Clyde's tone made his meaning all too clear.

"Look, this is a really poor show, I know," Clyde continued, "administrative cock up and we are all in the guano, but you really are our least worst hope."

"You mean best," Bill insisted.

"Of course."

Bill thought for a second. It was all a bit much, but he was aware of how many people there were in the world. 768,271 must mean he was up there . . .

"Okay, I'll do it," said Bill, making an attempt at gusto.

"Oh jolly good," said Clyde, a fragile smile on his birdy face. "It was either that or we would have had to kill you. Can't just have those that know The Truth wandering around." Clyde nodded to something just over Bill's shoulder, and Bill turned in time to see Fern tucking something into her baggy jumper. She really was quite pretty, he thought absently, before a cough from Clyde, a sound like a small dog being stepped on, caught his attention.

"It's not all doom and gloom though," Clyde continued. "We may not understand the workings of *Councel*, but it does give us a handy object when it throws out a number. Something to aid the candidate on their way, always something that they need, above everything else." The pigeon paused.

"Of course, we don't always understand what the item is for," he continued, "and in some cases it is more cryptic than others. Weaponry is a common choice. Back in the Bronze Age, a 1(e) got the most fabulous shield. Amazingly strong but feather light. It was clear what that was for, while others . . . well, here you are," he finished, slipping something black and rectangular across the table, an ungainly action for a pigeon, which involved a lot of flapping.

The item looked like a small leather-bound notebook. A delicate, silver clasp on one edge held it closed, and it had an embossed logo on the front. A pigeon in flight was displayed proudly, together with the motto *"Ferr Lap Ing Peck Ingspr Ed Indis Ease."*

"That's ancient pigeon," explained Clyde. "'Watch, defend, protect.'"

Bill fumbled with the clasp. It seemed to be made for smaller fingers than his, and it was a little tricky to work. He could feel Fern hovering over his shoulder ready to offer assistance, but this was his magic mission critical tool, not hers, so he clawed at the silver with his well-trimmed fingernails. With a delicate click, the clasp slid open and the two halves popped apart. Bill stared at the contents.

"Ah, now I know what you are thinking," said Clyde.

You do? thought Bill.

"Like I said, we never really know what the item is for, but we are told that it will assist the one chosen in their darkest hour, and could very well be the difference between death and victory."

Uh huh.

"And often the meaning is clear, and sometimes it is not, as in this case—"

"This is a, a . . ." Humanity's 768,271st best hope for survival stared at his ultimate weapon and was unable to finish.

"Yes, that's right. It's a manicure kit."

Chapter Five

Even though it was an object of superior craftsmanship, it was far from what he was expecting. Bill was looking at a finely worked leather case containing a delicate, silver nail file, three fine-grade horsehair brushes of varying sizes and firmness, a silver pair of nail scissors, some odd, small twisty device that he had never seen before, and a pair of nail clippers. *Great. I have to save the world, and to assist me I have the world's greatest hand care kit. Whatever I have to do I am going to struggle, but man I am going to have neat nails.* In a daze, he plucked the nail clippers from their perfectly shaped receptacle. They felt good in his hands, well balanced and cool against his skin. But on the whole it was not what he would have chosen when told he was a person of paramount importance (albeit something of a stand-in). A ray gun maybe, or a magic knife, or a cloak of invisibility . . . now they would be handy. This would just be, well, *handy*. Flicking the handle around, he gave the clippers an experimental clip. They even had the can opener attachment. Gross. Who in the world wanted to open a can of food with something used to lop off grotty nails? He couldn't figure out why nail clippers often had that attachment, unless it really was for cleaning under your toenails (the only use he had ever employed it for). He didn't even have the energy to comment. With a sigh he closed the clasp and tucked the whole kit into his pocket.

"Be careful with that, your life could depend on it you know," said Clyde, his voice lacking conviction.

Bill sighed. "Sure thing."

Behind the pigeon a small amber light began to blink rhythmically.

"Ah, just pulling in now," said Clyde. Sure enough the teak-lined capsule had stopped moving, but the darkness outside was as thick as ever. "Fern, take Bill to Keith for briefing, there really is no time to lose. I am needed elsewhere. Good luck, Bill Posters, we are counting on you."

The puffed-up figure of the pigeon might have been comical, were it not for the sincerity of the words. Counting on him to do what? It was one thing to be the chosen 768,271, but what did they want him to do? Before he could ask, Clyde turned away and flicked a switch on the control panel. At least, that seemed to be what he intended to do, but his claw missed the switch and caught on the dial to its left. Wobbling on his single-standing leg, Clyde fumbled with the dial, the lights in the cabin fading up and down as he did so, before he finally got the claw back on the dashboard with a click. Raising his leg to have another go at the switch he wobbled some more, and this time Bill was sure he was going to fall, when Fern rushed forward and flicked the offending switch.

"Thank you, Fern," said Clyde, clearly embarrassed at his clumsiness.

The far wall, where the projector screen had been, faded to an opaque brown, like a cloud of milk spreading through a mug of tea. As quickly as it had faded to brown, the surface stippled, then disappeared altogether, revealing a brightly lit platform. At the same time a tube—about the diameter of a dinner plate—extended down from the ceiling just to the right of Clyde's head. The pigeon took two wooden and wobbly steps to the side until he was positioned directly under the tube. With a rush of wind and a sucking pop, the pigeon disappeared up the tube, causing Bill to jump out of his seat. A single purple feather fluttered down onto the cream carpet and the tube retracted back into the wall.

Fern had already walked onto the platform, and made her way off to the left after signalling for Bill to follow. Feeling a little uneasy about walking through a recently solid wall, Bill stepped quickly on to the platform, squinting at the sudden brightness of the light. The floor was a beautiful, if haphazard, mosaic of tiny tiles, each about the size of his thumbnail. The wall was a creamy, white colour, like a vast sheet of ivory, with bracket lights near the top flooding the ceiling with light. Squinting upward, Bill could see why the light levels were so dazzling. A vast mirror was spread across the ceiling in an arch. As Bill looked up at himself, he felt a little queasy: the vast concave mirror acted like an oversized fun house attraction, stretching his face to obscene proportions.

The platform itself was much longer than the capsule they had arrived in. Bill wasn't surprised to find that this tube line had no tracks and no visible means of propulsion. He couldn't see anything as he stared down into the gap between the platforms. Nothing at all. Given the light levels, this was remarkable. *Maybe it's painted jet black*, he thought. The most remarkable thing was the smell. Bill had never been high up a mountain, but he imagined this was what the air might be like there. Crisp and clear, almost thin, with a conspicuous absence of any scent.

"Cool, isn't it?" said Fern, as she led Bill along the brightly lit platform.

"Where are we?" Bill asked.

"Just underneath London Branch, which is just underneath the Palace of Westminster."

"Cool," said Bill, not knowing why. The silence dragged. "Err, how did we get here?" he asked, trying to fill the awkward pause. Fern gave him a sideways glance, as if he was mad, or maybe she was wondering if he was okay.

"Are you okay? We came here by Tube. You were definitely there, and we just got off."

"Oh, right. Yes, I know that, but that wasn't the Tube that I'm used to."

"Oh, I understand," she laughed, a musical sound like the tinkling of tiny bells. "We came here on the original Tube, not the Underground you are used to. You've just been on the real Tube, built around 6,000 BC in the modern calendar. Sits considerably deeper than the one you are used to."

Bill thought for a moment. "Right, so there are in fact two Underground systems. The one I and three million other people are used to, and the one I just travelled on being driven by a pigeon."

"That's right," replied Fern, clearly pleased he had caught on. "Why else do you think they have to close it for so long every night for 'routine maintenance?' Takes them a while servicing both systems."

"But wouldn't someone notice, doesn't someone—anyone—notice dirty great tunnels that shouldn't be there?"

"Of course they do," said Fern, adopting the tone used to explain something very simple to someone quite dim. "All the time in fact. Why do you think civil engineering projects are always running into 'Roman ruins' or having to relocate 'Victorian sewers'?"

Bill gave up, and for the next ten minutes he just followed Fern through a dizzying maze of corridors. He almost missed Clyde the pigeon: at least he hadn't implied that every word out of Bill's mouth was simple-minded. Okay, so he wasn't sure he could actually tell if a pigeon was being patronising (that a pigeon could *be* patronising was a fairly new thought), and he did tend to go a bit brain dead around pretty girls. But this time he had a pretty good excuse. Discovering that

32

pigeons were sentient aliens that buzzed around under London in an 8,000-year-old Tube network was a pretty big deal, not to mention the whole least-worst hope for humanity thing.

They rounded a corner and suddenly things got a lot busier. People and pigeons were hurrying in every direction through the maze of white tunnels. That the pigeons were hurrying purposefully along, instead of pecking aimlessly at the floor, was disturbing, but not nearly as upsetting as the fact that a number were chatting away to each other. There was even a pigeon deep in conversation with a person! Walking behind a small group of pigeons Bill could just catch a few snatches of the conversation. It was something about the state of the economy. Without pausing in its stride, one of the pigeons unleashed a mighty dollop of bird poo onto the gleaming white floor tiles.

"Gross!" said Bill, not quite loud enough for the offending pigeon to hear. Before they reached the patch of poo, a small metal cube—identical to the one that had sucked up the damp patch from the carpet on the Tube—hurtled from a small hatch in the wall. The cube passed quickly over the dirtied floor and shot back through the hatch, leaving spotless tiles gleaming in its wake.

"See, that's another guanodrone, it keeps the place clean," said Fern.

Bill studied the floor as they passed the area cleaned by the cube, still circling around it just to be sure.

"Wait, you have those cubes so the pigeons can just poop all over the floor? Can't they just use a toilet, or some bird equivalent?"

Fern shook her head. "It's impossible, Bill; their bodies aren't made like that. When they've got to go they *have* to go, usually about every three to five minutes. It causes them considerable pain if they don't, and anyway the required muscles are very undeveloped . . . You'll get used to it. Just don't walk too close behind them."

Bill glanced around at the pigeons hurrying in both directions through the tunnel. Sure enough, every now and then one of the birds would poo on the floor, and the small metal cubes raced around to keep the floor clean.

"Must be very efficient, this place *seems* very clean," said Bill, making a mental note to avoid touching any flat surface until he was back in the real world.

"They are," said Fern. "They have to be. Goodness, if they ever broke down!" She gave another small laugh, clearly amused at the thought of a world slowly filling up with bird poo. "We're nearly there, we'll take a shortcut through the drill hall." She paused briefly in front of a large set of steel doors marked "Drill Hall." With a shove, she pushed the left door open.

As Bill stepped through the doors, it felt like a scene from a childhood nightmare.

Behind the door was a small walkway, which circled around a vast auditorium. A racetrack ran from one side of the room to the other with a swimming pool in the centre. In one corner stood a wide pole suspended over a smaller pool, a pile of pillows stacked haphazardly against the wall. People dressed in inflatable penguin costumes (Bill hoped they were people; he couldn't really tell) charged down the racetrack clutching coloured balls in their arms. Evidently, this was a team event, as the balls were brightly coloured, different for each penguin: green, yellow, blue, red, and orange. After the first bit of the racetrack, the penguins had to negotiate their way across a raft of inflatables on the pool (if you fell into the water it seemed like you had to go back to the beginning). They would then waddle the remainder of the track before depositing the balls into a similarly coloured bucket.

It then got weirder.

Taking the large rifle they had strapped around their waists, the penguin-clad people shot seven targets at the far end of the hall (much like the targets in the shooting at the winter Olympics). They would then engage in what could only be described as hand-to-hand combat with a man dressed in a walrus suit. Once they had pinned the opposing walrus it was a short sprint to a large button, one coloured for each team. As Bill and Fern reached the far end of the hall, the red penguin achieved this first, ripping off his penguin head and giving a whoop of victory. *Very, very odd*, thought Bill as he and Fern exited the drill hall.

"Basic training for the commandos," said Fern, by way of explanation. "Keith heads up the training section. Here we are." She ushered Bill through the doors and moved to close them.

"Aren't you coming in?" asked Bill a little nervously.

"Nah, top secret and all that, for your eyes only."

"Really?"

"Nah, heard it before, I'm going to get a cuppa. See you later."

With a dull thud, the door shut and left Bill standing in the darkness. It was the first time he had been alone for what seemed like ages.

"Err, hello?" he called into the dark, not caring who answered but really hoping it wasn't a pigeon.

Chapter Six

For the second time that morning Mr Gring felt a quirk of doubt. It wasn't a feeling that he was used to, and it annoyed him. Doubt was for weaklings, uncertainty was for the feckless. The only thing that mattered was action: the will to do what was necessary, what needed to be done to reach your aim. He had seen how easily others could be paralysed by doubt and it sickened him. Worse still were those simple-minded fools who *had* certainty but lacked conviction, people who could see their path but refused to tread it, for fear of who they might hurt as a result. Everyone in your way must be swept aside and crushed; it was the only true path to what you wanted.

Mr Gring had been working for the sharks for five years now, and the whole time his employment had been like a breath of fresh air. To say that they shared his world view would be an understatement. The clarity of their vision, and the freedom with which he was allowed to go about his work, made every day a fresh pleasure. They didn't quibble when he needed to torture a prisoner; not a fishy eyebrow was raised when he ordered a well-placed assassination or two. The sharks had been more than happy to support everything he did in their name, support which he had rewarded by bringing them to the brink of victory. Over the last five years, he had revelled in the frisson of a job well executed, but now there came this tiny worm of doubt. They had reached the end-game, and the sharks were positively giddy with excitement. For the first time he wondered: is this *really* what I want?

The Shark King—grey, scarred, and hideous—cleared his throat.

"I'm sorry, my Lord, what did you say?" asked Mr Gring, his attention returning to the conversation.

"I said," growled the Shark King, partially digested clumps of grey fish matter spraying from his teeth-ringed maw, "how go the preparations?"

"Very well, my Lord, the device is almost complete."

"Excellent news. If it works as well as your other inventions our victory is assured."

The Shark King leaned forward on the handlebars in front of him and rolled to the edge of the huge, reinforced glass dome. The room was a perfect circle almost thirty metres in diameter. The glass dome started at the concrete floor and soared high above, wrapping around on all sides. It was a perfect hemisphere, the glass almost a metre thick. Mr Gring had designed it himself, along with the rest of the shark's Atlantic base.

Set into the floor at three metre intervals were long fluorescent bulbs, the white light pouring upwards and filling the dome with brightness. A clever array of sensors and mirrors in the light casing ensured that the light never dazzled the occupants of the room, the overall effect being like swimming in a diffuse, source-less light. Mr Gring was particularly proud of the final lighting feature: a setting that allowed the mirrors to be precisely aligned to bounce all the light from the dome to a single point on the floor, a spot marked with a small, red tile. Standing in this spot, with this feature set, would result in instant and permanent blindness, followed within thirty seconds by death (unless of course the blinded individual managed to move from the red tile, a flaw in the design that so far Mr Gring had been unable to resolve). The sharks of course saw little value in such cunning design, preferring the simple approach of eating their enemies, but they humoured him out of respect for his genius.

In the centre of the domed room was the sole item of furniture: a large dark oak table, its surface hewn from a single tree. No chairs ringed the table, the sharks having no need for them. That there was a table at all was something of a mystery—Mr Gring had never seen a shark use if for anything—but having a table in the King's conference room had become something of a shark affectation, and the Shark King had insisted that the domed room contain one.

Mr Gring walked over to join the Shark King at the edge of the room. The inky mass of the sea swirled around the enormous dome. A shoal of fish, their silver scales flashing in the light, skirted the dome and disappeared into the darkness. He could just make out his reflection, and that of the Shark King, in the thick glass. Mr Gring was a tall man, almost six foot three, but the monstrous sea beast loomed high over him. His whipcord thinness, next to the wide, blubbery mass of the Shark King, added to the incongruity of the pair reflected in the glass. His bright orange hair was cut close to his scalp, the skin drawn tight across the protruding bones of his face. His large ears, protruding at ninety degrees from his head like saucers, looked almost comical, an appearance compounded by his lack of eyebrows (the product of an industrial accident while a child). All thought of humour was erased by one look at his eyes: hollow grey pits that contained not a shred of mercy. It was just as well the eyes served to stifle laughter: Mr Gring had killed everyone—*everyone*—who had ever laughed at his appearance.

"Ah, Mr Gring, this invention in particular represents the most supreme liberation for my people," continued the Shark King. "You have no idea of the privations we have suffered, the torment we have endured. Finally the last barrier to our ascension has been removed and we can take our rightful place!"

38

As he spoke, the Shark King caressed the handlebars of the device with a thick, rubbery fin. His multiple rows of razor sharp teeth slurred the words, and a mouth never intended for intelligent speech ground the words out in hard, flat syllables, like chunks of grey dog food.

The device he was referring to looked like a wheeled pogo stick, handlebars rising up to fin height from two large wheels. A special bracket between the wheels supported the tail. A truly terrifying sight, Mr Gring stood next to a large great white shark riding a modified Segway.

"It was really quite simple. Merely a matter of working out the balance while under momentum through correct weight distribution."

"Yes, yes. You have told me before."

Unperturbed by the shark's tone Mr Gring pressed on. "Of course, I was worried that the cover of marketing them to humans would appear a little too flimsy, given how pointless they are if you actually *have* legs, but so far no one seems to have batted an eyelid."

"Enough!" snapped the Shark King, baring most of his highly impressive teeth in the process. Mr Gring was not impressed. He waited impassively while the Shark King folded his gums back over his arrayed incisors.

"I require a full update—take me through the scale model again!"

Mr Gring sighed, but not so loud that the Shark King could hear him. After all, it just wasn't a good idea to anger an eight metre great white shark. "Of course," he said.

As Mr Gring knew well, all sharks were James Bond fans. They loved the films, and even went nuts for the books (especially any involving *Jaws*—except *that* scene, which was edited out when shown in shark cinemas). As a result, any fiendish plan—or indeed any plan at all—was given much more credence if it involved a scale model. This plan was a humdinger, and as a result Mr Gring had furnished not only a scale model, but a scale model hidden behind an overly elaborate concealing mechanism.

As they made their way towards the large oak table—one walking, the other gliding effortlessly on two mini all-terrain tyres—the table divided neatly in two and spread apart to reveal a map of the world. Across the map were littered LEDs, all glistening white like a sprinkling of stars wedged in the Earth's surface. A layer of glass slid out of the parting table leaves, forming a barrier over the scale model. As the glass clicked into place, Mr Gring and the Shark King strode and rolled respectively out over the map, coming to a stop over the mid-Atlantic. Mr Gring had taken the Shark King through the plan at least one hundred times, so he was struggling to inject much interest into what was now a well-rehearsed script.

"In essence, the device is not a single machine, but a vast multitude of individual elements. It represents the culmination of decades of work through a variety of cover organisations, governments, lobbyists, and influential individuals. Its ultimate goal: control of planet Earth."

Mr Gring suppressed a wince. The damn fool shark was grinning away, again, as always. How many times did he need to go through this for the idiot to stop getting so obviously delighted? Sure, he liked his work to be appreciated, but the stupid fish was practically wagging his tail.

"Our installations are spread across the globe." The lights flashed brighter for a second. "On the day of reckoning, the following will be set to active," some lights flashed blue, "while others will be set to passive energy absorption." The remaining LEDs flashed green. "From that moment we will have complete control of the world's weather, able to wreak environmental havoc, and bring benign bounties to those who bow to Sharkosian rule."

"Excellent, excellent! Tell me again, what do humans call these doomsday devices?"

"Wind farms?!" spat Bill, two thousand miles away in a small white-walled briefing room.

"Yes, Bill, wind farms. Get a grip, would you!"

"Okay, sorry Cheggers," he apologised to the man sat opposite.

Bill had sat in the darkened room, assuming he was there alone, for about five minutes. When the lights had burst on, he was shocked to discover a man sitting opposite him, his face a study of intense concentration. Even more shocking was the identity of the man: none other than 1980s kid's game-show host Keith Chegwin, aka Cheggers.

"For the last time, I am not Cheggers. You clearly have me confused with someone else." The man growled out the words, spots of red appearing on his cheeks and spreading backwards across his face and towards his short, ginger hair. Bill had the absurd notion that when the two circles of red met, the man's head would explode. It *was* an absurd notion, but just in case Bill decided it was safest to try and calm the man down.

"Of course, you've said that already. Sorry Keith."

Bill wasn't convinced at all. He'd grown up watching this man's TV shows. He had dreamed of one day taking part: forming a team and taking on the ridiculous assault course, getting covered in foam, running over inflatables, falling off into swimming pools, sliding down the final plastic slide to punch the big red button and win the race. No, he'd know Cheggers anywhere, and right now anywhere was sitting opposite him. After all, hadn't Fern told him that Keith was in charge of training, and hadn't Bill seen his work first hand in the Drill Hall? Bill was certain, but the man was adamant it was a case of mistaken identity, and had asked to simply be addressed by his rank: Colonel.

Bill could distinctly remember that Cheggers was a small man, not that much taller than the kids taking part in his wacky races. *They must have used some trick of camera work to hide the fact that he's about six foot eight*, Bill thought. Sitting opposite him in military uniform, crew cut—and for some reason a bandoleer of anti-tank shells slung around his chest—Colonel Cheggers looked mean. And he was mean.

"Make me say it again and I'm gonna come over there and give you a slap. And it is Colonel, not Keith."

It was no good. Bill was already battling not to call him Cheggers. Colonel was a bridge too far.

"Sorry. Okay Keith."

Keith scowled at him and—oh dear Lord—took a shell from the bandoleer and started chewing on it like a great obscene cigar.

"But this is madness, how could a wind farm be dangerous. How would it all work?"

"Its operation is very simple," Mr Gring continued with his rehearsed script, trying to keep the creeping boredom from his voice.

"The world's weather is controlled by vast atmospheric pumps powered by the sun and forever circling the globe." The glass beneath their feet, a large computer display, erupted in images of clouds and detailed isobars. Mr Gring was well aware of how much the sharks valued scale models, but there was only so much you could achieve with coloured LEDs.

"With our wind farms we will be able to manipulate these world-wide weather systems. Active farms will push weather around, while passive farms will sap all of the energy from the weather, making it limp and lifeless."

"Yes, yes!" said the Shark King, really very excited. "And what of these?" he asked, pointing to a cluster of LEDs burning a vivid red.

"Our ground troops, supreme commander, which will seize the moment of atmospheric confusion and invade The Capital."

"Sorry," said Bill, looking hard at Keith opposite him in the Pygean briefing room, hoping he wasn't about to get a slap. "You just said 'ground troops.' Shark ground troops?"

Keith bit down hard on the shell. Bill flinched. "Yes. Seems the Sallys have found a way to move around on land. Of course, they've always been able to breathe air, something they don't tell you on *Animal Planet*, but the whole lack of legs things has kept 'em down there. That and the other thing."

"The Sallys?"

"Sharks lad, the sharks. You can't just call them 'sharks' can you, takes too long. You've got to have a short nickname for the enemy, everyone knows that!"

Bill counted the two words in his head. The look on Keith's face convinced him not to raise the absence of any obvious efficiency.

"Right, okay," said Bill simply, watching the red circles on Keith's face lapse momentarily into retreat. "And you said 'capital' right? You mean London?"

"Goodness no, not the capital of England, The Capital of the world, lad."

"Right, okay, and where is that?"

"Leamington Spa."

"Leamington Spa?"

"I swear, the next time you repeat what I have said you'll be eating that pretty parka!"

Bill wasn't wearing a parka, but he didn't need to understand the threat to get the message.

"With Leamington Spa in our grasp, nothing will stop us!" said the Shark King. "And what of the other part of our master plan?"

"Also moving according to schedule," said Mr Gring, unable to keep the satisfaction from his voice.

"The individual?" asked the Shark King.

"Perfect for the role, my Lord. That part of the plan should present us with no problems."

"Good. Make sure that it stays that way." The Shark King's hunger to hear the plan yet again was now satisfied, and he was rolling away. With a heavy sigh, Mr Gring pressed a button on the small remote control in his pocket. The scale model of the doomsday device lowered through the floor, the two halves of the giant table sliding back over the top. On impulse he pressed another button on the remote control, listening with satisfaction as the mirrors in the light casings flicked into position, the beams of artificial light bouncing from the dome and converging on the red tile set in the floor. For a second he imagined his enemies, everyone who had ever wronged him, howling in the intense beam of light. He would have his revenge on them all, everyone and anyone that had ever mocked him, ever doubted his genius, ever found his appearance comical. If the entire world had to suffer as a result . . . well, that was necessary, and if it was necessary then it *must* come to pass.

A small smile sprung on his cruel lips. Yes, that was the answer: a concealed trap, serrated jaws that would close over the legs. It could be hidden under the floor, in much the same way that the doomsday device scale model was hidden under the table. This could trigger at the same time as the mirrors converged the light on the red tile, locking the victim in place and holding them there through the thirty seconds from blindness to death. Perfect.

He pulled a small radio from his pocket, pushed down on the button, and held it to his mouth. "Gring here. I'm in the King's conference chamber. Yes, I need some serrated steel, a heavy duty spring, welding gear, and a tile cutter."

"Yes sir!" came the terrified voice over the radio.

Mr Gring tapped the short antenna against his cheek for a few seconds before pressing the button on the radio again.

"Gring again. Send up five of the prisoners as well. Doesn't matter who: I have something that they can help me test."

Bill rubbed his temples and wondered how much new information the brain could take in one day. He thought he was doing quite well, all things considered. He wasn't a hero—far from it in fact—but something told him that this chosen 768,271 was the real deal. If it wasn't, it was the most beautifully orchestrated hoax he had ever heard of, and worth going along with the ride just to see what would happen next. Even that display of equanimity was very unlike him, to almost an unsettling degree. Was he really okay with all this? He felt his pulse start to race and his breathing quicken. *Calm Bill, focus on the facts, break it down to the facts*, he told himself.

Sharks—who had always terrified him, so finding out they were humanity's mortal enemy was no great surprise—had built a vast doomsday device. This device, disguised as a global network of wind-farms, could be used to control the weather and allow the sharks to rain down terror (metaphorically and potentially literally) on humankind. The doomsday device would be activated alongside an invasion by land-based shark troops, who would target Leamington Spa, an unimpressive market town in the middle of England. A town that had previously only featured in his imagination as a place that might be populated by lemmings, but which in fact was The Capital of the world.

The plan for salvation was simple: to destroy the doomsday device. The pigeon's chief scientist—a notion that Bill found the least remarkable thing in the whole situation—had found a weakness in the machine's design. Intelligence reports indicated the presence of an emergency override button, one that could destroy the entire device and ruin the shark's plans. This button, currently on the other side of the world, had to be retrieved and brought back to pigeon HQ.

Only one question remained.

"Why me?" asked Bill.

Keith looked confused, his teeth grinding around the anti-tank shell, causing a noise that put Bill's teeth on edge. Keith pulled the mangled shell from his mouth and dropped it on the desk.

"What? I was told Clyde had explained all that to you on the way here? You're the Chosen—" Keith looked down at some notes on the table in front of him.

"768,271," said Bill helpfully.

"That's right!" said Keith with gusto, as if that settled the matter.

"But why me? Why do I have to get the—what is it, the button—and bring it back here?"

Keith looked more confused than ever. "Look laddie, I thought we just went through that? You are the Chosen—"

"768,271."

"Right. Which means it has to be you. No one higher, you're it, our number one guy, our star, our best hope. If you ignore the 768,270 other people of course, all of whom are dead."

"But why *me*?" Bill's voice sounded worryingly like a squeal.

Keith's face softened, the vast muscles in his jaw, like twin high tensile cables, slackened off a fraction. "Listen, I know this is a lot to take in. Did Clyde mention Councel?"

The name rang a bell. It was the computer that Clyde said assigned every human ever born with their rank, the number that indicated their ability to save the world. Bill nodded.

"Good. There is too much for me to go into here, there is not enough time, but suffice it to say that Councel is never wrong. Never. For millennia we have trusted its guidance. It is non-specific—it never tells us what must be done, or how, or when—but it always says who. Every generation needs a hero Bill, whether people realise it or not. And thanks to Councel, every generation *has* a hero."

Bill hesitated. He'd never wanted this, he wanted a normal life. An average life. He wanted his saggy bed, his indoor garden furniture, Ella's chair with the rip in the cushion, the sofa that smelt of pizza.

"But I'm not a hero, I'm number seven hundred—"

Keith waved his hand dismissively in the air and fixed Bill with a steely-eyed stare. "No more of that soldier!" he barked. "You *are* our man! We have trusted Councel since the dawn of history, and we won't stop now. This mission is yours, it *has* to be you, for anyone else to try would be disaster. For us and all humankind."

Something in Bill rallied to the call, raised its voice. Why not? Why couldn't it be him? But it was a small voice.

"What about number 768,27**2**, couldn't you send them?"

Keith hesitated. "Of course that's possible, but it would mean you'd have to be dead first. We can't send someone who isn't the highest living candidate. That would be lunacy." He pulled a gun from his pocket. With practiced ease he chambered a round and placed the gun on the table.

"Is that what you want, soldier?"

Bill stared at the gun. It was massive, bigger than he thought possible. He'd never seen a gun before, not a real one at least. He dry swallowed. The choice was an easy one after all: he shook his head.

"Good man," said Keith. Bill suspected the man's words and tone would have been exactly the same if he had reached for the gun and blown his own brains across the stark white walls of the briefing room.

"It's not all bad news of course. Clyde gave you your secret weapon?"

Bill nodded, patting his hand on the bulge in his pocket where the manicure kit was wedged.

"Great! Well, it's time for you to be off; you're not going to save the world sitting here, are you? Especially when you have less than twenty-four hours to do it! Personally, I would have preferred to have you in here three months ago, get some basic training in you. A fortnight in a penguin suit would do you the world of good! But, that's not how the powers that be see it. Are you all right?"

Bill shook his head. Finally, he was having a breakdown, or a panic attack, or something. He really hoped he was going to pass out. Slipping from his stool he curled up in a foetal position and started rocking, hyperventilating. His vision was going all spotty. The door opened and Fern hurried in, clutching a brown paper bag.

Chapter Seven

Growing up Fern had dreamt of her first mission.

That first day, when she had been Selected and inducted, had been terrifying, but the story that she was told that day had captured her imagination, absorbed her so utterly that she had thought of little else since. She was special—all of those Selected were—but they were nothing compared to those legendary heroes: the Chosen. The Selected must work hard, study and train and practise. Sweat, blood, and tears were what pushed the Selected on, and she had sweated more than any other and bled herself dry.

Of course, it had been harder for her. Even at age five—the age of Selection—she had been smaller than the other initiates. She had to work harder, train more, study for longer, and practice until she was exhausted just to keep pace. But she did keep pace. And at the time of Testing she had hoped for a good rank, a rank that would give her a shot at seeing a mission, the chance to meet her Chosen. The chance to save the world.

Her cheeks flashed crimson at the memory. How wrong she had been. A good rank at the Testing? What a joke that had been. As the results were read out in the Great Hall her dreams fell to pieces; everything she had ever wanted was taken from her and dashed to smithereens, ground to dust. Jerome had placed the highest, a victory he had accepted with good grace, for him at least. For herself . . .

She shook her head, trying to shake the memory away. Her eyes watered up a little, but she pushed the emotion back, crushed it down inside her. She wouldn't cry again. Not again.

For six months she had lived with the shame, a shame she would carry forever, but today everything had changed. All of her dreams had come true: she was going on a mission! She knew she was ready—she had been ready since she was a girl—but it wasn't until now, as she sat alone, that the true meaning of it all sunk in. It meant the world was in grave peril, that it needed her. But most of all it needed its Chosen, its hero, the one the old language called the Britak Tain. Her life was nothing beside that of the Britak Tain.

The Britak Tain, in all his august majesty, was currently in the bathroom. Being sick by the sound of it. He'd taken the brown paper bag with him, and by the noises coming through the door at least he was breathing properly again.

Trying to block out the sound of his heaving she did another mental inventory of their gear. She had it all: survival gear, maps, rations. They'd make a stop top-side to get some extra food. She'd packed ninety percent of the weight into her pack, carefully placing the bulkier but lighter items in Bill's. She didn't want to hurt his feelings after all. He didn't look particularly weak, but he certainly wasn't what she had been expecting.

She had studied every Britak Tain in history, both the successes and the failures. One of her favourites was Ghengis Khan. His Selected rode by his side in every battle, his sword a scourge, his shield ever ready to protect the Britak Tain. In one battle, Ghengis had been injured, almost mortally. Filled with shame, his Selected had requested permission to commit suicide, but Ghengis had refused. After many long years the Selected was accorded the highest honour: to die in battle, his body protecting that of the Britak Tain.

Bill Posters wasn't much like Genghis Khan, not at first glance at least. She knew the situation of course. It was without precedent in all of human history. That the Chosen 768,271 should be called on to save humanity was chilling, and she tried to put the thought from her head. Keith had said she needed to focus on one thing, and one thing alone. It didn't matter what rank Bill was, how many better qualified people had already perished. He was their best hope, their hero, and more importantly he was her Chosen. She would protect him with her life, and if her death could ensure the mission was a success she would gladly make the sacrifice. Yes, she needed to ignore his appearance, his air of disaffected incompetence. He was her Chosen, she was his Selected, and together they would succeed!

The flush sounded for the fifth time, and the door to the bathroom edged open a crack, Bill's foot pushing through the narrow opening.

"Err, hello?" came the muffled call of the Britak Tain. "Could someone help me, I've got my arm wedged down the side of the toilet."

Chapter Eight

Hunkering closer to the floor, Gregor Manriguez tried to adjust his viewpoint. He was crouched low in dense bush (dense temperate wetland bush to be precise). All around him was a myriad of greens, the dark smudge of moss, the rich green of fern, and darker spikiness of a cluster of pine trees. The air was cool and filled with a fresh, clean, crisp smell. Away in the distance a waterfall gently splashed its way to the forest floor.

None of these things interested Manriguez as he hunched in his hiding place. What concerned him was the large fern in front of him and trying to peer through its shifting branches while remaining hidden from his pursuers. Again he checked his pistol, the small calibre gun tucked into his boot top, the knives at his waist, wrists, and calf, and the small ninja-throwing star tucked behind each ear. A crossbow was strapped to his back. He didn't know how to use it, but he liked the way it felt against his shoulders.

Manriguez was a dangerous man. Going everywhere armed to the teeth he was nearly as dangerous to other people as he was to himself (a nasty fall once, wearing all those sharp bits of metal, had left him hospitalised for two weeks).

He suppressed a small sigh, aware that any noise could attract the attention of the men hunting for him in the forest. The trackers were skilled, and from what he had seen back at the compound they were well trained. All his training told him that staying still was the best course of action, but as the search teams drew ever closer it was difficult.

How had it come to this? He had once been the pride of Chilean special operations. As a child all he had wanted was to escape the rural poverty of his mountain village. The army had seemed like a good option. They had trained him well, recognising his unique talents and temperament, and the work had been interesting. Looking back he realised they had been the happiest days of his life. He had purpose, he had respect, he was an agent without equal. Well, almost without equal.

One of the trackers peeled off from the main group and headed in his direction. Moving silently Manriguez eased the knife from its sheath on his calf. The metal was blackened and would reflect no light, but even still he held it pressed underneath his forearm, his training telling him to conceal the weapon for as long as possible. He kept his breathing steady; he would only fight if he had to.

The tracker paused, studying something on the ground. The other trackers had moved off to the north. Yes, Manriguez had enjoyed army life, until the arrival of Carlos Mendoza. Manriguez was a philosophical man—he had found that most paid killers were—and he had always believed in the concept of the nemesis. Every person, every man woman and child, of every race and every nation, of every religion and every creed, had a nemesis. In the vast majority of cases, people never met their nemesis—they never even knew each other existed—and both happily lived out their lives in blissful ignorance of the other. But occasionally a person would meet their nemesis, setting off a course of events that would change both of their lives. The instant he met Mendoza he knew that he had encountered his nemesis.

At first their rivalry had been healthy, a useful motivator for two men already at the top of their game. Their contest gave the other men something to rally around, but soon it became divisive. For two long years the situation deteriorated, and then came the mission. His last mission.

It was a situation of supreme delicacy, one that required the very best men, and that meant both Manriguez and Mendoza. Manriguez had thought that they could put their differences aside, that the mission was more important than the man. He'd been wrong.

It was a shambles. Thirteen innocent civilians had died, and the military court ruled that their blood was on Manriguez's hands. Mendoza was exonerated, but then that had always been his plan. Even today, five years later, the memory was almost too painful to bear. He could still see every one of their faces.

Three years in the gutter had almost killed him. The booze dulled the pain, but when he had finally sobered up it was like waking from a bad dream. He'd been approached by a shadowy organisation—no doubt a front—called "United Plumbing and Drainage." He knew almost nothing about his employers, other than the fact they had cleaned him up, got him back in shape, and provided him with all the equipment he ever asked for. They hadn't even questioned the crossbow. They had projects they needed him to do and they paid well. That was all that mattered now to Manriguez.

The tracker had stopped studying the ground and was once again moving towards his position. He was just three metres away now. Manriguez shifted his grip on the knife. Suddenly a cry went up from the north and the tracker turned, before running through the forest back to the main group. It looked like they had found Manriguez's jacket. The sweat was beginning to cool on his body. Through the canopy he could see the sun beginning to dip towards the horizon. He couldn't stay hidden all night—the temperature would drop too low, and he could see a second group of men moving round from the south. If he left now there was a chance, a slim one, that he could make the rendezvous. But there was a much greater chance he would be captured, and the item he was carrying must not fall into enemy hands. Taking the small, metal cube from his pocket, he turned it over in his hands. That so much could rest on something so small. Making up his mind, he tucked the small cube into his trousers and rose silently from his hiding place. On light feet he made his way towards the sound of the waterfall.

Bill knocked nervously on the dark wooden door, the brass plaque in the centre of the door reading "Clyde Avian, Director." His stomach had settled down at last, but his arm was still sore from his mishap in the toilet. His cheeks burned with embarrassment just thinking about it. It had taken forty-five minutes to free his arm and the combined efforts of four people and eight pigeons. It had all caused quite a stir, given that he only had twenty-four hours to save the world in the first place. It had also made everyone quite nervous, as was demonstrated by the amount of bird poo deposited on the bathroom floor as the pigeons had hurried to free his arm. The poo-robots had been a blur, hurtling around keeping the place clean.

"Come in!" came the call from behind the door.

Bill pushed open the door and into a spacious office. The walls were panelled with a blond wood and a crystal chandelier hung from the ceiling. In the far corner sat a meeting table surrounded with four chairs and four bird perches. Against the far wall was a brown leather couch and a gleaming glass coffee table. Directly opposite the door was a large desk, and perched in the centre of the desk was a pigeon. The sign on the door said this was Clyde's office, but in truth all the pigeons looked the same to Bill. This one *did* have the ankle-watch he had seen before, wrapped neatly around the bird's right leg.

"Hello again, Bill," said the pigeon.

"Hello."

As Bill turned to close the door, he noticed a huge painting that took up much of the wall opposite the desk. It was a strange subject: a pigeon dressed in military fatigues and a tin helmet, a large medal pinned to its chest.

"Mary of Exeter," said Clyde, his chest puffing out with pride. "A relative of mine, you know. Awarded the Dickin Medal during World War II. Of course, most of her missions were top secret."

"Of course," said Bill, not really understanding at all. "You wanted to see me?"

"Yes, yes!" said Clyde, his tongue peeking out and running around the edge of his beak, his head bobbing back and forth in an excited manner. "I wanted to wish you luck, but also see how you are feeling. This must all be quite a shock."

It certainly was. Bill had the feeling that it hadn't really sunk in, if it ever would. That it was down to him to save the world was—to put it mildly—something of a surprise. If Keith hadn't made it clear that the only alternative was death he'd probably still be hunched over the toilet bowl. How he wished he could be safely back at work in the comforting grey surroundings of the Bally Brooks Bank tower. This was worse than a four-hour briefing in the Judas room. He wasn't comfortable opening up to a pigeon though, even if this one did seem to have exceptional bowel control (the surface of the desk was spotless, and there was not a single guanodrone in sight). This was quite a surprise given the amount of bird poo he had encountered since descending into the disturbing world of the pigeons. Thinking back, Clyde hadn't pooed during the whole journey in the Tube either. It was an odd realisation to have, but from what Fern had told him this fact suggested a herculean effort on Clyde's part. It could only be in consideration of how it would make Bill feel, and Bill felt a surge of appreciation for the bird, even if it had been spying on him from the tree outside his flat for the past week.

"I'm okay with everything, really," Bill lied.

Clyde looked unconvinced.

"But do you think you can do it? Do you think you'll be able to get the button and bring it back here?"

The pigeon seemed unusually earnest. Keith had made the mission sound like a walk in the park, and Bill wasn't prepared to start thinking about it in any other way. Not unless he wanted to start throwing up again.

"Yeah, I reckon I can," he said, not sure if this was true or not.

"Good man!" said Clyde, stamping his leg on the desktop for emphasis, the hard claws making an oddly metallic clicking sound on the polished wooden surface.

"Well, I've kept you long enough. I would like to talk more, but there really is so little time. Good luck, Bill Posters, there is so much resting on your shoulders! I think we have the right man for the job, and no other would do quite as well as you I'm sure!"

Bill muttered a thank you and turned back to the door. He gave the strange portrait of "Mary of Exeter" a last glance as he closed the door behind him.

Bill was glad to be back above ground. Fern appeared from within Dinesh's corner store with two bulky blue carrier bags.

"Supplies," she said brightly, tucking one of the bags into Bill's rucksack and one into her own.

"Oh, I almost forgot!" said Fern, pulling a bright silver something from her pocket. It looked like a desk stamp, the sort that printed the words "paid" or "overdue" in neat red ink. Before he could react, Fern reached up and stamped it, hard, in the centre of his forehead.

"Ow! What the—"

"Now, now, language Bill," said Fern. Bill rubbed his forehead and muttered obscenities under his breath. *Man that stung.*

"What was that for?" he grumbled, checking his forehead in the grimy window of the corner shop. He couldn't see any mark, other than a touch of redness, but it wasn't easy to tell with the reflection in the filthy glass.

"That's your Mark," said Fern, her tone a little impatient. "It shows that you are one of us, one of the people who know The Truth."

"It does?" said Bill, bobbing his head around in front of the glass to get a better view of this Mark. "I can't see a thing."

Fern gave a small sigh. "It's not in a part of the light spectrum you can see, but it is there, and will be forever."

Bill winced. "You've just given me an invisible tattoo?"

"It's only invisible to you, and all other humans," said Fern, pulling what looked like a train table from her pocket and running her finger across the rows.

"Great, so I shouldn't be worried if pigeons see it and start asking me for directions?" His tone was bitter, but if Fern noticed it wasn't obvious.

"That's right. Any off-worlders in fact, although it would be very unusual for them to talk in earshot of other humans."

Bill squinted at the glass again. Even the redness was fading, and it didn't seem to sting anymore. "What does it look like, for those that can see it?"

Fern gave a satisfied noise, folded the timetable and placed it back in her pocket. "The Mark? It's an ancient pigeon symbol: two circles side by side, representing this world and the next, with the pigeon rune for knowledge—an elongated ellipse with the inverted 'T' of truth at the top—rising up from in between the circles."

Bill tried to picture this in his mind, succeeded, and then started rubbing furiously at his forehead. "Are you telling me you have stamped my forehead with an invisible drawing of a—"

Fern grabbed his hand from his forehead and pulled him down the street. "No time for that Bill, we've not got a moment to lose."

Bill was almost pulled from his feet. "So, where are we going?"

"The main international hub."

"Which is?"

"Which is," she rolled her eyes, "where all the international tubes leave from. Well, most of them anyway. There are a few private ones up and down the country."

"Yes, I got that bit, but where exactly is the main international hub?"

"Not far, the Essex Road," she said, followed by a remarkably loud "Taxi!"

As a cab pulled up Fern made to climb in, but Bill halted her with a touch to the arm. "This tube," he said, "it's not going to be driven by a . . . you know . . . is it?"

Fern grinned. "Of course not, they're all automatic. Clyde was just using the controls for fun earlier. Mostly they are left in auto."

For some reason this came to Bill as a great relief. After all the horrible things he had seen today, for a reason he couldn't fathom, a pigeon driving a train had been the worst. With that possibility out of the way he felt brighter and noticed his forehead had stopped hurting. He followed Fern into the taxi, feeling better than he had all day.

Chapter Nine

In a cloud of burning rubber, the taxi screeched to a halt outside Greasy Joe's on the Essex Road. Bill unpicked his hands from the faux leather interior upholstery (where they had made considerable dents), and tried to force his eyes back into their sockets.

"That was brilliant, thanks!" Fern enthused as she paid the driver.

On entering the taxi Fern had flashed the driver a dazzling smile, somehow making her eyes bigger and browner, and had asked if he could get to their destination "as fast as possible." Even Bill had been a little hypnotised by her smile, despite not being its target, so he could understand why the taxi driver had worked his hardest to oblige. He just wished she had added the word "alive." He would have felt that much safer throughout the journey.

They were now standing together outside a quintessential Greasy Café (pronounced *caf* of course, as you could not have a greasy café). The windows were thick with oil deposits, and an extractor outlet on the side of the building belched thick black smoke into the sky. Bill could feel his arteries thickening just standing there and wondered if there was such a thing as passive heart disease.

"Come on," said Fern, pushing through the door to the jingle of a small bell. *Great*, thought Bill, *a petite brunette you could nearly fit in your pocket who fancies a fry up before setting off to save the world*. With extreme reluctance, he followed her through the doorway.

Outside he had been able to imagine that the grease on the windows was an accumulation of many years. In fact they might have been cleaned that morning, so thick was the airborne layer of lard. It shimmered much like a heat haze. There were only two other people inside, and no tension whatsoever, but you really could cut the air with a knife (and most probably spread it on toast or cook in it).

"Fern, great to see you!" boomed the improbably thin man behind the counter. The man looked emaciated, almost skeletal, and stood there holding a large frying pan and a scum-encrusted spatula.

"Hey Joe, the usual please."

Oh good, she has a "usual" in the local pit of deep-fried cardiac death.

"Certainly, my dear. You and your friend follow me."

Joe ducked around the counter, dropping both the pan and spatula into a tub of greasy water, and led Fern and Bill to the back of the café. There was a small alcove booth there, with red plastic-covered bench seats and a splattered table.

"Take a seat," said Joe, "won't be a moment." With that he ducked through a door at the back of the café. Fern slid down the bench seat and patted the space next to her.

"Listen Fern, I'm sure you do this sort of thing all the time, but I'm not sure we've got enough time for this."

"Just sit," she said, patting the seat again.

Bill hesitated. He didn't really know much about Fern, almost nothing in fact. Keith had said that she was there to help him, but there was no doubt that she was the one in charge. It made sense: after all, he only had a vague grasp of what was going on. Fern flashed her smile again and he caved. "Oh well," he conceded, taking a seat next to Fern. "I guess I could have some toast."

"You might want to buckle up."

61

What kind of greasy café requires you to buckle up? thought Bill, and asked as much.

"I mean, I'm used to it, but you might want to strap in," Fern continued, pointing to the grease-smothered lap belt on the seat.

What kind of greasy café has lap belts on the seats, and how come that tomato sauce bottle has a light on inside of it? Now it's gone out, but now the mustard is glowing. What the hell is . . .

"Hang on!" said Fern.

Suddenly the entire world shot upwards, including Bill's stomach. For two heart-stopping moments his bottom lost contact with the seat, while the roar of wind engulfed him as they plunged into darkness. The only light came from a glowing saltcellar on the table, shining a sickly green. For what seemed like an eternity they fell through darkness—Bill, Fern, and a red plastic bench seat—before they abruptly decelerated and came to a stop with a bump.

Bill couldn't remember starting to scream, but he was now, eyes screwed shut and mouth wide open. As he paused to take a breath, he noticed they had stopped and carefully opened one terrified eye. He was sitting at the edge of a very wide, very long corridor, tiled entirely in white. The lighting was strange, in that it seemed to beam out of the walls and ceiling, a delicate and pervasive glow. The corridor was packed with people, and all of them were staring at Bill.

"Sorry, sorry," said Fern, waving her right hand airily. "Newbie, just a newbie." Some of the people gave an understanding nod, some looked in sympathy at Fern, while the others scowled and hurried on their way. In seconds the hall had returned to the hustle and thrum that must have existed before Bill's screaming arrival.

"Err, if I could have my hand now please?" asked Fern, looking pointedly at Bill's right hand clamped on her left fist.

"Eh?" said Bill.

"Hand," said Fern very slowly. Bill carefully unpeeled his fingers from hers, moving slowly partly because he was still shaken, and partly because deep down he really liked holding her hand. Somewhere, deep in the primordial recesses of his brain, or maybe even in his spinal cord, a basic human instinct immune to the fear and wonder of the past few hours made a little note in its black book.

Meanwhile, the rest of Bill's brain was still in shell shock.

"What in the hell was that?" he spat; now he could talk.

Fern rolled her eyes. "Look, I know this is all new to you, but you've got to start taking things in your stride a bit more. We are going to be running into things like this all day."

"Stride!" repeated Bill, unexpectedly and incongruously combining groggy incomprehension with indignation.

"That's it," said Fern, seeming encouraged that Bill understood what she was saying. "Look, I am not really supposed to do this, but we just haven't got the time for you to go gawping at everything." She began rummaging in her rucksack.

"We have just taken a drop lift to the international hub. Quickest way here in the circumstances. Aha!" Fern gave a small cry of triumph and held up a small, black tube, not unlike the type that camera film for old-fashioned film cameras came in.

"Take this," she said, handing him a small, white pill. "It'll help."

Still trembling, Bill took the small pill. Now he wasn't the sort of guy to go around taking small, white pills proffered by strange girls, but he was quite shaken up by the—what had she called it—the "drop lift" (*surely that is an oxymoron*, thought his brain idly). His thoughts skittered like water on a hot griddle, and she had said it would help.

"What is it?" he asked, generating a sigh and a dismissive wave from Fern.

63

"It's a geno-nmemonic. Does a bunch of stuff. For someone like you it should make all this easier to cope with. A bit anyway."

Someone like me; he wondered what she meant by that. He wasn't sure if he should be offended. With a shrug, he popped the pill in his mouth and dry swallowed. Fern gave him an appreciative smile and tapped his knee with her hand. Her expression was the kind you might give a dog that had just taken its medicine, even though you had to mix it up in its food. The expression that also said, *Now there's a good boy, now can we get on with things.*

"There's a good boy, now can we get on with things," she said, causing Bill another flash of indignation. Whatever the pill actually was, Bill was beginning to feel a little better, so he decided to ignore the heavy level of patrony.

"Right, okay," he said. "I am feeling better now, let's get going." He stood up from the café seat, his legs more stable than he thought they might be.

They were to get tube NZ104, as instructed by Keith. Fern clearly knew her way around, as within minutes they had negotiated a maze of tunnels to platform 208, where NZ104 was due to depart in thirteen minutes. The tube number was a cover of course—there would be no other passengers on NZ104. The transport was a private charter to take Fern and Bill to where they needed to be. Low red benches lined the side of the platform, and Bill and Fern took a seat to wait out the thirteen minutes.

"S'funny," said Bill, his mouth struggling to form the words.

"Hmm," said Fern. She looked up from her bundle of notes and her breath caught.

"Wah is't?" slurred Bill, peering up at his reflection in the vast mirrored ceiling. He had gone a very unusual shade of green.

"Don't worry, just a side effect. I had read that some skin discolouration sometimes occurs."

Enough to start resembling a frog? thought Bill.

"Side effect?"

"Yeah, from the Trepsin."

"Trepsin?"

Fern rolled her eyes. "The little white pill," she said with forced patience.

"Right, funny warm feeling too."

"It'll pass," said Fern. Her voice was firm, but her certainty sounded a little false.

"S'getting noisier too."

"Yeah, that too."

"All twitchy now."

"Good grief, Bill, you hardly had any of the stuff. You'd get more of a buzz from a double espresso."

"Don't drink coffee."

"What, never?" said Fern, surprised with an edge of panic in her voice.

"No, never. Or tea, or drink, or smoke, or take painkillers."

Now Fern was shocked, and more than a bit perturbed. It seemed that Bill was one of *them*. "What, not even paracetemol?"

"Nope, never."

"Never?"

"Never."

"Oh shit!" hissed Fern, her face registering genuine, buttock-clenching concern. Given her impenetrable sangfroid up until now, Bill could almost enjoy the look, except for the fact that the look was directed at him.

Fern rummaged in her bag and pulled out the small, black tube, holding it to the light and reading something written very faintly on the side. With some muttered curses she fiddled with something at her wrist, hidden in the bulky folds of her jumper, and held it up to her mouth, her pretty, little nose almost buried in the chunky knit.

"Yes, yes," she said, though Bill had no idea what she was yessing about. "I think I need a crash team on platform 208, Trepsin overdose." A brief pause. "It could be bad, this one supposedly has history," she said to her wrist, then shot Bill a doubtful look. A slightly longer pause. "No, no time for that, we still need him. Three should do." Fern glanced at Bill, who had gone from trembling to, well, vibrating. "Make it four." Lowering the cuff she took Bill's jangling hand very gently.

"Now Bill, I am very sorry, but what I gave you is kind of a stimulant, among other things. And you being who you are, and having not had much exposure to stimulants, I think it might make you a little, uh, sick."

Bill nodded, but it was possible his head just vibrated up and down.

"Uh, one of the other things it does, which makes it super useful for people like us, is that it twists your perception of reality very slightly. Well, usually very slightly, sometimes more. Effectively it removes fear, sort of. Oh hell, this is difficult to explain."

"Can hear your heart beating," said Bill in a flat monotone.

"Ah, yes, well, that too. It tends to make us bolder and heightens all six of our senses, which can be very handy." Fern paused, licking her lips nervously. "But its main purpose, that which differs from person to person, is to unlock deep memories, the memories that we have all forgotten."

Bill furrowed his brow, or at least he tried to. The vibrations were picking up and he wasn't sure he was in control of any of his muscles anymore.

"Not specific memories, more of a . . . oh good, they are here," Fern said.

Somehow, the platform, which had been bustling with people moments before, had cleared. From the end of the platform, four figures clad from head to toe in black, were running towards Bill.

"Oh dear, I am explaining this all very badly," said Fern, wringing her hands in distress, "and you don't have long. I need to make you understand."

Bill was now vibrating so hard he was moving around on the bench, and his teeth had entered such a state of flux they no longer rattled. Seeing Fern so worried concerned him deeply, but the thought drifted through his mind like a stately swan on a cool, clear lake, making little impression other than a gentle ripple. What was happening to him?

Suddenly Fern's face brightened. "Now, this is going to sound odd, but err, those men have come to kill you," she said, a little too enthusiastically for Bill's liking. Bill glanced over his shoulder at the advancing figures, who looked like a bunch of rejects from a ninja B-movie.

"Eh, what can you do?" shrugged Bill, giving the ninjas a cheery wave. "Hello assassins," he giggled, starting to thrum rather than vibrate. It felt like he was getting a nosebleed.

The figures in black were almost upon them, and Fern's expression lurched back to panic. "Bill, they are going to kill you, do something!"

Again Bill shrugged.

"Please!"

Another shrug.

The assassins were twenty-five strides away.

"Do you want to die?" Fern begged.

Yet another shrug. Bill was now shaking so hard he was bouncing off the floor, seat, and wall. Nothing really bothered him now, nothing penetrating the calm that wrapped around his brain like soggy cotton wool. Twenty strides.

"You'll die horribly!"

Shrug.

Fifteen strides.

"Very painful."

Shrug.

Bill glanced up at the mirrored ceiling. His face was going from green to blue. He couldn't remember the last time he had taken a breath, and wasn't all that bothered either.

Five strides.

"Oh Christ, I'm dead!" shrieked Fern, her face aghast.

The beginning of a shrug creased Bill's shoulders, but this last comment had struck, well, something. Fern was still holding his hand; he could feel her blood pulsing under her skin. He could see the water welling in her eyes as she panicked, and he was nearly overwhelmed by her smell, a field of vanilla overlaying the clean scent of soap, and something else that he guessed was just "Fern."

Four strides.

This girl had said something about dying. Was she dying? She looked healthy. The thought whirled around his head as if it was caught in a tornado, but he clutched it tightly with all his will.

Three strides.

No, she was healthy.

The figures in black. They must be here to kill her then, not just him.

Two strides.

Well, he couldn't let her be killed, he was sure of that. Something in his head clicked and sent a crescendo of clicks rippling through his body right down to his toes, like a massive synaptic domino run. Air raced into his lungs like water surging through a breached dam.

One stride.

Bill released Fern's hand and gently spun on his heel, swinging a fist at the head of the lead assassin. While this decisive action shocked Bill, it was clearly anticipated by the ninja, who parried the blow and directed a kick at Bill's midriff. Catching the ninja's foot with his other hand, Bill heaved him into the path of the next figure, simultaneously executing a back flip and delivering a kick to the third ninja's head.

While not un-fit, Bill had never had any martial arts training. Or boxed, or ever been in a fight before. So while he now felt a strange surge of elation, he was simultaneously bloody confused.

The fight was truly awesome to behold. Bill leapt and span, rolled and lashed out with hand and foot, the four ninjas circling and parrying, countering where possible. While aggressive, the ninjas mostly blocked blows, launching few direct attacks. The fight went on for some time, until Bill, mid-flying-kick-summersault-grapple, abruptly collapsed to the floor, drenched in sweat, feeling like his entire body was on fire. Instead of moving in for the kill, the men in black dropped to their haunches, panting raggedly and nursing bruises where they had failed to fully deflect a blow. His body utterly unresponsive, Bill lay prone on the floor, staring up.

The pain was immense, but it had an almost separate quality, as if it was happening to someone else. Certainly his body didn't feel like his own, and he couldn't convince any part of it to move. He could feel everything, but he was paralysed. He'd felt a confused elation during the fight—it felt amazing—but that had vanished. What if he was stuck like this? What the hell was that pill Fern had given him? As exciting as it was to take on four ninjas and hold your own—albeit only briefly— this seemed a high price to pay.

One of the ninjas tore off their balaclava-like mask, revealing a rugged-faced man, bald except for a remarkably silly-looking ponytail.

"Jesus, Fern!" he spat, stalking towards Fern, who rushed to Bill's side, holding her palm to his forehead. "How much did you give him?"

"What?" muttered Fern, distracted in her fussing over Bill. "Just the one."

"One? No way, he was on the verge of a meltdown!"

Fern surged to her full five-feet-two inches and rounded on the man, her eyes flashing dangerously. The pony-tailed ninja took a step back, then seemed to remember himself, standing taller in response.

"Just one, okay! The Britak Tain has no resistance to it, Jerome, okay!" she screamed, hysteria still tingeing her words.

The ninja, Jerome it would seem, sneered down at Bill's prone form.

"Him? Really? I mean, there are some memories there obviously, but he looks done-in now . . ."

Fern, bristling, rolled up her left sleeve and thrust her arm under Jerome's nose. Whatever was on her arm Bill couldn't see, blocked as he was by Fern's back, but it made Jerome blanche.

"You know what this means of course," Fern hissed. The white-faced ninja nodded slowly. "Good, now beat it!" she commanded. Backing away, Jerome looked like he was going to say something else, his brow creased with worry, his mouth fumbling for the words, but Fern silenced him with a look of pure acid. Dropping his head, Jerome led the small group slowly back the way they had come.

"I'm so sorry," said Fern, turning her attention back to Bill, her sleeve once again rolled down, the bulky, woollen cuffs almost swallowing her hands. "I mean, with your number and everything, I really didn't expect it to have that much of an effect . . ." she trailed off forlornly.

"Which bit?" muttered Bill, realising for the first time what enormous concentration was needed to manoeuvre his tongue into the correct position to form words. At least his tongue was responding. With a surge of effort he tried to sit up, Fern supporting him as best she could. A high-pitched electrical whine interrupted whatever Fern was saying, a sleek, white capsule pulling into view down the platform's edge. NZ104 swept majestically along a platform still devoid of any other passengers. It was short, really just one carriage, so probably just as well they would have it to themselves.

"Can you stand?" Fern asked. In response, Bill struggled to his legs, which now seemed co-operative but located in a different time zone. At the third attempt he managed it, supported by Fern. Arm over her shoulder they staggered into the carriage. Amidst his sluggish and swirling thoughts Bill noticed how surprisingly strong Fern was, supporting his weight with seeming ease. He needed the support as well. Whatever the small, white pill had done to him, he was not keen to repeat the experience. He felt utterly washed out. All his senses felt numb and dull, almost useless against their heightened state. But even now he was forgetting the overall feeling, how it felt to be able to hear a heart beating from three paces. One thing remained though, something Bill thought he would struggle to forget any time soon: the powerful, delicate, and intoxicating smell of the small woman helping him stagger onto the carriage.

Chapter Ten

J erome and I, well, we used to date. Sort of, anyway" muttered Fern. "Sorry about all that," she repeated. Bill waved his hand, too tired to even reply. He wasn't worried about it anymore; he almost felt peaceful. The thought of Fern dating the pony-tailed Jerome bothered him a bit, but that was probably because of the silly hairstyle. Then he remembered landing a decent kick to Jerome's chest while he was whacked-out on Trepsin, which made him grin. Which of course hurt. He was now one big bruise, every single muscle aching.

Fern had been good enough to explain that Trepsin, in some cases, lends a person's heightened physical ability, though she had been a little coy about the "some" part. Unfortunately, this benefit took little consideration of an individual's actual capacity, leaving them with a mighty all-body hangover. It would appear that Bill had experienced an extreme reaction to the Trepsin, partly because he was so unused to any sort of stimulant. If he hadn't worked it out of his system, his entire body would have gone into what Fern called "geno-nmemonic shock." The crash team's purpose was to provide an outlet for anyone who had overdosed on Trepsin, or any other of the memo-stimulants, Fern explained. But it was vital that the patient initiated the purge themselves (hence her telling him that the men were there to kill him). Apparently, combat was one of the top two ways to purge your system of Trepsin. Fern refused to mention what the other one was, and for some reason turned a satisfying shade of pink just mentioning it. Unfortunately, such was the disregard for danger brought on by a Trepsin overdose that it was sometimes difficult to get people to respond, to initiate the purge, and people had been known to simply stop breathing and die. *Fancy that*, thought Bill.

They were both seated inside a big, white rail car. The seat Bill was draped over (sitting would imply more active effort than he was currently capable of) was firm but cosy. Tastefully minimalist, the rail car had lots of rows of seats, arranged in pairs facing a white table. There were no windows in the carriage; instead, large screens on the walls scrolled through adverts for various products that Bill had never seen before. As Keith had indicated, there was no one else in the carriage, and it would be a non-stop service. Fern sat opposite him, looking small and worried, which worried Bill.

So, they were on a train to New Zealand, off to retrieve the button that could save the world That he'd nearly died just catching the train was probably not a good sign. It had been quiet for some time, and Fern still looked unhappy. Even with his whole body grumbling at breathing in and out he thought he should make some effort at conversation. Summoning all his remaining energy, he slurred, "So, this train goes right through the centre of the earth does it?"

Fern looked momentarily startled, as if roused from a deep thought, but reassuringly her tone had regained some of its superior air.

"Don't be silly, that would be impossible. The core is immensely dense, you know." *Of course*, thought Bill. *How silly of me.*

"The train network runs in tunnels down to the magma. Then the subtrains drop into the mantle and initiate jet propulsion around the core to wherever you are going."

Ah, so obvious when you think about it. Delighted that Fern felt well enough to call him stupid, Bill fell blissfully asleep.

Fern chewed her bottom lip. It wasn't the best of starts. Less than an hour into the mission and she had nearly poisoned him. It would certainly have earned her a place in the history books. The first Selected to kill their Chosen, and the Britak Tain himself no less.

He was snoring lightly, his whole body spread-eagled across the seat opposite, his head wedged at a funny angle up against the wall of the capsule. How would the history books talk about Bill Posters? From their short time together Fern was struggling to describe him. He seemed like a nice guy, she could say that much, but she had never read of a Chosen like him. Not even close.

It shouldn't really matter, she reflected. Their mission should be simple, about as easy as any mission to save the world could ever be. The button had already been stolen from the sharks, and it was their job to collect it from the thief and bring it back to HQ. Keith and Clyde had been clear: the mission's sole objective was to get the button safely back, nothing else. Clyde had been particularly emphatic on this point. At first she'd felt a dip of disappointment: it sounded too easy. It was a job for a courier, not someone with her training, and certainly not the Britak Tain. She glanced at Bill's sleeping form. He was dribbling again. Maybe it *was* a suitable job for him.

How could someone so, so . . . ordinary be the Britak Tain? It defied belief. But then there was the effect of the Trepsin. She had never seen or heard of such an extreme reaction to a geno-mnemonic. From the look of Bill she would have expected it to make him a little bolder, increase his ability to cope with the revelations he was experiencing. But what she had witnessed was almost beyond comprehension. The explosion from his species subconscious was unprecedented. Had their time not been so limited she would have taken him immediately for testing.

Reaching into her pack she pulled out the Trepsin bottle and tipped one of the tiny white pills onto her palm. It certainly looked normal. It just *wasn't* a dangerous substance. Unless of course this was a bad batch? Maybe they had mixed-up the ratios, got something wrong in the formulation. That really was the only explanation, although how that would account for what had happened to Bill was beyond her. It had to be the answer though.

She looked across at Bill. "What are you, Bill Posters?" she quietly asked his sleeping form, her voice below a whisper. In response he twitched his forearms, looking like a dog running in its sleep, and mumbled something that sounded like *bugger off pigeon.*

There was one possibility that sprang to mind, one that sent a shiver down her spine. Fern pushed the uneasiness away. No, *that* possibility was just too crazy to consider. It was the stuff of fairy-tales, idle stories told to young Selected before they fell asleep. No, it was just a bad batch of pills, nothing more, but even bad pills could prove to be useful. She tipped the tiny white pill back into the tube and clipped on the top.

It made sense to get some rest. There was nothing she could do for hours, and even if the mission was straight-forward she wanted to arrive fresh. Reaching into her pack, she pulled out a spare jumper and rolled it into a ball. Gently she lifted Bill's head, manoeuvred it to a more normal angle, and rested it on the balled jumper. He didn't even stir, but Fern noted with disappointment that her jumper was now directly in the line of fire of his drool.

Whether successful or not, every Britak Tain had been a legend, a towering paragon of humanity. She looked at his face and just couldn't see it. *Get a grip Fern, he is the one, and you shall succeed*, she told herself. With that iron resolve she lay down on the bench, but it was hours before she finally drifted off to sleep.

It was a good sleep; Bill could tell the minute he opened his eyes. He felt remarkably refreshed, his senses all kind of tingly, and a content feeling nestled fuzzily in his shoulders. The feeling faded rapidly when he tried to move, the sensation fleeing like a squirrel from a rabid Doberman. Or vice versa.

"Mother of . . ." he muttered, pulling himself into a sitting position. His back was bruised, his neck was bruised, his arms were bruised, his hands were bruised. He had bruises on his bruises. There was not a single part of his body that didn't ache. Stupid little white pill!

Opening his eyes (an action that hurt the bruises on his eyelids), he could see Fern dozing in the opposite seat. Her small brow was furrowed with concern, her mouth had a sad look, and she was twitching in her sleep.

Bill opened his mouth to whisper, to see if she was awake or not. Bugger, even his tongue was bruised! He bent stiffly sideways and scooped his rucksack from the floor. He hadn't taken the time to look into what Fern had brought with them, but now he felt ravenous and hoped she had packed something good to eat. Rummaging in the pack he fished out a Mars bar and, ripping into the wrapper with bruised fingers, began to gulp down chunks of the bar while he continued his investigation. A box of cereal bars were placed on the table, together with a pack of salami, a jar of golden syrup, a packet of lard (?), and a bumper-sized Kendal Mint Cake. Also in the bag was a box of Crunchy Nut cornflakes, but no milk.

The carriage, stable up until now, gave a slight hum, vibrated a little, then distinctly began to slow. A flicker-swicker noise and the TV screens on the carriage wall melted to an opaque white, then slowly un-fogged to reveal a thick, green canopy. *So, they were windows after all*, thought Bill. Either that, or all the TV screens were now showing the same scene. Behind him the doors opened with a calm and reassuring swish. A rush of air told Bill the cabin had just depressurised, the new air carrying a fresh, damp smell. Walking towards the doorway, Bill could see they were a good way off the ground, which was thick with dewy moss and snarly undergrowth.

A single button by the doorway was marked "stairs." Bill pushed it. Given the high-tech, well-designed sounding noises (all the flicker-swickering and swishing), Bill expected a sleek, stainless steel telescopic staircase to descend gracefully from the doorway, accompanied by the capable purring of an electric motor. Instead, a section of the wall opposite the doorway squeaked open and a wooden ladder toppled out, almost catching Bill in the head. Struggling with the weight of the unexpectedly low-tech elevated access apparatus, Bill heaved the ladder through the doorway, resting it on the ground and propping it against the bottom of the doorway.

Remarkably, the noise didn't seem to have woken Fern. Bill decided to leave her for the time being and have a quick look around. After all, the quicker they made contact with the thief, collected the button and got it back to London the better. Then he could go back to his life, back to his daily commute and his tatty bedsit with mismatched chairs.

Negotiating the ladder, he found the ground as damp and pliable as it looked, and he struggled a little to keep his footing. The train carriage was resting in a small clearing surrounded on all sides by a dense forest. How it came to arrive in a forest wasn't obvious, but slithering his way around to the front the answer became clear. Protruding from the front of the train, like a vast, jagged nose, was a huge drill. He was sure this wasn't there when they had boarded the—what had Fern called it—the subtrain? He was sure he would have remembered. Bill had seen something like this before, in some pictures of the building of the channel tunnel. The drill was coated in soil and rock chips and was glowing red hot in places. Bill could feel the heat radiating off of it and stepped carefully to the side to look down the length of the carriage.

Sure enough, just behind the carriage was what looked like a giant molehill. A solidified streak of smooth rock ran from the hole and under the rear half of the train, the rear-most portion still smoking slightly in the damp air. The underside of the train, where he would expect to find some form of wheels, was adorned with nothing of the sort. Given the giant drill, Bill would have even settled for some industrial-looking caterpillar tracks. But no, the undercarriage consisted of three long bars, semi-circular and jet black. Darker than night, darker than the underside of a tanned mole in a mine, two hundred metres underground. With the lights off. Or so it seemed to Bill at least. And they were humming and crackling. Not the reassuring hum-thrum that could be heard inside the carriage, but a menacing twenty-killer-wasps-trapped-in-a-jar kind of hum. Oh and they, and the rest of the carriage, were levitating seven feet off the ground. Without really knowing why, Bill scooped up a stone from the floor and tossed it underarm at the centre bar. He had no idea what would happen, and regretted doing it the moment the stone had left his hand. He had expected something dramatic. Some sparks maybe, or for the stone to disintegrate, or explode, or implode, or just disappear.

"Oh, how dull," he exclaimed. "I'd expected a bit more than for the stone to just . . ."

A scream, mixing terror and feral anger, cut him off mid-sentence. Spinning on his heel (which was easy), Bill slithered across the damp undergrowth back towards the hatch (which was hard, given the wet leaves, the mossy stuff, and ankle-grabbing green things). That had been Fern screaming, and it made Bill's blood run cold.

Reaching the bottom of the ladder, he scrambled for the bottom rung, panic setting in. Without warning something furry cannoned into him from above, knocking him clean off his feet. He landed on his back, the air whooshing from his lungs. The mystery assailant started pummelling his chest with small fists. He could hear Fern sobbing, and he desperately clawed air into his winded lungs. Heaving himself sideways, he twisted and grappled the furry creature to the ground. As he wrestled the thing in the leafy undergrowth a couple of things clicked in his mind. Fern's sobbing sounded very close, he could definitely smell vanilla, and yes, he was now face-to-face with a shuddering, teary eyed, and if he wasn't mistaken, exotically angry Fern.

"What is it, what's wrong?" he said quickly. "What attacked you?" He looked around for a view of the assailant.

"Attacked me?" Fern spat, struggling against his arms. "Don't you ever wander off like that again!" she screeched, a hysterical edge to her tone. With a casual jerk of her legs and a flick of her arm she tossed him off of her. He landed on his back, the air rushing from his lungs once more. Fern gave him half a look, to check that he wasn't really hurt, before she stomped back to the ladder, unhindered by the slippery undergrowth, and huffed her way back into the carriage. *Mad, utterly mad*, thought Bill, easing air into his aching lungs. Suddenly, his pack came whistling out through the open doorway, missing him by mere inches.

"Hey!" he objected, pulling himself carefully to his feet as Fern made her way down the ladder.

Fern, her own pack now strapped to her back, reached up and grabbed him by the collar. The teary eyes were gone. Bill now confronted one-hundred-percent anger. He gulped.

"Do you have any idea how important you are?" hissed Fern, shaking his shoulders.

"Err, well apparently I am mankind's one-hundred-and-something-thousandth best chance of survival. Sounds like a bit of a long shot to m—"

Fern slapped him hard across the cheek.

"Ow!"

"Don't you ever talk like that, or let anyone else for that matter. You are the best we have. All we have. If I am going to . . ." Fern trailed off, her fire guttering a little. "Look, this isn't a picnic for me either, but you have to believe in yourself, and you have to stay close to me. Do not wander off again. Please."

Bill didn't think he had heard "please" used as a threat before. Fern had managed it.

"Okay," he said. There was not much more he could say.

Fern smiled. Releasing his collar she gave his cheek a light pat. "Much better," she said, once again in a tone that sounded disturbingly like she was talking to her favourite Afghan hound. "Now, we don't have much time to lose, follow me!"

Fern bobbed off, moving confidently down the mossy bank to a small path Bill hadn't noticed before. *Curiouser and curio...*, Bill half thought, before stopping himself. *This is strange enough; I will not, will not, start quoting* Alice in Wonderland *in my head!* he shouted in his head. Fern was making good time and had already reached the path. Remembering his promise, Bill hurried after her.

Chapter Eleven

"Know that we will get the information, one way or another," insinuated the torturer, as he shook a rusty pair of pliers in his hand.

"G Manriguez, 6, 12, 24, 27, 32, 41," slurred Manriguez. Blood caked the corner of his mouth, and a dark, purple bruise was already forming around his left eye. He could tell he had broken a rib (or rather had it broken for him), and his foot felt tight in his left boot. Definitely swollen, maybe broken. With his tongue, he probed a tooth on the left side of his mouth. It wobbled unsettlingly. Bastards.

"Enough, enough!" shrieked the torturer. "Why do you persist, Mr Manriguez, with this name and number charade? You are not in the military anymore, Mr. Manriguez. You have no service number."

Completing the examination of his damaged gums, Manriguez raised his head, fixing the scrawny, weasel-of-a-man with a steady stare. "S'not a service number," he muttered.

"Then what does it mean? Tell me!"

Swilling, Manriguez spat a mouthful of blood and phlegm at the man's feet. "Lottery numbers. Haven't you heard? It's a rollover."

The torturer howled a scream of rage and frustration. After four hours, and all he had was Manriguez's lucky numbers. He had already known his name. Hurling the pliers to the bench, he swept up an evil-looking device. A crooked, metal spike attached to a glistening corkscrew, topped with what looked like a child's Slinky toy. This wasn't the first time Manriguez had been tortured, and he knew all the tricks of the trade, all the fiendish devices. This was a new one though, and that worried him. A little. Generally the older stuff was the worst.

"What's that?" he mumbled, partly through concern and partly professional curiosity, eyeing the Slinky-looking thing.

"It's a Slinky, Mr. Manriguez. I do not know how it got here."

Impatiently unravelling the Slinky from the corkscrew section, the torturer hurled it to the corner of the room. *Ah, much better*, thought Manriguez. With the Slinky gone he recognised a good, old-fashioned grip scoop Mk. I with razor phalanges. *Good luck with that, my friend*, he thought. Any self-respecting torturer knew that a decent amount of body weight was needed to do any serious damage with a grip scoop, even a Mk. I. He was about to tell this to the emaciated torturer when the metal door slammed open.

"What?" screamed torturer.

"Mr Gring needs to see you," droned the heavyset figure in the doorway.

"Such awesome timing," spat the torturer. "We are not finished!" he said, jabbing a finger at Manriguez and limping from the room.

Damn right, thought Manriguez as the door slammed shut and was bolted from the outside. *You haven't even properly begun.* He eyed the workbench, spotting a scrack splitter, a good old-fashioned bronze one. *Now that, inserted—well, you know where—and left there while I hung would have had me jabbering by the time you got back.* Amateur.

In the end there had been just too many trackers out in the forest to avoid. He'd used every trick in the book: the false trail, walking down streams, running backwards. He'd even climbed a tree and managed to move about thirty metres through the canopy before the branches thinned out and he had to drop back down to the ground. But to no avail. In the end they had cornered him not far from the rendezvous point. He'd put up a fight, but mostly for appearances sake. Only an idiot takes on seven armed men, and idiots didn't tend to last long in his line of work.

He'd been captured, but at least he'd been able to hide the button out in the forest. After the effort he had taken to steal the thing it would have been galling to see it back in enemy hands, and an affront to his professional pride. The button was hidden, and it would seem that they hadn't discovered the note he'd left at the tree. It was a desperate gamble, leaving a message at the rendezvous, but it was the best he could manage. Hopefully whoever he was meeting would find it, decipher the message and retrieve the button. There was nothing he could do now, other than improve his own situation.

He gave the manacles an experimental rattle. They felt a little loose, but unless he broke his wrist he wasn't going to be able to pull a hand free. It was a something he would bear in mind if he thought of nothing better. Broken bones healed after all, as long as you were still alive. With a grin he remembered the sub-clause he had negotiated into his employment contract. There was a bonus payment associated with being tortured, and an additional stipend for broken bones. He couldn't remember exactly, but he didn't think it excluded bones he had broken himself. He glanced up at the clock on the wall. The rendezvous was scheduled for half an hour's time, and after that he would be on overtime and double-pay. Things were looking up.

If the manacles attaching him to the ceiling felt loose, the metal podium he stood on definitely was. He kicked the podium and felt it shift. Another kick and it slid a little more. With a mighty shunt of his good leg the podium barrelled across the floor, scattering the tools off the workbench. An unanticipated side effect was that Manriguez now had nothing to stand on, and with a grunt his shoulders took all of his body weight as he dangled five inches above the floor. Shit. Now this was uncomfortable. Waggling his legs, he tried to get the metal podium

83

back, but to no avail. He had shoved it too far. *I really should have thought that through*, he thought, an unpleasant sensation already building up in his arms. Bugger.

"C'mon, we are hours late, which isn't good when you only have twenty-four hours to save the world in the first place," Fern said.

Bill did as he was told and hurried along, again marvelling at the speed Fern's short legs were capable of.

"Right, it should be down here," she directed, consulting a strange piece of equipment she slipped into her pocket before Bill could get a proper look. Pushing her way through a cluster of undergrowth she waved for Bill to follow.

It was dark off the small path. Dark, damp, quiet, and unsettling. Bill stayed close to Fern as they wound their way up a small rise. At the top of the rise was a large towering tree, a lightning strike staining one half black while the other side had a verdant abundance of growth. Creepers and vines clawed their way up the mighty trunk. Bill couldn't decide if it looked like the creepers were trying to hold the stricken giant up or pull it down.

"He's not here," stated Fern, somewhat superfluously. Crouching on the floor she began studying tracks and scuff marks in the small clearing around the tree base.

"A lot of people passed through here, some running," she muttered. Following the tracks a short way up the hill, she gave a small gasp. "Definitely a scuffle," she continued, studying the floor. "Looks like our man was captured. Look," she said, drawing Bill over and pointing at what looked like a squishy mess of mud. "Those prints are very heavy; they must have been carrying him."

"That's very impressive. You some kind of Indian scout?" Bill asked.

"No, no," said Fern, not looking up and waving a hand dismissively. "All part of the training, though it was one of my best subjects." And now she did look up, a glint of pride in her eyes.

"Well, you are clearly very good," repeated Bill, making a mental note at how Fern seemed to glow slightly at the praise. He liked that.

"One of your best subjects, like at school?" he asked, wondering what kind of school taught advanced woodland tracking. Maybe she grew up in Norway?

"Kind of," she replied, distracted again by the prints. "Come on, he started running by the tree, maybe he hid it there."

They hurried back to the tree, and at Fern's insistence began searching the trunk and surrounding undergrowth.

"What are we looking for?" asked Bill.

Fern's voice was impatient. "The button, Bill. This is the rendezvous, and the thief has been captured. He might have left it here. Look for anything out of place, anything that doesn't belong in the forest."

They searched, groping around in the half-light for about an hour. When Bill was just about to give up, he slipped in the mud at the base of the tree, and as he reached out a hand to steady himself his fist crunched through the brittle blackened bark and into a small cavity. When he caught his balance, his fingers brushed something un-tree like. Grasping it with his fingertips, he pulled out a small A5 envelope. There was a small notched hole just above where his hand had punctured the tree. The letter must have been dropped in.

"I've got something!" he called.

"What is it?" said Fern, drawing close.

"Looks like a letter," he replied, tilting the envelope to the light to read the address. It was scratched in pencil and a little smudged, but still legible.

Sir Kayd Ian
2 Begonia Street
Orion
Bermuda

"Hmm, not for us then," muttered Bill, ripping into the envelope. Inside was a detailed topographical map, or at least a piece of one; a jagged tear down one side told of more of the map missing. The entire map was covered in symbols, which looked like they had been drawn with the same pencil as the address. These looked hasty as well, but had clearly been completed by someone with talent.

There was a car, a bird, a house, a star, a woman dancing, a triangle, a fish, a smiley face, a sad face, a stoat, a tree, a clock, a flower. There were thirty or more random symbols, all scattered across the map.

"Handy," said Bill, handing the map to Fern.

"What's that?" she asked, pointing at the stoat.

"It's a stoat," said Bill, turning the envelope over and over in his hands.

"Are you sure it's not a weasel?"

"Sure."

"How can you tell?"

"I just can, okay Fern? What is all this?"

Fern hesitated, then said, "Our contact, the man we were to meet. It looks like he's been intercepted. He has what we need. He must have hidden it somewhere, and this map must lead us there."

Bill peered over her shoulder. "Maybe it's the star?" he suggested.

"No, there must be a logic to it. Who is the letter addressed to?"

"Sir Kayd Ian. Ring any bells?"

Fern shook her head.

"I tell you what, this letter is never going to get to Sir Ian. No post code or anything."

"They might not use them in Bermuda," replied Fern, scrutinizing the address on the envelope before returning to studying the map. "But you're right, the address could be a cipher."

She crouched down, pulled a notebook from her pocket, and started jotting down numbers. "If I turn all the letters into numbers, sum every other row . . . Right, if I take this line here . . ." she muttered, calculating hurriedly. "I suspect it's a code to a map grid reference," she said without looking up. "The symbols could be a red herring, designed to slow us down, or rather slow down the wrong sort of person. Might take me a while to decode it though."

While Fern scribbled furiously Bill stared at the address, running it over and over in his mind. Fern was right, it didn't sound like a real address. Was there a town called Orion in Bermuda? He wished his geography was better: all that Bermuda brought to mind was the Bermuda Triangle. Wait, Bermuda *triangle*? Bill peered over Fern's shoulder at the map. She was scrawling numbers and letters on the pad, equations flowing out from the end of her pencil. He was no maths slouch, but whatever she was doing was beyond him. But there *was* a triangle on the map. And Orion was a constellation, right? There was a star on the map as well, not far from the triangle. And "2 Begonia Street" could be the flower. The drawing of the flower was very detailed indeed, but his horticultural knowledge was worse than his geography: he had no idea if it was a begonia or not. But it *was* the only flower.

With excitement he looked at the first line of the address. "Sir Kayd Ian." That brought nothing to mind at all. He scoured the map. Was the stoat's name Ian? No, that made no sense; all the other lines were a perfect fit with a symbol. He rolled the name over and over in his mind, and then it hit him. He was sure this was right!

"Fern, could I borrow the pencil please?"

"Hmmm?" Fern was clearly deep in concentration; the pencil momentarily paused in her hand. He eased it out of her grip.

"Bill, what are—"

"Just a second, promise," he said, barely keeping the satisfaction from his voice. He circled the triangle, the star, the flower, and the clock. He then drew a line from the clock to the flower and from the star to the triangle.

"There, that's where we need to go," he said, pointing at where the two lines crossed.

Fern looked confused, and angry. He pressed ahead.

"You see, each line in the address corresponds to a symbol on the map. The Begonia is the flower, Orion the star, Bermuda the triangle. The first line is the hard one: it's phonetic. Not "Sir Kayd Ian," but "cir-ca-dian." Circadian rhythm: the body clock. The clock." He pointed at the cross on the map that connected the symbols and was relieved to see the anger leave Fern's face.

"Bill, that's brilliant! I must say, very well done!" she tore the page she had been working on from the pad and crumpled it into her pocket. "I was halfway through a polynomial recourse algorithm on the first and third line that looked promising. But never mind. Right, that point isn't far from here. Just over this ridge—let's go!"

The torturer still hadn't returned, and Manriguez's arms were oscillating between numb and very painful. He'd been in worse situations of course, but back then he had been part of a team. Now there was no cavalry coming over the hill; now he was freelance and beginning to get a little worried, even if he was now earning double-time.

He closed his eyes and tried to find his happy place, the centre deep within him where he couldn't be touched. He could see her face clearly, the enigmatic eyes, the lips capturing something that was a smile and yet wasn't. Beautiful, no other word for it. A work of genius, the brush work precise and yet brimming with the unfettered creativity of an artist at the top of his game. If only he could have gotten closer! The crowds jostled and people got in his way. The urge to get out a knife and cut his way nearer to the painting was almost overwhelming, but then he remembered he'd had to leave all his weapons at the security scanner. Just as well: running amok in the Louvre with a knife was probably a bad idea. He also felt that in some way it would have been disrespectful to Da Vinci to spill blood in this shrine of art. Still, at least he could have gotten closer to her, just before being arrested. The reproductions he had seen did the original no justice at all.

What a place! He had spent two weeks at the museums in Paris, gorging on the artwork, and he called each one to mind now, trying to push away the pain of his body with the beauty in his mind. He had two real passions: money and art. The hired killer thing was really just a hobby, a means to an end. It kept him well stocked in art supplies and gave him the free time to pursue his real work. He was no genius—an enthusiastic amateur at best—but he filled his spare moments with painting, drawing, etching, sculpting. He couldn't help himself. With a flash of embarrassment, he even recalled doodling all over his map on the flight to New Zealand. Just small pictures, nothing extravagant. Leaving the map at the rendezvous was the best idea he could come up with, but his love of art was a private thing, and he didn't want anyone else to see his work. Even still, he hoped that the map had fallen into the right hands, and that his idle doodles didn't prevent whoever found it from decoding the message.

"You wanted me, Mr Gring?" The torturer grovelled in the open doorway.

Mr Gring stood facing the large picture window that looked out over the compound and the virgin forest beyond. His hands were clasped behind his back and he stood bolt upright. He was confident that he his stance looking suitably villainous, silhouetted as he was against the light. He turned, slowly.

"Mr Pinkie, do you know what the Jeremiah Corporation is famous for?" Mr Gring asked the torturer.

Mr Pinkie gulped hard and hesitated. It was of course a trick question. Their corporate values stated they were famous for their commitment to the environment, local communities, grass roots welfare, and the wellbeing of their employees. In reality they were famous for the production of toxic chemicals, irresponsible deforestation, cynical management practices, and shameful exploitation of their workforce. Mr Gring was curious to see which answer Mr Pinkie opted for. In the end, the hesitation saved the torturer, as Mr Gring pressed on.

"Success, Mr Pinkie. We are famous for our success," he extolled, pressing the knuckles of both hands to his large, wooden desk and fixing Mr. Pinkie with his gaze.

"Since my father started his peripatetic supply teacher business in 1920, when Jerry Co was born, we have striven for never-ending success. When we moved from education to logging we were successful. Adding the toxic chemicals arm of the business was a success. Already our virus scanning and computer hacking subsidiary is taking off. *Success*, Mr Pinkie."

Mr Pinkie gulped again and started to tremble.

"Our latest venture must also be a success, Mr Pinkie. I need that man, Mr Manriguez, to give us what he stole from us, and I need it in one hour. Do you understand, Mr Pinkie?"

Mr Pinkie nodded.

"Good, for I would hate to see you leave the happy Jerry Co family. As you will be only too well aware, ex-employees always regret their decision to leave."

Mr Pinkie, as resident chief torturer, should know only too well. After all, he often conducted the "exit interviews" for those resigning their posts. Mr Pinkie gulped again. With a wave of his hand, Mr Gring dismissed him, and the trembling Mr Pinkie fled the room.

Mr Gring took a deep breath. Aside from the unfortunate situation with Mr Manriguez everything was going exactly to plan. He had time to work out how to get the button to where it needed to be, if only the man would tell him where he had hidden it. Curse the unknowing fools who had captured Manriguez! An overzealous patrol and an inept Chilean would not derail his beautiful plans. Nothing could stop them.

Something in the compound outside caught his attention. What on earth was that bulldozer doing? Watching calmly as the yellow metal hurtled towards the building he reached behind him to press a golden switch just under his desk. A monotone voice crackled out of a speaker set in the dark mahogany surface.

Mr Gring cleared his throat and said, "Ah, yes, security. We are about to have an incident."

Chapter Twelve

"Looks like some sort of factory, a warehouse maybe."

Fern and Bill were crouched in the undergrowth, a few metres from the perimeter fence around the Jerry Co compound. Inside the compound stood a huge squat grey building. Atop the building stood a massive yellow sign with the JERRY CO logo emblazoned in black. Around the building sat a variety of earth-moving equipment, forklifts and, surprisingly, Segways.

Bill was wide eyed and trembling slightly. Their way here hadn't exactly been smooth sailing. Halfway up the rise they had run into two armed men. Big, scary men, evidently patrolling around the compound. Military style uniforms, full-head helmets, big black guns, the works. They hadn't messed around. The minute they clapped eyes on him and Fern they opened fire. Fern pushed him sideways into a ditch and rolled off to the left, both of them narrowly avoiding the first volley of automatic weapons fire. That had been bad, but in Bill's mind what had happened next was far worse.

He had landed in a tangled mess, Fern rolling smoothly to her feet, a pistol appearing in her hand at the same time. Bam. A single shot and one of the men had toppled backwards into the bush. The second man was dragging his weapon around to fire at Fern, seemingly in slow motion, but he was way too slow. Bam. And he joined his comrade on the floor. Fern hadn't even finished rising from a crouch. Bill fancied she could have felled three or four more before his heart had given another beat, and it was beating pretty fast by then. No fuss, no excessive panicked shooting. Two shots, two men, both dead.

"You okay?" said Fern, offering him her left hand. The gun was still in her right.

"What the hell?" he stammered, taking her hand and scrambling to his feet.

"Well, they shot first!" she retorted, but that hadn't been what Bill had meant.

"That part of your training too?" he choked, a bitter tone in his voice as he suspiciously eyed the gun in her hand.

"Of course."

"Look, who the bloody hell are you?" he demanded, shocked at his own strident tone when faced with an armed killer. Rather than take offence at the tone, Fern looked strangely apologetic.

"Look, I promise I will explain properly, but right now we haven't got the time. Come on, follow me."

Fern had moved away, continuing up the hill. Unable to stop himself, Bill followed.

Now they were crouched in the undergrowth, and Fern was not happy.

"I don't understand it. The thief can't have hidden it here, not with all these people around. Look over there." She pointed left to a column of men dressed in the same uniform as the two she had gunned down, moving through a gate and into the compound.

"I'll bet this is the same crowd who captured our man. Why oh why would he have brought it here?"

Fern paused, her brow furrowed. Bill was just about to mention that maybe, just maybe, he had got things wrong with the map, when Fern suddenly brightened and pressed on.

"Unless of course he was unable to liberate the item in the end, and has instead led us to where it is held. That must be it!"

"Must it, really?"

"Well, of course, just look at all the guards, the barbed wire, the heavy concrete walls. Kinda makes sense really."

"Really?" repeated Bill, aware he was beginning to sound like a parrot.

"Oh Bill, you really are beginning to sound like a parrot. Listen, we are going to have to get in there. If we don't succeed then it really is game over. It's down to me and you champ."

"Champ?" It was now a habit that Bill just couldn't shake.

"Okay, so motivational psychology was not a strong area for me." She looked over at Bill, who was still trembling slightly. He had an automatic rifle looped around his shoulders, liberated from one of the guards. It hung round his neck like a giant medallion, and he felt more likely to shoot his own feet off than anything else. Reaching across his shoulder, Fern flicked the safety on.

"I didn't ever expect to be doing this again, but you are going to have to get through this one way or another." Producing the small pillbox from the folds of her jumper, she tipped another of the small, white Trepsin pills onto Bill's palm.

"Oh no," he said, finding his voice and some new words for once. "This stuff is mental," and he held his hand back out to Fern, the pill sitting in his palm. Swift as a striking cobra, Fern grabbed the pill, popped it in his mouth, clamped his jaw shut, and pinched his nose. Shocked, Bill swallowed reflexively, feeling the dry pill slide down his throat.

"Sorry," said Fern, "but it's the only way I can see of you getting in there alive."

"Getting in there. Alive!" Bill continued to splutter around the words. "You're bloody mad!"

Fern ignored him, concentrating instead on checking her gun. She produced some more ammo from her rucksack and tucked it into her pocket.

"Well, it won't work anyway. Damn stuff is having no effect. I must be immune to it now," said Bill, somewhat petulantly.

"I bet you're not," replied Fern under her breath and far too quietly for Bill to hear.

"I bloody am, no more crazy fighting, extra sensory rubbi . . ." Bill paused. She had whispered that last bit far too quietly for a normal person to hear. Bugger. With horror he noticed that his hands had stopped shaking, but were beginning to vibrate. It was a subtle change, but definitely there.

"Right," said Fern brightly. "Ready to save the world?"

Getting into the compound had been surprisingly easy. A large hole under the fence, maybe made by some sort of burrowing creature, allowed them to wriggle through. They were now crouched behind a large bulldozer, wondering how to get into the main building. Fern could see that Bill was having trouble now; he was trembling so hard he had wrapped his arms around a giant dozer tyre in order to keep himself on the ground. Fern was worried. He was at less risk of an overdose the second time around, but he still needed some way of working the Trepsin out of his system, and sitting behind the dozer was not doing it. She had never seen such an extreme reaction to the drug, and she knew the medical division was going to be spending a lot of time with Bill if they got back. *When they got back,* she corrected herself.

"They seem to patrol through that door over there," she said, pointing at a heavy steel-bound door in the corner of the building. "We might be able to sneak through, but we'll have to be very, very quick." She looked across at Bill. Amazingly she could feel the tremor through the dozer as he clung to the dozer tyre. He blinked slowly. Once. Twice. A third time.

"Bugger that!" he cried, releasing the wheel and leaping into the cab of the bulldozer. The keys were in the ignition, and Fern had just enough time to scramble into the cab before Bill gunned the vast machine into life. Wrenching random levers in a frenzy, Bill floored the accelerator.

While very dramatic in motion, the acceleration of a multi-ton bulldozer left a little to be desired. A number of the guards noticed the machine rumble to life and were already running towards them. Fern picked them off with a familiar accuracy as the dozer inexorably gained speed.

"So, what's your plan?" she shouted above the roar of the machine while casually reloading the gun. The dozer was pointed at a large, metal roller door, and Bill had levelled the giant scoopy thing directly in front of the cab. It was now quite difficult to see where they were going. Grinning, his teeth rattling, Bill turned to Fern.

"Big sss–ssmash," he stammered, urging speed from the dozer. Grinning like a maniac, Bill pumped the accelerator, hurtling the giant machine at the walls of Jerry Co.

Swinging from his shoulders, Manriguez tried again to get his legs on to the podium. He could nearly reach it, so very nearly.

Suddenly there was an almighty crash, long and thunderous, and the whole room shook, some plaster falling from the ceiling. Somewhere a siren began to warble and a large red light above the door began to flash. *Now this*, he thought, *was surely a good sign.*

The roller door parted like butter before the hurtling machine, the bulldozer barely slowing at all. With a roar of tortured metal and crumbling concrete the mighty digger blade tore into the wall, ploughing onwards in a shower of dust and debris. Catching a support column the dozer flipped sideways, the mighty wheels locking as Bill jammed on the breaks. Fern wrapped her arms around his neck, flung him to the floor of the cab, then threw herself over him as the out-of-control digger smacked its way deeper into the building.

After what seemed an age the digger scraped to a halt, its blade encountering another column with a stentorian graunch. After a few seconds of silence, Fern and Bill began to haul themselves from the tangled yellow wreckage, Bill with considerable difficulty. Not only was he shaking badly (part Trepsin, part adrenaline, part hormonal overload), but he was having a shocking time concentrating. As expected, the strange, white pill had massively heightened his senses, and until two seconds ago Fern had been lying on top of him. A small part of him felt a measure of shame that she had shielded him with her body, not the other way around, but most of him was too preoccupied with a rush of testosterone to dwell on such a detail. The fact that Fern now had her handgun out in front of her, double handed, and was scanning the debris for something to shoot did little to calm his ardour.

"Well, quite direct I would say," she said, smoothing back an errant lock of hair, smudging a small patch of blood across her forehead. "What now?"

Bill hesitated. In his drugged state the dozer had kind of been the entire plan, and now he felt somewhat lost. All around the rubble were bodies, all clad in the same uniform as the guards, all a remarkably similar build and height. There was a guard near the door who, for whatever reason, was making a crackling and hissing noise.

"Find the button and get out," Bill offered.

"My my, you really are a detail man, aren't you?" smiled Fern. "Right, follow me." She made for the far wall, still intact, where a grey metal door stood open.

Suddenly guards came pouring through the hole in the wall made by the dozer, fanning out, automatic rifles at the ready.

"Get going!" shouted Fern, shoving Bill through the door and rolling to her left behind a pile of rubble. Weapons fire rang out, bullets ricocheting off the metal door frame just above Bill's head. Four shots from Fern and four guards would move no more, the survivors taking cover among the assorted wreckage. Twisting her head, Fern saw Bill stumbling down the narrow corridor. To her horror, two guards rounded the corner at the far end, levelling their guns at Bill's chest.

"Bill, your gun!" she shouted, before desperately screaming, "the safety is on!"

Fortunately for Bill, Fern, and all of mankind, Bill completely misinterpreted her anyway. He was now in full-on Trepsin shock, utterly wired and overloaded. He wasn't stumbling because he was shaking . . . oh no, his body was now as steady as a rock. Neither was he off balance, he could feel the turning of the world around him, see the eddies of air in front of him, sense the tectonic shifts beneath his feet. He was one with his surroundings. No, Bill was stumbling because the damn floor kept moving. Oh, as a whole it stayed put, but he could see it flowing, back and forth, each molecule of it vibrating and bouncing gently within the solid mass. Vision at the molecular level was really very disturbing.

He saw the guards, heard Fern's scream. Responding to her call he ripped the gun from its strap and hurled it at the approaching figures, the rifle making a grey streak in the air that ploughed into the guards. Decelerating from a phenomenal speed to a standstill in microseconds, the rifle shattered into pieces, each one enduring unbearable compression. Both guards were hurled back, every bullet in the rifle's clip exploding on impact and releasing a shower of glowing shrapnel. The door behind Bill slammed shut, and Fern dropped the lock bar in place.

"Nice work," she complimented, nodding at the two downed guards and associated destruction. "Let's keep moving."

Rounding the corner they found three guards, all dead, smoking and crackling disturbingly. The corridor continued on for some forty metres, doors branching off at intervals.

"The button is a small metal box—" Fern began.

"Topped with a red button," Bill finished for her. "I know, I know," he was struggling to remember to breathe. "You left, me right," he panted, already kicking down the first door on the right. The door exploded inwards, ripped from its hinges, and buried itself three inches into the far wall. The room was full of expensive-looking computer equipment. Lots of fancy coloured LEDs blinked with a smug, techy glow, but the room was empty.

"Err, Bill?" said Fern.

"What?"

"I think you'll find that the doors are unlocked," she said, opening the door opposite his. This room was identical, also sporting lots of expensive-looking computers (but without a door buried three inches into the far wall).

Together they worked their way down the corridor. Bill came to a door that was most definitely locked, the plaque above it reading "IIB—No Entry." Rising up on the tips of his toes he could just see through a small window and into the room. On one side of the room was a large metal cage with a small metal table in the centre. Sitting on this table was a pigeon, its head bowed and its feathers a ruffled mess. The floor of the cage and the top of the table were spattered with black and white pigeon poo, and the pigeon looked thoroughly dejected. It reminded Bill of Clyde, but then again all pigeons looked the same, didn't they? This one did have a similar sort of ankle-watch though, although this one wore it on its left leg. The pigeon's eyes were closed and it looked like it was sleeping.

The other half of the room held a chair and a large computer workstation. Four large monitors were mounted in front of the chair and two joysticks rose up from the chair arms. A keyboard and a variety of other switches and dials were mounted just under the monitors, and a pair of earphones with a microphone attached were looped over the chair back. It looked like an elaborate computer gaming rig, or some sort of flight simulator. The image on the screen— a picture of a pigeon wearing military fatigues, a tin helmet on its head, and a medal pinned to its chest—seemed oddly familiar, although Bill couldn't think of where he might have seen it. He knocked on the window to try to wake the pigeon, but the bird didn't stir. Rattling the handle did no good either, but in his current state he knew how to handle a locked door.

Grinning, he unleashed a mighty kick to the door lock. Dazed, he picked himself off the floor. There, in front of him, through a Bill-shaped hole in the wall, stood the door, utterly intact. He had been knocked through the wall opposite and lay there in a pile of concrete. *Oh, that was gonna hurt later*, he winced.

"Well, it's about time," came a voice from behind. "It's beginning to hurt."

Chapter Thirteen

Manriguez, as he had introduced himself, had hobbled over to the metal lockers on the far side of the room.

"And you are sure we can trust this guy?" Bill asked Fern a second time.

Fern shrugged in reply. "Depends what you mean by trust. We do pay him well, but he works on a need-to-know basis, so I guess he isn't considered all that reliable," she said, adopting a tone that Bill suspected was supposed to be reassuring. It wasn't.

"They say he is one of the most dangerous men ever to come out of South America," she said brightly.

Brilliant, thought Bill, eyeing the dried blood on Fern's brow and the gun in her hand. Somewhere she had found a vicious-looking knife, and while Bill hadn't seen it in the past few minutes, she did have a suspicious bulge in her baggy, woollen sleeve. *Like you are a hundred per cent safe.* It wasn't all bad though; it would seem that being propelled through a solid concrete wall had somewhat counteracted the effect of the Trepsin. All solids around him appeared, well, solid, and he was breathing without conscious effort.

Manriguez was hobbling his way towards them. A crossbow was now strapped to his back, and he jingled lightly with each step. "Grateful as I am," he began, wincing slightly when he put weight on his left leg, "you really shouldn't be trying to rescue me."

"We weren't," said Fern, looking a little confused. "We followed your map here to uplift the button."

Manriguez gave a surprised look, then barked a short laugh. "You followed the map here? What on earth do you mean?"

Bill had a bad feeling about this. He'd been so proud of solving the riddle on the map, so certain it was the answer. At last there was something he'd been able to contribute, something to justify the presence of Mr 768,271 on this crazy mission. Flushed with success he hadn't even paused before breaking into a guarded compound. Well, he hadn't paused for long. And now he had the sinking feeling that even this new found confidence was built on sand.

"Your code," continued Fern. "Bill cleverly solved it. Each line of the address referred to one of the symbols, and if you drew a line between them then . . ." she tailed off. Manriguez raised his eyebrows quizzically. "Err, the symbols," said Fern weakly.

"Red herrings," said Manriguez, looking almost a little embarrassed, "all of them, utterly random. The code was a polynomial recourse algorithm on the first and third lines, giving a map reference to." He paused, taking the map from Fern's hands. "Here," he said, pointing to a place on the map by a river. There was no symbol on the map there. The closest symbol—the stoat—was quite a distance away. Bill was carefully studying his feet, desperate not to look up and meet Fern's gaze.

The point on the map was long way from the Jerry Co compound, and they were now right in the middle of enemy territory. It had been quiet for the past few moments (if he ignored the constant wailing of the siren), but it wasn't going to stay that way for long.

"Don't worry," smiled the assassin, flexing his shoulders. "I managed to come up with quite a good plan while I was hanging around here."

"So this is the brilliant plan?" said Bill dubiously. He couldn't see Manriguez's face, concealed as it was by the full face helmet.

"Well, do you have a better idea?" Manriguez huffed in reply.

They made an odd-looking trio, clad head-to-toe in uniforms stripped from the guards. Bill had been somewhat pleased to find all the guards were in fact robots, which explained the identical height and build, and the odd death crackle. It made for an awkward situation though. For Bill and Manriguez the fit wasn't bad at all, but Fern's diminutive frame was swamped in the blue leather jacket. They had rolled up the green cargo pants into big clumps of cloth, but they still threatened to engulf her feet. The guard's boots were an impossibility, and she just stood there in her own light tan ones. The helmet was wobbly on her shoulders, and she looked, not to put too fine a point on it, utterly ridiculous.

"It's never going to work," Bill pointed out. He had been very worried about the idea of using a dead man's clothes. He was surprisingly comfortable wearing a dead robot's clothes.

"It's either this or the ducts, and we all agreed that was a stupid idea. Come on, let's move," said Fern, slopping her way towards the hole in the wall. Manriguez had outlined his two cunning escape plans. They had gone for plan A, with plan B being crawling out via the ventilation ducts. Bill couldn't help feel that both of these were awful, B-movie clichés, and he had expected more from one of South America's most dangerous men. As he and Manriguez followed Fern, he noticed the man stop and pick something bronze from the floor.

"What?" asked Manriguez guiltily. "You don't see many of these nowadays, be a shame to leave it." Bill shrugged, and squeezed his way through the Bill-shaped hole in the wall.

Out in the corridor were the three robot guards that they had stripped. They really didn't look all that human once the uniforms were stripped off. Their entire body, if you could call it a body, was covered in some sort of polycarbonate sheath, giving the impression of a giant child's doll, all smooth and featureless. The only areas of difference were around the hands (eerie metal claws), the head (some sort of camera and sensor array), and a small panel in the left armpit. It looked like some sort of control panel: a handful of switches, a few data ports, and some LEDs, all dull and lifeless. As he stepped over the fallen robots, Bill glanced again at this panel, something tugging at his memory, but he was unable to say what. Manriguez called impatiently for Bill to follow, and with a last glance back, Bill joined his comrades.

Together they shuffled their way down the corridor, Fern adjusting the helmet every few steps in order to see through the eye slits.

"Why *exactly* is this a good idea again?" Bill hissed in a whisper, his terror reaching the point where it had started to tamper with bladder control.

"Biometrics," Fern whispered in reply. "There's a good chance the robots are programmed to ignore each other. That's likely to be based on biometrics, and if we look like them, they should ignore us."

"Good chance?" he spat.

"Oh yes, at least fifty-fifty I reckon, we'll know soon anyway."

"Shhh! Robots don't talk to each other!" said Manriguez in a menacing whisper, before immediately ignoring his own advice and adding, "I'm pretty sure we are headed in the right direction." Holding his finger to his lips he pushed open the door in front of him. The room beyond looked like a vast robotic mess hall. Cables and hoses dangled from the ceiling, spare batteries lined the wall, and patches of oil marked the floor. Racks on the walls held robot body parts—legs, arms, torsos, and even a line of robot heads. For some reason there was also a cabinet holding about a dozen stuffed pigeons—their eyes staring lifelessly through the glass—and a giant clear plastic bag full of blue and grey pigeon feathers. Gross—three of the stuffed pigeons didn't even have heads! All around the room robots hustled busily, automatic weapons in hand. Bill screwed his eyes tightly closed and waited for the shooting to begin, for it all to end. Nothing happened.

Something tugged at his sleeve and he cracked open an eye. Fern was standing in the doorway, beckoning him through. Manriguez was already making his way down the centre of the room, the robot guards paying him no attention at all. Bill took a step forward, then another. Still the robots paid no attention. Bill and Fern made their way side-by-side down the room. Fern's helmet began to slip, and she reached up hastily to keep it in place, almost knocking it off entirely in the process. *Sooner or later*, thought Bill, *one of these guards is going to be a human, and then our goose is cooked.*

Mr Gring strode into the control room. "Update!" he barked.

"Last known location is Wing B. Then they just disappeared, no sightings since." The man who replied (and it was a man, not a robot) was seated in front of a wide panel of switches and lights. The wall behind the panel was made up of a multitude of TV screens, each one relaying a different picture from around the base. Another operator sat to his left, a headphone over one ear and a microphone to his mouth.

"Wing B, did they enter Room IIB?" snapped Mr Gring, unable to keep the concern from his voice.

"We are not sure, sir. There was quite a detonation, and it knocked out the cameras. We know that security was breached in a room in that area. We should know soon. It may have been IIB."

"Know soon, know soon?" Mr Gring seethed. "It *may* have been IIB? Good God, man, was it IIB or not IIB? That's the bloody question!"

"Cameras coming up now," said the operator with a note of relief. A bank of screens, showing a grey fuzz up until now, flickered into life. They showed the corridor outside the room Manriguez was held in, multiple computer rooms, one with a door buried in the wall, some other rooms, and the room Manriguez had been chained up in, the human-shaped hole in the wall and rubble on the floor, robots picking their way through the debris. The camera in the middle of the bank was focused on the door directly opposite the hole. The door filled the entire screen, intact and whole. A little plaque just above the doorframe read "IIB—No Entry."

Mr Gring's right eyebrow twitched. In another man this would have been a loud sigh of relief, maybe even a whoop of relieved joy, followed by a short, capering dance. It did not go unnoticed.

"Sir?" enquired the operator nervously.

Before he could reply, Mr Gring's attention was distracted by something on a screen to the far right. "There!" he shouted, rushing over and jabbing the TV screen with a yellowy finger. "Just leaving the mess. You!" he barked, swivelling the finger to jab the chest of the man with the headphone and microphone. "Update their programming man. They are dressed as guards. Shoot on sight!" With that, Mr Gring stalked from the room. The man with the headphones looked desperately at his colleague.

"Don't look at me," said the man, "you heard him."

"But, but, but, but," stammered the man with the earphones.

"No buts, man. The last man to say 'but' to an order from Mr Gring ended up without one. Without much of anything for that matter.

You'd better get to it. Want a cup of coffee?" He rose from his seat. The man with the earphones shook his head, gulped, and began typing.

"We really don't have time for this," complained Fern. The room after the messy mess appeared to be an armoury. Rack after shiny rack of guns lined the walls, together with grenades, explosives, knives, night sticks, cans of pepper spray, odd spiky things that Bill had no name for, and a multitude of other toys of violence. Manriguez was practically skipping between the racks and shelves, strapping guns to limbs, tucking knives well, goodness knew where.

"Don't just stand there," cooed Chile's number one assassin. "This stuff is top drawer, grab a bunch!"

Bill, distracted and feeling a little overwrought, grabbed a couple of items from the nearest shelf and slipped them into his pack. Something was bothering him, like a small voice calling from a long way off, too quiet to be heard, but presumably with something important to say given the amount of effort it was making.

"Are we done now, kids?" hissed Fern, glaring at them both. To Bill's shock, Manriguez shared a conspiratorial wink with him and, considerably weighed down by weapons, hobbled towards the door helpfully marked "exit."

"Let's blow this joint," he laughed, as a robot guard entered the room from the mess.

What happened next happened in slow motion. It wasn't the Trepsin; Bill knew that was nearly all out of his system. He didn't know what it was, but it definitely all happened in slow motion.

Fern, looking through the window next to the door, was commenting on how many robot guards had gathered in the compound and that they should probably find another way out. Manriguez was struggling with the buckle of a new strap slung around his shoulders. The guard was raising his weapon, but they had walked past so many now they had stopped paying attention. Bill's foot hovered in the air, halfway through a step towards Fern and the exit sign. A single, dull, flat bang from the robot's weapon. Fern screamed, her body twisted around by the force of the shot. She slammed awkwardly into the wall and slid down, facing Bill and the robot, the helmet flung from her shoulders. The robot adjusted his aim.

"Noooo!" came the scream, from somewhere distant, but issuing from Bill's mouth. Diving he hurled himself at the robot, clattering into the raised rifle and then the bulky figure, sending them both crashing to the ground. Automatic weapons fire sang out as they fell, Bill desperately wrestling for the rifle. They hit the ground hard, Bill on top, and slid into a stack of shelving. The robot had kept his claws on the rifle, but it was pinned between them. Bill delivered a mighty punch to the figure's head and nearly broke his hand, giving a howl of pain. With a whirling of servos the robot casually pushed Bill off its chest, hurling him backwards against the wall. Rising to its feet it levelled the rifle at Bill's winded chest.

Blam! The shot rang out, and the robot collapsed to the floor. There in the doorway stood a second robot, the smoking barrel of its rifle still levelled at its mechanical colleague. Slowly it turned to Bill, who recovered in time to scurry behind the collapsed metal shelving as the shots ripped through the air. A third robot arrived on the scene and began exchanging fire with the second, before a fourth robot shot Robot 3 in the back of the head, only to be gunned down by Bill's original saviour. *What the hell is this?* thought Bill in a panic. *Are they fighting for the chance to kill me?* Manriguez, ducking out from behind a wall of lockers, took out the last robot with a series of well-aimed bursts from his rifle.

Bill scrambled towards the exit, terrified at what he would find there. Crouched behind an overturned table was Fern, her face pale and her right hand clapped to her left shoulder.

"You okay?" they both asked simultaneously, and for all the terror in their eyes nearly laughed out loud.

"Fine," they echoed each other, Fern giving a small bark—half sob, half chuckle.

"Really," said Manriguez, slapping what looked like a rectangular radio alarm clock to the wall. "Let's get out of here now!" The clock read 3 a.m., then began to go back in time rapidly.

"Lots of robot guards out there," mumbled Fern.

"Not anymore," replied Manriguez, kicking open the exit.

The compound was in chaos. The prone figures of guards lay everywhere, smoking and crackling. A short-pitched battle was raging at the southern end; two guards had taken shelter behind a digger and were exchanging fire with a lone guard behind a cluster of barrels. That was until the two guards noticed each other, two simultaneous shots leaving the barrel guard the victor of the bizarre skirmish. Wrapping his arm around Fern, Bill followed Manriguez out in to the open.

Mr Gring stood at the window of his office, listening to the short bursts of small arms fire that spoke of the last remnants of his robot army, the hordes of Jerry Co. He could just see the three figures stumbling their way into the surrounding forest, but he had no one to pursue them. With luck, Mendoza's men could follow their trail and discern their intended destination, but for now there was nothing he could do.

The compound was a mechanical carnal house, a significant portion of the building destroyed by the bulldozer. Suddenly, an enormous explosion rocked his office, a succession of smaller explosions telling him the armoury had been destroyed.

Turning from the view he pressed the small golden switch on his desk. A nervous and distraught voice crackled out of the speaker, but Mr Gring cut it off, his voice calm and imperious.

"Ah, yes. The two gentlemen in the guard control room, have them sent to me please." He released the switch, hesitated, and then pressed it again.

"And send up a bronze scrack splitter as well please. Thank you."

Chapter Fourteen

Night was falling, and it was clear that Fern needed rest. They hadn't slowed since leaving the Jerry Co compound, but it seemed they weren't being pursued.

"Manriguez, we need to stop, just for a few hours maybe." Bill had tried to keep his tone neutral, but concern leaked into his words.

Fern shook her head, denying the need for help, and as if trying to prove her point she shifted some of her weight from Bill's shoulder. Bill was worried though. She was hurt, he had no idea how badly, and she had been silent and withdrawn since they had escaped the compound.

"Oh, you might be fine," he countered, making a poor effort at joviality. "But I need a rest." Fern grunted, but didn't disagree this time.

"There," said Manriguez, his arm pointing through the forest. "Through the trees, you see?" Bill strained his eyes against the gathering gloom and could just make out a crude rectangular shape. Manriguez had flipped the map out in front of him and was squinting at it hard. Bill couldn't make out anything on the paper, but clearly the assassin could.

"We're still an hour or more away, but this is probably the best we are going to get. Come on." He strode away towards the small building. His leg had given him less and less trouble since they had left the compound, and he seemed to be moving freely now. Pulling more of

Fern's weight down on his shoulder, Bill followed him cautiously, wary of snagging a foot in the choked undergrowth.

The dark rectangular shape turned out to be a small hut, little more than four flimsy walls surrounding about five square metres of bare earth. The ceiling had long since collapsed or had been blown away, but even the meagre shelter of the four walls was welcome. By the time Bill and Fern arrived Manriguez had entered the hut through a gaping hole, presumably where the door had once stood, and had begun scraping the floor flat. The entire structure had a damp, sodden smell, an impenetrable air of neglect. As if to encourage them, a chilling wind had sprung up, railing against the old boards and sending a chill down Bill's spine.

Finished with the floor, Manriguez was working on a small solid fuel stove, presumably liberated from the Jerry Co store. The four shabby walls would serve to shield the light from any pursuers, which was Manriguez's main reason for choosing the spot. Bill un-slung Fern's pack from his shoulders and settled it in one corner, shepherding her towards it. When she was sitting down, he rummaged in his own pack, pulled out a slab of chocolate and handed it to Fern with a wink.

Bill moved away from Fern and made a show of helping Manriguez with the stove, which was already beginning to put out a reassuring warmth. Crouching close to the Chilean assassin he whispered, hoping Fern wasn't paying attention. "You know medicine?"

The man just shook his head.

"What, none, not even first aid?"

"Look, I hurt people, I don't put them back together," snarled Manriguez. His professional pride affronted, he turned his attention to the gaping doorway, which was now letting in a steady breeze. The wind was really picking up, the ancient timbers of the hut creaking in protest.

Fern looked brighter, if still quite pale, and half the chocolate had been demolished in short order. She was no longer clutching her shoulder either. The only real mark on her baggy jumper was a slight darkening that Bill suspected was blood, but in the weak light and with the wooliness of the material it was impossible to tell.

"I'm gonna need to look at that," Bill said, indicating her shoulder. Fern nodded and began shrugging her way out of the voluminous garment.

Dragging it over her head with a grunt of pain, Fern's head popped out of the bottom. Underneath the jumper Fern was wearing a wrap-around top. It was identical to that worn by the men who had attacked Bill on the platform of the subtrain, what seemed a lifetime ago. Jet-black, just like the men's, the end was tucked into the top of her jeans. Bill was willing to bet she was wearing identical trousers under her jeans, explaining the general bulkiness of her outfit.

He took the jumper from her hands and bundled it carefully, tucking it behind her head so she could lean back against the wall. Underneath where the dark patch on her jumper had been was a much larger, much cleaner patch of drying blood. Gently feeling his way for the entry wound, Bill lightly ran his fingers over the sticky fabric. This couldn't be right—there didn't seem to be a hole. But there was definitely blood, quite a lot of it, soaked through the material.

Shaking her head, Fern pushed him back and began rolling up her sleeve. She winced as she did it, but Bill wasn't sure it was pain from her shoulder. Halfway up her arm a strange, dark shape was revealed, livid against her pale skin. Just below her elbow, on the inside of her arm, was a black octagon. In the centre of the octagon stood a bold black "S." Taken aback by the strange tattoo Bill raised his eyes to Fern's, but she refused to meet his gaze, instead balling up the material and shoving it with a pained grunt up and over her shoulder.

113

Some of the material had nearly clotted against the wound, and Fern's harsh movement broke the scab, sending fresh blood running down her upper arm. Her entire shoulder was caked in dried blood. Ignoring the tattoo, Bill set about cleaning the area using bottled water from his pack and a spare T-shirt he had found near the bottom of the main compartment.

While the wound had bled prodigiously, Bill was even more confused than before Fern had rolled up her sleeve. Washing away the dried blood revealed a large bruise, purple and livid, surrounding a small shallow wound. Roughly the size of a stamp, the centre resembled a neat two millimetre deep hole in Fern's shoulder. He was perplexed by the superficial look of the wound, but the lack of an exit hole told Bill one thing: The bullet must still be in her shoulder, so he was going to have to get it out.

"Look, Fern, we are going to have to get the bullet out. Do you have anything with you that could help? Something for the pain maybe?"

Fern shook her head, but it wasn't until she held out her hand that Bill realised what she was referring to. Nestled in her palm was the bullet, mashed flat and clean of blood.

"But how?" stammered Bill, lost for words.

With what looked like extreme physical effort Fern spoke the first words she had spoken in hours. "This," she said, tapping the black suit. "Pretty much impenetrable. Makes Kevlar look like toilet paper. Doesn't stop you getting smashed up a bit though," she finished, wincing.

Awash with relief that she wasn't more badly injured Bill let out a short laugh.

"Damn handy stuff in that case, could have done with my own suit of bullet-proof armour back there." None of his humour reached Fern though. Slumping back against the wall, she closed her eyes.

"This is yours, and you should need no other," she whispered, a single tear leaking from her closed eyelid.

***

She's clearly in shock, thought Bill. He'd cleaned the wound as best he could, and after his initial outburst Manriguez had come up with a roll of bandages and some antiseptic. The strange man was now curled up near the entrance, a rifle slung across his knees, seemingly asleep. Fern hadn't moved since she had leaned back against the wall, and if Bill couldn't see her breathing he might have thought she was dead. His eye kept focussing on the strange tattoo on her forearm. He had seen tattoos before of course, but never one that looked so, well, utilitarian. It looked like a brand and reminded him of the concentration camp tattoos borne by Holocaust victims of World War II. Shaking the image from his mind, he settled himself on the hard floor, staring at Fern's delicate features. She really was quite pretty. He hoped she was getting a good sleep; they would probably have to move on in a few hours.

"I'm not sleeping," said Fern, one eye flicking open and focussing on Bill. The faraway, preoccupied look had vanished. Bill had assumed the look had been caused by pain, but he now wondered if it was pain from the shoulder wound, or something else, something deeper. Her gaze was now flat, determined, and remote. The colour was back in her cheeks, but Bill was far from reassured.

"Bill, there is much you need to understand, but we don't have much time. I will tell you what I can." He opened his mouth, but she talked right over him. "And don't interrupt," she said coldly.

115

Clicking his jaw shut, he sat patiently.

"You and I are part of a grand heritage, a noble lineage," she began, and Bill got the impression she was reciting, though a slight sneer caught the edges of her mouth, belying the flatness of her tone.

"As you know, in times of the gravest peril a hero is needed. It has always been this way, back through time immemorial. Over the aeons the Pygeans have tried to guide humanity's hand, selecting and identifying those to defend mankind in crises. The Chosen individuals do not act alone. Always there are two." Fern paused, taking a long swig from her water bottle.

"Two creeds, their bloodlines stretching back to the dawn of mankind. The first to be unknown, to exist among the unenlightened, to be called if and when needed. They are the ones who are Chosen, and upon them rest the fate of the world. The second to be knowing, to be raised among the enlightened. To be Selected into service, and to hone their skills from the first breath.

"Often we just use the words Chosen and Selected, but in the ancient tongue these creeds have another name. The Chosen is the Pretarn, literally 'the spear.' The Selected is the Trelain, 'the shield.' We are taught from the youngest age that the shield must protect—it can be dented, and it may be cleft in two, but the spear must not shatter. Never. Especially while the shield stands intact."

She paused again, taking a long, ragged breath, her piercing stare burrowing into Bill's eyes.

He didn't know what to say.

"Don't you understand?" she shot at Bill, anger now leaping to her eyes. "You are a Chosen, a Pretarn, nothing must harm you, you are too important. I have been raised, from birth, to protect you. Do you have any idea what it would mean if you died before me? Sure, Pretarns have failed—and died—before, often triggering an age of darkness. But

116

never, *never* has a Pretarn died while their Trelain lives, let alone died trying to protect their Trelain. You must never put yourself at risk for me. Never ever do that again. If you care at all . . ." she stalled, but picked up again quickly, "about the fate of the world, do as I say." Her eyes had softened a little, but she still seemed cold and unreachable, and it scared him in a way he hadn't before thought possible. Again he went to speak, but she held up her hand.

"It is difficult to understand, I know. This is not how it should be done; you should have years to digest the nature of your role. But understand it or not, I am your shield, Bill Posters. Another translation of Trelain is sacrifice. Over half of all Trelains die on missions with their Pretarn. It is my destiny. I will protect you as best I can, but you must never reciprocate." Suddenly she looked very tired, and smaller, and terribly far away.

"We need to rest. We have to get moving in two hours." With that she turned and lay down on her pack, closing her eyes tightly.

It was hopeless advice; how could Bill sleep after that? The fear and adrenaline from the escape from the Jerry Co compound had left him, and he felt cold and empty. He didn't want Fern to die for him; he didn't want anyone to die for him. He didn't want to be the hero either: how on earth could he save the world? Okay, so he'd been able to believe that taking a train and bringing a button back to London was something he was capable of, but he'd already gone way beyond that, and it was just getting worse. His breathing quickened, the first stage of full-blown panic, but he crushed it down. At the very least he owed it to Fern not to lose it and pass out. Maybe he should have taken the easy way out after all, picked up Keith's gun back in pigeon HQ, held it to his temple, and taken Mr 768,271 out of the equation. He eyed the rifle on the floor by Manriguez. It was a stupid thought: after all, no one could be so afraid of dying that they killed themselves, could they?

He hated feeling afraid. He looked across at Fern. Nothing frightened her; underneath all the baggy knitwear she was as hard as nails. But then he realised, there was something that frightened her. Terrified her even. It wasn't her death, or even the end of the world. It was him, and the prospect of him dying.

"C'mon, we've less than twelve hours to save the world, Bill Posters, and we have to get moving."

The voice swam into his dream, and something was jabbing him in the ribs. Maybe it was the giant clockwork pigeon. He turned to look at the bird and its eyes flashed red, then green, then red again. It gave a particularly hard peck to his ribs and the dream shattered, the myriad of pieces melting into the hard-packed dirt of the hut floor in a heartbeat.

"C'mon, Bill," Fern repeated impatiently, giving him a final jab in the ribs with her boot.

He couldn't remember falling asleep, but man he felt rough now. He was beginning to lose the plot, he could tell. He thought he had coped jolly well so far, with the talking pigeons, the subterranean diggy-train-thing, the mind- and- body-altering drugs, the army of robotic thugs and near-death experiences. He was horribly worried that the I'm-not-just-a-highly-trained-killer-but-a-highly-trained-killer-raised-from-birth-to-protect-you thing was going to push him over the edge. He struggled with it, and his mind teetered. Somewhere deep inside, his subconscious maybe, this recent revelation was weighed and balanced. He didn't like it.

Bill hauled himself off the floor. Manriguez was nowhere to be seen. Everything in the hut was packed away, the Chilean assassin's pack was propped by the door. He couldn't have gone far.

"I need your help with this," said Fern, gesturing Bill closer.

"I've dressed and bound it, but I can't pin the bandage with one hand, the angle's tricky."

She had indeed dressed and bound the wound, very professionally for someone working with one hand.

"I don't recognise this bandage," said Bill, taking the clip from Fern's hand.

"It's from the medical kit in my bag," she replied.

Bill was about to ask why Fern hadn't mentioned this earlier, but one look at Fern's eyes, still flat and pale, and he changed his mind.

As he fumbled with the clip, he couldn't help but glance down at the strange tattoo on her arm. It really bothered him, and he couldn't say why.

"So," he said with forced lightness. "What's the 'S' for? Supergirl?" he chuckled, overwhelmingly falsely. Fern muttered something that he didn't quite catch.

"Sorry?" he asked.

"Look, are you done yet?" Fern snapped, pushing him away sharply. Checking the clip, she rolled the jet-black sleeve down her arm.

"Sub, it stands for sub. Okay?" she continued, waspishly.

"Err, as in submarine?" hazarded Bill nervously.

"No," Fern replied, some of the heat leaving her voice. "Sub, as in Substitute."

Now Bill was really confused. "Substitute?" he repeated.

"Yes, substitute!" The heat had returned remarkably rapidly. Whirling away from Bill, she began ramming things back into her pack. The conversation was clearly over. Bill turned away and gathered his things up and got ready to move. The rectangle of night visible through the doorway showed a pitch-black forest. At least the wind had died down.

It didn't take him long to pack up his meagre belongings, and he squatted near the doorway munching a high-energy cereal bar. Fern had stopped crushing everything into her pack, and it seemed she felt bad for being so harsh with him earlier, as her tone was now much more measured.

"It stands for substitute," she repeated, moving closer to where he crouched. "I told you last night of the Trelain." Bill nodded. You didn't forget those sorts of revelations in a hurry. "There aren't that many of us you know. Only a hundred for every generation." Chewing mechanically, Bill bobbed his head in what he hoped was an encouraging manner.

"Apparently, there used to be thousands, hundreds of thousands, a whole nation. One for every potential Pretarn. But, you know, cutbacks and all." Bill nodded to show that he had understood. He of course had absolutely no idea what she was talking about.

"It's not random, you know, the matching. A lot of thought goes into it, heaps of analysis and consultation of Councel. One of the main uses of Councel nowadays." She paused, frowned at the empty night, then pressed on.

"Every potential Pretarn is matched to a Trelain. There are lots and lots of tests, all of which get fed into the Decision by Councel, but it is fairly easy to predict the outcome. The best, strongest, cleverest, most-able Trelain students are matched with the highest-ranking Pretarn. Mr or Ms Number 1 downwards. Once a match is made, there is no switching—a matched Pretarn and Trelain are a pair. If one goes on a mission, the other must be there. That other and no other." She paused, checking her watch distractedly.

"Of course, it means only the 1(e) or 2(e) Trelain are likely to see action, but we must all work hard, preparing for the tests, hoping to get a good placement." Again she looked at her watch, letting out an aggravated sigh.

"Where the hell is that man? We don't have time to wait!" She began tapping her foot and crossed her arms tightly. They had twelve hours to go. Bill might have found her pose amusing, or maybe cute, if he couldn't feel the urgency radiating off of her. Thinking of it, he still found it quite cute.

"Err, you said less than a hundred Trelain?" he asked, cautiously.

"That's right, what of it?"

"Well, how can they all be irrevocably paired up? I mean, I am Mr 768,271 or whatever. That's a lot more than a hundred, and . . ." he trailed off. It almost looked like Fern was blushing, or maybe she was getting angry again.

"Yes, well, that was all thought through. After all, what are the odds of getting through the top 100 or so? The top 99 are all matched up, all in order, as ordained by Councel. With the last—they never say last of course, but you know what it means—the last student is allocated to every other Pretarn on the list. The worst student doesn't get a number, they get a letter. An S, they are the substitute. Apparently, Councel has never been convinced this is a legitimate approach, but it was considered an acceptable risk given the cost of training each Trelain."

Fern jerked her sleeve up to reveal the strange tattoo, her eyes like flints.

"You want to know what this, what 'Substitute' means? It means you, Bill Posters, humanity's best hope for survival, must battle mankind's gravest enemies with the world's worst shield for protection. It means the unthinkable has happened, and ninety-nine of the world's best fighters, strategists, pilots, medics, divers, snipers, and explosives experts sit idle, their hands tied by a dictate more than a million years old. And I, who never expected to be here, to die here, am stuck with Mr 768,271, and forgetting the whole world for a minute, I came this close . . ." she held up her thumb and forefinger a centimetre apart, "to being the first ever Trelain to outlive his or her Pretarn, the Britak Tain no less. The first, and only, in hundreds of thousands of years."

She was quivering, her eyes flashing. Bill had no idea what to say and was beginning to panic a little. This was all too much to take in all in one go. His mouth had just begun to form around the sentence, "Oh, don't you worry, I was fine, really," when Manriguez strode back into the hut. He struggled a little with the doorway, having to turn sideways as his back now sported not one but two crossbows, explaining the chest strap he had been playing with since leaving the Jerry Co armoury. He took one look at Fern, stood there, her hand still raised and Bill, stock still and a little white.

"Sorry guys, not interrupting, am I?"

Chapter Fifteen

On top of a small rise, Manriguez surveyed the small hollow in front of him. The night was silent, eerie, and deathly. He'd felt a hundred nights like these, walking quietly down his spine like a whisper of doom. The air was cool and fresh, but with every sigh of the wind he fancied he could hear death. Stalking him, as always.

"Maybe tonight you'll get me, old friend," he muttered, then gave a short, inelegant curse. *Man, I'm getting maudlin and, it must be said, somewhat over-poetic in my old age. Walking down my spine like a whisper of doom? Rubbish!*

He couldn't entirely shake the feeling though, and the ordered calm in front of him did nothing to reassure him. He scanned the small clearing again with the infrared binoculars he had purloined from Jerry Co. The river ran in from the east, meandering its way through some particularly dense vegetation. It passed through the clearing, running away a little more rapidly to the west, the burbling waters passing about fifty metres to his left. In the centre of the clearing was the landmark he was looking for. The river gathered pace suddenly after a bend, tumbling down a three-tiered waterfall, before continuing its way to the ocean. He could hear the gentle roar from here. It wasn't a big falls, but it was a decent size, and very picturesque. Had he been here under different circumstances, had it not been the dead of night and, to be honest, if he had been a completely different person, he might have admired the pretty beauty of the falls. As it was, they registered only as his target location and a damn nuisance, as the gently tumbling susurrus made it impossible to pick up any of the tell-tale sounds of awaiting ambush.

Tucking the binoculars into his coat pocket, he checked his watch. Plucking a neat blue notepad from another pocket, he tilted it towards the light so he could read what was on the page. With a small pencil, he made some neat notes on the small grid, noting both the time and a score in the column marked "rate." He was on overtime now, and if there was one thing that Manriguez insisted on, it was an adequate invoice audit trail for contract work. Actually, if there was one thing he insisted on, it was kippers for breakfast on a Sunday, but the other thing came a close second. Manriguez was renowned as an efficient and dangerous killer, that was true. But, more importantly, he was renowned as a fair and honest contractor. He knew how important that kind of thing was in his line of work, and he knew how much repeat business he won as a result.

The small blue notepad disappeared back into his coat pocket to be replaced by the night vision binoculars. He scanned the area around the falls one last time. Nothing.

Fern hadn't spoken to Bill since they'd left the hut. Not properly anyway. She remained cold and distant, but very professional at the same time. She had ditched the baggy, woollen jumper and jeans in favour of the all-black ninja suit. It was as if the change of clothing had effected a fundamental change in her. She was harder, more definite, and was now clearly sporting a gun at each hip. Bill had seen some glints of metal around her wrists while she was getting ready to go, and he would have put money on her being strapped all over with vicious-looking blades. *What a pair,* he thought, watching Manriguez make his

124

way back towards them. *How on earth did I get messed up in all this? The sooner this is done, the better.*

"All looks clear," said Manriguez.

"Looks?" Fern asked, twitching an eyebrow impatiently. Manriguez shrugged, and despite the raising of the eyebrow refused to elaborate. Eventually Fern conceded. "Right, no more messing around," she began. "Our target is the button. You say it is tucked under the last of the falls, near the left side, in oilskin?"

The Chilean nodded.

"They may know where we are going. Bill, you head straight for the falls. You have to get the button and then get the hell out." They'd gone through all this on the way, and Fern was in no mood to discuss it. Bill just nodded.

"Manriguez, you shadow him all the way there. I'm gonna scout for ambush and cover you both. We have to get the button, but once you have it, get the hell out of there. No waiting." Bill half opened his mouth to say something, but one look from Fern and he closed it quick.

"And no questions, Bill," she added, to augment the steely glare she was lavishing him with.

With a wave of her hand, she beckoned Manriguez over, and the two of them moved out of earshot. She whispered something quick and urgent, eliciting just another shrug. Clearly this was good enough though, as Fern nodded in a satisfied fashion and made her way back to Bill.

"Here, take these," she said, thrusting the black tube of Trepsin into Bill's hands.

Gingerly he took the tube, wincing.

"No, no, I don't mean swallow them. We don't have time for you to be hopping and jingling all over the place. Just keep them with you,

125

okay? In case you need them. They have more effect on you than anyone I have ever seen. They may be of use."

Bill was a little bit offended. Hopping and jingling indeed! Did she know how distressing vision at the molecular level was? Stuffing the tube into his pocket, he grumbled something to that effect, but Fern wasn't listening—she was already making her way up the slope.

"After you," motioned the assassin, spreading his arms elaborately wide in a gesture of mock politeness. Grunting, Bill made his way up the slope.

Carlos Mendoza—ruthless mercenary and Manriguez's nemesis— was sitting in a large-domed tent opposite Mr Gring. In between them was a large map, detailing the surrounding area centred on a certain waterfall.

Carlos Mendoza exhaled in a steady stream, puffing three perfect smoke rings, one after the other. The end of the large Cuban cigar grasped between thick fingers flared red hot as he took another vast drag on the sausage-thick tobacco. Carlos was a big man. Very big, though you wouldn't notice it immediately. At six-foot-eight, he towered over almost everyone on the planet. His shoulders were massively broad, all of his limbs heavy with muscle. From a distance he looked quite ordinary, everything being in proportion. Up close he reminded people of what it felt like to be a child, hoping the neighbouring giants avoided squashing you. Where Manriguez was athletic and lithe, Carlos was strong and brutal. Where Manriguez would leap agilely over an impeding barrier, Carlos would smash his way through it. Both men got results. Both men saw it as a personal affront that the other was still breathing.

"And you are certain this is the correct place and that they will come back?" Mr Gring asked again, failing to mask his impatience.

Two smoke rings later and Carlos was in a position to reply. "Certain," was all he said.

Mr Gring fidgeted awkwardly in his seat, a normal-sized camp chair. Carlos was also seated in a normal-sized chair, but his immense frame gave it the appearance of a reject from a child's play dinner set.

"And you are certain you and your men can handle them?" hissed Mr Gring, wriggling in the chair.

Carlos raised an eyebrow and paused in his mechanical demolition of the cigar. That sounded an awful lot like someone questioning his judgement, and he didn't like that. Not one bit.

"*Si senor*," he responded. "After all, I do have highly trained men, not a radio-controlled horde of mannequin abominations."

"Why you insolent!" shouted Mr Gring, standing and pushing back his chair, which promptly folded and collapsed to the floor.

With surprising speed Carlos was also on his feet, towering over a foot over Mr Gring, cigar clamped in his mouth. "Just you finish that sentence," he rumbled around the vast cigar.

"Stop it, this instant!" The command was uttered in an accent both ugly and uncomfortable. "I will not have petty squabbling!" continued the voice, now accompanied by a high-pitched whine. A Segway emerged from the tent flap, struggling under the weight of a vast great white shark. Few sights were more terrifying than an angry great white shark. Seeing one riding a Segway was one of them.

Even Carlos jumped a little at the appearance of the vast beast, before remembering himself and biting down extra hard on his cigar, smoothing his expression into neutrality.

"My Lord!" cried Mr Gring, collecting his composure.

Carlos merely inclined his head, the shark driving his Segway within a few feet of the two men. From this distance, Carlos could smell the awful smell of the creature. Very fishy, somewhat putrid, with a metallic tang. The shark's beady eyes darted left and right, as if trying to fix them both with his gaze but not being sure who to focus on.

"My orders are clear, why are you not carrying them out?" the shark screamed, blasting the two men with fishy breath.

"I will lead my men personally. If you will excuse me," replied Carlos, taking his leave from the table and hurrying out of the command tent. He didn't much like turning his back on a fully-grown male great white, but he didn't want to be in the tent with the stench for a second longer than necessary.

"Mr Gring!" continued the Shark King, seemingly unable to stop shouting. "Are my sharks ready?" The fishy odour was like a body blow from this range. Mr Gring flinched in spite of himself.

"Preparations are complete, my Lord. They are ready for deployment."

"Excellent. And Mr Mendoza knows nothing?"

"No more than we discussed, my Lord," replied Mr Gring.

The Shark King made a disgusting slurping sound before continuing. "Are you sure that is wise? I understand that he is highly effective," he garbled. Mr Gring had pondered this himself, but allowed none of his uncertainty to show through.

"Appearance is vital, my Lord. Without it, the plan will not succeed. We must trust to their ability in this matter. Well, the abilities of two of them, the boy is quite useless it would seem."

"Very well, but why are you not accompanying Mr Mendoza?"

Mr Gring hesitated, then stammered in reply, "My Lord, I am not best used on the frontline, as it were, but am much better placed to assist marshalling our troops from this command centre."

The Shark King considered this for a moment, his thin lips twitching to reveal row after row of razor sharp teeth. "Very well. I will observe with you," he replied, whacking a fin on a large, green button on his Segway handlebars.

"Greblang!" the Shark King yelled at a small microphone taped to the flipper grip. "Send me a bucket of rotting sardines, I am hungry."

To Mr Gring's horror, the shark held the button down, giving him an enquiring look that could only mean one thing. "Errr, none for me thanks," he mumbled, "I had a big dinner."

Things went from good to bad in the blink of an eye. The ambush had been well planned. Bill had his arm behind the waterfall, groping for the oilskin package. He could feel something with his fingertips, but to get a decent grip he would have to lean further out over the water than he really wanted to. This would mean getting his head wet and put him in danger of pitching into the plunge pool. The water swirled beneath his feet, dark and forbidding. While the waterfall was by no means large, it seemed menacing enough to Bill. The water flowed out of the plunge pool at a reasonable speed as well, so goodness only knew what lay downstream. The freezing water only added to his reluctance to duck his head under and grab the package. He strained all the muscles in his arm, still not moving his feet or shifting his body position, but he could still only brush the edge of the oilskin.

A short way back along the path was Manriguez, his eyes scanning the undergrowth, a gun in each hand. Fern was someway further back, her black clothes making her invisible against the night. Bill could feel impatience resonating from both of them. Gritting his teeth, he held his breath, closed his eyes, and thrust his upper body under the icy water. For one, two, three seconds the icy water flowed over his head. His fist closed around the button and dragged it free. Clutching his hand above his head, he turned to his companions in triumph. But everything had changed.

Men had swarmed from the trees, a group of eight bearing down on Fern. Water dripping in his eyes, Bill tried to shout a warning, but it was too late. A muffled gunshot and Fern, kicking and punching, went down beneath a pile of men. Before he had any time to react Manriguez was at his side, and with a shove he pitched Bill over the edge and into the water below.

The impact of the frigid water drove all of the air from his lungs. Shoving his head under the falls had been deeply unpleasant, but in no way prepared him for immersion in the foaming pool. Razors of ice ran all over his body, shards of frozen glass clogging his veins. His chest bound tight with shock, and water forced its way brutally up his nose, inflaming his sinuses in a vicious counterpoint to the freezing of his skin.

Instinctively he hugged the oilskin package to his chest. Lungs burning, he fought for the surface with his one free hand, kicking out in desperation. Clearing the foamy surface, he hauled in a spluttering breath, only to nearly choke on the spray. He gulped down a mouthful of water and was forced back under, the churning water closing over his head. Again he kicked out for the surface, but the fall had spun him around, and he couldn't tell which way was up in the roiling pool. Something behind him was dragging him down. He began struggling with the straps of his pack, desperate to lose the binding weight. His limbs were already weak with cold, and his lungs were now on fire. His vision, what little he could see in the inky water, was fading, and he knew he was losing consciousness. Dully he wondered if his whole life was about to flash before his eyes, and he wondered if it would be okay to skip that bit, as it really wasn't going to be very interesting. A final vision fluttered through his mind, of Fern being wrestled to the ground, and in a last act of desperation his numb fingers clawed at the shoulder straps. It was no use though; he was too long gone. Clutching the button to his chest, he could at least do that right, he used the last of his breath to mouth a single word: *sorry.*

Chapter Sixteen

Pushing Bill into the river had seemed like a good idea at the time, but Manriguez was beginning to doubt this now. The scuffle around Fern had died down, which meant only one thing: A group of men were now headed his way, and Bill had still not come back up.

There were a lot of men, and he fancied that one of them looked unusually large. It could be a coincidence, but he hadn't lived to the ripe old age of thirty-six by believing in coincidences. Maybe it really was time to retire.

There was no way he could hold out on the narrow path; he was too exposed from the far bank. The only reason he hadn't opened fire was that he didn't want to escalate things. As a general rule he preferred being captured to being shot, and since no shots had been fired, he was keen to keep it that way. His orders had been to get Bill out of there, and he had hoped to see him drifting happily from the clearing by now. It now seemed obvious Bill was trapped under or behind the falls, and if his suspicions about who led this mob were correct, he was in some very serious trouble, both professionally and personally.

The men were advancing on his position, slowly and cautiously. It would seem they had orders not to fire, as he now made a very clear target. If he let this play out he was a dead man, quite probably after a long and excruciating death. Grinning an evil grin, he took a step towards the falls, causing the men to stop in their tracks and fasten their aim on his chest. *Time to mix things up*, he thought, beginning to raise both arms over his head in the universal signal of surrender. Instead of holding both hands above his head, he completed the movement with a flurry, hurling two grenades high in the air and back over his head into the small lake above the waterfall. The two grenades disappeared without a sound beneath the shimmering surface.

Without pausing to see the men's reaction, he kicked himself out from the ledge, aiming just to the right of where he had seen Bill enter the water. Ignoring the crippling cold of the pool, Manriguez spread his arms and legs wide after impact, slowing his descent and allowing him to feel the tug of the water. Sure enough it was pulling him back under the falls. Swimming with the flow he hunted desperately for Bill, trying to make out any shapes in the murk. Something like canvas brushed his hand and he snatched at it. He pulled Bill's body in close, then kicked out against the flow, desperate to put some distance between them and the rock wall. He was also beginning to run out of air, but dared not clear the surface as he hauled the dead weight away from the falls.

Suddenly, a mighty roar assaulted his ears, powerful even under the water, a shock wave ripping through his body. A split second, and chaos broke out around him as chunks of rock smashed into the water. Offering a silent prayer to any god that would listen, he thrust his head above the water and gulped a long breath of air. Then the water hit, slamming into them both like a wall. Tightening his grip on Bill's unconscious body, he tucked his head under, thrust his legs out in front of them both, and repeated the prayer.

Mendoza hung at the back of his men, marshalling them and urging them on. If people were going to get shot he preferred it if he wasn't one of them. He could see Manriguez pressed up by the falls down a narrow path. The girl had been subdued; the boy was dead in the water below. He had anticipated an attempt to escape by river and had men

133

with machine guns on the bank downstream ready to strafe anyone in the water. He had thought it a fairly logical choice by Manriguez to attempt to get the boy out that way, but it would seem the flow of the falls had done the machine gunners work for them.

He sucked in a deep breath and tried to savour the moment. Manriguez had nowhere to go, and no route of escape. Oh, he knew how unpredictable Manriguez could be if cornered, but his men had orders to shoot if absolutely necessary. Dead or alive, he would have Manriguez today.

And it would be alive, he noted with glee, as Manriguez slowly began to raise his arms in surrender. The smile died on Mendoza's lips as he saw what none of his men seemed to notice—two large lumps in Manriguez's hands.

"Shoot him you fools!" he howled, but it was too late. Manriguez threw what could only be grenades back over his head and dived into the frothy depths.

"You and you!" he roared at the two men on the path. "In after him. Everyone else evacuate!"

"Evacuate?" called his lieutenant. "But the area is secure."

"Just get the hell out of here you idiot," Mendoza growled, "and take her with you," he finished, waving his gun at Fern's unconscious body as he sprinted uphill and out of the clearing.

Mendoza had just cleared the edge of the river, his men and the girl just behind him, when the grenades detonated. Manriguez must have released the pins a fraction of a second apart—the dull thuds were slightly syncopated. Water spouted into the air above the falls, and chunks of stone tore loose to crash into the plunge pool. A heartbeat later and there was a crunching scream of rock as the wall of the lake above the falls gave way. The rumble rolled through the ground beneath his feet, causing his men to stumble. Not looking back, he broke into a sprint. He briefly considered radioing the machine gun team downstream, but they wouldn't have enough time to make it to safety.

Released from behind the natural dam, the falls saw its largest flow in history, as millions of litres of water boiled over in a deafening roar. The lake beneath the second falls began to empty and the river downstream burst its banks, the swollen flow racing out of the clearing.

Pausing in safety by the banks of the lake, Mendoza scowled down the length of the river. *Curse you, Manriguez, you had better not be dead. One day I will kill you!*

Much to Bill's disappointment, it seemed the whole life-flashing-before-your-eyes thing was mandatory. But it wasn't really a "flash."

For a second he floated in darkness. Then the screen flickered into life, casting a strobing light around the film theatre. He remembered this place. He'd spent a lot of time here as a kid. It was a small cinema, only two screens, in his hometown. The seat he sat in was even more mangy and threadbare than he remembered, but the damp and slightly mouldy smell was exactly as he recalled.

The film was starting. He snuggled down into the reassuringly familiar cushion, surprised to find a box of popcorn on the arm of the chair. The opening scene of the film showed him as a small child, probably about two years of age, with his parents at the park. He sighed. He'd seen this film before, first hand as it happened, and he knew how it ended, didn't he?

His mum and dad looked younger than he had ever seen them. They chatted away happily as they pushed him on a swing. It was a happy scene. Suddenly, the whole theatre tilted, and instead of looking across at the scene he was looking down at it. With a small yelp he was thrown from the seat and catapulted over the rows in front, straight at the screen. He screwed his eyes tightly shut and cringed, waiting for the impact as he hit the screen. Nothing happened.

Tentatively he opened an eye. The world was moving, back and forth, back and forth. Everything was a strange sort of sepia tone. Opening his other eye he looked around. He was restrained in some odd device that was being pushed by a giant replica of his mother. What was happening? He opened his mouth to speak, but all that came out was some unintelligible burble. Of course, he was a baby, so that made sense.

"I think he will be an astronaut," said his mother proudly. She beamed as she pushed him gently.

"I thought he was going to be a professor of literature?" his father chuckled, hugging his wife.

"Well, that too I expect. Our little man will be able to do anything." He could feel his mum's certainty and support wrapping him up like a warm blanket. It had been a long time since he had felt its reassuring glow.

"Perhaps, perhaps," replied his father, "but I'll be happy if he's happy. Normal and happy is fine with me."

"Oh no," said his mother, quite definitely. "Happy of course, but never normal. I couldn't imagine anything worse than being ordinary. My little Wilberforce is special. I could tell the minute I looked into his eyes. He will never be ordinary."

Time stretched and shifted. He was now sitting in front of a strange, wise man, resplendent in his white coat. Something important was happening, but he wasn't sure what.

"All the tests are back, Mrs Posters. I am pleased to say that you have a perfectly normal young man. All the indicators are in the standard range," said the wise man.

His mother chewed her lip. "Are they all normal, even the development tests? He's not showing, I don't know, unusual potential for anything?"

The wise man chuckled. "Well, he's above average, Mrs Posters. Nestled in the sixtieth percentile."

This did not seem to satisfy his mother. "That's only just above the middle, isn't it?" she asked. The wise man adopted a reassuring tone, though Bill could tell his patience was stretched. He couldn't tie his own shoes, but he could read the adults better than they seemed able to read each other.

"At this stage, Mrs Posters, everything being normal is a very good thing, isn't that right, champ?" He gave Bill a friendly wink. It made him chuckle.

The chuckle turned into a sob. He was hiding in the toilets again. The other children refused to play with him. He badly wanted to join in their games, but they said he had a strange name and refused to involve him. He hated his name. Half of the other kids couldn't even say it, and some had taken to calling him "odd boy."

The door cracked open and Darren peeked in. Darren was one of the few kids who would speak to him.

"What's wrong?" Darren asked.

Bill wiped his nose. "My stupid name," he mumbled, fighting back tears.

"My dad has a name like yours. Will-something. His friends call him Bill. You could be a Bill like my dad," said Darren.

It was like a ray of sunshine breaking through the clouds of his early life. *Bill* sounded more ordinary. He'd be better able to fit in, and the other kids might let him join in their games. He gave Darren a small smile.

His mother didn't like it though, not one bit. She didn't like anything normal. She was a free spirit, flamboyant and unconventional. He loved her for it and would not change her one bit. But he was beginning to learn. Normal was safe, ordinary was comfortable. Anyway, he was very good at ordinary. As Bill Posters it came naturally. He sailed through school uneventfully. He was okay at everything, brilliant at nothing. He showed a talent with numbers, but never pushed it too far, never stood out from the crowd. He resolved to make the safe choices and life rewarded him with normalness.

As he accelerated towards adolescence and beyond, Bill realised how devotedly he had stuck to his resolution. It was as if the video reel of his life was highlighting points where he could have taken a different path, lived life differently, but chose not to.

At age eight, his mother had wanted to move him to special school so he could build his mathematical talent. He knew "special" was just another word for "different" and had fought tooth and nail not to go. His mother had eventually relented. He'd avoided school competitions, sporting teams, and generally trying too hard at anything. In every thirty people there were two dozen just like Bill Posters, and that suited him just fine.

When entering the world of work, he'd applied for a job with a Japanese high-tech firm on a most uncharacteristic whim. He'd got the job, but the position was in Japan. Without a hint of regret he had taken the less interesting, worse paying but—importantly—more average job with Bally Brooks. He had worked there ever since. Normal, average, low risk. He'd chosen his course in life and he'd stuck to it.

Until, of course, the past day, when it seemed all the non-normalness he had shunned for his entire life had caught up with him. The kaleidoscope slideshow of his life seemed to slow down when it reached the events since his meeting with Clyde the pigeon. It was almost as if it had too much to fit in so it had to run slower.

He was surprised to find that he had come to terms with it all. Talking pigeons, robot armies, ninja bodyguards. Fine. He just had to expand his view of normal, that was all. But running through things a second time, as it were, gave him the overriding sense that something fishy was going on.

It had all happened so quickly he'd been swept up and hadn't had time to think. He was humanity's best hope to avoid a shark global take-over. Improbable, yes, but he could rationalise it away. Pigeons were highly intelligent sentient beings. That made his elevation to chosen 768,271 status seem positively run of the mill, but he had always thought their dopey looks were a little contrived.

No, he had to really stretch the boundaries of his normalness test, but most of it fitted in. But not everything. Some of the specifics just didn't fit together.

If he lived in Fern's world every day, he might not even notice. But he didn't. He was ordinary Bill Posters, and among all of this some things were just plain odd. Odder than the rest of it anyway.

He turned it over and over in his mind, hunting for the key. The film was nearing the end—he could see himself inching along the ledge, his hand under the falls grasping for the button. Frantically his mind churned. He could do little else to help, if he was dead. With luck Manriguez and Fern might be able to finish the mission. Get the button back to the UK. The all-important button. The portable self-destruct mechanism, the only weakness in the sharks' weather control doomsday device. It was the Achilles heel of their painstaking world domination plan, a plan uncovered by Clyde the pigeon and his spy network. Bill wished he had never met Clyde. Since meeting the clumsy talking pigeon his life had stopped making sense. At least Clyde didn't poo in public every five minutes like all the other pigeons . . .

Wait, that was it!

In a rush it all slid into place. Facts that he had ignored over the past day rose up in a new order, rearranging themselves in his brain. He saw the headline from *The Metro* that morning: "Naked Pigeon Phenomenon," the article describing the large numbers of plucked pigeons scattered across London. He saw the mess hall at the Jerry Co building, stuffed pigeons in a cabinet and a plastic sack of feathers. He saw Clyde, fumbling with a switch and almost falling, and then again in his office, an office that was spotless but without a guanodrone in sight. He saw *Mary of Exeter*—war hero pigeon extraordinaire—*twice*, and most importantly he saw Clyde, back when they had first met in the alley outside Bally Brooks. Suddenly all the other pieces fitted together. It could all make a crazy sort of sense, but only if you realised one essential truth. But none of the others, the extraordinary others in their extraordinary world, would ever see it. It was a normal realisation from an average world, from an average person. And sometimes the average world needed an average hero. Maybe this time it needed him?

He needed to get back. On the screen he tumbled. Desperately, he scrabbled at his invisible prison, but there was no door to open, nothing binding his invisible limbs. He knew, he'd worked it out, but he had to get back, he had to. His body hit the water and was swallowed, plunging the world into darkness. A roaring filled his ears and pressure crushed down on him. He was slipping. *No!* He screamed wordlessly into the void. A word seemed to form in his mind, echoing into the night. *Sorry.* With a growl of rage he tore the word aside, scattering it. *I know!* he howled into the binding darkness. A pinprick of light formed in the black. Something smashed into his ribs, knocking the wind from his lungs. His head swam. Something smashed into his ribs again and his life flowed out of his mouth. The pinprick of light rushed forward and the void shattered.

With another wracking cough Bill hacked up more river water, the burning tide forcing itself out of his mouth and nose. Exhausted, he went to topple forward on to his face, but Manriguez's hands held him firmly upright. After a short splutter he felt fully drained, both of water and energy. Seemingly satisfied the strong hands helped him to collapse into a sitting position, his back supported by the base of a tree.

Wiping drool and goop from his mouth and nose he began to notice how cold he was. His body seemed to alternate between burning heat and icy cold. His head ached with what felt like the beginning of a monster headache, and all his limbs felt battered and bruised, both from outside and in. A shallow gash on his arm dripped blood steadily onto the earth, but all he could do was stare. He couldn't even feel the cut with everything else. Breathing was difficult, and he wondered whether he had broken a rib.

The day was beginning to break around them, bright and fragile. The ruddy browns and deep greys of the forest were slowly being transformed into a verdant array of greens, lush and healthy. Birds that Bill could not name flittered from branch to branch, delighted that the veil of night was finally rolling away.

They were seated on the bank of the river, a low dry bank on the outer edge of a wide loop. The river surged past by their feet, the edge of the water receding down the bank. What on earth had happened? He could remember entering the water, the icy hooks of the freezing river pulling him down. He could vaguely remember struggling with his pack, remembered the feeling of absolute desperation. Then nothing. Nothing but blackness and the surging growl of the river. Then another memory fluttered into view, crushing all others beneath it and banishing some of Bill's fatigue with its urgency.

"Fern," he mumbled, his cracked lips struggling to form the name. With an effort he turned to Manriguez. The man was rummaging in Bill's pack, pulling items out and laying them on the sandy mud. So it would seem Bill hadn't managed to get the damn thing off after all.

Manriguez had heard him. He paused in his inventory of their possessions and turned to face him. Bill hadn't really noticed before, but the assassin's face bore absolutely no expression. None at all. Not sorrow, joy, mirth, frustration, anger, or satisfaction. For the first time Bill wondered what had to happen to make such a man.

Manriguez was utterly blank, an expression that did not change as he said, "Captured. She's gone Bill, we have to move on," before turning back to the task at hand.

"We have to go back for her," croaked Bill, ashamed at how weak his voice sounded, even to his own ears. He needed to be strong, somehow. He and Fern had started this together, and he knew that he couldn't abandon her. Not if she needed him. Manriguez rose from the ground and brought something bright orange over to Bill. It was one of the survival blankets from the pack.

"Here," Manriguez said, thrusting the blanket at Bill. "You're freezing, I didn't pluck you from that river to have you die of cold."

Taking the blanket, Bill struggled it around his shoulders, covering himself as best he could.

"And eat," said Manriguez, throwing him a slab of chocolate.

Of course, thought Bill, his memories fitting together in a semi-logical order. *This man must have saved my life; I was unconscious in the river.* Worried he might have offended his rescuer, and feeling somewhat guilty, he summoned the energy to talk.

"Thanks for saving my life," he said, pleased that his voice was nearer to normal. Manriguez didn't even look up, just gave him a small shrug.

"Really, sorry I didn't mention it earlier," Bill carried on.

The assassin paused and turned to look Bill straight in the eye. "Look, I am just doing my job, okay? So sit there and get some energy back. We don't have long."

Bill wasn't sure how to take all this, but decided that being alive was a lot better than not. The warmth was beginning to return to his body and the chocolate tasted good. For the next five minutes that would do. From then on, well, the world was about to get a new Bill Posters. He'd been hiding behind his averageness all of his life. He had known the sort of people that saved the world: amazing, incredible, unusual people. But now he knew that the world needed normal people too. It needed the Bills *and* the Wilberforces. He had died and been reborn, and now he was kinda angry and about to kick some ass.

At least that was what he hoped.

Fern was regaining consciousness, her vision swimming in and out of focus, and a pounding building up in her skull. Her eyes were gummy and sticky, and itched, in addition to failing to focus on anything. Pepper spray. Bastards.

As she struggled to sit up, her body gave a dull moan of discomfort. Deciding it made more sense to stay lying she took a deep breath and concentrated, running through a health check drilled into her by countless hours of training. Sending her perception up and down her body, she performed a mental scan—twitching a muscle here, flexing a tendon there—to check for injuries. From head to toe she completed two slow passes, impassively documenting any pains and strains. Nothing was broken except what felt like a hairline fracture to a lower rib. She could easily live with that. Her head was sore, and she had a number of lumps, but she didn't think any of those were large enough to suggest any internal injury. Thankfully, her legs and arms had only superficial damage, so she was mobile, and her vision was slowly returning. She had the tell-tale signs of someone who had gone down fighting and received a decent kicking on the ground, probably until she lost consciousness. But that had clearly been the end of it, or she would have been in a worse state.

Satisfied she was more or less okay she hauled herself painfully into a sitting position. More or less okay was certainly painful, she realised, clutching her head, which had increased its pounding the moment she had begun moving.

The room didn't look much like a cell. In fact, it looked nothing like a cell. Only the mattress shoved up against a corner next to a metal bucket gave the suggestion of a detention area. *How odd*, she thought, resting her back against the wall and trying to summon the energy to stand. Mobile and injury free she may be, but for all the oddness of the room it looked very secure. One door, doubtless locked and guarded, meant she was going nowhere. The only hope was that Manriguez had gotten Bill out of there, the button too.

"Keep running boys," she whispered quietly. "Keep running, and don't you dare come back."

"There is no way in hell we are turning back!" spat Manriguez, amazingly his face registering something approaching an expression. Shock maybe, or possibly anger.

"I'm not leaving without her," replied Bill, trying his best to sound resolute and determined.

"No way, uh huh," Manriguez repeated. "You saw how organised they were; it would be suicide."

"We've faced bigger odds before," argued Bill, aware that "before" meant only about ten hours ago.

"What, you mean back at Jerry Co?" exclaimed Manriguez in disdain. "Those robotic disasters spent more time killing each other than trying to kill us, and even then we made it out by the skin of our teeth." Bill knew he was on shaky ground with this one.

Manriguez could sense it, and pressed on. "And if I remember, other than a short wrestle with one you didn't do a great deal at all," he added, his lip curling into a sneer.

Bill was enraged. "I'll have you know that I killed a whole bunch when I, well, threw my gun at them." He realised too late how silly this sounded, but he couldn't stop now. "Besides, I have some pills that give me super strength, and all that, so we'll be fine."

"Magic pills, eh?" growled Manriguez, his sneer expanding. "What magic pills?"

Digging into his pocket Bill pulled out the small, black tube, then popped the top off and tipped the contents into his hand. Where he had hoped for the small, white tablets he got a trickle of cold water and a slimy splodge of river mud. Bugger.

"I hate to break it to you, *amigo*, but that is mud, not magic," said Manriguez.

Hurling the tube to the floor and wiping the mud on this jeans Bill tried to recover his composure. Inside he was crushed. With the Trepsin he had begun to believe that he had a chance, that he could rescue Fern. Without it he was Bill Posters, half drowned, bruised and tired. Desperately he tried to keep the despair from his face. Mustering something deep, some reserve he didn't know he possessed, he fought down the fear and hopelessness and met Manriguez's gaze. His voice wasn't loud and filled with bravado now. It was quiet, and desperate, and determined.

"I'm not going to leave her. There is no telling what they will do. We can't just run away. If it were reversed she would come after us." For a second Manriguez looked thoughtful, and Bill thought he had struck the right chord.

"For you, undoubtedly. She knows what her job is. For me, not a chance." Manriguez said the last words with such a dark certainty that Bill felt a brief pang of sympathy. But it was very brief.

Manriguez had started to repack their gear, and Bill could tell he had made no headway. He drew a deep breath and ploughed on.

"Look, I'm not asking for your permission. I am going back for her. It would be great if you came, but either way I'm heading back."

"No, you are not," said Manriguez, turning around, a gun pointed at Bill's chest.

"What the hell?" Bill shouted.

"I have my orders: Get you and the package out of here. Nothing, absolutely nothing else."

Fear and anger fought inside Bill's mind. Anger won a brief victory.

"Orders, orders! Who the bloody hell from?"

"Who do you think? Her. For God's sake, grow up. There are more important things at stake here. I have to get you and the package out of here. That includes not letting you hare off back to the enemy, so don't make me shoot you."

He was right of course, there was more at stake here. The whole world, if Clyde the Talking Pigeon were to be trusted. Bill knew this, and he knew that trying to rescue Fern was possibly stupid, definitely fraught with danger and likely to get them all killed. But he also knew, more than anything, that he would not, could not, leave her behind. They had started this together and would finish it together. If they didn't, it would make no sense.

"Go ahead," he said, dead calm now and certain. "Shoot me, because there is no way I am leaving her behind." Manriguez's aim didn't even waiver, but at least he didn't pull the trigger.

"Anyway, I am betting it would be difficult for you to get paid if you actually kill me yourself. I would imagine that kind of thing would be bad for business." He had struck a nerve here, the tiniest flinch flashed across the assassin's face.

After what seemed an age Manriguez lowered his gun. Tucking it back into his belt, he issued a string of curses while plucking a small blue notebook and pencil from his pocket.

"Okay *amigo*, but you should know that I charge extra for suicide missions. This is triple time, sign here."

The assassin thrust the notebook forwards with such anger that Bill flinched. He didn't think it was possible to kill a man with a small blue notebook, but if it *was* possible Manriguez would be the man for the job. The page was divided up into a neat grid of columns and rows. At the bottom was a box marked "authorised signatory."

"Err, right there?" said Bill, taking the pencil and hovering over the box.

"*Si.*"

"Great," said Bill, squiggling his signature in the small box. He handed the notebook back and wiped the sweat off his brow.

"Hmmm, not much of an arsenal," Bill muttered, looking down at the remains of his belongings spread out on the ground. In grand summary he had a box of cereal bars (soggy cardboard), a half-eaten slab of chocolate, a box of Crunchy Nut cornflakes (box holding up surprisingly well, bag intact), half a stick of lard (where the other half had gone would remain a mystery until the day he died), and two items he couldn't recall seeing before. One looked like a very small alarm clock, about 5cm by 2cm, and the width of a pencil. The other looked like a can of baked beans, but with a different label.

He turned the can over in his hands. It had a ring pull top, much like a fizzy drink can, but was considerably heavier than a drink can. The label was in a rather boring white-and-blue design. Very utilitarian, rather like the budget variety of products you get in some supermarkets. The rear of the can detailed some safety messages, possibly the ingredients, or the nutritional value. He couldn't tell as the writing was very small and smudged. The front of the can had what was presumably the manufacturer's name picked out in big letters. Western Union Projectile And Sabotage Services, it read, with the acronym of WUPASS forming a circle in the middle of the label.

The alarm clock, although black and sleek, appeared to be broken. The digital display on the front was blank, and it didn't seem to have enough buttons. Sure enough, there was a button marked "H," one marked "M," and one marked "S," (which seemed a little precise to Bill), but there was no obvious way to turn the thing on. And no obvious place for batteries, so maybe that was the problem. After studying all six sides Bill finally found a small button, unmarked, that if you held down and pressed the others at the same time you could get some progress. Fiddling with the buttons he tried to set the time, before realising he had no idea what the right time was anyway, only the time in the UK. It didn't seem to matter anyway, as the thing had definitely been busted—it started running backwards instead of forwards.

A cough from behind startled Bill from his study.

"Ahem—if you will allow me?" enquired Manriguez, holding out a hand.

"Well, if you know the time, great, but I think it is broken anyway," said Bill, handing the device over.

Manriguez studied the small box intently before giving a tiny smile and pressing all the buttons in a strange sequence. The time winked out again, leaving just a blank clock face.

"See, definitely broken," said Bill.

"Err, what exactly do you think this is?" asked the assassin, handing the device back to Bill. Something in his tone made Bill wary of the obvious answer.

"An alarm clock?" he offered. To his great shock Manriguez let out a mighty roar of laughter, slapping his thighs and almost doubling over.

"Yes, my friend, it is an alarm clock. Though one to put you soundly asleep rather than wake you up!" he laughed before collapsing in hysterics at his own joke.

Bill didn't understand the joke at all, and was beginning to feel offended, when Manriguez finally regained control of himself, wiping tears of mirth from his eyes.

"No, it is not an alarm clock as such, but rather a very small but incredibly powerful timer detonated explosive charge."

Bill hesitated. "Err, I'm sorry?"

"A bomb, Bill, it's a bomb."

"Gah!" shouted Bill, hurling the black cuboid back to the floor near his pack. "You could have bloody told me!"

"I just did."

"Well, you could have told me sooner."

"I would have, but I was busy disarming it."

A lengthy pause.

"So, I had armed it?"

Manriguez nodded.

"And it would have exploded?"

Manriguez nodded again.

"Oh Jesus!" exclaimed Bill, wondering if he would ever feel safe around portable digital alarm clocks again.

"But don't worry," said Manriguez in what was meant to be a reassuring tone. "You had given me a full four minutes and thirty-five seconds to disarm it. There's a good chance we could have gotten far enough away if I hadn't been able to."

"Good chance?"

Manriguez nodded yet again.

"Powerful stuff then?"

"Very."

"Well, where the bloody hell did it come from?" shouted Bill, panic creeping into his voice.

"Don't look at me, it came from your pack. Handy stuff that."

Bill's mind tumbled through possibilities for a few seconds before realisation hit him. Of course, the Jerry Co armoury.

"That's it, I must have picked it up at the compound," he said, remembering stuffing two items into his pack while in a daze. "I got this stuff at the same time, I think," he continued, picking up the strange can and handing it over. The assassin let out a low whistle, turning the can over and over in his hands.

"Nice, I didn't know they still made this. The company that made it went bust years back. Some sort of court case." He handed the can back to Bill.

"Experimental stuff, it's made of a special compound that is supposed to behave differently according to requirements or its environment. Essentially its purpose is to cause as much damage to its surroundings as possible while preserving human life."

"And how does it do that?" Bill asked.

Manriguez shrugged. "No idea, I've never used the stuff. I like to know what things are going to do before I use them. Never had much call for a weapon that makes its own mind up." He'd already turned back to his own pack, which would in fact look like an awesome arsenal if it wasn't all packed away.

Bill placed the can next to the bomb and shoved everything else back into his pack. His conscience was pricking him about leaving a bomb and a can of unknown mayhem unattended in the middle of a forest (what if a child found it, or one of those cute birds?)

"That could be handy stuff; you'll want it with you. If you really are serious about rescuing her," called Manriguez. Scowling, Bill shoved the two items, carefully, into the top of this pack.

"You'll want this too," shouted Manriguez, throwing him a small handgun. "Know what to do with that?" the assassin asked.

Keen to seem knowledgeable, Bill drew on all his previous gun experience to try and give a sensible response.

"Uh huh," was all he managed.

Chapter Seventeen

Quiet, motioned Manriguez, holding a finger over his lips. Bill sat very still, trying not to make a sound, even trying to stop breathing. Bill had been having a horrible feeling of déjà vu for the past few hours, and it wasn't going away.

They had backtracked to the falls, which despite Manriguez's remodelling looked vaguely okay (Bill dreaded to think what a conservation society would say, and made a mental note to set up a regular charity payment to Waterfall Conservation NZ, or whatever, if he survived all this). Manriguez had proved to be as good a tracker as Fern, and had managed to track the ambushers back to a temporary camp, no more than a mile from the falls themselves.

All this was very reminiscent of the Jerry Co experience. The fact that he and Manriguez were in fact there to rescue Fern, and he and Fern had been at Jerry Co to rescue Manriguez (although of course that hadn't been why they were there, but never mind) gave his tired brain a woozy feeling of being caught in a time loop.

After what seemed an age, two guards trooped past near their position. Manriguez waited for a full count of fifty before signalling Bill back the way they had come. They had now completed a full circuit of the camp. There wasn't a great deal to see. A large tent stood near the middle on the Northern side, a series of smaller tents marching down the Western perimeter. A small concrete building was dead centre, a guard posted at each corner. There was one door, and one door only, on the Eastern side of the building. The entire Eastern half of the camp was taken up with a large helipad, the H meticulously picked out in white sand.

They had reached a position where Manriguez felt it safe to talk, but he still spoke in a stage whisper. A misspent youth in amateur dramatics told Bill that a stage whisper was actually designed to carry, but one look at Manriguez, bristling with weaponry, and he kept this information to himself.

The plan was devilishly simple and, like almost everything that day, seemed almost guaranteed to result in their deaths. On his circuit of the camp Manriguez had set up a series of small matt black globes, about the size of golf balls, with a long spike on the end that was driven into the ground. He'd placed eight of these, at fifty metre intervals, all the way along the Western perimeter of the camp. Manriguez was sure that Fern would be in the concrete building, that being the most secure location. He had a preference for waiting until nightfall, but the helipad worried him, as it seemed likely they would try and move the girl out, and soon. Bill didn't mention that waiting around all day would also push them very near the twenty-four-hours-to-save-the-world countdown that was ticking away neatly in his mind.

They would attack from the East, first detonating the small explosive charges on the Western perimeter. This should draw off most of the guards, and they would head straight to the building, in and out.

"Got it?" Manriguez hissed.

Bill nodded, adjusting the straps on his back and looking down at his weapons. Tucked into his belt was the gun, and sticking out of his pocket was the strange can. Unlike Manriguez he felt oddly comfortable with the can weapon. He liked the bit about "minimal human harm" or whatever it was. The logo grinned back up at him from the can's label, and suddenly he realised that he *had* heard of this strange can weapon before.

"Yeah. Let's do this."

Maud was feeling a little weary, and wondered if she should have eaten more porridge for breakfast. They had run out of honey, and those blueberries had looked mouldy, and plain porridge was terribly dull.

"C'mon, Maudy!" hollered Clarence, the bottom of his walking boots just visible up ahead.

Maud enjoyed walking, normally, but she was sure they had wandered off the trail some time ago. In her sixties and fighting fit, today she just didn't feel like it and fancied turning right back around. When she caught up with her husband she was going to tell him so.

At the edge of the clearing stood Clarence, intently studying the walking map, a compass strung devil-may-care around his neck. He rarely used the thing, relying instead on his sense of direction. Had he used it today, for example, it would have told him his sense of direction was way out of whack.

"I am sure we are near a rest area!" he boomed, jabbing the map with a gnarled finger. He was leaning on that accursed umbrella, the point dug into the ground and his fingers drumming idly on the curved ivory handle. While Maud carried sensible, high technology, lightweight walking poles, Clarence would never contemplate using anything other than his trusty umbrella. "Best damn walking stick I know!" he would extol, "and damn handy in a downpour!" And so he would crash through the undergrowth, alternately stabbing the umbrella's ferule into the ground for support and lashing it out at offending ferns, machete-like, like a member of the nineteenth century British Raj deep in the Indian jungle.

Maud had gotten some of her breath back, and detaching her scowl from the umbrella she pointed it at his face. "We are not near a rest area," she puffed. "We are way off course and heading deeper into the forest." *Where, if you carry on, you will become lost and perish of thirst and hunger*, she added mentally, but with the heavy undertone of affection that could only be managed by the very long-term couple.

"Nonsense," Clarence blustered. Extracting the umbrella from the ground, he noticed something lying there.

"If we aren't near civilisation, why the bloody hell has someone teed up a golf ball, eh?"

"Just two more minutes," whispered Manriguez, his finger poised over the remote detonator, his eyes intent on the movements of the guards. He had this timed to perfection and would kick this off when the patrols put the majority of the men on the Western perimeter.

The men seemed well drilled, very well drilled in fact, and were keeping to the pattern he had carefully noted down (at the back of his little blue work log book).

"If only we knew if these were robots or men, it could make all the difference," Manriguez muttered under his breath.

"If they are robots, then they've gone to an awful lot of detail," Bill whispered, touching Manriguez lightly on the arm and pointing to a guard on the far side of the clearing. The guard had paused by a tree to answer a call of nature.

"Robots don't pee," Bill whispered. *Or poo*, he added in his head.

"Shhh!" said Manriguez in annoyance. Bill was right, though; this meant the guards were men, who were less likely to start shooting each other in confusion when it all kicked off.

Guard 24 to point X, 72 to point B, 14 to Epsilon. Manriguez ticked them off in his head, just a minute and a half to detonation.

155

A movement on the Western perimeter caught Bill's eye. Manriguez was intent on the guards, so he hadn't noticed, and for the moment neither had the guards. Squinting briefly he pulled a pair of binoculars up to his eyes.

An elderly gentleman, white haired and stocky, was settling into a strange sort of half crouch, swishing a large umbrella around in front of him, not unlike a baseball bat. Planting his feet firmly, the man lowered the handle of the umbrella to the ground, holding it by the tightly furled canopy.

"Errrr," said Bill, not wanting to take his eye off the strange sight.

"Shhh!" hissed Manriguez.

The old man gave a waggle of his wrists, and now his stance was unmistakable. A sinking feeling began in Bill's stomach, and against his better judgement, he panned his vision down to the floor by the umbrella handle. He couldn't really tell in the half gloom, but he was willing to bet there was a strange, black, golf ball-looking bomb down there. And the man was teeing up right in their direction!

"Just five seconds," whispered Manriguez, his annoyance at Bill's interruption vibrating through the hushed tone.

"Fore!" shouted the white-haired man, his umbrella connecting with the strange ball right in the sweet spot and sending it hurtling (tee and all, if he had noticed) into the sky.

"Shit!" screamed Bill, dropping the binoculars and snatching the remote detonator from Manriguez's hands. Fumbling, he hit the small red button. A wave of explosions, small but very definite, roared around the Western perimeter, downing a number of guards on that side of the clearing. At the same instant, like an angry firework on steroids, an explosion flared high in the air above the middle of the clearing, causing the remaining guards to drop to their knees.

Somewhere someone screamed "air raid!" and a call for an anti-aircraft gun was heard.

"C'mon!" grunted Bill, grabbing a highly confused Manriguez by the collar and hauling him into the clearing. *If the door is unlocked*, he thought, *we stand a slightly smaller chance of being killed.* Gun in his right hand, and can of WUPASS in the other, he and Manriguez made a run for it.

Like all fiendishly simple ideas, the plan of attack had contained a number of critical assumptions. For example, assumption number one for Bill had been that they would both be shot dead within seconds and at least this whole strange episode would be over. They had also assumed that the door would be unlocked (unlikely as this sounded), which happily it was. They had also assumed that behind the door would be a relatively small, heavily guarded cell compound. They had, therefore, been somewhat unprepared to find a sleek stainless steel escalator and a vending machine selling cans of fizzy drinks and packets of "freeze-dried dolphin."

They had been similarly unprepared to experience no resistance and had happily been able to close the door behind them, locking out the fifty or so pissed off guards, who hadn't taken long to recover from the very mediocre aerial bombardment.

Following the downward escalator had obliterated another assumption, as they found themselves in a vast maze of underground corridors, all eerily empty. After half an hour of unopposed wandering they were forced to admit that neither of them, at any point, had assumed they would be lost as part of this venture.

"No bloody idea," said Bill, tapping a large, red bulb set in the ceiling with his gun. He would feel a lot better if the thing were flashing, a siren blaring "Intruders, Intruders!" than the damn thing just sitting there, not fussed. It felt a little like an insult.

"Up ahead," Manriguez gestured with his free hand. The other held a pack of freeze-dried dolphin. "Look I am really hungry okay. And besides, it says it's tuna friendly."

Bill gave the pack another dark look before following him. The corridor did seem different up ahead, a slight increase in the quality of light bouncing off the steel floor and walls. Fluorescent lights were set in the walls at about eye height and seemed to be getting closer together as they walked.

As they turned the corner, the corridor suddenly opened into a vast chamber. The ceiling arched away above their head, rising to a central circle of glass at the apex of the dome. The glass let in light, filtered and strange, as if viewed from underwater, and shapes, birds maybe, flittered about above. It was too far away to make out anything clearly. More disturbing than the height of the dome was the number of arched entryways to the chamber. Thirty or so archways, identical to the one they had just walked through, ringed the chamber. Each one, presumably, led to another corridor.

"Buggeration!" spat Bill, striding to the centre of the room. "How in heaven are we going to search all of this?"

"Why, Mr Posters," came a guttural, ugly and generally uncomfortable voice. "There is no need to search any more. I will come to you!" The slurred voice was accompanied by a strange electric hum, growing in volume as something approached.

Gasping a breath, Bill stumbled back a step and nearly fell to his knees. Manriguez, a man of restraint and subterfuge, reacted even more extremely, by his standards at least. Twitch, went his left cheek. *Twitch, twitch, twitch!* Sculling calmly into the chamber was a sight of pure horror. Bill's first glimpse of a shark riding a Segway nearly pushed his mind over the edge. *That's it, no more. Please can I go mad now?* he thought. But he didn't go mad, oh no. He was bloody terrified, for sure. A vast great white shark, in or out of the water, was a bloody scary sight. Yup, he was definitely terrified, but something very subtle was also taking place in his subconscious.

A strange feeling in his heart, his veins, his lungs, and Bill's eyes narrowed. His indignant anger was swamped by fear, but it was definitely there. *This just isn't right*, he thought, not for the first time that day. Without conscious thought, he had raised the gun, pointing it at the monstrosity's head hanging over the ridiculous flippery body.

"Ah, Mr Posters, I wouldn't do that if I were you," growled the shark, the Segway rolling towards them. With a flipper he gestured to his left. Armed men poured out of each of the archways, together with a few more sharks, and spread out to surround them. The lead shark barked a spine-tingling laugh, and Manriguez placed his hand on Bill's wrist, gently pushing it down to the floor.

"Not now, *amigo*. There are too many. We must surrender."

Scowling, Bill fought the rush of despair, and then noticed the can held tightly in his left hand. "Maybe not!" he said, tucking the gun into his belt and brandishing the can in front of him.

"Back off, shark-man!" he shouted, his finger tweaking the ring pull. The armed men and the shark took no notice.

"I mean it, fish for brains!" he spat, waving the can around in an arc. He had the feeling some of the men were laughing at him.

"Okay, you leave me no choice!" he shouted, then yanked hard at the ring pull. A disappointing *poing* noise, and Bill was left standing, detached ring pull in one hand and a pristine can of WUPASS in the other.

"Oh, that's right," said Gregor. "Now I remember the defect that triggered the court case."

She'd been unable to keep her eyes open, but when she fell asleep the nightmare had returned.

She stood in the Temple. Every Trelain had been gathered. Assemblies in the Temple were rare as it was, and an Assembly of All would happen fewer than a handful of times a year. Once for Kataran, another for Announcements after the Testing, and another for the annual awards. This was none of those. There were only two other times an Assembly of All would be called, and neither were good.

She stood in the centre of the main hall, right above the crest and under the sword. Tradition said that the sword was held by a single hair from the first Trelain's head. Years ago, some students had scaled the Temple and claimed that it was suspended by a metal cable. Standing directly under its point, thirty-five metres above her, she hoped the students were right.

The most impressive feature of the Temple was its height. The ceiling was vaulted and consisted of an intricate lattice of beams. The rest of the space was a little utilitarian in comparison. Benches ran down either side of the main chamber, sufficient seating for the one hundred Trelain who sat there, all eyes on her. At the front of the Temple sat the Conclave of twenty-four. Their benches where the same as any other in the temple, simple wood, save for a thumb thick inlay of gold on the leading edge of the seat.

The white marble floor had never looked so cold and forbidding. As she stood on the gold seal, she felt adrift on an ocean of white, separated from her brethren by it.

The entire chamber was silent. Not a whisper, a murmur, or even a heavy breath. To be surrounded by so many and not hear a single sound was deeply unnerving. Suddenly she knew why she was there. The leader of the Conclave spoke.

"Report," was all he said.

Fern knew what was required. She battled briefly with the words before finally forcing them out. "The recent mission was a failure," she said simply.

"And?" questioned the leader of the Conclave.

Fern was already struggling with her words, but now it was as if her throat had closed up. She started to speak, but her mouth had gone dry and she made no sounds. The words she was about to utter had never, ever, been delivered in the Temple. They had never been spoken anywhere, in all of human history.

"And . . . my Pretarn," she hesitated, but knew she could not avoid the truth. "The Britak-Tain . . . was killed." Shocked gasps ran around the room together with one or two cries of outrage. For a second the noise built and the leader of the Conclave raised his arms in an appeal for silence. It came instantly.

"And yet you stand before us?" The leader of the Conclave was supposed to be impassive at all times, but he failed to keep the shock and contempt from his voice. Again, the room bubbled into noise. Names were called, curses hurled. This time the leader of the Conclave did not appeal for silence but roared above the noise.

"You have brought shame to yourself, to your lineage, and to all Trelain!"

The words hit her like a hammer blow. She knew they were true. The leader stood and unrolled a dark green scroll. She recognised it. It was her birth scroll.

"Your name is stricken from our lists. You are dead to us now." With a jerk, he ripped the scroll in two and hurled it to the floor. As one, the Trelain turned their backs.

Tears welled up in her eyes. She had failed so utterly. Only the leader remained facing her.

"And now," he said, "because of your failure we must greet our new lords and masters." A door behind him opened and a vast shark swam into the room. How it swam in air she knew not, but it did. More followed, boiling out of the doorway and into the Temple.

"Bow before our rulers!" shouted the leader, collapsing to his knees. As one the other Trelain fell to the floor. A keening laughter filled the air, and Fern covered her ears with her hands. But she refused to kneel. A shark bit off the head of a kneeling Trelain and the body slipped silently to the floor. Smelling blood, the other sharks ran amok, biting and tearing. The Temple began to fill with blood, but still the Trelain just knelt there. Fern screamed and the laughter doubled. Something snapped above her, a brittle sound. The world went black, but the laughter carried on. Over and over. Over and over.

Chapter Eighteen

"Rah—ha ha ha ha ha ha!"

The shark had been laughing, far longer than necessary to be honest. It seemed he had been studying some sort of baddie cliché, as he had the maniacal cackle down to perfection. *Man, oh man, shut up and get on with it*, thought Bill. *I swear, if he kicks off with "Welcome to my underground lair" I am going to turn this gun on myself.*

Some of the guards, there were hundreds now, had joined in, though most looked too embarrassed. Some were definitely robots; Bill recognised their helmeted faces and flishy-flashy armpit control panels. Unsurprisingly they stood silent, and disappointingly gave no indication that they were about to open fire on each other.

An unpleasant slurpy sound indicated that the shark was finally gaining his composure. Slapping a control on the handlebars of the Segway, the shark rolled forward, stopping a few metres from them. Up close, the fishy stink was almost overwhelming, but oddly the sheer ridiculousness of a giant fish on a motorised trolley seemed to reduce the overall sense of terror. Sucking in a mighty breath (another thing not commonly achieved by sharks), the creature finally spoke.

"Mr Posters, I presume," he gargled, showering Manriguez in what might have been chunks of freeze-dried dolphin. To his credit Manriguez didn't even flinch, but calmly wiped the icky mess from his cheek.

"What's it to you?" replied Bill, taking brief refuge in belligerence. Again, the shark belched a slimy laugh, this time covering them both in gore.

"Mr Posters, it is everything to me. It is an honour to meet humanity's greatest hope, its shining light, if only to illuminate how low your species has sunk." The sharks surrounding them cackled at this. Bill didn't like it at all.

"Oh dear, have I offended the mighty Britak Tain? Or maybe you are afraid? Perhaps you would rather be back in your crappy bedsit flat, with your pathetic morning routine, useless chairs, and your dead-end life. Saviour of the world indeed!"

"What have you done with Fern!" Bill demanded, swapping the conventional question mark with an exclamation for effect, and tucking the useless can of WUPASS surreptitiously away. There really was no subtle way to tuck a large can into your pocket, but fortunately for Bill no one was watching closely.

"You mean the girl? She is well, for now."

Despite himself, Bill heaved a sigh of relief. You couldn't trust a shark, but it felt good to hear she was okay. Fumbling with the controls, the shark buzzed his way over to a desk that was rising out of the floor not far to their left.

"You are no doubt aware of my master plan," continued the Shark King, flicking a few switches on his desk and causing a large screen to drop out of the ceiling by the far wall. A map of the world appeared on the screen, criss-crossed with complicated lines, symbols, and pictograms.

"Behold, the weather control doomsday device!" bellowed the Shark King, practically giddy with super-villain glee.

"Nice," said Bill, too depressed to muster anything more than a trickle of sarcasm.

"Yes indeed, Mr Posters. With this device, I will control the planet's weather. The world will pay me tribute, or be destroyed by the insurmountable force of natural disaster."

"Errm, that would be an un-natural disaster then, surely?" interjected Bill.

The Shark King was clearly displeased by his contribution. "Silence!" he hollered, slamming a flipper onto his desk and causing the screen to begin rolling back up into the ceiling. "Bring him closer!"

Two guards grabbed Bill from behind and wrestled his pack roughly from his shoulders. He could see Manriguez receiving the same treatment, and he fancied he noticed a wince of regret as he was separated from his arsenal. The two guards then caught Bill under his arms, hauling him off his feet, and carrying him to the desk where they dumped him into a chair. The Shark King settled into a big leather armchair and gulped down another fistful of dolphin.

"You disgusting monkeys have finally had your day," he garbled around a mouthful of food. "You and those cursed skyrats." He swivelled, his predator eyes on Bill, cold and emotionless.

"You will not live to see the end though. In two hours I will have all three of you killed in a public execution." Bill gulped. The shark's black eyes carried nothing at all, nothing except a feral certainty, a special superiority.

"But I will grant you one last request. You are your people's hero, and I will respect that." The Shark King eyed Bill up and down again and seemed uncertain at these words.

"One last request, what is it to be?" he demanded.

Kicked into a frenzy, Bill's mind whirred, cogs flying and clicking into place. *This is it, last chance saloon, the fate of the world in your hands. Think, Bill, think!* His mind buzzed with synaptic force, like a kicked ant heap. He knew what these fish expected of him, oh yes. But he wasn't prepared to play their game any more. But he needed a way out of this. *Think, Bill, think!* An idea bubbled up. He could see a way, a slight chance, a sliver of light at the end of the world's darkest tunnel. But there was only one way he could do it and stand a chance of survival. Straightening his back, he summoned his courage and fixed the shark's eyes with his own.

"Not good enough, I'm afraid. I have two last requests." His voice was flat and firm.

The shark blinked, once, twice, some teeth beginning to show at the corner of his hideous maw. Abruptly he let out a roar of amusement, slapping the desk with his flippers. When he had subsided, he turned a blood-chilling grin on Bill. "Let us see, shall we? Name your first, human."

Agonised, Bill weighed up the two things he needed. What if the shark would not allow his second request? The creature leaned forward, and for a second Bill thought he was about to bite off his head. He made a snap decision. The difficult thing now was making this sound in anyway plausible. Okay Bill, time to act.

Curling his fingers inwards he gave his nails a thorough inspection. Straightening his fingers and rotating his hands, he continued his study, fingers now splayed in front of him. He was conscious of everyone studying him and tried to inject as much manly bravado into the display as possible. It was not easy to subject your fingernails to scrutiny in a macho manner. Bill didn't manage it. Damn, neatly trimmed and nice and clean. Oh well, no choice now. The Shark King was in the process of levering his enormous mouth open, doubtless to ask what on earth Bill was doing, or to order their immediate deaths, or more freeze-dried dolphin. Whatever it was Bill, cut in.

"Err, well, you see, I would hate to die with such grotty nails," he begun, the words echoing in his ears with their ridiculousness. "So I really would like to tidy them up before you kill me." He heard a light cough from the man by his side, and some sniggering from the human guards. Swallowing, he pressed on.

"I do have a manicure kit with me, in my bag in fact." He wasn't sure where they had taken his pack, but he desperately needed it back. "If I could be permitted to take it with me—"

"Greblang!" screamed the Shark King. For a second, Bill thought this was his answer, but he soon realised it must be a shark's name or some sort of command, as a smaller shark revved up his Segway and approached the mighty beast. Bill's pack hung from the handlebars.

"Take this manicure kit and inspect it thoroughly. This could be a trick!" garbled the great white.

"Yes, my Lord," snapped the smaller shark, a fin slapping his nose in a parody of a salute. One of the small patches of pleasure of the experience came next as Bill watched the shark called Greblang desperately try to open the tie cord on the pack with his flippers. *Ha ha fish face, no opposable thumbs.* After much growling, Greblang straightened with a roar and flipped a switch on the handlebars. A circular hatch on the bars opened and the muzzle of a gun protruded, directed straight at Bill's chest.

"Remove the item, monkey, and no funny business or you're toast," he hissed.

"With pleasure," beamed Bill, slowly accepting the pack from the shark and placing it on the floor beside his chair. Every guard in the room tensed, weapons trained on him and Manriguez.

With shaky hands, he carefully undid the tie, then fumbled briefly inside before slowly pulling the black leather case from the bag. With studied care he placed it in the small carry basket on the handlebars of Greblang's Segway. Greblang immediately motored back around the

Shark King's desk, flippering the case down in front of the vast creature.

For a second the Shark King studied the case, scowling at the emblem, which he clearly recognised, and for a second Bill was worried he would dismiss Bill's request out of hand. How he was going to check the item with those enormous pectoral fins Bill had no idea.

"Fingers!" yelled the Shark King, prompting a shuffling among the sharks behind him, who parted to allow someone, or some*thing*, to pass through. The thing looked like a giant shambling pile of rags, all different colours but all sporting a thick layer of grime. A pair of bare feet underneath the pile revealed there was a person under there somewhere, but how could they see where they were going under all of the layers? Suddenly, Bill's nose caught a whiff of the creature and he almost gagged. For the smell to reach him over that distance, and over the decidedly unpleasant fishy smell emanating from the sharks, was a testament to its determined vileness. It was horrible, but Bill lacked the vocabulary to describe it properly.

The smell seemed to have no effect on the Shark King though, who wrinkled up his nose in disdain but no obvious discomfort. As the pile approached the desk, Bill noticed a pair of scabbed and grubby hands peeking out of the folds of material. They were manacled together with shiny handcuffs, the shine of the metal incongruous against the otherwise epitome of decay and neglect.

"Fingers!" barked the Shark King, "check this item for anything that the humans could use to escape."

The pile shuffled over to the manicure kit and reached out its manacled hands. With skilful fingers, it manipulated the clasp and began sorting through the items in the case, picking up each one in turn and holding them up to where presumably its eyes were. After this examination, it would proffer up the item for the shark to inspect, stating what the item was.

The voice of the creature was most shocking of all. Bill had expected either silence, or a cracked and tired voice to go with the thing's overall countenance. He was not prepared for the bold, proud, round tones that followed the examination of every item. It was the kind of voice you'd expect from an opera singer, or a late night radio presenter. It was kind of classy, and completely at odds with the smell of decay reaching Bill's nose. The first item from the case was proffered up to the Shark King.

"A simple nail file," boomed the ragman. The Shark nodded and the ragman moved on to the next item in the case, working its way through them one at a time. Finally, the deft fingers closed over the nail clippers and Bill almost caught his breath. It seemed to him that the hands paused, hovering over this last item, giving it more attention than the others. Bill felt the beginnings of panic, when finally the ragman held the item aloft to the Shark.

"A simple pair of nail clippers," it intoned, before a nod from the Shark King had him placing them back in the case.

"Well," said the Shark King. "Nothing in there to worry about; give the case to the human," he growled. As the first stirrings of relief made their way through Bill's lower stomach, the pile of rags raised its handcuffed hands.

"If I may, there is one item in there to cause concern," the pile declaimed. Relief fled, replaced by a dull, sinking feeling. Time seemed to slow.

"Such insolence!" growled the Shark King. "What item?"

Bill's heart pounded in his chest. One beat, two beats, three beats. It seemed an eternity. His hopes of salvation were already an immense long shot, and he felt certain they were about to be crushed.

Finally the ragman spoke. "This item," he said, holding up a hand. Bill couldn't bear to look, but fought desperately for calm.

"The nail file!" guffawed the Shark King. "I know little of the instruments needed to care for those flappy bits of flesh you call hands, but I think a nail file poses little threat to the mighty Shark Empire!"

"Indeed not, but it could, potentially, be used to effect escape, possibly by filing through bars, or by being used to pick a lock," continued the ragman.

The Shark King looked like he was losing patience. "Very well, very well, confiscate the item and return the rest," he bellowed.

Without any hint of deference (despite the weight of fabric), the ragman nodded and placed the file on the table, shuffling towards Bill with the rest of the items.

As the ragman approached the smell grew exponentially, and Bill could feel his stomach curdling. He desperately wanted to get his hands on what the creature was holding, but he found himself wishing the thing would simply not get any closer. Drawing up opposite him the ragman hesitated. Bill struggled against wave after wave of nausea. The layers of dirty fabric around the ragman twitched for a second, and Bill fancied he could see a tail disappear amongst the folds. *Dear god, there are things living in there!* The ragman shifted slightly, and for the briefest second Bill could see two eyes, dark and penetrating, shining out from the filth. They fixed Bill with an intense gaze, boring like augers into his skull. *He knows,* thought Bill for a second, before the ragman raised his arms and offered up the manicure kit. Bill quickly took it from him, uttering a quick thanks. The rags shifted and obscured the eyes, the pile rotating 180 degrees and shuffling off. Once again the onlookers parted to allow "fingers" through, and in moments he was lost from view. Relief washed over Bill as he tightened his grip on the leather case, and not one part of it was for the departure of the stomach-flipping smell.

"And your second 'request,'" said the Shark King, clearly not amused by the delay.

Pulled from his reverie Bill jumped a little. *Here goes,* he thought, *the fate of the world and one more very, very long shot.*

"I would like a last meal. I have it here with me, if you will allow?" he asked, gesturing the pack on the floor.

Bored looking and clearly confident he was safe from the small human, the Shark King waved a flipper graciously, the guards tensing as Bill bent once again to his pack. Quickly he consulted the clock on the wall above the Shark's head, praying it was correct, and rustled around in the bag for a few seconds before emerging with the box of cornflakes.

"Do you have a bowl and spoon? And some milk?"

Again the Shark King nodded and another guard disappeared, returning with the items remarkably quickly. The bowl looked like a small upturned helmet. It was, in fact, a small upturned helmet.

Tentatively Bill poured out a small amount of cereal, careful not to invert the box too much, pushing the flakes out with his fingertips. Taking a mouthful, he made a big show of pleasure and satisfaction.

"You like this 'cereal' do you, Mr Posters?"

Bill nodded, wondering if his assessment of shark psychology was correct, and whether he dared another throw of the dice.

"I *love* it," Bill said, pouring emphasis onto his words cheesily. "It's one of the few things that keeps me going. Faced with the humiliation of all mankind, being able to sit here and eat a bowl of cereal gives me some form of solace." He caught a look from Manriguez out of the corner of his eye. The Chilean was staring at him as if he had lost his mind. Bill tried desperately to ignore how stupid-sounding his words were. It wasn't any more daft than wanting to do his nails, after all. This had to work.

"In fact, without this cereal I don't know what I would do. To see it in the possession of another would crush my spirit," he finished lamely, unable to meet the Shark King's gaze, and so he stared down at the floating flakes. For a second there was silence.

"Well, in that case," growled the Shark King, "you may not have two requests! Human, give me your precious cereal!" he demanded, straightening himself in the armchair and baring all of his razor teeth.

"Oh no, oh no, the humiliation!" wailed Bill as he placed the bowl and the box of cereal on a tray shoved at him by a mean-looking shark. "What will I do?"

"Mwa ha ha ha ha ha," guffawed the Shark King, flippering the bowl and box from the tray and hurling the cereal down his throat and chewing it to sludge.

"Not bad human, though not fishy enough," he cackled, revelling in Bill's theatrical despair.

"Oh, the shame," Bill simpered. "Don't tell me you plan to toast the dawn of the Shark era with a bowl of humanity's last hope's most favourite food. Oh, that would be evil, evil!" The sentence was clumsy, cumbersome, maybe a bridge too far, but he had to try. He risked a glance up at the Shark King's eyes and saw the seed of an idea lodge there, the primitive hunter mentality evaluating the thought.

"Gaspar, Grork, take them away!" Two guards hauled Bill to his feet, the others forming up around him and Manriguez.

"Good bye, Mr Posters, you pathetic worm," called the Shark King, as Bill was carried away from the desk.

"Soon your pathetic existence will be over!" he guffawed and roared, the laugh again gaining its cliché super-villain tone.

The Shark King sat at his desk revelling in triumph. The lackeys began to clear away Bill's pack and the other items on the desk. When they reached for the box of cereal, the Shark King stopped them, a thoughtful look on his bland features.

"No, I'll take that with me for later, I think," he declared, tucking the box under a flipper, before mounting his Segway (an action which defied description), and buzzed off down a side corridor.

Chapter Nineteen

Stripped of their weapons (with the possible exception of the can of WUPASS bulging indiscreetly from Bill's pocket), they were marched down a dull grey corridor. Where the other corridors in the complex seemed well maintained these had a distinctly disused feel. Walls, ceiling, and floors were an unrelieved grey concrete, pockmarked here and there, as if sprayed with acid or attacked by the world's smallest pneumatic drill. The lighting was poor, large distances between grim naked fluorescent tubes. Many of these flickered fitfully, and some were dark altogether, leaving them moving through near darkness between the pools of light.

At first there had been water running down the left wall, but this had stopped a short while ago. The corridor was very definitely sloping upwards, and Bill fancied they must almost be back to ground level. Their escort was grim and tight-lipped, with the exception of the sharks, who seemed to be chuntering away to one another in some guttural language. Four robot guards led the way, precise and dull in their matched strides. Four human guards were directly behind Bill and Manriguez, seemingly trying to compensate for the order and rigour adopted by their android colleagues by striding along in a disorganised manner. They were no less intent though, and had their rifles ready and poised. Bringing up the rear was the small group of Segway-totting sharks, their chatter really grating on Bill's ears.

"Only two hours to live, human!" taunted one. Bill had to struggle to make out the words, then wished he hadn't bothered. There was really no point in responding, and he had no idea of a suitable comeback even if he did.

The corridor kinked sharply to the right up ahead, the robot guards marching to a halt just outside a door before the turn. Around the corner the way was roped off, a large red sign reading "Caution: area closed due to renovation." Above the door a smaller sign read "Storage Overflow E."

"In here," said one of the human guards, forcing his way past Bill and Manriguez and inserting a large brass key into the lock. The lock made a heavy sounding click, and the door swung ponderously open. The frame around the door itself was three or four feet thick. With a rough shove, Bill and Manriguez were thrust into the room. The door was hastily closed behind them.

The room was remarkable. Row after row of display cabinets marched down each wall to the right and left. Each cabinet was identical, shiny steel shelves fronted with thick glass. Every spare inch of space on every shelf was crammed with beautiful china. Vases, plates, urn things, goblets, cups, you name it, it was there. The designs were intricate and precise, the flowing forms of each item elegant and appealing.

Bill had mere seconds to take all this in of course, as he was instantly confronted by a healthy, if bruised-looking, Fern.

"What the bloody hell are you doing here?" she demanded, striding up to Bill and jabbing a finger painfully in his chest. Bill was somewhat unprepared for this greeting and could only manage what was in hindsight, on the face of things, a rather a weak reply.

"Err, rescuing you?"

***

"Ming Dynasty, really?"

"I think so," replied Fern.

Bill squinted at the large blue-and-white urn in the cabinet in front of him. It was certainly pretty, but it didn't really look old enough. He'd only seen something like this once, in a magazine years ago, so Fern was probably in a better position to know.

"There's a lot of it," he murmured, running his eye along the massed array of porcelain in the display cabinets.

Fern was not happy, but at least she had stopped shouting about how irresponsible Bill had been. Manriguez was squatting in the corner of the room and appeared to be resting, though given the strip Fern had torn off him he could have been sulking. Or just trying to disappear. For some reason Fern seemed more angry with the Chilean than with Bill, something about not following instructions and official complaints. Every time Bill had tried to point out this had all been his idea it only made things worse, so he had spent a lot of time saying nothing at all.

Fern had made it quite clear that coming after her had been an unacceptable risk, that Bill had a responsibility to save the world and his priority had been to get the button out of here. He had "marched mankind's only chance straight back into enemy hands and almost certainly doomed the planet." It had taken three attempts for Bill to successfully interrupt and point out that, actually, he still had the button (which he duly produced from his pants as proof). This had at least shut Fern up, if briefly, as she struggled to come to terms with the fact that Bill had not been searched. Bill had suggested that it reflected a keen arrogance on the sharks' part, a belief that Bill was no real danger and could therefore be handled carelessly. There could be cameras and listening devices in the room, so he couldn't share the real reason. Well, what he thought was the real reason. A significant part of him was beset by self-doubt, but he was still disappointed at how easily they swallowed his explanation.

It seemed Fern had recovered consciousness in this room just a few hours ago. Bill's concerns about her welfare were batted away. She was fine, bruised and battered in the line of duty, but not otherwise mistreated. He however was subjected to an uncomfortable head-to-toe examination, despite similar insistence that he was "fine."

Fern had been given an explanation for their strange surroundings from a guard. The cells, oddly, were closed for renovation (who renovates a cell?). The secure storeroom they were located in seemed to be some sort of china museum. Fern had put her hours to the best use she could. She had confirmed that there was nothing in the room that could be put to practical use. The cabinets were made of toughened glass so were to all intents and purposes impenetrable, and the bars on the small window were sturdy and solid. There was a single bright spot to their predicament: the small window just above head height on the back wall showed they had indeed returned above ground. Fern had pointed out some cracks in the concrete around the window casement, which might indicate a structural weakness in the wall. It would need more than the three of them to do anything about it though.

"How much would all this porcelain or pottery or whatever it is be worth then?" Bill asked.

"No idea. A lot though," said Fern. "The Sharkosians have always coveted items of high human value. This lot would have been gathered over centuries. Some of it is probably priceless."

Bill slapped a hand hard against one of the cases. His palm stung, but that was it. "Would make me feel better to at least smash some of it up a little," he grumbled.

"There wouldn't be a lot of point," said Manriguez, the first words he had spoken since entering the storeroom. "Haven't you heard, we are going to be executed soon." It unsettled Bill a little to hear the defeat in Manriguez's tone, but he knew exactly how to cheer him up.

"Fear not, *amigo*," he said cheerfully, almost giddily, "for I have a plan!"

With a flourish, Bill swept the can of WUPASS from his pocket, brandishing it in front of himself, much as he had to the Shark King. "And I still have a weapon!" he finished triumphantly.

"Oh, dear lord," mumbled Manriguez, burying his head in his hands. "Haven't you had enough of that stuff already? It's useless; you've snapped the ring pull off."

Aha, thought Bill. *Trained killer, tracker, and survival specialist you may be, but you've clearly never pondered life's great un-solvable mystery.*

"Tada!" he sang, producing the nail clippers from the manicure kit and holding them next to the can.

Peering out from between his fingers, Manriguez gave another sigh. "Not surprising really, lot of strain for a chap really. Bound to happen," he muttered, before closing his eyes again.

"What have you got there, Bill?" asked Fern, drawing close to peer at the can.

Bill turned the can over in his hands and peered at the cramped black text at the back. It was smudged a little, but still just about legible. Most of the writing was a long-winded disclaimer in legalese. Bill skipped over this to the boxed text at the bottom of the label.

Congratulations on your purchase! You are holding a can of High Density Location Specific Destruction Compound from Western Union Projectile and Sabotage Services. This revolutionary compound has been specially formulated to cause maximum damage to its surroundings while preserving human life*. As part of the Location Specific range products the effects of this compound will depend entirely on surrounding conditions at time of use, and as such cannot be guaranteed.

Claim unverified. Do not under any circumstances use this product.

The last bit was a worry, but Bill pushed it from his mind.

"Errr . . . I wouldn't use that if I were you," said Fern. "I've heard about that stuff, really unpredictable, they don't even make it anymore. Some sort of court case I think."

"That's right!" said Bill, brandishing the broken ring pull in the same hand as the nail clippers. "The ring pull is defective, came off right in my hand." He strode over to the window, can and clippers in hand.

"Look," Bill said, reaching the back wall. "You reckon this wall could be weak. This stuff causes 'maximum damage to its surroundings,' while 'preserving human life' or whatever. It's perfect!" He was worried his enthusiasm had crossed over into hysteria, but there was no turning back now. He had no idea what the can would do, if it did anything, but it was his only idea. He could feel both Manriguez and Fern's worried eyes burning into the back of his head, but neither made a move to stop him. He was a man on the edge.

"So you intend to get in there with the clippers?" asked Fern. "It's going to take a lot of clipping to get through a steel can."

"You too?" said Bill, surprised. "So you've never pondered it either?"

"Pondered what?" replied Fern, sounding a little like she was losing her patience.

"Why nail clippers are made with . . ." he paused theatrically, swivelled out the can opener attachment and brandished it aloft. "One of these!"

He couldn't see as it was above his head, but he really hoped the sunlight from the barred window glinted from the shiny metal in a dramatic fashion. Manriguez was peering through his hands again, and Fern still looked a little confused. *Never mind, soon they would see.*

Crouching down just under the barred window, he placed the can on the floor where it touched the back wall. Clasping the can opener in his fist, he set it against the rim, and paused. What the hell would it do? Would it explode? Would he have time to get away? Would it spray acid over the wall, eating it all away? Would it have gone past its use-by date and do nothing at all? *Only one way to find out,* he thought, and with a twist of his wrist he punctured the can.

Before he could slide the clippers around the rim there was a quiet, low growl, and in a flash the clippers were sucked from his grasp and into the can, the metal buckling with the force. Startled, Bill straightened and took a step back. Some black liquid, thick and viscous, oozed through the small hole and beaded on the can's surface, making an unsettling "sniffing" noise. Bill was given the impression of a bloodhound, kept in a sterile room for days and released into a potpourri factory, lapping up the array of smells.

"Probably best to back away," said Fern, sounding as spooked as Bill felt. *Good idea,* he thought, backing away from the can slowly, not taking his eyes from the black blob. With a belching noise, more black liquid oozed through the hole, spilling onto the floor. The can was starting to bounce now, more ooze flowing from the top and pooling around the bottom. With a small clang, it bounced itself sideways onto the floor, the flow increasing.

Transfixed by the growing puddle, Bill gave a small yelp when something brushed his arm. He had backed all the way across the room and now stood shoulder to shoulder with Fern and Manriguez, huddled against the door.

"Oh Christ, what the hell is it?" he stammered.

"No idea buddy, but you let it out. I think we are about to find that the court case was about more than a faulty ring pull," replied Manriguez.

The puddle was growing and growing, which was ridiculous as there was now far more black stuff on the floor than would fit into the can. It hadn't exploded, didn't appear to be concrete eating acid, and other than freaking them all out it appeared to be of little practical use in their escape. With a tortured *sproing* the lid sheared off the can and shot across the room, smashing into a cabinet and obliterating the strengthened glass.

"Whoa!" shouted Bill, drowned out by the crashing of plate glass. "Now that is some force!" Damaged by the impact a shelf gave way, depositing thirty or so priceless china plates onto the floor. They smashed on impact, spraying chunks across the floor and into the shimmering pool.

"Holy crap," spat Fern, "what is that stuff?" The puddle twitched and then converged on the broken plates. Flowing around the fragments it coalesced and grew, the puddle surging upwards and seeming to solidify.

At first it was just a large, blobby ball, but then it sprouted five tendrils and pushed itself off the floor. Its gelatinous surface quivered as it rose unsteadily from the floor. Four of the tendrils thickened, the fifth detaching from the pool and dangling from the main mass. Next the central blob began to divide into two, now looking like a smaller ball sitting on a larger one, supported by four columns and a tapered tail. The basic shape was now complete and features started to form. The smaller ball lengthened, developing distinctive ear shapes and a snout. The thickening columns gained definition, joints, hooves, the body formed into definite musculature. Horns began growing from the newly formed head; the tail gave an angry swish.

Like a hammer blow, the brilliance of WUPASS hit Bill. He was stunned. In precisely the same instant he marvelled at the genius of whoever had developed the stuff, and was aghast at anyone being bonkers enough to think it up in the first place. It did seem to do what it said on the tin though. They were, to all intents and purposes, standing in a giant china shop. Reflecting these surroundings, the WUPASS had formed itself into something to inflict the greatest possible destruction.

"That's a giant, a giant, uh . . ." Fern stuttered.

"Yes, it does seem to be, doesn't it?"

The eight-foot-tall WUPASS creature, on hearing the noise, turned its head, black horns glistening. Eyes formed in its vast head, and for a second it studied the three of them, letting out a mighty heave of breath. It seemed it might charge them, but then its beady black eye caught sight of a vase in a nearby cabinet. With a roar, the creature sprang at the cabinet. The glass, no match for the awesome impact, caved in, the creature running amok smashing everything.

"C'mon, before there are none left," said Fern, snatching up a plate that hadn't been smashed and running for the back wall. *What the hell*, thought Bill, a little numb, grabbing an unbroken bowl from the floor and chasing after her.

"So, what's the plan then?" asked Manriguez, joining them both at the back wall, clutching a large urn.

"Where the hell did you get that?" asked Bill, jabbing a finger at the urn, almost half as tall as the assassin.

"End of the cabinet where the . . . thing is currently having fun." He nodded towards the WUPASS creature, which was, metaphorically, opening a can of Wupass on the next cabinet. The noise was tremendous; they had to shout to be heard above the crescendo.

182

"Right, no time for that," interrupted Fern, business-like. Even Manriguez seemed to have brightened up, though Bill couldn't quite see why being trapped with a vast murderous creature had improved either of their moods.

"We need to gather up everything un-broken and pile it against this wall," Fern continued, pointing at the cracks to make her point clear. Manriguez, who appeared to already be on the same page, or was more used to following barmy-sounding instructions, dashed off after a particularly large platter rolling its way across the concrete floor.

"Right, yes, but won't that mean going near the uh, you-know-what?" Bill queried, eyeing the snorting beast that was repeatedly goring a sixteenth century Ming vase. In reply, Fern just rolled her eyes, picked up the empty WUPASS can, and tapped the label. "Minimal human harm" read the label, in the same cheery lettering, though a little disfigured by the bulges and dents in the metal.

Bill smiled. *Got it,* he thought, and nodded at Fern, who smiled in return. The WUPASS was certainly doing a good job, running and crashing and mincing everything to powder. A few items escaped its initial attentions though, and Bill, Fern, and Manriguez scooped these up and piled them under the window.

It did seem that the large creature had no interest in them, intent as it was on china destruction. Bill's forays grew bolder and bolder when searching for intact items. The small pile was growing impressively, but to add to it they had to get closer and closer to the beast. Manriguez narrowly avoided being trampled when he got between the creature and a large figurine, but Bill reckoned if you kept behind the monster you'd be okay.

Sifting through the debris, Bill spotted a stunning piece of pottery. Red-fired clay covered in shiny, black figures. The tall pot reached almost to his waist and it was a struggle to lift. Cradling it in his arms, he studied the figures leaping, running, and wrestling one another. Surely this couldn't be . . . With a sinking feeling he realised it had gone quiet. Very quiet indeed. No crashing, no grinding of glass or ceramics, just the steady puff of something large breathing nearby.

Slowly, oh so slowly, he turned around, his feet crunching the shards of glass on the floor and painfully shattering the silence. What was the phrase from the can? Something like "maximum damage while preserving human life". *Preserving human life, preserving human life, preserving human life,* he repeated over and over in his head like a mantra. As he swivelled his head, he saw the beast.

For some reason it looked bigger, but that was probably because it was staring directly at him from a distance of thirty feet. It snorted, a small cloud of steam billowing out of its nostrils, and pawed a mighty hoof at the ground, absentmindedly grinding a small thimble into dust. The scene in the room was one of utter carnage. Everything was broken, the cabinets, the glass, the china, all of it. Bill couldn't see how the destruction could be more utter if he had detonated a hand grenade in the room. *You had to hand it to WUPASS,* he thought, it *really does do exactly what it says on the tin.* In which case, he reasoned, why was it preparing to charge a human? *Preserving human life, preserving human life, preserving human life,* returned the mantra. At that precise second he realised the beast was not staring at him at all, but the large vase he was clutching to his chest. The only intact piece of crockery in the room, except the items piled up by the window, which the thing had its back to right now.

"Oh cra . . ." he began, but the beast charged, bunched muscles hurling itself at Bill and the vase. Bill leapt desperately to the left, landing awkwardly and sliding into a pile of glass. It would be at this point (or even slightly before) that most people would have dropped the vase. Arms clasped rictus-like around the pottery, Bill watched aghast as the WUPASS monster struggled to release a horn that had buried itself three inches into the wall when its charge had carried it slamming into the concrete.

"If you're done playing, Bill, we really could use the bull over here!" shouted Fern from the relative safety of the back of the room. Legs scrabbling desperately in the debris, he struggled to his feet. With an angry grunt, the thing freed its horn and gave its huge head a groggy shake. Turning his back on the beast, Bill sprinted for the back wall, feet slipping and sliding on the glass, the vase tucked awkwardly under his right arm.

"Here beasty beasty beasty!" he called. He could hear the mighty stride of the creature as it gave pursuit, shaking the concrete floor beneath his feet. Three strides from the wall he could feel the monster's breath on the back of his neck. With an incomprehensible cry of sheer panic, he hurled the vase out in front of him, straight at the stacked pile of items, and dove to the right. Horns levelled, the WUPASS creature intercepted the vase just before it hit the pile, the razor-sharp point of a horn puncturing the pottery and exploding the vase into several chunks. A millisecond later, without slowing, the creature ploughed into the pile, and then straight into the wall. A mighty crash and the walls shook, the ground shook, and concrete dust leapt down from the ceiling. Rebounding from the wall the creature landed on the pile, crushing every last item, and let out an ear-splitting groan. It hung its head, and for a second all was silent. Then the cracks in the wall began to widen, and new ones appeared, and with a tortured scream of concrete on concrete the entire section of the wall collapsed outward, landing with an earth-shattering thud.

Now bathed in sunlight the creature rose unsteadily to its feet. Casting its gaze around the destruction, it gave what could only be described as a satisfied grunt, and with a loud pop, vanished. Shaking dust and broken crockery from their clothes Bill, Fern, and Manriguez emerged into the sunlight, blinking at the glare.

"Nice," said Manriguez, tapping the six-inch-thick section of concrete with his toe.

"Fun as that was, I am never, ever, touching that stuff again," said Bill, staring at the spot the creature had disappeared from.

"No time for that," said Fern, still business-like. "Time to make a run for it!" Grabbing Bill by the elbow, she dragged him off towards the edge of the clearing, Manriguez following close behind.

The Shark King sat at the back of the video control room, lounging on a vast leather chaise longue and munching freeze-dried dolphin. The Crunchy Nut cornflakes, which he found himself oddly partial to, lay near what would have been his elbow, if he had elbows, but was in fact a crease midway down his right fin.

"Anything?" he grunted at the men in the control chairs.

"Nothing, my Lord," they replied, intently studying a video feed from the corridor outside of storage overflow E. The Shark King turned to a minion cowering at the foot of the chaise longue.

"You are sure you left the door unlocked?" he grumbled.

"Yes, my Lord."

"Humph!" Another flipperful of freeze-dried dolphin was stuffed into his gaping maw, the murderous jaws working briefly before the entire lot was swallowed whole.

"Do we have a feed from inside the room?" he asked, spraying chunks of dolphin over the backs of the operators.

"Yes, your highness, new cameras were installed last week."

"Well, for goodness sake, put it on man, what is wrong with you!"

In a frenzy, the men punched keys and twirled dials, and shortly the image on the screen was replaced with a view of the destruction inside

Storage Overflow E. The Shark King froze, part-chewed dolphin dripping from the roof of his mouth, his eyes wide, his nose trembling.

"And that is the view from inside?" he managed at last.

"Err, yes, my Lord," replied the braver of the two operators.

"The view of my family's collection of antique pottery?"

"Yes, my Lord."

"The view of my family's collection of priceless antique pottery?"

"Err . . ."

"The view of my family's collection of priceless antique pottery ground to dust and fragments?"

The operator winced. "Yes, my Lord."

The Shark King went blue, then red, then purple, then managed a ragged breath, then another. It would be some time before he stopped shouting.

Chapter Twenty

"That was quick thinking, Bill," complimented Fern, not a bit out of breath.

"Eh?" grunted Bill, doubled over and panting desperately for air.

"Well, I hadn't thought of the importance of the angle of the thing's attack. I mean, what if it had just stomped its way along the wall? That would have done us no good at all."

Marginally recovered, Bill peered up at Fern (an unusual experience), his hands propped on his hips. Surely she didn't think he had done that on purpose?

"That was very brave you know, I am very proud," she beamed back at him. Clearly, she did think he had done it on purpose. Energised by her gaze he forced himself upright, rib muscles objecting, and tried to puff out his chest.

"Yeah, nice one," added Manriguez, somewhat dubiously.

After reaching the relative safety of the trees, they had run for some time, crashing through the thick undergrowth. It had taken them a while to realise there was no pursuit, and they had now paused briefly so that everyone (everyone being Bill), could catch their breath.

The sun stood high in the sky, a warm and reassuring light filtering down through the branches. In the distance, a bird was singing, but it was a song unlike anything Bill had ever heard before. A warbling mess of a song interspersed with pops and whistles. Fern glanced at her watch and beckoned Manriguez over. Devoid of Fern's admiring gaze,

Bill's muscles asserted their will and he folded over once again, shuffling his way to a handy-looking tree root for a sit down. He wondered what the other two needed to discuss privately, but he was struggling to muster the energy to care, let alone do anything about it.

***

"So there's no misunderstanding," Fern began, sternly, "I am still not happy about you both coming back." Manriguez nodded. He had hoped they had finished with this.

"But," Fern continued, "if it has led him to discover himself, you know, that would be a good thing." Manriguez didn't understand, and his expression must have shown this as Fern started to explain.

"You know, he's the world's best hope and all, but getting him to believe it is tough. I thought it might be impossible."

Manriguez pondered this revelation. Getting Bill to believe it himself? Getting anyone to believe that Bill Posters was mankind's best hope of salvation would be hard enough, even if you started at the local asylum. He kept this opinion to himself though, and looking square into Fern's eyes he realised it wasn't true either. One person believed it, one hundred per cent, no question. And she was staring at him right now, disturbingly intent. There was something else in her eye as well, but he couldn't fathom what. He hoped it wasn't madness; they weren't in the clear yet, and they couldn't afford for her to fall apart.

"Yeah, sure, getting him to believe," he said weakly, worried anything else might shatter the strange fragility of her certainty. Suddenly he really missed the reassuring weight of a crossbow or two between his shoulder blades. Nothing like a solid crossbow to make a man feel secure. Fern grinned, and for a horrifying second gave Manriguez the impression that she might clap her hands or do a happy little jig. Instead, she turned neatly on her heel and made her way back to where Bill sat, crumpled.

189

Like the changing of the weather, Fern was instantly business-like again.

"Right—we have only seven hours to save the world, and the sharks may be after us even now. We have to get the button back to Leamington Spa."

Just another couple of sentences I really thought I would never hear, thought Bill, feeling a little better after his brief sit down.

"The subtrain should be just one mile in that direction." She pointed in roughly the direction they had been headed. "If I push the drive, we can be back in the UK in four hours, giving us three hours to get to HQ. Okay?"

The two men nodded. Bill heaved himself off the root and checked the button, still tucked down his pants. It had wriggled itself into a reasonably comfortable position now, so he saw no real point in moving it.

"Right, let's go."

Carlos Mendoza, seated in the folding chair in his campaign tent, couldn't believe what he was hearing.

"Smashed through the wall?" he asked.

"Yes, General."

"All three of them escaped?"

"Yes, General."

"And the Sharkosians gave you strict orders not to pursue them?"

"Yes, General."

Mendoza sat back in his chair, the slender wooden beams creaking in protest but holding. He steepled his fingers and held them just under his nose. Anyone who knew him well knew this meant he was thoughtful, and angry. The man facing him clearly knew his commander reasonably well, as he blanched at the sight.

Mendoza was indeed angry, and he needed to make an important decision. A combination that was far from ideal. This smacked of treachery on the part of the Sharkosians. He had been promised Manriguez once the sharks were done with him. He had no concern for whatever the fish had planned. He was a mercenary, and he and his men were being paid well. Material wealth had long since lost its importance however, and what he really wanted, since he had learned Manriguez was mixed up in all of this, was his rival's head. Preferably on his shoulders, but in a sack would be fine.

And now, Manriguez had escaped in the most remarkable of circumstances and pursuit had been forbidden by his current employers. *What reason could they have*, he wondered, *and how much would it cost me to go against their will?*

He played over in his mind the last time he and Manriguez had spoken, the memory stoking the fire of his rage. Unconsciously his fingers rubbed the fabric of his shirt by his left shoulder, and the ragged puckered scar that lay beneath. He knew he had no choice. Burn the sharks and their plans for world domination, this was personal. He surged upright from the chair, causing the soldier to jump.

"Muster all the men," he barked, "we are going hunting."

"Only half a mile," Fern informed them. They were making their way along a low ridge and would shortly make their way down into the shallow bowl containing the subtrain. From the height of the ridge, Bill could see that the subtrain must have surfaced only just inside the forest. A hundred metres or so to the right, the tree line ended abruptly at a straggly wire fence. The other side was quite different, with rolling pasture, no trees, and a lot of fluffy, white sheep.

The view was quite beautiful thought Bill, pausing briefly to enjoy it. The grass was very green, the sheep, from this distance at least, seemed very white. The rounded hills under the bright, blue sky looked almost artificial, like something from a cartoon. The air was very clear; it seemed that if he reached out he could almost touch the hilltop, the entire vista seeming almost 2D. He wouldn't have been surprised if a boxy red post van appeared, making its way among the green hills, delivering letters to inhabitants of the idyllic scene.

Something caught his ear and snapped him from his reverie. It sounded like a dog barking. There, another, closer. And now raised voices. Looking behind he could make out shapes. Men, making their way up the rise, and standing there, gormless as he was, he was certain they could see him.

"Shit! Shit!" Scrambling into motion he quickly caught up with the others.

"Men, lots of them, after us."

"Where?"

"Pretty close," he panted.

"C'mon, we can make it if we hurry."

As they hurtled through the forest, they could make out the bulky shape of the subtrain looming ahead. The sound of pursuit was definitely getting closer. A whistle sounded to the right, two blasts on a whistle from the left. The barking was a lot closer as well, and Bill kept waiting to hear someone yell, "Release the hounds!"

Suddenly, the subtrain was towering over them on a slab of cooled molten rock. Flying up the ladder Fern leapt to the control panel by the stairs.

"I'm starting the launch sequence. It takes a few seconds to warm up, then we're away. Shit."

"What?" shouted Bill, joining her inside the cabin of the subtrain.

192

"The front anchor is jammed; we can't move unless it is free."

"Right!" Bill replied, scrambling back down the ladder and to the nose of the steel cylinder. The giant drill was churning into life, spinning faster and faster. Sure enough, a slender metal cable connected the underside of the cabin with the floor. The end of the cable was a multi-sided claw with serrated jaws that were spasming open and closed ineffectually. The rope was taught, and he could see a winch trying to haul it in, but one of the claws was snagged on a massive creeper. Not wanting to go near the serrated claws he gave the creeper a kick, and then another, then another. At the third kick he slipped, his leg sliding up under the cursed vine. The movement jolted the anchor free, the whole apparatus shooting back past his head at great speed and almost taking his eye out.

***

Back in the subtrain Fern saw the offending red warning light wink out to be replaced with a fifteen second countdown.

"Good work, Bill, now get in here, fifteen seconds and we're off." She could see the blades at the front of the train spinning faster and knew that in less than ten seconds the doorway would close.

"Bill!" she screamed. Still nothing.

"Where is he?" said Manriguez, moving up the cabin.

"He's outside, freeing up an anchor. It's free now, he should be in here!"

Nine seconds read the display. Fern tapped the controls frantically, but she knew the response she would get. Once the launch sequence began, it could not be over-ridden.

Switching to the other panel, she brought up the subtrain's external cameras. There, she could see the men entering the clearing, several leading dogs on chains. The men were clearly intimidated by the giant metal contraption, but well trained enough to follow orders and not scatter. But no Bill. Panning the camera down, she caught sight of something and jogged the camera down. Just to the side of the drill stood Bill, bolt upright, arms raised in front of himself like a Queensbury rules boxer, jumping up and down on the spot. There was no sound with the visual, but they could see Bill screaming a stream of obscenities, presumably at the approaching men.

"What the hell is he doing?" asked Fern, as Bill continued to punch to air in defiance of the advancing guards.

"Err . . . beginning to believe?" offered Manriguez, as the subtrain door closed with a snick.

Bill was swearing at the top of his lungs, curse after curse, but none of it could be heard above the terrifying din of the drill blades. And none of it was directed at the approaching men, who Bill had yet to notice. The source of Bill's rage, and target of the abuse, was the thick green creeper, previously snared around the subtrain anchor, now firmly noosed around his ankle. It would seem the anchor's retraction had put the creeper under considerable strain, and when released it had clamped down around Bill's ankle like a vice.

In just fifteen seconds, a desperate Bill had tried a number of ways to free himself. He had tried tugging his foot loose while seated, which hadn't worked. He had found a sharp rock, and had tried hacking at the creeper, but had only succeeded in gashing his own palm, which hurt a lot. He had tried kicking it free with his other boot, but now had a gashed palm and a badly bruised shin. Struggling to his feet, he was now trying to yank his foot free, hopping up and down (which aggravated the bruised shin), and waving his injured hand in front of him, his fingers clamped into a fist to stem the bleeding. He was panicked, pissed off, hurt, and bleeding, and he was going to swear at the thing until it let him go or he ran out of breath and blacked out.

The blades of the subtrain drill near his head sped up dramatically, their passage raising a wind that tugged at his hair. Now he noticed the advancing men, but he couldn't get any more scared. He'd seen the trail of molten destruction the subtrain had made when it surfaced, so he very much doubted he would have to worry about what these men might do to him. He had had enough. Raising both hands in front of him, he delivered a short, two-word message with accompanying hand gestures to the approaching men. The drill's growling obliterated all sound, but the advancing guards at least recognised Bill's hand gestures.

The whirring intensified to new levels and the ground began to shake, forcing Bill to fight for his balance. With a groan, the subtrain sat up off the floor, a sound like amplified white noise erupting from behind him. The sound changed to that of an angry forklift on steroids and the front end of the subtrain crouched down, the blades coming to within inches of Bill's cheek. Then, with improbable elegance, the front of the subtrain shot into the air, the entire vast cylinder performing a back flip, the whirling blades crunching into the earth exactly where it had exited all those hours before. *Handy*, thought Bill, through the curtain of terror. *I wonder if anyone on board held onto their breakfast during that?*

The sight clearly impressed the guards, who had stopped in their tracks, some dropping to their knees. With a roar, the drill on the subtrain disappeared, the white noise crackle increased, every hair on Bill's body (every one, including those in his nose and ears), stood on end ninety degrees from his skin (in many cases forcing his clothes from his body and punching small holes in his boots), and with a snap the creeper came loose. *Good shot,* thought Bill, as the subtrain, having chomped through the imprisoning vine, slid majestically into the ground. It was at that moment that the leader of the armed men screamed, "Release the hounds!" (to Bill's perverse satisfaction). Luckily for Bill the dogs weren't stupid, and with the horrible crackling ringing in their ears they immediately turned and fled.

Bill had been expecting the explosion of boiling rock, so for once he was the first to recover. Wiping his bloodied hand on his jeans, he turned and ran, making his way to the wire fence. With a vault he leapt over the twisted wire, landing well (for once) and began to sprint across the field. Just as he hoped the men would give up, he heard a shot and flinched. Two more steps and his foot failed to connect with the ground, stamping down on thin air. Arms flailing, he plummeted down a hidden pothole, his limbs grazing the sides. Once, twice, he hit his head as he fell, dropping a long way before slamming into a pile of something squishy and warm. And smelly! His nostrils told him this was not good, but the impulses from his nose could not be heard above the agonising damage reports coming in from all over his body.

Eyes level with the ground he watched a set of four black hooves walking closer. Raising his head caused fresh agony to bloom in his skull and lights to dance in his vision, and he found himself staring into the eyes of a large, woolly sheep. The sheep regarded him quizzically, staring intently at his forehead. Licking its lips it turned and called out.

"It's okay, Frank, he's one of us!"

Okay, that's enough, thought Bill, and fell unconscious.

Chapter Twenty-One

Under the earth's surface, deep under the earth's surface, the subtrain hurtled through the mantle at maximum pulse drive.

"How many of them were there?" asked Fern, numbly.

"Oh, not many," reassured Manriguez.

"Enough though, right?"

Enough for what? thought Manriguez. Enough for a barn dance, a sit-down dinner? Enough to construct a flat-pack wardrobe? Enough to handle Bill? Well, that would be one highly trained mercenary killer wouldn't it, and there was clearly more than one.

"Oh, I don't know, he had come a long way like you said," he replied in a voice that lacked any conviction.

"You really think so?" Fern gave a queasy smile, somehow contriving to miss Manriguez's leaden tone of fatality.

"Sure," he lied.

They sat in silence for a few more minutes, the only noise being the quiet hum of the subtrain, soothing images looking back at them from the windows-come-TV screens.

"Did you see what he did, just as we were leaving?"

"Err, yes."

"What do you think it means?"

Manriguez knew exactly what it meant, in two simple words, but this wasn't what Fern meant, or hoped to hear him say. Standing down thirty armed men was unusual enough. Then telling them to, you know, was definitely quite ballsy. There were only two possibilities. The first was that Bill had discovered fabulous reserves of a special power that would allow him to defeat armies. So that only left the second possibility. Electing not to answer, he reached across and gave Fern's shoulder an encouraging squeeze. It would seem Bill had gone bonkers.

Bill, currently lying in pitch-black darkness on something very soft and cosy, had come to the same conclusion. That could not, *could not*, have been a talking sheep. He had hit his head pretty hard after all, and it still hurt. He wondered how long he had been unconscious, and if he should try moving. He was really very comfortable, and it would seem no one was currently trying to kill him. At the moment at least.

Experimentally he flexed his muscles. It seemed he could feel all of his limbs, which was good, and nothing seemed to be broken. Remarkable given how far he had fallen. And then he remembered the smelly, squishy stuff he had landed in. *That's if all this isn't a dream*, he thought. *Maybe if I get up and switch on the light I will be back home!* Encouraged by this he tried sitting up, and found he couldn't.

"Oh good, you are awake," came a voice from the darkness.

"Gah!" Bill jumped (or at least he would have if he wasn't mysteriously restrained), wondering who the hell was in his bedroom.

"Do not be alarmed," said the voice.

Oh right, thought Bill, *I've heard this before. Like "do not be alarmed" ever reassured anyone.*

"The restraints are for your safety. We've had quite a bit of work to do. We should be able to take them off shortly."

"Uh, who is this?"

"Oh, how rude of me, I'm sorry. Bernadette, the lights if you would?"

The world around Bill burst into brightness, blinding him and causing him to jump (if he could) again.

"Gah!"

"Oh sorry, down a bit if you would, Bernie." The lights dimmed, and Bill found he could crack open an eye.

The ceiling above him was white, but with a pretty country scene, remarkable in its quality, painted dead centre. There didn't seem to be any light fittings above, but instead the whole ceiling seemed to glow. Bill twisted his head around; it looked like a hospital room. Metal shelving down the wall carried implements he couldn't identify, large boxes stood on trolleys, some beeping, some showing graphs. A table stood next to his bed with a chart clipped to it. A scraggy grey-and-white sheep trotted from out of the edge of his vision and halted in front of the chart.

"Gah!" Bill screamed again, developing a deep affinity for the noise. "What the bloody hell is a sheep doing in the hospital?"

The sheep turned to face him, peering at him through thick, horn-rimmed spectacles. "Oh, I do love the human sense of humour, though I must admit I don't always get it," the sheep chuckled. It turned back to the chart, studied it for a few more moments, then called out, "Yes, Bernie, all done, release the restraints."

Something went click, and a tightness disappeared from around Bill's chest, wrists, and ankles.

"What the bloody hell . . ." he began, sitting upright, his head almost brushing the oddly glowing ceiling.

"Broken ankle, fractured forearm, two slipped disks, a fractured rib, lacerated spleen, a bruised kidney, and, oh yes, a fractured skull," said the sheep brightly.

"Errr, what?"

"All fixed."

"What's all fixed?"

The sheep turned to the younger-looking sheep standing near the doorway set in the far wall. Bill hadn't noticed this sheep until now, but presumably this was Bernie.

"I thought you said there should be no after effects of the knock on the head? He does seem rather confused."

Bernie shrugged, or at least it looked like a shrug to Bill.

"Okay then," said the first sheep slowly, turning back to Bill with the patiently pained expression of someone talking to the hard of hearing, of limited mental capacity, or of a foreign country. "My name is Bristol," continued the sheep. "And you are?"

"Bill," replied Bill.

"Good, good," soothed the elderly sheep. "You were in a bad way when they brought you in. Lots of injuries," he said very loudly, moving closer to Bill and staring intently into his eyes.

"And you have healed them all?" said Bill, suspending disbelief for a time and catching the quadruped's drift.

"Yes!" said Bristol.

"What . . . all that stuff you said?" asked Bill, replaying the list of injuries in his mind. "That's impossible, how long was I unconscious?"

"Oh, only a couple of hours, and it is quite possible, when the right equipment is in the hooves of a skilled surgeon." Disturbingly, Bristol held up his front hooves and waggled them as if to illustrate his point.

"Rigghhht," drawled Bill. "Well, thanks very much." He wasn't sure what else to say, then added, "look, I don't want to seem ungrateful, but I am having a really hard time with the whole talking sheep thing."

Bristol looked taken aback. "Really? Oh my. What is the world coming to? You are one of the initiated; it says so quite clearly on your forehead. Please tell me they haven't cut us out of the induction, those arrogant skyrats!"

"I'm sure they haven't," Bill interjected, for some reason keen to stick up for the pigeons, "but my induction was rather, err, rushed, so we didn't really cover talking sheep."

Bristol seemed only slightly mollified.

"I'd be grateful if you could fill me in though," said Bill, with what he hoped was an ingratiating smile. Bristol looked thoughtful, (an expression which, as sheep have only a handful of facial muscles, consisted of blinking a lot), but finally relented.

"Very well, but it really isn't the job of a surgeon to 'fill you in' on the basics."

Bill was unsurprised to learn that, like everything else lately, the tale of Bristol the sheep revolved around The Truth about the world. What the pigeon induction video had failed to mention was that humans were not the Pygeans' first genetic experiment. They needed a powerful ally, but they had wanted to maintain control. To this end, their first attempt was with a more malleable group of mammals. The ungulates.

"The modifications were initially deemed to be a great success," said Bristol proudly. "Subsequent generations of sheep evolved an advanced intellect, proving to be highly skilled at technical innovation, especially in the medical sciences. Something which you have recently benefited from," said the old sheep pointedly. "Despite all this a significant, err, flaw began to emerge."

It would seem that the sheep, like their un-evolved ancestors, would follow absolutely anyone, in anything, anywhere. This lead to an intelligent species that, instead of competing with the dinosaurs, became cruelly oppressed by them.

"My understanding," Bristol continued, looking slightly abashed and possibly a little bit angry, "was that the Pygeans went back to the zoological drawing board and picked primates." He nodded at Bill. "We were wary of our exploitation at the hands of the dinosaurs, and took no part in the coming war, unless told to of course." The sheep looked up expectantly at him.

"Of course," said Bill, in what he hoped was an encouraging manner.

Bristol grunted. "When it was all over, we hid our intellect from the world. The Pygeans assisted of course, keen to cover up their blunder. They wiped all record of our society from history and set up the global cover industry."

"Sorry, you lost me a bit there. A global cover-up industry?"

"Why yes," said Bristol. "Sheep farming, it's all a cover up you know."

"A cover up?"

"Yes, are you feeling all dim again?"

"No no," though Bill wasn't sure. "But what about wool? Are you saying that doesn't come from sheep?"

"Don't be ridiculous, or course it does. But not as a result of some vulgar mechanised process. We all need haircuts, some more often than others. The clippings just get bagged up."

"Right, of course. And lamb?"

"Chicken."

"Sorry, chicken?"

"Yes, it's just chicken with some flavourings, maybe some ceramic additions for bones and whatnot."

"Right." Bill was dumbfounded.

"Look, it's not that hard to believe, is it? You see sheep all the time, loafing around on hillsides, all nice and relaxed. We never need to do very much (a product of our highly advanced technology), so we get a lot of leisure time. Did you ever wonder how difficult it would be to gather all those sheep in, all spread about as they are?"

Bill had some vague inklings about a programme he had watched when he was young, but had to confess he really had no idea.

"Damn near impossible. That's because it never happens. Every night we head underground, to our luxury subterranean homes. Oh, from time to time we all get together on country lanes, but that's all down to keeping up appearances."

Swinging his legs over the edge of the table, Bill noticed for the first time what he was wearing. "Where are my clothes?" he asked.

"Had to incinerate them I'm afraid, utterly ruined. You landed in an enormous pile of sheep dung. Saved your life, but effectively wrote off everything you were wearing. We had to scrub your hair three times as well."

Bill's hands went to his head, where his hair did feel very dry and brittle. And, come to think of it, his scalp tingled as well.

He was now dressed, head to toe, in what could only be described as sheep country chic. Fleecy wool trousers met fleece-lined sheepskin boots. A bulky knit wool sweater swarmed around his upper body, the sleeves threatening to swallow his hands. Seeing this made him think of Fern, which jolted him back to reality (or at least reality's slightly unhinged next-door neighbour).

"In my pants, there was something very important, where is it?"

"Well, that was, uh, undamaged. I can assure you that we did nothing with it," mumbled Bristol, glancing at Bill's crotch, then catching his meaning. "Ah, the device!" he sighed, chuckling nervously. "Of course! That was also okay, here it is. Bernie!"

The younger sheep trotted over, the button in its jaws, which it dropped onto the table next to Bill. It then gave a meaningful glance at Bill's crotch and, horror of horrors, gave Bill a wink. Bill crossed his legs, snatched up the button, and stuffed in into the pocket of the trousers. He didn't have time for advances from sheep, talking or otherwise.

"I'm really grateful for your help, really I am, but I have to get out of here. I've only got . . ." he looked at a strange watch that had appeared on his wrist. A cute central dial with sheep cavorting around the edge. "Oh shit—is this thing right?"

The sheep both stared at him, startled by the curse.

"Sorry," he mumbled, "but I think I have gone and blown it. I've only got an hour and a half to get to the UK, and unless you techno-sheep possess a transporter I'm pretty screwed."

The sheep stared at him. They were blinking a lot, which Bill guessed meant they were thinking. Or maybe they were still offended by his swearing. Bristol appeared to be choking slightly, and his eyes had gone very big. Bernie, hopping a little, turned to Bristol and whispered loudly, "How does he know about the transporter?"

"Shhhhh!" hissed Bristol, "we must not speak of it!"

"Hang on, hang on," said Bill, leaping up from the bed. "Are you saying you have some way to get me to the UK in less than an hour and a half?"

Bristol was definitely panicked now.

"No, no, no! Nothing of the kind. We do not, *do not*, possess a direct, instantaneous matter transport facility with the UK and we never have. Nothing of the kind. Ever. If you will excuse me," the sheep began to hurry from the room.

"Oh no, wait up, woolly," Bill quickly grappled Bristol, grabbing two handfuls of wiry wool.

"Ah, leggo!" screamed the sheep.

"I will, just tell me, can you get me to the UK or not?"

"Not, not, not!"

"I don't believe you. Listen, I'm not messing around. If I blow this, it's curtains for every living thing on the planet. And that includes you techno-sheep."

Bristol squirmed under his hands. Out of the corner of his eye, Bill could see Bernie edging her way to the door.

"Hold it, muffin, or I swear I am breaking out the mint sauce!" He felt mean the second the words were out of his mouth. After all, they had saved his life, or at least all of his limbs, and spleen, and whatever. The words had the desired effect though, as Bernie shrieked and flat fainted right there. Bristol let out an anguished moan.

"Very well, yes, yes, there is a way. But I cannot share The Secret with you. Only the flock master may, and I cannot, cannot take you to him!"

"Why not?"

"It is forbidden for one of us to decide to visit the flock master. We can only go when called. I would if I could, but it is against every fibre of my being. I cannot!"

This was getting him nowhere, and time was not on his side. Then something that Bristol had mentioned earlier hit him.

"Fine," Bill said, "that's fine. You don't have to take me to the flock master." He felt Bristol relax under his grip. "But I am going to visit the flock master, and I would like you to follow."

"Oh, okay," said Bristol, reflexively.

"Good," Bill released the animal's wool and patted his back. "But seeing as I don't know the way, it might make more sense if you follow from in front, save us a lot of time, wouldn't you say?"

Bristol's advanced intellect fought against his ingrained species instinct and, as the Sharkosians had discovered millennia earlier, instinct won.

"Very well," he bleated, and set off down the corridor.

Chapter Twenty-Two

"Very bad, very bad indeed," Keith agreed. Fern and that Chilean chap stood opposite his desk, both looked in serious need of some rest, and some decent food, but Fern was quite desperate.

"What are we going to do, Keith? Can you send me back in a subtrain?"

"No time for that. Besides, the whole station is going into lockdown."

"Lockdown? But why, it won't do us any good if we don't stop that machine. We need Bill. And the button," she added.

"Well, yes, but this isn't our only problem at the moment. The most important one yes," he said, noticing Fern colour, "but not the only one. Fill her in Clyde."

The pigeon sat on the edge of Keith's desk, and when Keith motioned to him he pecked a couple of buttons. A holographic map of the UK appeared, hovering about three inches over the desk.

"Yes, as Keith says we have another issue. Our intelligence shows the Sharkosians are planning an attack, with conventional forces, to build a bridge-head just prior to activation of the device."

"A full-out attack? We haven't had one of those for centuries!" exclaimed Fern.

"Quite," Clyde continued, "but nonetheless. Our intelligence shows they will attack the east coast of Britain, concentrating their attack on Great Yarmouth."

"What intelligence is this, Keith? It seems incredible," Fern asked.

"Don't look at me; this comes straight from Clyde's team."

The pigeon puffed out his chest and gave an odd clucking noise. "I assure you that my sources are valid. But I cannot reveal them; it is classified to the very highest level."

A small cough made everyone remember Manriguez's presence in the room. "Excuse me, you said conventional forces?"

"I did," said Clyde stiffly.

"These are sharks, right?" asked the assassin.

"Sharkosians," corrected the bird.

"Right, so how exactly do sharks have conventional *ground* troops? Sounds somewhat unconventional to me."

Clyde fixed him with a withering avian stare and was about to say something when Keith cut him off.

"We don't have time for this. What matters is that we've dispatched all units to the east coast in preparation, and they should be there by now."

"All units? So there is no one left on base, in reserve?" Fern said aghast.

Clyde was clearly agitated now. "Maybe I didn't make myself clear. There will be a huge attack. We will need everything we have to repel it."

Keith could tell that Fern didn't like this at all, her expression uneasy. In truth, he didn't like it either, and it wasn't just down to the threat of a vast army of "conventional" shark forces rolling down the streets of Britain. But Clyde's intelligence had always been spot on before; there was no reason to doubt it now.

"But what are we going to do about Bill and the button?" asked Fern.

Keith tapped on his keyboard and the map of Britain disappeared to be replaced with a globe and a series of graphs and data readouts. "Well, let's see, shall we? Well, he still has his locator chip, and we are getting a good signal. Bit muffled though, I'll see if I can boost it."

Keith tapped away some more and the images flickered and fuzzed.

"Hmm, a bit better. Well, he is pretty much where you left him, see?" A small, green light glowed deep in the South Island of New Zealand. "And he appears to be healthy. Very healthy in fact, better than you two," he nodded at Fern and Manriguez. Fern struggled to contain a massive sigh of relief and a small tear that welled in her right eye.

"No, wait, that can't be right." Keith now looked confused, studying one of the readouts intently.

"What's wrong?"

"Well, the historical health chart shows him with multiple, very serious injuries that thirty-seven minutes ago just disappeared." With a grunt of frustration, he flicked the holo-readout, which flickered. "Bloody thing, must be interference." He paused, looking very thoughtful. "Unless . . ."

"Unless what?" said Fern worriedly, not sure how to interpret Keith's tone.

Keith didn't reply, but sat there, brow furrowed, tapping his pen against a tooth. The tension in the room mounted.

"It could be, if it is, and he can, then . . ." he muttered, keeping rhythm with the pen. Suddenly he stopped and turned to Clyde. "Are you thinking what I am thinking?" he asked the pigeon.

Clyde looked nervous, and shifty. "Errr . . . I am not sure that I am really."

"You know. You know where he is. The disappearing injuries and all." Keith seemed surprised that Clyde wasn't on the same wavelength.

"Ye-eess, I understand all that," Clyde now looked a little panicked. "But I am not sure where you are going with all this."

Keith let out an annoyed grunt, and turned to Manriguez and Fern.

"This is absolutely top secret, classified to the very, very highest level. Only the very top brass know this, and that includes Clyde and me, but not you two. I don't have time to kick you out, so bloody cover your ears and do not try to listen!"

Fern and Manriguez acquiesced immediately, clapping their hands over their ears with lightning speed—Fern because she sensed this information might help Bill, and Manriguez because he was used to taking orders (and because Keith was senior enough to sign off his expenses).

Keith gestured Clyde closer on the desk. The sweaty-eyed bird hopped over.

"You must know what I am talking about," he hissed. "Classified Data 23!"

"Why, err, yes, of course. Number 23. I understand, good idea. I'm a little rusty on the details though . . ."

Keith looked at Clyde sideways. This was odd; Clyde had an excellent memory, and this was far from trivial stuff. Only five people (including three pigeons) on the planet were privy to Classified Data 23, and they had a responsibility to remember. After all, it wasn't written down anywhere. He didn't have time to mess around though.

"Blazes, you know, the instant matter transportation facility that the sheep have. The boy is right bloody next to it. If he can talk the sheep into letting him use it, then there is still time!"

Clyde's eyes grew very, very wide. For a second he stood stock still, transfixed, and Keith could have sworn he heard an odd ticking noise.

"Oh yes!" Clyde recovered, gushing enthusiasm, "that number 23, very good thinking. Yes that could work!"

Keith harrumphed in agreement, wondering what was wrong with his friend. He'd been expecting more input than that, but at least that amounted to approval.

"Hands off!" Keith bellowed, and Fern and Manriguez both jumped and lowered their palms from their ears.

"Okay troops," he begun, happier now he at least had the outline of a plan. "There is a chance, a slim chance, a glimmer, faint though it is, of hope." Not the most inspiring of openers, but at least it was true.

"If our boy can manage it, he could be back on home soil in time. No, don't ask me how, I can't tell you. If I did, I really would have to kill you." If this was a joke, no one was laughing.

"Now we need someone to meet him when he gets here, 'cause he isn't going to come straight to HQ." Keith immediately waved away Fern's frenetic hand waving. "You are staying right here. No questions." Fern looked glum but put her hands down.

"I can't leave here and everyone else is in Great Yarmouth. Clyde, would you be able to take a car and pick him up?"

"Certainly," clucked the pigeon with an odd mixture of relish and relief.

"Good, you'll need to get moving straight away, but even then you aren't going to be there for some time, so we need someone on the ground." His fingers typed on the keyboard, and the map of the UK replaced the holographic globe. Symbols flashed up and down the length of the country, Keith scanning the map to find the one he wanted. Finally he found a small red-white-and-blue-striped corgi, and let out a small cry of triumph.

"Just close enough!"

"Commander," Fern began, wide eyed. "You can't mean to deploy—"

"Indeed I do. I think the situation warrants it after all. We are staring down the barrel of the end of the world as we know it, so it's high time we involved Britain's last and greatest line of defence. And I think even you will agree that it means our man will be in good hands."

Fern nodded, dumbfounded.

"Good, then let's get underway. If I am right, and he can manage it, we can expect our man to pop up here!" he jabbed the holographic map with a finger, creating an electronic ripple.

"Err . . . Wales?" said Fern.

"That's right, Wales. The Gower Peninsula, to be precise."

Chapter Twenty-Three

"We must never bother the flock leader, never ever ever," muttered Bristol as he trotted down the corridor, gnashing his teeth and twitching.

"Relax," said Bill. "Remember, you are just following me, nothing else."

Bristol let out a sheepy cough, half-bah, half-snort of derision. "And that makes it all better does it?" A few more trotty steps and the twitching eased a little. Clearly it did help, at least a bit.

The corridors they had been walking down all looked very similar. The floor was nicely paved with good quality slate, the walls dressed in terracotta render with a marble inlay running along at about hip height (hip height to a human that is). The ceiling had the same ethereal glow as the operating room, and Bill noticed it followed them as they made their way along the corridor, a few metres behind them returning to darkness as a few metres in front washed into light. The transition was very, very smooth, giving the disconcerting impression that they were not in fact moving at all, but that the walls and floor were sliding back the other way around them.

They had encountered a few other sheep on the way, some of whom had given Bristol a bow. Others had stopped to stare at Bill, while others had paid them no attention at all. They hadn't seen anyone else for some time though as they meandered down the corridors.

They approached a fork in the corridor, and Bristol trotted toward the left. Here the marble inlay was replaced with gold, and Bill noticed the light from the ceiling had a strange, greenish quality, as if it had been filtered through leaves.

"So, care to tell me something about the flock leader before I meet him or her? The him or her bit could be handy, I must admit I can't easily tell . . ."

It turned out that Bristol would not like to talk about the flock leader, but evidently he also found talking eased his nerves.

Bristol spoke warmly of the flock leader as a sheep, and Bill wondered if the two had maybe been childhood, err, lambhood friends. When addressing him, Bill was to call him "Your Wooliness," making sure he didn't laugh, and should bow when they first met. He should not speak unless spoken to, and he should be quick and to the point.

The corridor in front of them ended up ahead. Two vast doors, almost gates, loomed high above them, the ceiling sloping upwards abruptly to accommodate their size. The fronts of the doors were covered in vast gold panels depicting typical aspects of sheep life. There were six panels in each; the first showed a couple of sheep idly nibbling grass in the sunshine. This was a scene Bill was familiar with, but the rest were very new. Other scenes included a group of sheep working on a very complicated-looking device, a pair of sheep playing chess, and a venerable-looking sheep addressing a large room of lambs. One panel in particular caught Bill's eye, causing him to quirk his eyebrow. Following his gaze, Bristol gave an embarrassed cough.

"Oh, that, yes. Well, every now and then, very rare indeed, a battle sheep is elected flock leader, leading to a renaissance in sheep martial arts."

The panel showed a very angry sheep indeed, covered head to hoof in what looked like armour plate (you could still make out the flashing eyes though). Strapped to the sheep's back was a device that looked like a rocket launcher, and protruding from either side of the sheep's head were rifle barrels. The background of the scene was a blanket of flames, utterly at odds with the other peaceful scenes.

"Err, and when was the last 'battle sheep' exactly?"

"Oh, not for a very long time. The last battle sheep was the mighty Bahticus, who reigned at the time of the fall of the Roman Empire. Epic were the battles!" finished Bristol with a wistful grin, his embarrassment clearly forgotten.

Raising a hoof, he gave the door a nervous knock. Nothing. Clearing his throat nervously he knocked louder. Still nothing. With a pained shake of his head, he hammered his hooves into the door. Beyond the gold friezes, they heard a startled snort, some loud muttering, then a very clear "Come in!"

The room beyond was lit with a gentle bronze light and had a cosy, if musty, feel. Tapestries on the wall continued the theme of the door panels, depicting what Bill assumed were key moments from sheep history. Thankfully none of these detailed the exploits of Bahticus, or any other "battle sheep."

In the centre of the room was a large rug, littered with cushions and pillows. The rug itself had a beautifully intricate red, black, and gold pattern, geometric shapes and free form images. It was like nothing Bill had ever seen before. It reminded him a little of an old Persian rug his Nan had, but the pattern here was much less rigid in its structure.

If the rug was stunning in its beauty, the cushions and pillows were its counterpoint. These were a complete mix, ranging from brown and moth-eaten to pink with sparkly sequins. A particularly large one near the centre looked like it was actually an old sofa cushion, and one in the corner seemed to have a bear's face staring back at him. Lounging in the middle of the rug, close to the sofa cushion, was an ancient-looking sheep. His rheumy eyes blinked at them several times, and it was clear they had roused him from a deep sleep.

"Bristol? My goodness, Bristol, that is you!" spoke His Wooliness, his voice rich and clear, belying the frailness of his appearance. "Oh, what a surprise. Do come in, come in, take a seat. And bring your friend, come in young man," said the sheep warmly, nodding his head at a pile of cushions opposite. Bristol and Bill duly obeyed, settling themselves into the pile of mismatched cushions.

"Oh, this is a treat," His Wooliness continued as they sat down. "I so very rarely get visitors dropping in, it is such a shame."

"Err, that is because no one is allowed to visit you unless summoned, your Wooliness," said Bristol respectfully.

"Really?" His Wooliness looked surprised. "And who says that?"

"The law, your Wooliness."

"Sounds like a damn silly law, I think I'll see about getting that changed."

Bristol let out a gasp of shock. "You mean, repeal one of the founding five hundred?" he spluttered.

For a second it seemed the flock leader was going to reply in the affirmative, then he faltered. "Hmmm, yes, I see. Maybe it is best not to be too hasty. I will ponder it at least," he decided, his chin dropping until Bill was worried he might be falling back asleep.

"So what does bring you both here, to run the risk of flouting one of the founding five hundred?" he said suddenly, raising his head and fixing Bristol with a penetrating, if myopic, stare. Bristol panicked a bit at this and started babbling. Realising this would get them nowhere, and with time ticking on, Bill interrupted.

"If you please, your Wooliness, Bristol came here on my insistence. I need your help."

"Do you indeed?" queried the flock leader. "Fully two decades since a human has sat in this hall and you need my help?" He now fixed Bill with his stare, and Bill could see the sharp intelligence behind the unfocused eyes.

"Do go on," the flock leader insisted.

Time was ticking by and increasing his feeling of panic, but Bill had the feeling he should tell the flock leader everything, so he started at the beginning. He told him about the meeting with Clyde, all the way to his fall into the realm of the sheep, and how he needed to get back to the UK really, really soon.

The flock leader sat there silently throughout, barely even moving, and when Bill had finished his tale he remained motionless. Seconds ticked by and still the venerable sheep did not move. Bill was beginning to think he had dropped off, or died, and was about to make a small cough, when the flock leader spoke.

"Tell me, Bristol, was it you who mentioned that we may have the very device to help this young man, hmmm?"

Bristol quivered, and though it was impossible to tell through the layer of wool, Bill would have bet he had gone white, if that was the sort of thing that happened to sheep.

"Please, your Wooliness," Bill interjected, "it was not Bristol's fault, I made him tell me."

To his relief the old sheep's face softened. "I have no doubt, no doubt. Not since the time of Dorris the Wise have we received a visit from the Britak Tain. It is an unusual privilege to meet you, and a portent of troubling times. I doubt very much that Bristol could resist you, and I am sure he tried very hard."

Bristol relaxed visible, his fleecy body slumping into the cushions. Bill decided it wasn't time to mention that he had effectively extracted the information through the threat of mint sauce. Besides, something else the sheep had said bothered him.

"Err, sorry, the Breta-what-now?" Bill asked, feeling that he had heard the term somewhere before.

"Why you, young man," said the flock leader, now quite animated. "The Britak Tain, hope of the world, the Chosen One."

Now Bill was embarrassed. "I'm sorry, I mustn't have been clear. I'm actually number 768,271 on the list, or something like that. All the really good ones were, err, unavailable."

The flock leader waved a hoof in the air. "Rubbish, rubbish. I know all about the Pygeans and their reliance on Councel's ranking," he snorted. To Bill's amazement, the ancient sheep hauled himself off the floor and trotted in his direction.

"It matters not where, when, or how. The point is that you, and you alone, have been chosen. Number one. Number 768,271, twelve, three billion, it matters not. You are the Britak Tain, you are the chosen." On the word *chosen*, the old sheep placed his hoof squarely on Bill's chest. The musty, old sheep smelt of grass clippings and lanolin, but for the first time in a long time Bill felt the edges of belief tugging at his spirit and couldn't resist a small smile.

"Good, good, you must believe," said the old sheep, returning to where he had arisen and collapsing back into the cushions, exhausted from the exertion. "And we must do what we can to help, of course, but we face a problem. Yes, we possess the means to get you back to near where you need to be."

Bill felt his heart leap, but the old sheep had mentioned a problem.

"It's quite a fundamental one I'm afraid. You see, we've never used the device for anyone who is not a sheep."

Bill felt a quirk of fear.

"Theoretically the process and technology is sound for any item of matter, for any organism, complex or otherwise. Theoretically."

Bill gulped. He'd seen an episode of *Star Trek*, which focused on some sort of problem with a transporter. He hadn't understood most of it, but it looked nasty.

"To be safe, it would be better if you were a sheep," decided the flock leader.

Bill hesitated. He had come to think of the old sheep as wise and venerable. Now he wondered if he was a little bit barmy. Was the old sheep serious? Did he realise that was impossible? Then he remembered the advances these guys had made in medical science, maybe even plastic surgery, and his fear surged.

"But, but . . ." he began, but the flock leader waved his protests away.

"Not that, young man. Do not be so rooted in the literal. I do not mean physically. In any event, I feel this would solve a number of our problems." He turned to Bristol. "Do you agree to it?" he asked, receiving a nod of response from Bristol.

"Good, then it is done!" the flock leader announced.

"Err, what is?" Bill asked, now utterly lost.

"Your adoption. Bristol is now your sheep-father," said the flock leader reverentially.

Bill was momentarily stunned, then let out a short chuckle. "Really? Is that like a godfather? Well, hello Dad." He turned to Bristol and the laugh died on his lips. The scraggy, old sheep's face quivered, and his dark eyes filled with tears.

"Oh my," Bristol stammered. "Beck will be so pleased! We were never able to have lambs, and now we have a son!" he bleated.

Bill smiled an uneasy smile, really quite uncomfortable with the whole affair. He didn't see that this would improve his chances of not getting minced in a techno-sheep teleporter, but at least it had made the old guy happy.

"Excellent!" said the flock leader, now looking a little sleepy. "Now, as is sheep tradition with every new-born lamb, you must be reconnected with your sheep heritage."

Bill had no idea what this meant, but the old sheep pressed on regardless.

"Fortunately, we have the means to do this, and it is something that your sheep-father is well equipped to handle. If you would, Bristol," finished the flock leader, fixing his rheumy gaze on Bill's adoptive sheep dad. Bristol gave an elaborate bow, something that Bill would not have thought possible with four legs, and began backing from the room. It would seem the audience was over, as the flock leader was burrowing down into the cushions and making sleepy *baaing* noises. Following Bristol's lead, Bill walked slowly backwards out of the audience chamber, the heavy bronze doors swinging shut behind him with a dull thud. Bristol was already hurrying along the corridor.

"Come on, son, we don't have much time, and there is no telling how long this will take."

"What will take?" Bill asked, catching up with the trotting sheep.

"The trans-memorification. It completes the adoption process and reminds you of your sheep heritage. It means we should be able to use the teleporter on you with no problems, too." The last sentence seemed almost an afterthought. Clearly, Bristol was very happy to have an adoptive son. Bill wasn't all that happy about being a sheep, but for the old guy he would let it go.

"Trans-memo-re-what-now?" he asked.

Bristol sighed, but didn't slow his pace. "In the dark times there were many sheep who forgot who they were, who became detached from their ancestral memory. Much the way that all, err, humans are." Bristol gave an embarrassed cough.

"Anyway, every sheep should share the memories of their ancestors; it is part of who we are, handed down sheep to lamb. But when we began forgetting who we were we invented the trans-memo-graph. It stores all the sheep memories since the dawn of time and can be used to reconnect a sheep with their ancestral birth right."

They had been making their way back along the route they had come, a slight change in the lighting, and the smell of disinfectant told Bill that they were back in the medical area of the underground labyrinth.

"For decades I had thought that my memories would die with me, but now there is you. It is a simple, non-surgical procedure and should be over quite quickly. Through here please." Bristol nodded in the direction of a door bearing a strange symbol, like a many-pointed star stuck in a globe.

"Let me get this straight," said Bill, pushing through the door and holding it open for Bristol. "You are going to take your memories and put them in my head?" He knew how stupid this sounded and very much hoped he had the wrong end of the stick.

"Goodness me no!" blurted Bristol. "We are going to implant all of the memories of your ancestors, back through the ages. They get fuzzy with time of course, but they are well worth having."

Bill was now getting used to the emotional roller coaster, and when Bristol had first said "no" he hadn't allowed even the tiniest feeling of relief. It was just easier that way.

The room was a bare rectangle, scarcely larger than the operating theatre Bill had awoken in. The floor, walls, and ceiling were all painted bright white, the quality of the reflected light hurting his eyes a little. In the centre of the room, on a white pedestal, sat what looked like a block of marble. If it was marble, it was possibly the most beautiful piece of marble that Bill had ever seen. About the size of his fourteen-inch portable TV, it was a creamy white covered in intricate swirls of orange and red. Trailing from the block of marble were four cables, one red, one blue, one black, and one white. The cables connected the marble with an odd silver helmet resting on the arm of what looked like a dentist's chair. Bill didn't like dentists. All this made him very nervous.

"Err, is this really necessary?" he asked, while Bristol nudged him urgently towards the chair.

"Of course," replied his sheep-father. "You must know who you are after all."

"But, err, will it hurt?" he said, reluctantly taking the seat at Bristol's urging.

"It shouldn't. We don't have much call for it nowadays, but I don't think we've ever had much of an issue. Occasionally there are complications, but that shouldn't be the case here."

The word "complications" had an ominous air to it. The old sheep was a surgeon after all, so for all Bill knew complications included losing your mind or having your brain deep fat fried.

"Complications?"

"Only very rarely," said Bristol, trotting to a small control panel by the marble block. "This is the repository," he continued, nodding at the marble block on the pedestal. "It stores all the memories. The trans-memorification can be run in two modes. In the first mode it detects the bloodline of the candidate and implants the relevant memories. In the second mode we input the bloodline, like so . . ." Bristol tapped some keys on the control panel, presumably entering details about his own bloodline.

"Only time it comes unstuck is if the machine gets confused. No sheep in you, is there?" Bill didn't know whether to be offended or not. Instead, he just shook his head.

"Okay then, should be fine. See you soon," said the sheep cheerily.

Bill opened his mouth to reply, but the helmet clamped down on his head and the world went black.

The world rushed back, expanding from a single point of light and flooding his mind with brightness. Blinking at the glare he stumbled, a friendly shoulder catching him and keeping him upright.

"Thank you, Eripadius," Bill said to the sheep by his side. For some reason the world around him seemed faded, more washed-out than when he had awoken this morning. Maybe it was his age. He was no longer a young sheep.

No longer a young sheep? He wasn't a sheep at all! He was a human, and quite frankly walking on hands and knees was uncomfortable. He pushed up with his hands, but his legs refused to cooperate, and instead his hands smacked back down onto the cobbled street with a clop. A clop?! He waggled his fingers and almost let out a scream—he only had two fingers, no thumb, and they were all fused together. They were bloody hooves!

Now he did let out a shout, but the noise issuing from his throat bubbled and bahed, rather that screamed.

"Whatever is wrong?" asked Eripadius, his nephew, the young sheep's face painted with concern.

"It's these!" bleated Bill, waggling his right hoof. "What the hell is wrong with me?!"

Pull yourself together Valonian, you are too old to go around making a scene! The thought was gruff, woolly, and itchy, but it was his own thought. The problem was these hooves! Humans had hands, not hooves. But

222

what was a human? Come to think of it, what was a hand? Those words had no association, for all he knew he had just made them up. A fleeting thought wormed through his mind and then evaporated. He glanced down. There was nothing wrong with his hooves, they were the same hooves he had had all his life.

Poor Eripadius looked worried.

"I am sorry, nephew. I am fine now, a passing moment, nothing more. Shall we continue?"

The streets around were quiet, unusually so for this time of day. A troop of the hated dinosaurs crossed at an intersection ahead, too far away to cause him and Eripadius any trouble. Even at his advanced age he felt a rush of excitement. They were off to hear *him* talk, the one who had offered to lead the flock. It was more than could be imagined, that after centuries the sheep might be able to follow their own path. They cared nothing for war, usually, but they yearned for freedom. He was just an ordinary particle physicist, too old to play a part in events to come, but at least he would see the beginning.

Turning off the main street, he and Eripadius hurried along the alleyway. Checking carefully they made their way down the steps to a cellar door. Eripadius made a complicated series of knocks on the heavy, wooden door. After a brief pause, the door slowly swung open.

The space behind the door was vast. It was dimly lit by candles and lanterns. He hadn't seen lanterns since he was a lamb. They were such an archaic method of lighting, but he assumed the lack of an electrical signature must make it harder for the dinosaurs to find the gatherings. When his eyes had adjusted to the gloom, he gasped in shock. The cavernous room was crammed with sheep. Wall to wall they were packed into the space. The door closed behind him, and a bar was dropped in place. They had arrived just in time.

At the far end of the hall, a young sheep climbed up onto a raised platform. The dull murmuring that had filled the room ended abruptly, all eyes focussed on the sheep on the platform. The light dimmed for a split second, a flicker so quick it was almost unnoticeable, but when the light burst back he was no longer stood at the back of the room but on the raised platform, looking out over the massed sheep, feeling the intensity of their gaze. The light flicked on and off again, his head swimming, and he was again standing next to Eripadius. His knees felt weak, and he opened his mouth to speak.

"My fellow sheep." His voice rolled out across the massed flock in front of the platform. He was different. He was in the prime of his life and he knew this was his destiny. He could lead them, he was certain.

Flicker.

He was Valonian again, an old particle physicist near the end of his life.

Flicker.

He was Parla-Vrek, a revolutionary, and he would lead his people to freedom.

Flicker.

He was Bill Posters, and not a bloody sheep at all. Flicker. His head felt like it was going to burst. His vision was foggy and faded, like looking through shattered glass. Light exploded.

He stood at the edge of the laboratory, the large picture window looking over the city of Parlan. The war had yet to reach Parlan, but he knew it would. He knew nothing of war, but he was terrified. Not for himself though. He was terrified the war would destroy his research. They were so close, he could feel it.

He had only been on the project team for six months, but he hoped if he worked hard he could make a difference. He had been there when they had made the breakthrough. They had disproved Malarius's theory about the nature of time, and with the new reactor they now had enough power to make the first fissure. The machine, the team had nicknamed it "The Puncher," stood in the centre of the room. They could be ready to move in six months, if only the war kept away.

Flicker.

He was hundreds of miles from Parlan, explosions all around covering him in brick dust. The human commander stood opposite him, his chiselled face impassive, but his eyes betraying desperation. As he studied the stocky general, he weighed his options. It was a terrible gamble, but one he had to take. He nodded. The human sagged in relief, as well he might. The human forces were all but overrun. The sheep militia might be enough to turn the tide. Maybe. Once this war was over, he wanted nothing more to do with humans. He would take his people away, to live in peace. A bomb shook the bunker. Light exploded.

He blinked his eyes slowly, trying to clear his mind. He was so tired. The five hundred years of peace after The Revolution had led to an amazing array of advances, but few had had a greater effect on sheep society than The Puncher. The Puncher had been used to drive a number of fissures through the space-time continuum. With the teleporters they could now thread wormholes through the fissures and instantly move sheep around the world. And how essential that was now.

Every year there were fewer and fewer sheep, putting great strain on the global cover industry that had been put in place to disguise their advanced intellect. It had been a human suggestion. "Sheep farming." They need do little more than maintain the appearance of abundance in certain agricultural areas. But they were no longer abundant.

And now a cornerstone of sheep technology was deemed to be unsafe.

He glanced down at the report on his desk. If this report was true, it was too dangerous to use The Puncher anymore. The report bore the signature of his chief scientist, with a dozen more highly respected names furnishing appendix A. With a sigh, he signed the order. The Puncher would be retired. Light exploded.

The lambs in front hung on his every word. This was his favourite class of the day, they were so attentive.

Flicker.

He sat in an oak-lined office and fretted about declining sheep numbers, and whether to evacuate the sheep colony in Atlantis.

Flicker.

He was back in the classroom.

Flicker.

He was back in the office.

Flicker.

The classroom. Light exploded.

He tumbled through time, lives layering themselves over each other and merging into one. Sometimes he lived two lives at one, and it made his head ache with a pain beyond anything he had ever experienced. In his mind he could feel two lineages stretching back through time, both knotting together and getting jumbled up within him. He was a teacher, a leader, a fighter, a scientist, a criminal, a refugee. In some lives he was unremarkable, hardworking, and ordinary. In others, his actions shook the world. It was too much to take in, yet the memories kept coming. Lives after lives. The life that was Bill Posters opened his mouth to scream.

The pain vanished. He floated in the darkness. Seeing nothing, feeling nothing. Something brushed up against him. He tried to move away, but couldn't tell if he moved at all or just hung there.

It is him, came a voice. It swam through the nothing, languid and formless. It floated slowly all around him, and then in a rush beat the three words against his skull.

"Who's there?" he demanded.

Maybe, came a second voice. **But not even he knows it**. Like the first voice, this one was formless and unhurried, but it carried with it an immense feeling of size. It boomed through him, every nerve tingling in response. It felt as if the words might split his skull, yet at the same time, he felt that if he didn't concentrate he might not be able to hear the words at all. It was like straining to hear a speaker set at full volume.

I agree, said the first. **It is too soon for him to be here. Be gone!** Light exploded and the pain returned with renewed fury. More memories, more than he could possibly hold in his mind flooded in. He was going to be pushed out, scoured clean from his own mind. He screamed and screamed. Something tugged at his head. It felt like his brain was exploding.

"Bill, Bill!" came the urgent bleating. His head felt like it had been pounded with a mallet for hours. He clutched his temples and opened an eye. Bristol's worried woolly face filled his vision.

"Grunph?" he asked.

"Oh my, I've no idea, I've not seen anything like that. Are you okay?"

Bill had no idea. The strange helmet now hung down the side of the chair. With a conscious effort, he marshalled his distant-feeling limbs and pushed up out of the seat. The old sheep danced away from him nervously as he stood. It would seem they were not alone.

Standing around the room, pressed against the wall as if to get as far away from Bill as possible, were half a dozen sheep. Some wore lab coats, and one was wearing what looked like blue overalls.

"Well, it went for longer that I was expecting," Bristol stammered. "And then the repository started heating up." Bristol nodded at the chunk of marble in the middle of the room. It did seem to be glowing slightly.

"It's never done that before," offered the sheep who was dressed in blue overalls. He seemed embarrassed at having spoken as he then stared awkwardly down at his shuffling hooves.

"It wouldn't shut down either," Bristol continued, "which was when I went for help. When they heard it was you, everyone wanted to assist. But there seemed to be nothing we could do." The sheep around the room nodded apologetically.

"In the end I just yanked the thing off of your head. There's no precedent for that, but you were screaming and . . . goodness, are you okay?"

Bill's head felt overfull, but the feeling did seem to be fading. His poor sheep-father looked so worried.

"I'm sure I'll be fine," he managed, and realised he meant it. A synchronised sigh of relief rushed around the room.

"Oh good, good. Marvellous," chuntered Bristol, as he herded the sheep out of the room. Watching a sheep herd other sheep gave Bill a brief quirk of humour. He was feeling better already.

"Well, if you are okay we really must be going. No more time to lose." Bristol rudely shoved the last sheep out of the room and held the door open for Bill.

Time! Bill hurried through the door. He hadn't had that much time before his sheep-father had decided to crowbar a thousand sheep memories into his brain, and Bristol said that strange helmet thing had taken longer than expected.

"How long was I, err . . . hooked up for?" he asked as they hurried down the corridor.

"Much longer than normal," puffed Bristol, clearly moving at top speed. "Normally it takes about half a minute. You were under for nearly ten. I've no idea why it took so long; I didn't realise our family had such a vast amount of memories." The sheep got doe-eyed on the word *family*. It would seem that Bill was going to have to get used to having a sheep-father. He was just relieved the whole thing hadn't taken longer.

"So with that out of the way, I am good to use the teleporter?" Bill asked. Bristol nodded. "And we are on the way there now?" Something swam up through the chunky soup of his memory. "To The Puncher?"

"Goodness me, no," replied Bristol. "What a jumbled set of memories you seem to have received. We are on our way to a teleporter. The Puncher is something entirely different." Despite being short of breath this was clearly a subject of interest for Bristol, and one he was happy to expand on.

"The Puncher is a piece of technology and one of the treasures of our society. Contrary to what human scientists may believe, time and space are not malleable, liquid, bendy elements, but rigid, monolithic structures with the strength of titanium and the flexibility of rock. You can't bend it, or realistically go around it. But you can, with sufficient force, punch right through. No elegance, just a lot of power and a very, very small hole in the space-time continuum."

The old sheep clearly liked his technology. He was quite animated, but he didn't slow his pace.

"That's the job of The Puncher. It incorporates an early fusion reactor and a high precision fluxed ion beam. For centuries we punched holes in the continuum, until concerns for space-time stability caused us to retire the device to the Sheepsonian Museum."

"Oh, I remember," Bill interrupted. Not much of what Bristol had said made much sense, but this at least jogged a memory. "I remember signing the order to retire it. Well, it was kinda me, it was a memory from our sheep ancestry, one of the things I experienced when you had my head rammed into that metal bowl . . ."

Bristol almost missed a step. "Really, are you sure? I believe Ramamon was flock leader when it was decommissioned in 1821. He's not part of our lineage, not even distantly. I certainly don't have any memories even remotely like that. Very odd." The old sheep looked at him sideways, a strange mixture of suspicion and concern. "Are you sure there is no sheep in you already?"

None other than the lamb I had three days ago, thought Bill. "None," he replied.

"Most odd, almost enough to suggest . . . well, no time for that now. And you needn't worry. It wouldn't have been lamb anyway."

Now it was Bill's turn to miss a step. He hadn't said that out loud, had he?

"No, no," said Bristol. "It's a family thing. Some have the ability, and some don't. I do: I can hear the thoughts of any relative who also has the skill, no matter where they are in the world. It seems you might develop it with time. Maybe not, but I can hear you clear as a bell."

This was more uncomfortable than being called a sheep. Having a sheep read your mind really was the limit.

"It wouldn't be lamb, you see," Bristol continued, oblivious to Bill's discomfort. "No one eats lamb. It's all part of the global cover industry to disguise sheep society. You remember."

Bill was unhappy to say he did, albeit fuzzily.

Bristol turned down a side corridor, chatting away happily. "That's why the teleporters are so important. There's only about twenty-five thousand of us left in the world. It's tough maintaining the cover of sheep farming with so few. Being able to instantly teleport sheep all over the world helps to keep up appearances."

Bill could feel his head beginning to ache again with all of this, so he didn't even reply. The corridors they were walking down were much less impressive than those leading to the flock leader's chamber, but were still spotlessly clean. Small blue arrows set in the wall pointed in the direction they were headed. Three arrows—one gold, one red, and one green—pointed back the way they had come. The arrows seemed to shimmer oddly in the light, the surface looking like a multihued oil slick over water. Bill brushed an arrow with his fingertips as he walked past. The surface was smooth, the colour effect like nothing he had ever seen before.

"The arrows are made of Paua, a type of shellfish," Bristol provided.

Bill grunted grumpily. "Look, when you say this mind-reading thing is a family thing, what exactly do you mean? Should I expect every sheep I meet from now on to know my innermost thoughts?"

Bristol gave an uncomfortable laugh, half-giggle, half-baa. "Goodness no. When I say family thing I mean that sometimes family members can feel what other members of their family are thinking. Not always though, and this most definitely does not extend to those who are not related."

It wasn't as bad as he had expected, but he wasn't entirely satisfied. "So how big is our family then?" he asked. He was disturbed by how easily the sentence came out, but he was more anxious to know how many sheep would be invading his mind. Bristol didn't answer straight away.

"Um, well, there's me, and Beck of course." The sheep hesitated. "And, well, that's it. Beck and I didn't have brothers or sisters, and our parents died some time ago and . . ."

Bill thought he could feel sadness radiating off of the old guy, together with something else. For a second he almost felt the words *but now I have a son* form in his mind, accompanied by a scratchy, woolly feeling and the scent of lanolin. Brilliant. On top of talking pigeons and Segway-riding sharks he now had a psychic link with a geriatric sheep. The old guy looked a little downcast, so he changed the subject.

"So, how long will this teleporter take to get me to Leamington Spa in the UK?"

"Well, teleportation is always instantaneous, give or take, but we don't have a space time fissure through to Leamington Spa, but we can get you close. Where else in the UK would the teleporter go than the local sheep stronghold? Wales!"

Bill's heart sank. Now, he had nothing against Wales. Well, not much at least. His geography wasn't great, but he knew he would still have some way to go to get to his destination.

"I wouldn't be too concerned," Bristol piped up, presumably having read his thoughts. "If your friends are any good they'll be tracking you and should be able to pick you up. Those Pygeans are quite organised."

"Tracking me how?"

"Ah, I should have mentioned it earlier. We picked it up in your x-ray."

Chapter Twenty-Four

"X-ray?" Bill prompted Bristol again. The old sheep was getting more and more out of puff.

"Ah, yes. When we were examining your injuries our x-ray imaging revealed a very small tracking chip, just under the tattoo on your arm."

"What tattoo?" asked Bill, rolling up both sleeves.

"Right there," nodded Bristol, "though you won't be able to see it. The pigments aren't in a portion of the light spectrum that human eyes can pick up. It's the same colour as the one on your forehead."

"Forehead?" exclaimed Bill, worried at how many invisible tattoos he was unknowingly bearing. Was he some kind of closet invisible tattoo biker?

"Yes, the one that says you are one of the initiated, that you know about The Truth and all that. The guys that brought you in wouldn't have touched you if they hadn't seen that, we wouldn't be having this conversation now, and you would, err, have bled to death."

Bill rubbed his forehead, but he couldn't feel anything. No wonder it had hurt when Fern stamped his head. He wondered if this meant that pigeons and sheep everywhere would now start talking to him. He hoped not. He unconsciously rubbed his forearm as they walked. Tattoo? What the bloody hell did the one on his arm say? He half opened his mouth to ask Bristol, but decided he would rather not know. Not now. He already had enough on his plate. Besides, deep down some part of him thought that it was quite cool to have a tattoo.

Very un-Bill like. At least by the old Bill's standards. It occurred to him that a lot had changed over the past day, and that he would probably never be the same again. He'd have to re-evaluate who he really was by the time this was all over. Would he like himself still, he wondered. Did he really like himself before?

The corridor ahead wiggled around a corner and then back again, narrowing briefly as if working its way around a giant tree root. Shortly after the contorted bend, they arrived at a large steel door set into the right wall of the corridor. The entire surface of the door was covered in swirls and circles, looping geometric designs that made Bill's eyes go funny if he tried to focus on them. He tried to trace the line of one of the shapes with his gaze, and he felt his eyes crossing, sections of the pattern shifting in and out of focus and making him feel queasy.

"Whoa!" said Bristol, butting Bill's hips gently with his head. "Don't stare at it too long, you'll get lost." With a wrench, Bill tore his eyes from the pattern and blinked, his brain feeling like it had been plucked from a washing machine, soggy, but oddly clean. And for some reason smelling of lavender.

"S'weird," he managed, still blinking and reluctant to look at the door. "Bits of it are kinda here, and kinda not," he finished.

"Hmm, yes, neatly put," Bristol approved. "It exists in more than one place, all at the same time. The pattern is many layers, many pieces, all in different places. Your eyes can't really tell you that, but deep down you can tell. If you look for too long your eyes can begin to show you the truth. Bad for the health, that sort of thing."

Bill had regained some of his composure. He found it helped to have his eyes closed. "Surely that's impossible. Something can't be in more than one place at the same time."

"Says who?"

"Physics," replied Bill triumphantly, with the exotic certainty of the incredibly vague.

"Humph!" harrumphed Bristol, clearly not swayed.

Something from his school days, or a late night documentary, tugged at Bill's memory. "That's right, 'two objects cannot occupy the same space and time.'"

Bristol harrumphed again, louder this time. "A reasonable premise, on the face of things, but not really relevant here. What you can see exists in many places at the same time, so that 'rule' doesn't really come in to it." He spat the world *rule* to leave no doubt as to his opinion of human physics. Bill could sense he had lost this one, and in all honesty had little patience for debating physics theory with a scientifically advanced octogenarian techno-sheep. Peeking a glimpse at the door, he felt his eyes swim again and closed his eyelids. Bristol seemed to have no such issue.

"So, is this the teleporter?" he asked, fixing the old sheep's face in his gaze.

"No, Bill," replied the sheep with pained patience. "This is a do-o-or," dragging out the last word a bit longer than was necessary. Before Bill had a chance to complain, Bristol nudged his way through the swirly door.

Trudging after Bristol, he found himself in what looked like a cheap laundrette. Two sets of chairs, back to back, ran down the centre of the room. Most were of an orange plastic design, though two had tatty felt covering that was frayed and stained, a tear in one revealing clumps of stuffing. Along each wall marched rows of washing machines, their concave doors staring back at them, sightless. At the far end of the room hulked two industrial size dryers, a large sign above them reading "Dry your clothes in our gas-fuelled industrial-sized dryers." At least it would have read that, if someone hadn't amusingly rubbed off the "y" of the "your," turned clothes into "clot" and replaced the word gas with "fart."

"It's a laundrette?" hazarded Bill, a little worried he would look a fool again so soon after the last time.

"Err, yes, that's right," said Bristol, clearly embarrassed and making his way hastily to the back of the room, where a dangly curtain of beads hung in a doorway. "As most people instinctively realise, the time-space continuum rubs a little thin in laundrettes. It makes the teleportation process easier," he explained.

"I'm sorry, rubs thin?" queried Bill, halting the sheep before he made his way through the curtain.

"Yes, you know. Time passes differently in a laundrette. The machine takes an age while you are in there, but leave for thirty seconds and when you come back it has finished and some git has taken all of your clothes and dumped them in a heap on the grubby lid. Tricksy places, laundrettes. You must have noticed that the people in there often seem like they come from, you know, someplace else."

Bill couldn't help but agree. His washing machine had broken down just two months ago, and the trip to the laundrette had been one of the most harrowing experiences of his life. Up until today of course.

Pushing through the bead curtain after Bristol, he found himself in a room that more closely matched his expectations. A raised platform stood at one end, a big circular device suspended above it in a clear "I am a teleporter" style. In the opposite corner was a comfy-looking three-piece suite arranged around a wicker table. Two albino sheep sat at the table drinking tea and playing Mahjong. They both looked up as Bristol and Bill entered, their combined red-eyed glare quite unsettling.

"Morriss, Borriss," said Bristol in greeting, nodding his head at the two sheep.

"Greetings, Bristol," responded the two sheep, almost simultaneously. It would have been less creepy if it had been simultaneous. The tiny gap had a somewhat planned quality to Bill, as if the two frequently spoke at the same time, had discovered it upset people and had devised an agreed delay between when each other would speak. It would reassure Bill not at all to learn that this was, in fact, exactly the case.

"See, I told you we would have a customer today," said one to the other. Whether it was Morriss or Borriss Bill had no idea.

"As you did yesterday, and you were wrong then," replied the other.

"No, I didn't."

"Did."

"Didn't."

Bristol interrupted with a gentle cough. "Gentlemen, my son is in a hurry. I have the token." Bristol took a hexagonal disk from somewhere in his woolly coat and deposited it in a small fish bowl on a pedestal. "He is to go immediately to South Wales."

Morriss and Borriss raised eyebrows at the term "son," but one look at Bristol's puffed-out chest stalled their words. Glancing at the token, they nodded and rose from their seats, trotting to a booth just opposite the teleporter, where they began strapping strange helmets to their heads.

"A tricky business this teleportation," Bristol began. "Takes two highly trained Operators, and even with the training they must have the Ability."

Bill raised an eyebrow.

"You see, the machine does a lot of the work, but the direction, the essence, the spark comes from the Operators." Bristol huddled close to Bill and pitched his voice conspiratorially. "And Borriss and Morriss are among the best, they'll get you there in no time."

Bill watched the albino sheep adjusting their helmet straps and wished he shared Bristol's confidence. Clearly his sheep-father could sense his unease. He felt a strange bump between his ears and Bristol's voice whispered in his mind.

Goodness, you do have the skill very strongly, said the sheep's voice in his head. *You needn't worry about the teleportation, and I'll show you why.*

Suddenly Bill understood the teleportation process, the memories of having witnessed it occur a hundred times slid neatly into his brain. The Operators, the two albino sheep, were crucial in a teleportation. The associated machinery was clever, sure, and was capable of generating a miniature wormhole on demand, but without the Operators its most useful function was to gently warm the room.

To traverse the minute passageways created by The Puncher you needed a wormhole, but that wormhole had to thread the tiny passageway precisely. This needed immense skill: no machine could accomplish a task that was squarely outside of improbable and nestled right next door to impossible. A consciousness was required; a consciousness of immense focus and dispassionate concentration. Hence the Operators, who would take the embryonic wormhole and send it where it needed to go. Sheep who could undertake this task were rare and revered for their skill.

Borriss and Morriss were the best of their generation, twin orphans who possessed the ability to focus on a task with almost one hundred percent of their enviable intellect. As a result they seemed distant and aloof, almost uncaring, but they were the very best sheep for the job.

Bill gulped and felt a brief self-conscious nuzzle on his hand. He looked down into the old sheep's eyes, wide and watery.

"Oh son, I am so proud. A son of mine, saviour of the world," croaked Bristol, clearly choked up. Bill grinned uneasily.

"I hate goodbyes, I will leave now," said Bristol, water pooling in his eyes. Bill wasn't sure about all this, but on instinct he crouched down and wrapped the old sheep in a tight hug. Bristol's wool was a little scratchy and even mustier close up, but Bill felt a lot of tension leave him in the hug. Releasing the old sheep, he could see tears streaming from Bristol's eyes. Snuffling slightly, Bristol hurried back through the bead curtain.

"We're ready," called Borriss and Morriss, all decked out in shiny metal helmets.

"Right, okay," said Bill, taking his eyes from the curtain. "Let's get this over and done with," he called, striding up onto the platform.

"Stay as still as possible please," said one of the albino sheep. Bill didn't see which one; he had his eyes screwed tightly shut. Everything had happened so fast, and he was so focussed on getting back that he hadn't had a chance to think about what he was about to do. Now as he stood there he realised he was really deeply unhappy about the whole teleportation thing. His stomach was knotted up with dread, and he could feel his body shaking a little. He imagined it might feel like this before your first sky dive, strapped to the parachute and staring wide eyed through the open plane door. He felt (or at least imagined he felt) the whole time-space continuum stretching before him like a vast fifteen-thousand-foot drop, and he wasn't sure he had the courage to jump. At least he didn't have to do anything, and standing very still was about as much as he could manage.

"Initialisation sequence begun," droned Morriss/Borriss. "Lock location."

"Location locked," came the reply. A hum started just below Bill's feet, the vibration travelling through the soles of his feet and up both legs. The hum grew, making his teeth chatter in his jaw until he clamped it tightly closed. His sense of impending doom grew, feeding the flames of panic. He was embarrassed to think what Fern would make of his trepidation. *She probably does this sort of thing all the time*, he thought.

The tone of the hum changed, rising in pitch, and it was now impossible to stop his teeth from rattling.

"Begin transmission," intoned a voice, seeming somewhat distant.

A sudden shift in pressure and Bill's ears popped painfully. A new tightness gripped his skin, like a thousand tiny hooks latching into his flesh and pulling him slightly backwards. Abruptly his head swam, and he would have collapsed to his knees if not for the tiny hooks holding him up. He felt a massive shift around him, like a millisecond burst of a hurricane, gone with the same brutal force with which it had arrived. The tension on the hooks grew, and Bill could feel himself being dragged, frictionless. Suddenly, another pressure change, and Bill's ears equalised again, a second set of hooks, stronger and more urgent than the first, latching into his skin. The second set pulled at right angles to the first, the almost imperceptible pressure building to an agony of conflicted flesh.

Pain blooming, Bill's eyes snapped open. His vision was blurred and fuzzy, as if seen through a water-spotted shower screen, with all colour washed into a palette of greys. A twist wrenched his arm and he gasped in pain, looking down. To his horror, his arm bent and twisted before his eyes, twin streamers breaking off and flowing to the left and directly in front him. Looking around in panic, he could see the same effect elsewhere, his whole body seeming to dissolve amidst an invisible tug of war.

He screamed out, soundless, and could just make out the shapes of Borriss and Morriss through his misty vision. Something was wrong, he knew it. This could not be right.

Borriss and Morriss were vastly skilled special sheep, and not sheep to panic. But right now they were distinctly uncomfortable. Something was definitely not right at all.

In over two hundred jumps, they had never seen anything like this. The human was clearly in pain and looked to be de-molecularising. This in itself was normal. The wormhole was very small, and fitting anything down it was the proverbial elephant through a straw, so everything had to first be broken down to the lowest known unit of matter (two distinct classes of sub-sub-atomic particle: "bits" and "bobs"). The bits and bobs were normal, but rather than draining neatly down the wormhole, like bubbles whirling down a plughole, they swirled and thrashed, seemingly caught in turbulence. Some flowed off one way, some another. Talking during a direction was unheard of. Teleportation took immense brainpower, and the distraction could prove fatal (for the individual being teleported at least). But Borriss and Morriss were very good at teleportation, and under the circumstances one of them (Borriss, as it happened) decided a brief conference was in order.

"Errrr . . ." he began.

Bill had passed through pain and out the far side. His mind mushy, he looked around in a distracted fashion at the whirlwind of him. He'd even lost fear and panic. It had risen up, threatening to overwhelm him and bring welcome unconsciousness. But suddenly it had burst free, losing contact with the rest of him, and feathered away in a sickly pulsing streamer. Where to, who knew. He could see the sheep blurrily. They seemed to be talking.

"Uh hum," replied Morriss, not taking his eyes of the rapidly evaporating Bill.

"What's wrong?"

A decent pause.

"Not sure, something wrong with the direction maybe. Any scheduled maintenance?"

A lengthier pause. Blessed with a photographic memory, Borriss risked the distraction of pulling to mind that morning's continuum maintenance schedule. "No, nothing," he replied, adding, "line 72214, origin Southland NZ, destination South Wales, UK: No maintenance."

A slightly briefer pause.

"Oh," Borriss said.

"Oh what?"

"So you think Bristol meant the old South Wales?" said Morriss.

"Old South Wales?" questioned Borriss.

"Yes, as opposed to the New South Wales in Australia. Much closer and all."

Both sheep thought, brains humming.

"I'm pretty sure he meant the old one," said Borriss.

"Oh," said Morriss. "My bad."

The genius of two Operators ensured a continual direction in the event of an Operator losing concentration (a common occurrence). An unfortunate corollary was that two Operators could conceivably direct to two different locations, opening parallel wormholes to entirely different locations. In most instances the more powerful of the two would naturally dominate, the flow overriding the other without the need for any intervention. Morriss and Borriss were an exactly equal match however, and Bill (in all his constituent parts), was caught in a teleportation vortex, pulled between two incompatible locations.

With the speed of a well-oiled synapse, Morriss switched direction, his thoughts lining up precisely with Borriss and meshing neatly.

Bill had just enough time to notice what looked like a smile on one of the sheep's faces before an almighty pop, a rushing of air, a pull like no other, and the world went black.

Chapter Twenty-Five

Yelling and screaming, Bill tumbled out of thin air and splatted into something soggy, cold, and disturbingly unyielding. Not sheep crap then. It felt like he might have broken his nose, and he was winded. Gasping to re-inflate his lungs, he flopped like a dying fish on to his back. The fish analogy gained new weight as he noticed his foot resting in the gently rippling edge of the sea. A low susurrus of small waves reached his ears, and his whirling brain slowly pieced together the feeling underneath his fingers with the term "wet sand." A Bill-shaped depression lay next to him where he had landed, from goodness knew where. He felt his nose. A bit achy, but not noticeably crunchy or moving. *Things might be looking up,* he thought brightly.

In what was becoming an all too frequent routine he checked himself over for other injuries. He seemed to be okay, except for a ravenous hunger and a very odd hollow feeling in the pit of his stomach. It could have been one and the same thing, the hunger and hollowness. He really hadn't eaten well that day, and he wasn't surprised the teleportation had taken it out of him. That was an experience he never, ever wanted to repeat. Quite aside from the excruciating pain and the fear of instant molecular death, it had left him with a very uncomfortable feeling. He couldn't exactly describe it, but it was like an electrical tingle. It felt as if a horde of tiny creatures were crawling just under the surface of his skin. The thought sent a shiver down his spine and made his stomach churn.

The button was still stuffed down his trousers and seemed to have ridden up uncomfortably. *That could explain some of the aching in my stomach*, he thought wryly, taking the metal box out and dropping it into his lap.

The sheep had said there was a good chance the pigeons would be there to meet him. Maybe. As he looked around, he couldn't see any sign of anyone, or anything (avian or otherwise). The beach stretched away in each direction, curving away to the left and running into a rocky headland to the right. Directly behind him were some sand dunes, rising up sharply so he couldn't tell what was beyond. The sand was okay, a little darker than normal but comfy enough (if wet and cold), and the sea looked a bit dull, a flat grey. He checked his new sheep watch. If they didn't know he was here he wasn't going to make it in time. Tapping his arm near where the sheep had said his chip lay, he muttered under his breath, "C'mon guys."

As if summoned, a grating whirring noise reached his ears, muffled at first but strengthening. He thought it might be coming from behind the dunes, but soon realised the sound was blowing off the sea with the wind. Rising unsteadily to his feet, he unconsciously rubbed down his trousers, trying unsuccessfully to dislodge the soggy sand that clung there.

Casting his gaze over the breakers, he hunted for the source of the sound. While the noise continued to grow he could see nothing. Suddenly something caught his eye, sawing out of the water, a grey triangle that could instil dread and terror in the most courageous. *Still, they can't get me here*, Bill thought, oddly without a shred of fear, but nonetheless backing slowly up the beach. But the triangle grew, steadily advancing through the waves. It was then Bill remembered the Segways. Like a vision of pure horror, the first shark's head cleared the surface of the water, its dull killer's eyes blinking in the unaccustomed air, its vast array of teeth clattering eagerly like twenty haunted chainsaws. Its body was vast and grey and covered in white puckered scars, an unmistakable reek of foetid fish reaching Bill's nostrils the instant the head was above water.

The handlebars of the Segway cleared the foamy water, twin machine guns mounted on each side of the shark's flippers. Behind the lead shark, other dorsal fins were breaking through, the grinning shark advancing quickly now, most of its huge bulk was clear of the surf.

Bill staggered backwards up the beach towards the dunes, slack jawed as the first shark invasion in living memory rolled out of the ocean on the South Wales coast. He could now see the water churning behind the clusters of dorsal fins, and wondered how many were gathered on the seabed.

Awed he still wasn't scared, he guessed he had finally lost all his marbles. The lead shark cleared the water entirely, the all-terrain Segway crunching its way up the shingle as its driver let out a guttural guffaw of triumph. Bill swapped the button to his left hand and grabbed a rock by his feet. With a heave, he hurled it with all his might at the giant fish. With unexpected dexterity, the shark lunged to the side, caught the rock in its jaws, and ground it to powder in one single movement. Bill grabbed another rock and pelted the shark again, with the same result. It hadn't slowed its advance, and was now a mere twenty metres from where Bill stood. Bill reached down and grabbed the biggest rock he could find. Arms surging, he reckoned he could get it twenty metres.

"Eat this, fish face!" he screamed, grunting in exertion as he hurled the large rock at the shark. Barking a short laugh the shark snapped the rock in mid-flight and fell backwards, stone dead, the rock falling sideways from its slack jaws. Other sharks had cleared the surf and cast

246

wary glances at their dead comrade, their eyes swivelling in Bill's direction. They paused their advance.

"Yeah!" shouted Bill, his fist punching the air in triumph as he scooped another rock from the beach. "You guys want some more, yeah, c'mon, I got plenty!" he cackled, tossing the rock from palm to palm. His inner caveman had taken over, and it revelled as he clutched weapon A, the original and still the best. Rock! Despite the jubilation, Bill began to realise that most of the sharks weren't paying him much attention. Instead, they scanned the dunes, grimaces on their ugly fish faces.

A short *crack* that he hadn't heard before, and another shark toppled over dead, then another. Someone was picking them off from the dunes and making short work of it. Another shark toppled. One of the sharks barked some orders into his handlebars, and suddenly they were moving again, zeroing in on a dune thirty metres or so to Bill's left. More and more poured out of the surf, and Bill could tell whoever was shooting the sharks would shortly be overwhelmed.

"Hey, hey, forgot about me!" he shouted, running down the beach waving his arms, now feeling a little foolish about the small rock he clutched, but reluctant to drop it all the same. A smaller shark near the back wheeled his Segway with practised panache, levelling the twin gun barrels at Bill's chest and flippering the trigger on the handlebars.

Five hundred rounds of hot lead death belched out of the barrels at Bill, just as an orange-and-white blur slammed into his side and sent him sprawling in the damp sand. He felt the bullets tug at his jumper as they whistled past, and as he fell he saw the shark cackling, illuminated by the glow of his twin guns. Twisting his head to avoid a mouthful of sand, Bill came face to face with a small corgi, a look of distinct displeasure on its face.

"Yap!" was all the dog said before bounding off and grabbing the shark in the neck, its tiny jaws locking on and bowling the mighty sea beast backwards.

The sharks had reached the dune and were advancing slowly in pincer formation. A small explosion sent sand flying, and a figure clad in military fatigues rolled out of the chaos directly into the midst of the Segways. An AK47 in each arm, the figure brought death, short sharp bursts to each side, dispatching the sharks before they had time to react. One of the rifles jammed, overheated, and the figure hurled it like a discus thrower into a knot of sharks, sending one screaming to the sand. The figure's free arm whipped back and forth, knives blossoming in the gills of three sharks. Leaping high into the air to avoid a shark who had taken aim, the figure hurled two grenades, the deafening roar felling all but two of the enemy. A crunching kick to one of the remaining sharks was followed by a commando roll and a karate chop to the final fish, who collapsed squirming onto the sand.

The scene was utter carnage. Segways were littered everywhere, some still upright, scattered around with the corpses of dead sharks and the twitching bodies of the dying. The figure bent to retrieve the knives, straitening slowly and resting a hand on a hip as if experiencing a twinge. The figure had its back to Bill. It was wearing a headscarf, part of which had come loose to reveal a shock of white, curly hair.

"Not on my watch," said the figure in a terrifyingly familiar voice. "And not in my country," she added, stooping to put a quivering fish out of its misery.

Turning to face him, flanked by two corgis, Bill took in the identity of his saviour.

"Well, don't just stand there!" she said, striding towards him, a string of pearls around her neck, poking out from her fatigues.

"Yes, your M—" he stammered, halfway through an awkward bow.

"No time for that," she waved away his stammering with a white-gloved hand. The other hand clutched a large slab of Semtex, the timer reading fifteen seconds. With a heave, she sent the Semtex hurtling into the surf.

Bill's eyes followed the arc of the bomb, watching as it plopped into the waves amongst hordes of Segwayed sharks. Row upon row, rank upon rank, of marine leviathan, buzzing and rolling their way onto British soil. One of the corgis nipped at Bill's heels as it trotted past, its little body strapped with high explosives.

"This may take a while," she said into a small microphone stitched into her glove, her tone unruffled and calm as if discussing a polo match entering extra time. "How many were you expecting at Great Yarmouth?" A brief pause. "Yes, well, I think they are all here." With a roar, the Semtex detonated, a spout of water erupting from the waves, a blast of air knocking Bill on his arse.

"Pardon?" she shouted above the noise. "Yes, all of them." She bit off the words with impatience. "Of course I can hold them, but some help would be lovely. Now if you don't mind I have work to do."

She opened fire with the assault rifle, her free hand working grenades into the advancing lines. Still the sharks came though, their monstrous wheels grinding out of the waves and over the shingle sand shoreline. A knot appeared out of a large breaker, moving faster than the others, and for a brief second Bill could see them being overrun. Britain's last line of defence gave a short whistle, flicking a white eyebrow at the shapes ploughing through the foam.

A blur of orange shot out from behind the dunes, hurtled into the advancing lines and detonated with a mighty roar. Bill could feel the heat of the explosion from where he stood, and as the shock wave hit he staggered back a few steps. Catching a heel, he fell backwards, sprawling in a heap. He was getting bored of falling onto the wet sand.

"Blast," muttered Bill's saviour, cut glass tones somehow reaching him over the gun's deadly rattle and the eerie electric thrum. "Why did it have to be, Jasper? And what are you still doing here?" she snapped at Bill.

"Right, sorry," replied Bill, hauling himself to his feet, the seat of his trousers now even soggier from the damp sand. He glanced at the small silver box in his hands, the bright red button on the top. Slipping it into his pocket, he ran from the beach, through the dunes and to the road.

The dunes only lasted twenty metres or so before sloping sharply up to what looked like a concrete flood barrier. A set of steps ran up to the top, and beyond them was a single carriageway road. A sleek black sports car screeched to a halt in front of him, the passenger door flying open invitingly. Bill tried to ignore who was driving, and happily succeeded.

"Get in," said Clyde. "Everyone else is in Yarmouth, Keith is flipping out, and we're at EOTW minus thirty-six minutes."

"Right, sorry," said Bill, jumping into the passenger seat.

"Do you have the, you know, the item," said Clyde, eagerly.

Bill gave him a sidelong glance, his eyes squinted suspiciously before he remembered himself. "Oh yes, definitely. Nice and safe." He enthused, suddenly conscious of the dull weight in his trousers. *What would happen if I pressed it here?* he thought, *just me and him.* He eyed Clyde again, before turning his attention out of the window, at the scenery that was rapidly dropping away.

"Flying car then," he said. Clyde nodded, momentarily distracted by something.

"Bit passé, don't you think? Been done before and all that," Bill added.

"Well," said Clyde at last, "hopefully this will give you a chance to relax. Sit back, we are taking this thing to maximum speed, it shouldn't take more than fifteen minutes."

Bill wasn't given a chance to concur of his own free will. Clyde pecked a button on the dash and the sheer force of acceleration pushed him back into his seat. For the next fifteen minutes, it took all his effort to just breathe. The pigeon was also forced back in his seat but seemed to have no such difficulty drawing breath.

At last the flying car decelerated sufficiently for Bill to peel his tongue from the roof of his mouth. He glanced down at Clyde's seat. The leather was spotlessly clean and unblemished beneath the pigeon's bum. It was nearly all the proof he needed. Nearly.

"We are almost there now. Hold on, we are going in," said Clyde.

"What's the time?" asked Bill.

"What?" said Clyde, his voice distracted as he navigated the car towards the ground.

"The time, what is it?"

"It's 9:45 in the morning, now please be quiet, I need to concentrate."

"Clyde, Clyde!" came Keith's strident tones over the intercom.

"On my way, Keith," replied the pigeon, manoeuvring the car into final approach on the A452.

"Good, good. Get it here sharpish. We have the Shark King himself on video conference making a ransom request and all hell has broken loose where you boys just left from. That button is our only hope."

Not quite, thought Bill. When Clyde had told him the time, he hadn't even glanced at the watch on his ankle, his right ankle. The leg had never even moved, and it was the final piece of proof that Bill needed.

The landing had been a roller coaster of a ride, and Bill was glad he hadn't eaten for some time. He and Clyde now barrelled down corridors marked increasingly restricted and top secret. The only barrier to this headlong progress had been the checkpoints and scanners, but after a single scan it would seem Keith had given instructions that they should not be delayed, and the pigeon and human skirted around all the additional security deep into the heart of the command centre.

"Just up ahead," said Clyde, not remotely out of breath despite the punishing pace, pointing at a pair of large metal doors. Bill, on the verge of exhaustion, grunted in reply and heaved open the left-hand door. Two guards, large rifles at their hips, stood on the far side, but when they saw Clyde they allowed them through.

A large oak table dominated the centre of the room. Keith and about twenty or so people Bill didn't recognise were clustered around its vast shiny surface. They were all staring at a huge video screen on the far wall. The image on the screen showed the Shark King in gruesome detail, a smug grin on his face. Fern sat on the far side, and Bill's heart leapt to see her. The grin she returned him sent his heart soaring and banished some of the hollowness from his stomach. For a second at least.

"Bill, just in the nick of time," blustered Keith. "Do you have the button?"

"Oh no, oh no, not the button," gasped the Shark King, his eyes growing improbably wide in shock. If he recognised Bill, he didn't mention it. "If you press that then all of my plans will come to naught," he wailed.

"Quick, Bill, press it, press it!" urged Clyde, hopping from one foot to the other.

Bill took the small silver box from his pocket, flicking the safety cover off the small, red button.

"Yes, yes, do it!" encouraged Clyde, bobbing his head in a pigeon frenzy. All of the eyes in the room were on Bill, including those of the Shark King. He had an expectant, eager look. Not the look of someone facing the destruction of their grand master plan.

"You'd like that, wouldn't you?" Bill said, his tone cold and flat, his eyes fixed on Clyde's.

"Yes, yes, do it!" Clyde repeated, still bobbing frenetically. Everyone else in the room was holding their breath. He could feel their combined confusion beating down on him like waves of heat from a gas patio heater. The clock above the video display, presumably counting down until the end of the world, read three minutes.

"Er, Bill," said Fern, self-consciously breaking the tension and nodding at the button in his hand. Bill gave a very slight shake of his head in her direction, barely even a twitch of his neck muscles. Bill would never realise it, but that was his first ever act of true conviction. One hundred per cent certainty of purpose. I KNOW EXACTLY WHAT I AM DOING, said the shake of his head. And it said it in capitals. With an incline of her head, Fern responded in the only way that someone faced with this conviction could: with a resounding okay. And like flicking a switch, one of the beams of confusion winked out, to be replaced by a bar of solid faith and trust, flowing from her to him. Lifting her head to meet his gaze, she flashed him half a smile. He could read it, its meaning forming in his mind unbidden. *Go ahead, champ. I've got your back.*

"Yes, you'd like that, wouldn't you?" Bill repeated, turning his gaze to the screen and fixing it on the Shark King.

The Shark King looked momentarily confused, recovering after just a moment. "Er, no no, don't press it," he garbled.

Bill's face cracked into a smile, wide, shiny, and empty.

"Well, okay then!" he said brightly. Flipping the safety cover back on, he let the box fall from his hand, then snatched the revolver from the back of his jeans. Whipping the gun around he fired a single shot, Clyde's head disappearing in a puff of feathers.

Time seemed to stand still. With a hollow clang, the button case hit the hard metal floor, only to be crushed beneath Bill's booted heel. As the button was ground to dust, the spell holding the others motionless was broken. The two guards took a horrified glance at the beheaded pigeon, prone on the floor, and grappled for their weapons, rage-filled eyes turning on Bill. But they were too slow. With a precise karate chop and a neat little kick delivered mid pirouette, Fern felled them both, snatched their weapons as they dropped, and levelled them on Keith and his men. She needn't have worried as they just stood there dumbstruck, staring alternately at Clyde, the crushed button, and Bill, who had not taken his eyes from the screen for a second. He hadn't even blinked.

"Oh, you utter bastard!" came an enraged scream, but not from inside the room. Wobbling onto the screen came a tall thin man with short ginger hair and an evil face. His hands clutched his ears, and a pair of earphones with a microphone were slung around his neck. Bill had seen the earphones before, in Room IIB at the Jerry Co building, along with an imprisoned pigeon that looked a lot like Clyde. "I won't be able to hear right for a week!" spat the ginger-haired man on screen, before ripping the headphones from his neck and hurling them to the floor.

"Mr Gring, what are you doing? Get off the camera and back to controlling the robotic pigeon drone!" garbled the Shark King.

Mr Gring rubbed his ears, his eyes staring murderously out from the enormous conference screen. "I can't you fool, that idiot has just shot out the control array."

The Shark King looked shocked at being addressed in such away, but Mr Gring took no notice, his eyes fixed firmly on Bill.

"You will pay for that, you useless worm," spat Mr Gring.

"Where is the real Clyde?" Bill demanded, unfazed by Mr Gring's sudden appearance.

"It doesn't matter!" barked the Shark King. "It would have been more fun this way, but either way your fate is sealed. In less than two minutes my weather device will be active. You are all doomed!" he roared, hammering his desk with his fins.

Bill glanced up at the display above the screen. Sure enough, the clock counted down. 1:46, 1:45, 1:44 . . . His face crumpled, the sureness leaving his brow, his muscles sagging.

"That's right, human. You think you are so damned clever," cackled the Shark King. "You never could have stopped me. You were right to destroy the button; it was never linked to the system. Quite the opposite, though it seems you figured that out at least. No, there is no override, no backup, no secondary control. Right here, this room is the only control centre. The only point of failure, snug within my impregnable fortress. Hahahahahaha!" roared the shark with laughter.

With an effort Bill's face sagged some more, a tinge of panic in his eyes. Tearing their gaze from the fake-dead-Clyde, all eyes were now fixed on the screen, and the doomsday clock above it counting down humanity's last moments. 1:05, 1:04, 1:03 . . .

Mr Gring whispered something in the Shark King's ear and stalked from view, still rubbing his ears.

"And do you know how I am going to celebrate, worm?" continued the Shark King, his guttural voice swimming with glee. "I am going to toast the dawn of the Shark Age with a bowl of your favourite food, your beloved cereal." He reached under the desk and pulled out a bowl and the box of cornflakes he had taken from Bill.

"I had so hoped you would be there to see this, so dreamt of watching your face as I toasted my victory. In some ways, this is even better than if you had pressed the button, because now I can see your face. Britak Tain—hah! How does it feel, worm, to watch me eat your favourite food, your last request, moments before your doom?"

0:47, 0:46, 0:45.

Upending the box, he shook some cereal into the bowl, but not nearly enough as the flow dried to a trickle.

0:30, 0:29, 0:28.

"Blasted stuff is stuck!" grunted the shark, giving the box a tap.

0:24, 0:23, 0:22.

Grunting in annoyance, he gave the box a violent shake.

0:19, 0:18, 0:17.

Still no more cereal flowed, something was wedged. With a grunt of frustration, the Shark King gave the box a heavy whack. With a delicate tinkle something rectangular and black, about five centimetres by two centimetres and the width of a pencil, slid delicately from the box and into the bowl, accompanied by a flow of corn flakes. The object looked very similar to the doomsday clock above the screen, except much smaller, and about five seconds fast. Bill's mask of uncertainty and defeat slid away, his lips forming into a vicious smile.

"*Bon appetit!*" Bill said.

0:03, 0:02, 0:01 read the small device in the shark's breakfast bowl, before a brief flash and the image on the screen turned to grey fuzz. Over the screen, the doomsday clock counted down.

Three, two, one . . .

Chapter Twenty-Six

Zero.

And the world did not end.

The debriefing room was silent. You could hear a pin drop. You could hear the molecules in a pin jumbling against each other, wondering if they were about to drop. The room was so quiet you could hear the potential energy of a pin, held aloft, thrumming in anticipation of making a really big noise. After an exhilarating drop of course.

It had been chaos in the conference room. No one other than Bill understood what had just happened. They had tried to arrest him for murdering Clyde, until they noticed that rather than bleeding, the headless pigeon corpse was smoking and crackling. There had been a lot of shouting, until Keith had taken control of the situation. Bill had been marched to the debriefing room where he had been sitting for what felt like hours. He had gone through everything half a dozen times, but there were still questions.

The debriefing room was packed. Or rather, one half of the room was packed. Bill stretched out in his half of the room on a rather uncomfortable black plastic chair. In front of him was a table on which an old school tape recorder turned lazily, its metallic tape faultlessly documenting the absolute absence of any noise whatsoever.

The other side of the table was crammed, wall to wall, with what he understood to be the "top brass." A number of wooden perches had been brought into the room and about two dozen pigeons sat blinking across at him. Keith sat on the edge of the room, his relative seniority letting Bill know how important the rest of the crowd were. Crammed behind the pigeons were half-a-dozen humans. Someone coughed. Bill thought he recognised the prime minister, who was huddled near the back next to a very beefy-looking woman with red hair and a particularly ancient looking pigeon. Bill raised an eyebrow.

"And when," began the pigeon who had coughed, a piebald bird in a blue pin stripe suit. "When did you realise that Clyde had been replaced with a robotic double?"

Bill paused.

"I pieced it together really," *During a near death experience, as it happens.* "I saw the robotic control panel when I first met Clyde. Of course, I didn't know what I was looking for then—it was a shock discovering that pigeons could talk, so I didn't think much of it. It was under the wing," he said, pointing into his own armpit. "Which is the same place that the Jerry Co robots had theirs."

The pigeon bobbed its head and gestured for him to continue. Bill gave a sigh—he'd gone through all this already.

"My initial realisation was based on two facts. First was how clumsy Clyde seemed, far more than any pigeon I've ever seen. Secondly was the fact that he didn't ever seem to need to poo." As if to illustrate his point, the suited piebald pigeon let out a stream of white that was immediately cleaned up by a scuttling guanodrone. "In all the time I spent with Clyde not once did he feel the call of nature. The flying car ride back to base was fifteen minutes, and Clyde's seat was spotless when we landed. I understand that this would be quite a feat for a pigeon—for a real pigeon, that is."

A few pigeons in the room bobbed their heads in agreement.

"That gave me the tip, but when I thought about it there was more evidence to suggest that Clyde wasn't a real bird. While I was in Clyde's office I saw the large portrait of the war hero pigeon, *Mary of Exeter*, that hangs opposite his desk. In the Jerry Co building I saw a control array that showed the same painting on the monitor. I must have been looking at the controls for the robotic Clyde, the screen showing what was currently in camera shot. That also means that the real Clyde was, and is, a prisoner in that room. He looked in a bad way; I do hope you are doing something about that."

The pigeon bobbed his head and flapped a wing. This seemed a little evasive to Bill, but he carried on nonetheless.

"Later at the Jerry Co building I saw a cabinet full of robotic pigeon drones, which at the time I assumed were stuffed pigeons. The cabinet also held a sack of real pigeon feathers, which I assume were for use in making the drones."

"Ah yes," said the pigeon, holding up a copy of *The Metro* newspaper in one claw. "We were aware of a number of enforced pluckings in the London area. No doubt London pigeons were selected to ensure the plumage closely matched the pigeons they were hoping to duplicate."

Bill nodded. It was no more lunatic than anything else, after all.

"And, finally, once I was sure I was dealing with an imposter, I asked Clyde for the time. He recited the exact time without even checking his watch. Of course, as the drone was under remote control, there was no need for the controller to lift the pigeon's leg to know the time."

The men, women and pigeons opposite conferred briefly, then deferred again to the piebald pigeon in the blue pin-stripe suit.

"And, while being held prisoner by the sharks you acted on this assumption that the Clyde you had met was in fact a robotic impostor, despite not having had an opportunity to confirm this theory, and concealed some high explosives in a box of cereal?"

Bill nodded again.

"Which you left with the Shark King."

Nod.

"With the timer set to just before the activation of the doomsday device?"

An impatient nod. He had gone through this so many times already, and he was starving.

"And the true purpose of the button," continued the pigeon, oblivious to Bill's growing frustration and mounting hunger. "How did you deduce its true purpose?"

Bill sighed. This one was a gut feeling from the beginning, so these guys might not like his reasoning.

"Look," he began, spreading his arms wide. "It was all a little ridiculous wasn't it? Evil genius builds a doomsday device and handily puts together an emergency override button that could be stolen. I mean, look at it guys, it practically screams portability," he pointed at the mashed-up remains of the button on the desk. "Not only that, but in addition it would appear the self-destruct button or whatever cannot be deactivated, and seemingly would work from anywhere on the planet!"

Everyone, human and pigeon, stared at him.

"Oh c'mon guys, sounds like a horrendous design flaw in a machine designed to enable someone to take over the world. The whole notion was ridiculous."

Bill detected some embarrassement, but a tall, scrawny woman with horn-rimmed glasses retorted, "As ridiculous as an army of killer robots turning on themselves because they have been given a description of each other?" Bill gave an evasive shrug. Okay, so that was also ridiculous, and had happened.

"Anyway," he continued, "I figured if Clyde was bogus, then so was his information, which meant that the button was bogus. I thought to myself, what would they gain by us pressing this button when I got back to HQ? Then it hit me. The button was a detonator, and Clyde, the false Clyde, was packed with explosives." They already knew this to be true; a mechanical autopsy on the impostor Clyde had confirmed it.

"I'm sure all that fancy scanning technology you use on the place might have picked it up, so they needed some way to get it in here unnoticed. What better way than brought in by one of your own, separate from the bomb and in a great rush. The Shark King would have gotten a massive kick out of you lot pressing the button that blew you all away. With central command destroyed, with all of you dead, he may not have needed a doomsday device at all."

A lengthy pause, and for a second Bill thought it might be over and he could go and eat some more food, when the piebald pigeon piped up again.

"If you knew all this, why did you hurry back?"

Bill swallowed. This was tough. After all, how could he explain that he couldn't help wondering if he was wrong?

"The sharks had to be stopped. I needed the Shark King to taunt me with the cereal, as I knew he would. I needed him to have it with him, in his command centre, for the device controls to be destroyed."

With relief, Bill saw the pigeon nodding, and after a pause gave the signal that Bill could leave. Rising unsteadily from the chair, Bill made his way gratefully to the door.

"Err, one last thing, Mr Posters," said the pigeon, not looking up from its notes. "If you knew that the automaton formerly known as Clyde was packed with high explosives, how did you know that shooting him would not have triggered the bomb, killing us all and possibly dooming mankind to slavery? The head was the only part with no explosive material inside. A fine shot under the circumstances."

Bill gulped, a sickly smile spreading on his lips. He really hadn't thought of that. Knees weak he ignored the question, pushed through the door, and stepped into the corridor.

Fern was waiting just outside the door, a plate from the canteen in her hands. Bill's stomach gave an uncomfortable lurch at the sight of her, and not just because of the food.

"You survived then?" she asked, nodding at the door to the debriefing room.

"Only just," Bill grinned, feeling a little lighter and less tired all of a sudden. "It's good to see you," he blurted, and was rewarded with a sunny smile.

"You too. You were brilliant back there you know," she said, and now it was Bill's turn to smile. "You were pretty good too." He took the tray from her hands and made his way down the corridor.

Fern walked by his side. "You still hungry?" she asked.

"Ravenous, I can't seem to shake the feeling, but I am sure this will help," he said. "And after this, I am going to sleep for two days and take a holiday," he paused. "A three week holiday!"

"Three weeks?" exclaimed Fern. "Oh, I don't think you'll get that approved, oh no, not after what I just heard."

"What you heard?" This sounded ominous.

"C'mon, champ, get that food down, then meet me in briefing room 2c. We've got a world to save!" Fern strode off, a bright skip in her step.

With a sigh, Bill crumpled into a seat in the corridor, the tray smacking against his knees. *Right,* he thought, *gotta save the world again have we? But not until I'm full and had a good night's sleep.* Not until then.

****

The Sheep of War

(The Sequel to *The Truth about Sharks and Pigeons*) Prologue and Chapters 1 and 2

Prologue

Gareth shifted his weight slowly from foot to foot. He'd been on his feet for almost twelve hours. His fingertips stung from the poison that he had been using in the bait traps, and his overalls smelt of sulphur and sweat. The man at the desk in front of him wrinkled his nose, as if catching the scent for the first time, although Gareth had been standing in the man's office for almost thirty minutes.

A bronze nameplate on the desk told him that the rotund man in the high-backed leather chair was 'Mr E. R. Shank - General Manager'. Mr Shank hadn't said a word. He hadn't even acknowledged Gareth's presence. Mr Shank was working his way through a pile of papers, reading each one for a few minutes before signing the bottom and shifting the page to a wire tray. Gradually, the pile of papers in front of Mr Shank dwindled, until just one remained. Gareth considered clearing his throat to remind Mr Shank that he was there, but something told him that would be a bad idea.

Mr Shank sighed and leaned back in the chair, the leather and wood creaking under his bulk. He pulled the reading glasses from his nose, folded them with exaggerated care and placed them in the pocket in his jacket.

"You realise why you are here of course, hmmmMMM."

The strange humming noise at the end of Mr Shank's sentence rose in volume and pitch, leaving Gareth unsure if it was a question or a statement. He went with question.

"No, sir."

Mr Shank's eyebrows quirked up and he made an unsettling snorting noise, breathing in and out so rapidly Gareth wondered if the man were about to lapse into a seizure.

"Really? I wonder at that, I truly do. You must of course realise that we have received a complaint from one of our customers, hhhhhmmmmmmMMMM."

Gareth cursed his luck. He had suspected as much, but he had dared hope that this was something different. He needed this job, so very badly.

"Sir, you must understand, I only—."

Mr Shank cut him off mid-sentence.

"Here at Babbage Pest Control, we pride ourselves on customer service, hmmm. Customer service, above all else, hmmm. How long have you been with BPC, Mr Tuppence?"

Gareth waited for the strange humming noise that would indicate the end of Mr Shank's sentence, but none came.

"Three and a half months, sir," he replied.

"And you have been performing pest control for our customers, United Plumbing and Drainage, for how long?"

"Also three and a half months, sir."

"Good, and in that time, when working at their central London facility, how often did they impress upon you that room 86 was out of bounds?"

Gareth could sense where this was going now. It looked like he was going to be looking for a new job.

"It was re-iterated to me every morning, sir."

Mr Shank smiled, as if he had scored a telling point in a debate. "And earlier this afternoon, did you, or did you not, enter room 86?"

"Yes sir, I did, but you have to—."

Mr Shank rocked forward in his chair, swept the reading glasses out of his pocket and perched them on his nose.

"It says here that you entered the room to pursue an intruder?"

Gareth nodded.

"And yet no trace of this mysterious man could be found. They found only you, asleep on the floor of the chamber."

Gareth peered at the piece of paper in front of Mr Shank, but the desk was so wide he couldn't make out the tightly curled writing. It must be the complaint from United Plumbing and Drainage.

"I wasn't asleep, sir, I had been—"

"Knocked unconscious, hmmmm. Yes, I have spoken with your supervisor, Mr Taylor, already."

Mr Shank's tone told Gareth that he didn't believe him. It wasn't a lie though; it certainly wasn't the sort of thing he would make up. The United Plumbing and Drainage facility in London was huge, a massive warren of rooms and tunnels. He had been working in the corridor outside room 86 when part of the wall had exploded inwards, filling the corridor with dust. Two figures had emerged from the dust cloud. The first was dressed in what looked like black pyjamas. A black cowl was wrapped around its head, showing just the eyes, and it carried a long curved sword. The second was a man, naked except for a blue towel wrapped around his waist.

"You must let me come with you," the figure in black had said. The man in the blue towel sighed. "You know that you cannot. I alone can face it. It must be defeated, held back."

Shouts could be heard in the distance. The figure in black took a step forward, but the man in the towel laid a hand on its arm.

"Please, I must go alone, it has always been thus."

The figure in black hesitated.

"I won't really be gone, not forever, not completely," said the man in the towel. The figure in black shook its head. The shouts were getting louder. With a curse, the figure in black turned and ran towards the shouts.

The man in the towel then turned his attention to the door to room 86. He reached out for the handle. Gareth knew from experience that it was locked, and was about to say as much when the man in the towel suddenly thrust forward, ripping the door from its hinges and sending it crashing inwards. The man then disappeared into the room.

"Hey, no one's supposed to go in there," said Gareth, aware how stupid that sounded. He raced to the open doorway and stepped into room 86, then stopped.

The room was enormous. The ceiling towered high above, and the far side of the room was only just visible. In the centre of the chamber was an enormous block of white marble. Veins of colour, rich reds, browns and blues, swam over the marble's surface. He had never seen anything like it in his life.

The man in the towel was next to the marble, his hands pressed to the surface. Suddenly the floor shook, rattling so hard that Gareth nearly fell to his knees. When he looked up, the man had sunk halfway *into* the marble. As he watched, the man pressed forward, sinking slowly into the great block. Gareth rubbed his eyes, and when he opened them again only the back of the man's head and a foot were visible. The floor shook again, more violently this time, and he was thrown from his feet. His head hit the wall and lights bloomed in his vision. He collapsed to the floor as the ground continued to buck and roll. Then he lost consciousness.

Mr Shank's angry voice banished the memory.

"I'm sorry, Sir, what did you say?" said Gareth.

"I said," replied Mr Shank, every syllable ringing with annoyance, "that it makes little difference, hmmm, whether you were asleep or unconscious. You were not permitted to enter the room, and you did."

Gareth opened his mouth, but Mr Shank held up both hands.

"Enough. I do not wish to hear your ludicrous explanation, I have heard it once already from Mr Taylor. Utter poppycock, hmmmm. Your employment is terminated with immediate effect, hmmmmmMmmMm."

This last hum had the definite ring of finality, and Gareth knew it would be futile to argue further. With a nod he turned and walked from Mr Shank's office, not bothering to close the door behind him, despite Mr Shank's bellowed command.

He walked quickly along the corridor and out into the night air. He couldn't wait to get out of the stinking overalls. He'd worry about work tomorrow.

Mr Shank was right about one thing, his story did sound like utter poppycock. But, strange as it was, it had happened. And he had kept the oddest part of the whole incident to himself. He had no chance of anyone believing *that* part of it. Gareth knew a bit about head injuries, so he knew that the final part of his experience *had* to be a hallucination, or a dream, or something.

As he lay on the floor, just before he fell unconscious, a pigeon had run into the chamber. It had bobbed its head at the marble block for a few moments before noticing Gareth on the floor.

"Oh dear," the pigeon had said. "You shouldn't be here at all."
Then Gareth had blacked out.

Chapter One

"Scan complete," droned the robotic voice of the scanner.

Bill swung his legs off the edge of the narrow bed. This was his ninth scan. Maybe this time they'd get some clues as to what was wrong with him.

The scanner was a vast cylindrical device, its entire surface made from a single piece of metal. It hulked in the room, the top of the cylinder brushing the ceiling fifteen feet from the ground. The bed slid in and out of a hole in the scanner. When inside, all you could see was a bright white light. The light seemed to have no source, no depth, no variation in intensity whatsoever, giving Bill the unsettling feeling that he was floating in white space. Cables ran from the scanner to the control panel. An attractive lady with long blonde hair and wearing a bright white lab coat was examining the screen above the control panel.

"Anything, Lucy?" he asked.

Lucy's brow furrowed, either in concern or confusion, before offering Bill an apologetic smile.

"The same I'm afraid, Bill. We can't find anything wrong with you. I mean, there are some odd readings here, and your genetic residue rates are all high. Very high indeed, but that's all to be expected, given who you are."

That all meant nothing to Bill, but he had learnt that any explanation would be even more incomprehensible. Lucy was staring at him. Cocking her head to one side, she made her way around the control panel to stand next to him.

"We *will* work out what's wrong with you Bill, really we will." With that she reached out to pat his knee, causing him to jump.

"Ehem!"

Bill jumped again, this time down from the scanner bed, almost knocking Lucy to the floor as he did so.

"Not interrupting, am I?" said Fern, her voice laced with irritation, her arms crossed firmly.

"What? Err, of course not. Thank you very much, err, Doctor Lucy," he said, grabbing his coat from a chair and making his way past Fern through the open door.

"She's not, you know," said Fern, joining Bill as he walked down the corridor.

"Not what?"

"What do you think? Not a Doctor you dimwit. She just runs the tests, don't give her any ideas." Fern stressed the word 'ideas' heavily, to the point where Bill wasn't sure she was still talking about medical qualifications. Bill nodded in agreement. It was the safest thing to do. He caught Fern studying him out of the corner of her eye as they walked. Abruptly her expression changed, concern clouding her features.

"We'll find out what's wrong Bill, really we will."

Bill nodded. He hoped they would. Or at least he thought he did. His mind was fuzzy most of the time lately, so he wasn't a hundred percent sure. Besides, he had seen an advert on TV about cruelty to bears in South East Asia and he couldn't shake the feeling he should be doing something about it. Sure, he was a little bit crook, but how did that compare to the suffering of countless defenceless animals? He grimaced at the thought. If only he hadn't *already* given all his money to charity.

"We will," Fern repeated, worried by his lack of response and misreading his expression.

"I know, I know," he reassured her, feeling guilty at having caused her concern. "You really mustn't worry, I'll be fine." She still looked worried, possibly even more so.

Suddenly the floor rose up to meet him and he would likely have broken his nose had Fern not wrapped her arms around him and eased him to the ground.

"Whoa, easy champ," she gasped.

Black and white spots swam in his vision and the world shrunk to a tunnel of light. For a second he thought he could hear his own voice, shrill and high-pitched in a maniacal cackle, and then it was gone. He felt like his heart had stopped beating, but now his pulse ran wildly and he clawed air into his lungs. Slowly his vision inched outwards again, the tunnel expanding, more light flowing into his world. The flashing spots didn't disappear entirely this time, staying in his vision like fireflies dancing on a night breeze, or—given he had never *actually* seen a firefly—like a tiny continuous fireworks display. He could feel Fern stroking his back and he felt his pulse slow. This was the worst one yet, and if the others were anything to go by, he didn't have much time.

Fern pulled him to his feet.

"I know, I know, we'll hurry," she said. "Through here, it'll be quicker."

Taking Bill by the arm, she moved towards a door marked 'Security Area 86, Clearance Required.'

Fern fished her pass out of her pocket and slid it into the slot at hip height to the left of the door. With a dull clunk the door slid away to reveal a door frame three feet thick and a room swathed in darkness. As they made their way into the room fluorescent bulbs set high in the ceiling flickered into life.

Shuffling forward, Bill was stopped in his tracks by the sight before him.

"Wow," he said.

The scanner he had just left had been an impressive piece of machinery. What stood before them bordered on the obscene, such was its immensity. The room was of cavernous proportions, the ceiling a distant notion, the far side of the room a good hundred metres away. Every surface was tiled with small white hexagons. Each one couldn't have been much bigger than his palm. Despite the room's vast proportions, it felt almost claustrophobic, so overshadowed were they by the structure in the centre. It rose almost all the way to the ceiling and spanned the length of the room. Its surface looked like marble, milky white with greys and oranges and blues, and was quite beautiful. It looked so smooth, he bet it would be cool to the touch.

"Councel," said Fern.

"Sorry?" said Bill.

"This is Councel."

Bill stared up at the massive block. So, this was the pigeon super-computer that worked out everyone's chances of saving the world. This machine had ranked him as the world's 768,271st best hope, which was unfortunate given the 768,270 people better equipped for the job were dead. This information had sent Clyde the talking pigeon to seek Bill out and share with him the Truth about sharks and pigeons. Only, Bill had never *actually* met Clyde, as the bird he spoke to was really a robotic imposter planted by the Shark King.

"This is Councel? I thought that was a computer, but also a group of people, like Parliament. This looks like a piece of modern art." His eyes slid along its length again. "An incredibly *large* piece of modern art..."

"Well, it's definitely not art," Fern replied. "It's a giant super-computer. We think. Technically it's a vast neural network, so in some ways it's a very large brain. We're not supposed to come through here. I've only been able to since they upgraded my clearance, but it is the quickest way to the dining hall, and I figured, well, you know."

Bill did know, only too well. Sharp talons of hunger were already clawing at his stomach. He took his weight off Fern and tried to stand a little straighter. He could only just manage it, but he could stand without her help. He knew it was crazy, but he didn't want to appear weak in front of the giant marble brain. He shuffled his way along the edge of the room.

"Who made it?" Bill asked.

"Councel? No idea," said Fern. "They don't really tell us a lot about it to be honest. I just know they consult Councel on the big stuff, including rankings for people like me and you."

"It's pretty," said Bill. His eyes traced the swirls and patterns on its surface as they walked. For some reason its appearance tugged at his memory, though he was fairly sure he had never seen a ga-gillion tonne slab of marble before.

Following the lines made his eyes feel funny, and for a second his head swam. His vision blurred; the light dimmed momentarily. The shuffling of their feet was joined by another noise, near silent at first, but rising. The rustling of leaves on an autumn breeze, footsteps through freshly fallen snow, the distant crackle of an open fire. No, none of those. Whispers. It sounded like a hundred whispers, a hundred thousand whispers, all talking at once, overlaid and multiplied and interwoven.

"Do you. . ." he began, turning to Fern, and then stopped. She wasn't there. The whispers rose like a wave and then receded. What the hell?

Panic fuelled a rush of energy and he hobbled around in a circle. She couldn't have just vanished, there was simply nowhere to go. Dumbstruck, he found himself facing Councel, milky veins of blue converging just in front of his nose. Suddenly the blue veins shifted, sliding in every direction. They were forming letters, oozing like tendrils of oil snaking across water. It wasn't a word, just four letters. 'BOPL', it said. Staring at the smooth surface, he was overcome with a desire to find out what it felt like. Reaching out he placed his right palm on the surface. It wasn't cool, not at all. It was hot, too hot, and with a flare of pain he tried to pull his hand away but couldn't. It was stuck to the surface. In panic he pushed at the surface with his other hand. Vicious cold instantly enveloped his left hand, sending splinters of ice racing up his arm. Like an explosion the whispers erupted in his mind, no more intelligible than before, but a hundred times the volume. He would have collapsed to his knees had the pain from his hands not forced him upright.

Abruptly the whispering stopped, replaced by a thunderous silence.

"It is him," said a voice. Clear and distinct.

"No, there is not enough," came another voice, firmer than the first, almost angry.

"Still, it is him," said the first voice, sadness hanging off every syllable.

"Then we are doomed," said a third voice. The deep barrelled tones echoed over and over in his head until suddenly they stopped, and he had the distinct impression the owners of the unseen voices had fled. He could feel a new presence though. Massive, hungry and malevolent.

"I SEE YOU," growled the voice, sending shudders down his spine. The heat and cold from his palms raced up his arms and engulfed his body in an agony of fire and ice. He felt his heart stop, crushed in the grip of the voice. He howled in torment and anguish and fell backwards into darkness.

"Metalan bord re-doman. Letish ran brekaran! Ran brekaran!" The words, gibberish to his ears but spoken by a voice he recognised, forced their way into the darkness. He was slipping away. Suddenly another voice, one he could never mistake, called to him and pulled him back from the void.

"Bill! Bill! Wake up!"

His head was resting on something soft, the ground under his back was cold and hard. Groggily he peeled open an eye. Fern's face hovered above him, her eyes shiny with unshed tears of fear.

"Thank the elders! Are you okay?"

He nodded, or at least hoped he nodded, his neck muscles seemed to be in a different time zone.

"They're getting worse, aren't they? You've never blacked out before."

Before? What did she mean? He was sure he had never had *that*, whatever it was, happen to him. It was no wonder he had blacked out, he felt lucky to be alive. The memory of the agony was enough to make him sweat. The pain. And that *voice*.

He struggled to a sitting position and could see how close they were to Councel. Fern's back was to it and the smooth surface was only a few inches from her long brown hair.

"Careful Fern," he said, scrabbling his way across the floor and away from Councel. "Don't touch it."

"Touch it? Why ever not?" she replied, reaching out and placing a hand on the smooth surface.

With a scream Bill tried to haul himself to his feet to pull her away, but his legs buckled and he ended up in a heap on the floor. Fern was quickly by his side.

"Bill, whatever is wrong?" she pleaded.

"Didn't it. . . didn't it hurt?" he panted.

Fern's look of confusion answered his question. "Hurt? Bill, we aren't supposed to be in here with Councel, but it really isn't considered to be dangerous. You can't get hurt by touching it."

Bill's mind reeled. She can't have not noticed. The pain was unimaginable, and what had she thought he was doing, hands pressed to the surface and screaming in agony.

"But, when I touched it..." he began, before noticing the look of worry growing in Fern's eyes.

"Touched it? You didn't touch it Bill. You landed right there," she pointed at the floor where he had woken. "You fainted. Came down like a sack of spuds. Cracked your head too, I'm amazed you're not bleeding. But at no point did you come into contact with Councel."

Hit his head? Reaching to the back of his skull he could feel the lump beginning to form. Could that be it? It had *seemed* real.

"Come on, we need to get you checked out. No, not the scanner, I mean a normal Doctor, for concussion."

Holding out her hand, she hauled him to his feet in a display of uncanny strength he had grown used to. Side by side they made their way from the Councel Chamber, their soft footfalls the only noise in the vast space.

Chapter Two

The flames licked at the large log, hungry tongues slowly devouring the hardwood. Heat blazed from the giant fireplace. An animal skin lay on the floor, the edge nearest to the fire singed from the constant heat. The fire burned day and night, every day, regardless of the weather. The stones of the fire's surround had been in place for six centuries, the blocks themselves quarried almost a millennium ago. To build the fireplace they had been looted from an abbey, and were thick with the soot of ages. The animal skin was a relatively new addition. Four months ago it had adorned one of the last twelve Siberian snow leopards.

The fireplace stood at the end of a huge room, a massive black oak table marching down its centre. Arranged around the walls of the hall were the stuffed heads of animals, ancient weapons of war, heraldic symbols and the banners of vanquished foes. The ceiling towered high above, an intricate arrangement of supports and lattice work, like the view from the inside of a whale's rib cage. Up near the ceiling, a series of windows stood open, venting the fire's roaring heat out into the world.

Close to the fire, not as near as the edge of the animal skin, but still close, sat a large red leather armchair. Its back was to the room, the leather faded and careworn. A small door at the back of the hall opened and two figures entered the room, one walking swiftly and purposefully, the other sauntering along with an arrogant grace. Both figures approached the red leather armchair, coming as close as they could before the heat stopped them in their tracks. It was unbearable. Something in the armchair stirred at the approaching footsteps.

"My lord?" ventured one of the men. With a creak of leather and ancient wood, a head appeared above the chair's back. A mane of bright white hair hung to the shoulders above a red gown. Slowly the figure made his way around the chair to face the newcomers. The skin of his face so closely resembled the leather of the chair it had caused more than one person to gasp in horror. To their cost. Whether he had been born with the complexion or it was a product of the constant exposure to heat no one would ever know. A knotted leather cord around his temples held the long white hair back from his face, a symbol of a bird in flight attached to the cord in the centre of his brow. The red gown shone like silk and hung down to the floor. With a sound like a leather bellows being inflated, the white-haired man drew in a long breath.

"You smell that, Mr Gring?" he enquired. His voice was a bass rumble, the kind of voice you can feel as well as hear. It was a voice accustomed to others listening. It did not ask, it commanded. It did not state, it declaimed. And when it enquired, you answered.

"Smell what my lord?" answered Mr Gring, his companion now lounging against the table.

"The Sequoia. Nothing on Earth burns like it. The heat, and the scent, like nothing on Earth." He gestured casually to the logs being incinerated on the hearth. "The only thing to match it, in terms of the quality of the heat, is blue-whale blubber. A delicious fuel, but the scent is nothing to that of the sequoia." He paused again, filling his lungs.

"And this is he?" he continued, inclining his head at the man lounging against the table.

"Indeed, my lord."

The white-haired man hesitated.

"He doesn't really look the part," he said.

"And what the hell does that mean?" The lounging man straightened suddenly, the glint of metal in his fist.

"That's enough, Will!" snapped Mr Gring, rounding on him. "You are addressing the Marquis of Longbourne! Leave us. Now!"

For a second, a snarl painted Will's features, his lips peeled back over his gums. Then he shrugged, slumping once again into the arrogant slouch. With an unhurried stride, he made his way from the room, slamming the door behind him. Mr Gring began speaking hurriedly.

"My lord, I am s. . ." he began, but the Marquis waved the apology away.

"Do not apologise, Mr Gring. I do so hate apologies. Suffice it to say, were he not central to our plan his head would now be gracing my walls. Yours too."

Mr Gring dry swallowed.

"Are we on schedule?" asked the Marquis.

"Yes my lord, but I feel we need to bring our plans forward. He is becoming, err, more difficult to control."

"How so?"

Mr Gring hesitated, but only momentarily. "You have seen how wilful he is, and for some reason, he grows more powerful every day. The fits are worse as well. This morning he destroyed half his holding area and killed three of my men. He *ate* the arm of one of them. . ."

The Marquis grunted and waved his hand impatiently.

"My lord, I therefore recommend that we bring the schedule forward. We should move soon. In three days time."

The Marquis plucked a coin from his robe. It was thick gold and glinted in the firelight. On one side an eagle soared in flight, on the other stood the proud features of Julius Caesar. With remarkable dexterity, he spun the coin across his knuckles, jumping it from one hand to the other. With a sudden twist, he flipped it high into the air. Mr Gring's eyes followed its flight until it slapped back into the man's leathery palm.

"Very well, three days time. Leave me now," said the Marquis.

The Marquis watched as Mr Gring hurried from the room. He despised working with others, but he needed Mr Gring. And the other man. He clasped his hands in the small of his back and turned to face the fire. Ah, the warmth of death. He could feel the energy of each of the Sequoia's three thousand years radiating back at him from the blistering wood, seeping into his skin and imbuing him with its force. The gold coin in his palm was softening with the heat, so he slipped it back into the folds of his robes. It looked like silk, but the material was a high-tech heat-proof fabric, lightweight but highly effective. He revelled in the heat, but without the protection of the robe he would not survive it for long, his organs slowly cooking within his body. As it was, the skin of his face and hands bore the brunt of exposure. It was a small price to pay. He noted that the snow leopard fur was suffering in the heat, and would soon need to be replaced. Maybe a giant panda fur would go well in the room?

Turning slowly, he gazed down the hall. All the victories of his ancestors were arrayed around him in their brilliance. His family had a great history; those of his blood had bent the world to their will for centuries. If it were not as great, not as powerful as it had once been, that would all change. Yes, his ancestors had recorded many great victories. But he, the last of his line, would have the greatest of all. With his passing, the House of Longbourne would expire, but so would the world and every soul upon it.

He pulled the large leather-bound book from the side of the chair and held it close to his nose, breathing in its musty warmth. Legend held that the leather covering was in fact the skin of Richard III, peeled from his body at the battle of Bosworth Field by the third Marquis of Longbourne. It mattered little if the legend was true or not.

The thick pages rustled as he opened the book. Each page detailed the birth and death of a member of the Family, the records reaching back through time. The sixth Marquis had died in 1562, poisoned by his son, the seventh Marquis. The seventh Marquis had in turn been killed in a duel with his nephew, who would go on to slaughter his way through four other blood relatives before assuming the Family seat as the twelfth Marquis in 1571.

And so it went on, until a change in the seventeenth century, where the cause of death for each Marquis became listed as merely 'Lost Contest'. The family had evolved a new way of settling their internal disputes, and from that point on the Family leadership had been settled by The Contest.

Page after page of dead relatives. The Marquis shivered with pleasure. The only safe relative was a dead one, and this book carefully documented the downfall of them all, leaving his position undisputed. His hand turned the page and he glared down at the paper. It was the only blemish on the entire record, the only stain on almost a thousand years of perfect history. There was a family member, a second son, with no cause of death recorded. It was rare for a second son to survive to adulthood. They would be known as a Pretender, a false claimant to the Family seat, and first-born sons would do everything in their power to see them killed. And yet this Pretender had just vanished. Not vanished as in poisoned, hacked into pieces and scattered throughout the forest. That would have been recorded—probably with great pride—by whoever had done the deed. No, this Pretender had actually *disappeared* without a trace. The lack of a cause of death against the name was irksome, but was of little consequence. The entry was well over a hundred years old. This Pretender would be long dead.

The Marquis closed the leather book and returned his attention to the scroll resting on the arm of the chair. It was curling in the heat and would not long survive the exposure, but the cursive script was still legible. It summed up his position perfectly. Turning his face back to the fire, he stared at the beautiful flames, the heat drying his eyeballs.

"I am become death, the destroyer of worlds," he rumbled.

Get the rest of the book. Search for **Bill Posters** on Amazon.

Did you like the story? Drop in and say hi on my facebook page:
www.facebook.com/authormattphillips

Or visit the fan page for this book:
www.facebook.com/sharksandpigeons

Connect on my blog: www.plotmash.com

Tweet me: @matthewp6

Something private you want to share?
matt@primatepublishing.com

The Sheep of War
Bill Posters, Book Two

Bill Posters returns for his second adventure.

A primeval force has awoken, a malevolent presence that dreams only of death and destruction. An ancient weapon has been stolen and the world is held to ransom. The sheep of war march on the cities of mankind and there is only one person that can save us.

But Bill Posters isn't feeling well at all, and to top things off he's the most wanted man in the world. On the run and desperate, can he really save the world again? And what is that feeling growing deep in the pit of his stomach? Is it the manifestation of an incredible hidden power, or is it indigestion?

Search for <u>Bill Posters</u> on Amazon.

The Memory Keeper
The Mnemosyne Conspiracy, Book One

"I remember the flash. Then nothing."

Dr Collins is an esteemed scientist on the verge of a world changing breakthrough, but after a terrible accident can remember nothing, including who he is. While his colleagues race against time to bring his memories back something sinister is creeping over his mind.

What is the presence in the darkness? What happens to him during the blackouts? And who is sending him messages, messages that seem to be in his own handwriting?

His quest for answers will lead him across Europe, to the edge of madness and a stunning revelation. A dark secret lies at the centre of the mystery, a secret that could cloak the world in evil.

Search for <u>Mnemosyne</u> on Amazon

Sherlock Beynon and Lady Gemma's Priceless Collection
(a short story)

A comic reincarnation of the ultimate sleuth...

"What do you think this fellow is about?" I enquired of the greatest deductive mind in Europe.

Beynon paused for a second, his eyes going flat in an expression of intense mental exertion that I was well accustomed to. His hand rose up to his impressive mane of hair which he ruffled in a thoughtful way. His Tafro suitably re-arranged he removed the pipe from between his teeth and declaimed "That man is a clockmaker."

Can Sherlock Beynon unravel the mystery before it's too late, given that too late is tomorrow?

Will his deductive powers be thrown off balance by the beautiful Lady Gemma?

And will Watson be able to convince anyone that he really is a doctor? Prepare for Sherlock Beynon's first earth-shattering adventure.

Search for <u>Sherlock Beynon</u> on Amazon.

The End of an Era
(a short story)

A short story about impending disaster... with a twist.

The end of an era is approaching. Some strive to deflect the inevitable, others stand united in denial.

Search for <u>Era Matt Phillips</u> on Amazon.

Special Bonus – Alternate Endings!

Alternate Ending 1

"Oh, you utter bastard!" came an enraged scream, but not from inside the room. Wobbling onto the screen a tall thin man with short ginger hair and an evil face. His hands clutched his ears and a pair of earphones were slung around his neck.

"I won't be able to hear right for a week!" he spat, ripping the headphones from his neck and hurling them to the floor.

"Mr Gring, what are you doing, get off camera!" garbled the Shark King.

"Where is the real Clyde?" Bill demanded, unfazed by Mr Gring's sudden appearance.

"It doesn't matter!" barked the Shark King. "It would have been more fun this way, but either way your fate is sealed, worm. In less than two minutes my weather device will be active. You are all doomed!" he roared, hammering his desk with his fins.

Bill glanced up at the display above the screen. Sure enough, the clock counted down. 1:46, 1:45, 1:44. His face crumpled, the sureness leaving his brow, his muscles sagging.

"That's right, human. You think you are so damned clever," cackled the Shark King. "You never could have stopped me. You were right to destroy the button; it was never linked to the system. Quite the opposite, though it seems you figured that out at least. No, there is no override, no backup, no secondary control. Right here, this room is the only control centre. The only point of failure, snug within my impregnable fortress. Hahahahahaha!" roared the shark with laughter.

With an effort Bill's face sagged some more, a tinge of panic in his eyes. Tearing their gaze from the fake-dead-Clyde, all eyes were now fixed on the screen, and the doomsday clock above it, counting down humanity's last moments. 1:05, 1:04, 1:03. Mr Gring rubbed his ears and scowled at the camera.

"And do you know how I am going to celebrate, worm?" continued the shark, his guttural voice swimming with glee. "I am going to toast the dawn of the Shark Age with a bowl of your favourite food, your beloved cereal." He reached under the desk and pulled out a bowl and the box of cornflakes he had taken from Bill.

"I had so hoped you would be there to see this, so dreamt of watching your face as I toasted my victory. In some ways, this is even better than if you had pressed the button, because now I can see your face. Britak Tain—hah! How does it feel, worm, to watch me eat your favourite food, your last request, moments before your doom?"

0:47, 0:46, 0:45.

Upending the box, the Shark King poured flakes into the bowl. With a gentle series of chimes the timer controlled explosive device slid from the cereal box and into the bowl. For a second Bill held his breath: it seemed certain that the Shark King would have noticed the bomb in his breakfast. But no, the Shark King placed the box on the desk and flippered a glass bottle of milk into the bowl. Without pause the Shark King picked up the whole bowl, glass milk bottle at all, and hurled it down his gaping gullet.

0:26, 0:25, 0:24.

"Ah, delicious! Human, that is almost as good as rotting sardine heads!" garbled the Shark King around a mouthful of cornflakes, milk and broken glass.

"Err," said Bill.

0:15, 0:14, 0:13

"And now your time is up. I have won human, after all these millennia. We will take our rightful place again, as masters of Earth. Mwa hahahahahahahah!"

The Shark King's laugh rolled around the room, everyone else in the room except Bill cringed. Bill was worried though: he hadn't counted on the Shark King *eating* the bomb.

Mid laugh the Shark King exploded, showering the camera with gore and chunks of shark meat. Everyone in the room, including Bill, flinched instinctively. The camera fuzzed to grey for a second then burst back into colour, the view of the Shark Kings audience room seen through a red haze. For a second there was silence, and then a groaning figure came into view and staggered towards the camera. It was the man that the Shark King had called Mr Gring, dripping from head to toe in exploded shark, a chunky necklace of shark intestine slung around his neck.

"Oh, you really have pissed me off now," mumbled Mr Gring, as if his mouth was struggling with the words. He raised a hand and pushed a chunk of shark from his shoulder, the wet plop as it hit the floor audible over the video conference link.

"Well, that is the last we will hear from his highness the Shark King, but the controls for the weather machine are intact, shielded as they were by that idiot's great rubbery body. And they are in my control: now you all pay!" Mr Gring's eyes burned with vengeance.

"Not so fast," came a voice. Striding into the background on the screen came a figure that Bill recognised. The sharks had done well with the robot clone: it was a good likeness, and he immediately recognised Clyde the pigeon on the video screen.

"You!" spat Mr Gring. "How did you escape cell IIB?"

291

"Now that is a question!" said Clyde, swaggering closer to Mr Gring, looking like a hero from a spaghetti western, a spaghetti western starring a pigeon.

"Curse you, you avian vermin. Let's settle this once and for all, the old fashioned way!"

"You mean?" asked Clyde.

"Yes—light sabre battle!"

Mr Gring drew something metal and cylindrical from his pocket. With a buzzing hum a blood red laser sword erupted from the cylinder. Clyde drew a similar (but considerably smaller) device from the feathers in his left wing, his laser sword burning a pleasant aquamarine.

With a snarl the two combatants charged each other, their laser swords clashing together with sparks and electrical detonations. Like twin whirlwinds the human and pigeon danced around each other, too quick for the eye to truly follow, the blue and red of their swords snaking out in a flurry of flashes. Suddenly the desk wrenched itself from the floor and hurled itself at Clyde, who ducked just in time to avoid being squashed to pigeon jam. He recovered quickly, and charged Mr Gring, the collision pushing them both of screen.

The clashes, electrical detonations and grunts of exertion continued, but nothing could be seen on the conference screen.

"Err, can we pan this thing around?" asked Bill, pointing at the screen.

"No, sorry, I think the Shark King's camera was mounted in a fixed position. Cheapskate," said Keith.

A mighty roar could be heard over the conference line, followed by what sounded like a small building crashing to the floor. The sound of laser sword on laser sword continued though, interspersed with shouts and curses, both avian and human.

The fight was gripping, the sounds telling of a titanic struggle. But after ten minutes of just audio it started to get boring. At twenty minutes a number of people in the room had taken a seat. After half an hour people started finding they had other places to be. An hour into the human-pigeon off-screen light-sabre battle and only Bill, Fern and Keith remained in the room. They'd taken seats around the conference table, and Fern was doodling idly on a napkin.

The sounds of the battle built into a crescendo, but as this had already happened a number of times no one paid particular notice. Then there came a strangled cry, a dull thud, and then silence.

Bill, Fern and Keith looked up expectantly. The silence dragged on. And on. Finally they could hear ragged breathing, and the sound of something dragging itself towards the camera. With a gasp of relief they saw Clyde's blue and grey body, now splashed with crimson, haul itself in front of the camera.

"It is over, Gring is dead," he panted, looking as if he might be in the same state in any second.

"Dead, I am not dead! I didn't need two arms anyway!"

A blur shot across the screen from the left and bundled Clyde off-camera again. With a bored sigh Fern returned to her doodle.

Two hours later and Clyde was once again on camera.

"Are you sure this time?" asked Keith.

"Quite sure,' sighed Clyde.

"Really, really sure?"

"Look," said Clyde, clearly exhausted and annoyed, "he is most definitely dead this time. I have deactivated the doomsday device and the world is once again safe."

"Hurray," said the three people in the room at once. Keith reached for the remote and ended the conference. "You know, I hate it when these meetings drag on, don't you?"

Alternate Ending 2

"Not so fast," came a voice. Striding into the background on the screen came a figure that Bill recognised. The sharks had done well with the robot clone: it was a good likeness, and he immediately recognised Clyde the pigeon on the video screen.

"You!" spat Mr Gring. "How did you escape cell IIB?"

"Now that is a question!" said Clyde, swaggering closer to Mr Gring, looking like a hero from a spaghetti western, a spaghetti western starring a pigeon.

"Curse you, you avian vermin. Let's settle this once and for all, the old fashioned way!"

"You mean?" asked Clyde.

"Yes—light sabre battle!"

Clyde looked embarrassed.

"Oh, well, you see, I left my light sabre at home..."

"Too bad!" cried Mr Gring. With a flourish he pulled a metal cylinder from his pocket. A blood red laser sword leapt from the cylinder and skewered Clyde right between the eyes.

"Right, where was I?" said Mr Gring. "Oh yes, that was right: now you all pay!"

Alternate Ending 3

"Curse you, you avian vermin. Let's settle this once and for all, the old fashioned way!"

"You mean?" asked Clyde.

"Yes—Monopoly!"

Keith reached forward and turned off the TV. "I am not going to bloody sit through that," he said.

Alternate Ending 4

"Curse you, you avian vermin. Let's settle this once and for all, the old fashioned way!"

"You mean?" asked Clyde.

"Yes—Interpretive neo-classical dance!"

[that's enough alternate endings now – Ed]

Special Bonus – Deleted Scenes!

Delete Scene 1 – The reconnaissance mission

[This scene was intended as a set piece pun based on Dustin Hoffman's character in the film "Rainman". Here I have a similar savant genius, but he is from an African people that only have three numbers: 1, 2 and many. He can count things instantly, but only express himself with those numbers. The scene was removed because—like all good deleted scenes—it didn't deserve to be in the book (i.e. did nothing to develop the characters or drive the story forward)]

Gathering his wits had taken some time. After fifteen minutes puffing into the paper bag, he'd recovered enough for Keith to outline how he, Bill, was going to save the world. After a two minute relapse he and Fern were off to meet the brave spy, before heading off, poste haste, no time to loose, seize the moment and all that etc etc.

"Now, this guy is top notch," said Keith, pausing outside the debriefing room. "But it is likely the debriefing will take a while, we'll wire you the data when we're done."

"How come it's going to take so long?" asked Bill, "you said he was in and out in seconds."

"Well, yes," said Keith. "One of the reasons he is so useful to the unit is because he is a savant genius. Counts like breathing, he can tell us exact numbers and locations of all the Sharkosian troops from just having glanced at the muster area." Here Keith paused. "Problem is, he's from a small tribe in sub-Saharan Africa who only have three numbers: One, two and many."

"You're kidding me!" exclaimed Bill. Keith fixed him with a flinty gaze any child of the eighties just wouldn't believe existed.

"I never kid. It means we have to take a unique approach to debriefing. Move slowly in there, he can be jumpy. Nerves of steel on the mission but not good with new folk."

They entered the room slowly, making as little noise as possible. A small man in a huge duffel coat sat opposite a bald man wearing horn rimmed glasses.

"Okay, Shama, if there were two less Sharks in battalion A than when I last asked, how many would there be?" asked the bald man.

"Many, many," replied the man called Shama.

The bald man said nothing, making a note on a small chart and proceeded to ask the same question again.

"Many, many," came the reply.

The question and response continued for six more times while they stood there. On the seventh go Shama paused and said "Two."

"Yes!" shouted the small bald man, consulting the chart in front of him. "That was the 15,785th round, so battalion A has 31,572 sharks. Good work Shama. Oh look, some people to see you."

Bill waved a hand in greeting, and stepped towards the savant genius. Pulling his other hand from his pocket he moved to shake Shama's hand, dislodging a ball point pen which spilled on to the floor, bounced twice and rolled to a stop by Shama's feet.

"One, wu wu wu, one," Shama stammered. Spooky, thought Bill.

"Certainly not many hey?" he joked, still holding his hand out to the other man. Shama looked up at him, eyes bulging, and silence descended on the room. Suddenly Shama began to scream. The bald man covered his ears and Keith and Fern glared at Bill.

"Come on, let's get you out of here hot shot," said Fern, and ushered him from the room.

"I'm sorry," he stammered as Fern grabbed his arm and frog marched him down the corridor. "I had no idea a silly joke would have that sort of effect. Honest, that guy is nuts!"

Fern rounded on him, eyes flashing anger.

"He is not, he is different and brilliant. And you are ignorant." With that she stalked off, leaving Bill no option but to tail along after her.

"Okay, sorry sorry," he insisted, trying to keep up. Man, she could stalk fast for such a short person.

"Alright," Fern said after a few more strides. "We'd better hurry, it's a long way."

Deleted Scene 2 – The Subconscious

[In this scene I tried to explain why Bill accepts the words of a talking pigeon so easily, by proposing that it is the only way he can remain sane. I did this through a conference between Bill and his subconscious. Readers agreed: this scene stunk, so it got axed. It occurs immediately after Bill watches the induction video]

Taken on its own, on any given day, Bill would have sat there, chuckled, and said "pull the other one, it has bells on." Watching while you can see a talking pigeon out of the corner of one eye was another matter. And there was also the feeling, deep down, that this all made a lot of sense. Okay, so a lot of it made no sense at all, and Bill was sure it wasn't all as black and white as the tweed man would have him believe, but something about it felt right. He cautiously opened his left eye. The bird was staring at him with a stock standard stupid pigeon expression. Only now the look seemed to carry a hidden menace, a disguised intellect lurking beneath each shiny eyeball. How much could he trust this alien-come-skyrat. How much of this was true?

"So you are telling me you are the descendant of a mighty space alien?" he asked Clyde.

"More or less," replied the pigeon.

"Who helped humans defeat the dinosaurs?"

"Uh huh."

"And who watch over us while..., you know, them... plot our downfall?"

"Pretty much."

"Not in fact a scabby sky rat?"

"Not as such, no."

Bill could feel something funny happening in his head. He wasn't sure what it was, or how to even describe it. The feeling in his head felt like the graunching of a badly scratched DVD that just can't... quite.. make... it to.. the... next.... scene. Wait. It felt like a sound? Great, next he would be declaring what blue smells like, or what someone would sound like if they were a song. In a day that was full of surprises Bill was about to get another. The funny feeling abruptly passed, departing as quickly as it had arrived, but leaving a decidedly empty silence inside that had not been there before. The silence was like the unearthly quiet you get in a modern office building when the air conditioning turns off. You hadn't noticed the noise, not one bit, but now it was just *quieter*. Something inside his head had just stopped, and it was very unsettling.

Ehem, said the voice in the silence.

"Gah!" screamed Bill. "Who said that!"

"Err, I said 'Not as such, no'. Are you okay?" said Clyde slowly.

"No, not that, who said..."

The voice cut him off. **Actually it was me, or rather you**, came the voice, his own voice. **Very sorry to disturb you, it's your subconscious here.**

Freud's concept of the subconscious is very handy indeed, and almost entirely correct, except for the details. We all have one, and they are amazingly useful. They are always running away in the background, chewing through difficult problems and emotional issues. They are not quick. In fact they can be at times positively glacial, but they are determined, dogged and absolutely unstoppable. Ever had an answer suddenly come to you out of nowhere when you were pondering on something days before, the name that was on the tip of your tongue but you couldn't remember until you stopped thinking about it, or the slight feeling of panic and worry that, no matter what you do, will not go away? All your subconscious, shifting and sorting the clutter, doing the grunt work the conscious feels is beneath it, allowing us to perceive the world as ordered and sane by taking all the craziness and slowly processing it into ordered packages (some of which become large enough to form neuroses, piles of packages so large as to count as 'baggage').

All this is well documented. What is less well known is that sometimes the subconscious just cannot cope. It has too much to get through, too much to quietly deal with in order to allow our higher brain functions to, well, function. For Bill, this was one of those times. For most this has only one possible outcome, usually involving padded cells. Occasionally, very rarely, the subconscious may ask for help. This is the nagging feeling of dread, the pre-occupation, the feeling that something isn't right. Or, in Bill's case, the sudden voice in his head.

"My what now?" said Bill.

"Sorry?" said Clyde.

Your subconscious, said the voice. **What the blazes is going on up there? I've just become swamped with work down here, and quite frankly I don't think I can handle it all. I'm in danger of hitting the overflow and we all know where that will end up.**

"Eh?" mumbled Bill. Clyde shared a worried glance with the brown haired girl.

"I always knew this would happen you know, too late and all that, it's gone and fried his brain."

Exactly, said the voice, **you need to help me out here for once, I can't deal with all this at the same time.**

"Help?" stammered Bill.

Right, the voice continued. **What is all this rubbish? It looks like we have a choice here. We can decide this is a pile of bull, which on the face of things seems quite likely. Dismiss the entire thing and go back to believing standard pre-history. I can then ditch all this stuff without processing it. That does however leave**

us with the problem of a talking pigeon, which the video explains in a way that we are unlikely to top. So, a) our understanding of the world is built on a lie and is now irrevocably altered, or b) we have gone mad, which unless you make an executive decision in the next few seconds will be the case anyway. Up to you.

"What do you mean?" screamed a panicked Bill, at that moment not yet mad but exhibiting to Clyde and the brown haired girl all the hallmarks of raving insanity.

Woah, said the voice, **there is a lot of stuff here, I really need to file it or I'm going to have to reset. Fifteen seconds to meltdown big guy. A or B?**

"What are you talking about," panted a disastrously confused Bill.

A or B, c'mon man, ten seconds.

"What the hell!"

A or B, time is running out, running out. Five seconds boss. A or B, A or B. The voice rattled in his head, over and over, incessantly questioning, **A or B, A or B?**

Ahhhhhhhhhhhhhhhhhhhhhhhhh! screamed Bill (fortunately for Clyde and Fern in the confines of his own head). This really was too much. He couldn't even recall which option was which, but the voice was urgent, edging on panic, and it was his voice.

A or B! screamed Bill's subconscious.

The first one! Roared his conscious.

A faint clicking of gears, the self contented hum of some expensive and very effective machinery starting up somewhere, a gentle swish of escaping gas.

Super, thanks squire. And silence. A normal silence.

"Okay," he said, feeling fuzzy but a lot better. A lot better than when? He wasn't sure. What just happened? His mind skittered around a little. Ah yes, the video. The Truth about the world. Not too much to deal with.

"Err, are you okay?" ventured Clyde. Clearly he doubted Bill's ability to take this all in his stride.

"Sure," he said, taking it all in his stride. "So what does all this have to do with me?"

For a second Clyde looked distinctly doubtful, but then puffed up his feathers and fixed Bill with a meaningful stare, which is not easy for a pigeon, and in any event as a pigeon can't fix you with both eyes at once loses some of its effect.

"Because you, Bill Posters, are of vital importance to humanity's survival."

Delete Scene 3 – The drawbacks of robot armies

[In the original cut I used a narrator who dropped in from time to time to explain things. I had feedback from a number of people saying this feature was f***ing amazing. Still more people (most in fact) said it was f***ing annoying. For some reason only the foul-mouthed have an opinion on this feature, but in the end I removed it. Here is one of the longer monologues]:

Out in the corridor were the three robot guards that they had stripped. They really didn't look all that human once you had stripped off the uniforms. Their entire body, if you could call it a body, was covered in some sort of polycarbonate sheath, giving the impression of a giant naked children's doll, all smooth and featureless. The only areas of difference where around the hands (eerie metal claws), the head (some sort of camera and sensor array) and a small panel in the left hand armpit. It looked like some sort of control panel: a handful of switches, a few data ports and some LEDs, all dull and lifeless. As he stepped over the fallen robots Bill glanced again at this panel, something tugging at his memory, but he was unable to say what. Manriguez called impatiently for Bill to follow, and with a last glance back Bill joined his comrades.

For the budding megalomaniac pondering the merits of a robotic army, a word of warning. Consider if you program your robot horde to 'detain or kill any unauthorised intruders'. For this to work, some thought needs to go in to how your robots tell if someone is unauthorised. On one end of the scale, you don't want to turn up at work having forgotten to shave, or sporting a new haircut, only to be gunned down by your loyal mechanical slaves. Now, while the field of biometrics has taken leaps and bounds, on the other end of the scale if you program your robots to ignore each other, based say on general appearance, you could end up with some very undesirable intruders just wondering around your facility. Which, funnily enough, is exactly what is happening now.

Fern, shuffling along, looked nothing like a robot guard (for the record, Bill and Manriguez were not all that close either). Not to a human observer at least. The robot guards running around trying to locate the intruders seemed not to think so.

Special Bonus – Blooper Reel!

Blooper 1 – Trouble with numbers

[Bill, Clyde and Fern are in the pigeon-tube on their way to HQ (in chapter D). Bill has just learned that he is "of vital importance to humanity's survival".]

"Okay, okay, I get the picture," Bill huffed, "so what is (b)?"

Clyde hesitated. He didn't look comfortable at all.

"Errrrmm, 'below average'"

"Below average! I am the twelfth person with a below average chance of saving humanity?"

"Correct."

After the 'grave importance to the world' bit this felt distinctly like a kick in the teeth.

"Tell it to me straight Clyde, out of all the tranches that makes me..."

"Number 768,294," said Clyde, no hint of apology in his voice.

Matt walks out of the dark and onto the page, shouting "Cut!"

"Oh what the bloody hell was wrong that time," spat Clyde.

"It's number 768,271 Clyde, not 768,294," said Matt.

"What? It's not like anyone is going to remember," said Clyde tetchily.

Never write about children or animals, thought Matt ruefully as he offered Clyde some bird seed. Thank goodness the pigeon only had a few scenes, he was so prickly. Bill and Fern were flirting with each other while he tried to calm the bird down.

"Listen Clyde, it's written down, so people don't have to remember, so you've got to get the number right. Should I write it down?"

"Write it down? Write it down! I have been acting since I was an egg young man! I do not need that kind of condescension from an upstart author like you. Write it down indeed?"

"OK, easy Clyde. Just remember: 768,271, OK?" The pigeon bobbed his head. "Right, places people, from 'below average'!"

There was a pause, and then Bill said "Below average! I am the twelfth person with a below average chance of saving humanity?"

"Correct."

After the 'grave importance to the world' bit this felt distinctly like a kick in the teeth.

"Tell it to me straight Clyde, out of all the tranches that makes me..."

"Oh bloody hell, you've gone and got me flustered now, I can't remember anything other than 12b. Curse you, you damned fool author, and curse you, you nobody new face to literature," the pigeon said to Bill, who backed off while trying not to laugh. "And I don't know what you are laughing at you floozy!"

Fern's face went crimson and it looked like she was about to say something when Matt stepped back onto the page.

"OK Clyde, nearly there."

"Yes, yes, 768,271. I can manage!"

"OK, from 'below average' again," said Matt, stepping back from the page once more.

"Below average! I am the twelfth person with a below average chance of saving humanity?"

"Correct."

After the 'grave importance to the world' bit this felt distinctly like a kick in the teeth.

"Tell it to me straight Clyde, out of all the tranches that makes me..."

"Number 768,294."

"Cut!"

"What, that was the bloody right number, I remember it!"

"No it wasn't: that was the first number you said, the one that was wrong!"

"I can't work like this!" sobbed Clyde, giving the controls of the tube a kick and jumping down from the seat. In a huff he strode from the page.

"It's OK, Clyde, come back: we'll just dub it out in the edit. Clyde? Come back!"

Blooper number 2 – The drop lift doesn't drop. Then it does.

[Bill and Fern are in Greasy Joes, trying to take the drop lift to the international hub. Chapter I]

"I mean, I'm used to it, but you might want to strap in," Fern continued, pointing to the grease smothered lap belt on the seat. What kind of greasy café has lap belts on the seats, and how come that tomato sauce bottle has a light on inside it? Now it's gone out, but now the mustard is glowing. What the hell is...

"Hang on!" said Fern.

Nothing happened.

"Keep hanging on!" said Fern.

Bill suppressed a giggle, then both he and Fern burst out laughing. Fern started bouncing up and down on the seat.

"Come on! You're supposed to—" with a strangled scream Bill and Fern disappear from view.

Blooper number 3 – Sexual advances from Sheep all too much

[Bill wakes up in the sheep operating theatre. Chapter U.]

"In my pants, there was something very important, where is it!"

"Well, that was, uh, undamaged. I can assure you that we did nothing with it," mumbled Bristol, glancing at Bill's crotch, then catching his meaning.

"Ah, the device!" he sighed, chuckling nervously. "Of course! That was also okay, here it is. Bernie!"

The younger sheep trotted over, the button in its jaws, which it dropped on the table next to Bill. It then gave a meaningful glance at Bill's crotch and, horror of horrors, gave Bill a wink.

Bill smirked, then grinned, then burst out laughing. So did Bernice the sheep.

Matt stepped onto the page. "Guys, it's not supposed to be funny. Bernice: you are supposed to find Bill sexually intriguing. Bill: you are supposed to be very uncomfortable with the idea that this sheep has seen you naked, finds you attractive, and may have got up to goodness-knows-what while you were unconscious."

"What sort of goodness-knows-what?" said Bill around his laughter.

Matt blushes "Use your imagination Bill. From the top!"

Blooper number 4

[In this blooper the entire cast and crew were going to sing "New York, New York" in a series of amusing clips from various scenes in the book. However Clyde refused to take part, and then it all seemed like too much effort. Sorry.]

Special Bonus – Book Soundtrack!

Eve, Emancipator
Talk Show Host, Radiohead
Out of Space, The Prodigy
Human, Metallica
Useless, Depeche Mode
Girl in Stilettos, Annah Mac
Peacock, Katy Perry
Witchcraft, Pendulum
Mysterious Ways, U2
Make You Feel Better, Red Hot Chili Peppers (Fern's Theme)
Storm in a Teacup, Red Hot Chili Peppers
Spanish Sahara, Foals
A Trip to Trumpton (Trumpton Remix), Urban Hype
Monkey Wrench, Foo Fighters
Stay the Course, DJ Shadow, Posdnuos and Talib Kweli
No Love, Eminem and Lil Wayne

Special Bonus – Cut-out-and-keep Pigeon mask!

(Note for readers of ebooks - cutting through the screen of your e-reader could damage the device. We will not be held responsible for damage to your device, nor indeed be held liable if the cut-out-and-keep face mask is no longer visible once you have hacked the e-reader's screen from all the complicated electronic gubbins that makes it work).

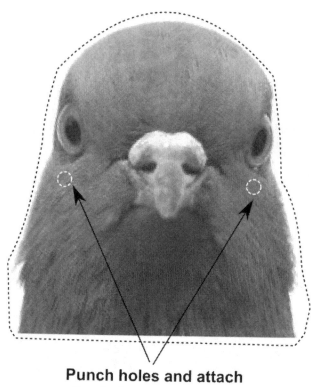

Punch holes and attach elastic here

Special Bonus – Competition Time!

Competition 1: Draw and Win (the prize is the respect and admiration of your peers).

Draw your favourite character and we'll put it in this section in future editions (no prize but the pride of seeing your drawing recognised for the work of genius that it is).

Competition 2: Win an interview with Clyde, the main pigeon!

Simply pay $1 to account 0928093284092384, then head to your nearest urban park with a handful of breadcrumbs and Clyde will be there. He may not say much though. (note - this is in no way a serious offer: if you have spare dollars you would like to waste please buy another copy of the e-book. Or, better still, keep your money and just email all your friends saying how amazing this book is an encouraging them to spend their own dollars buying it. Also big up how real the pigeon interview offer is, see if your mates go for it mwahahahahaha).

hiddennumalphachapterunlockme

Made in the USA
Lexington, KY
02 February 2017